FOOTPRINTS
in the
DESERT

FOOTPRINTS
in the
DESERT

A Novel

MAHA AKHTAR

**BARCELONA
EDITIONS**

Originally published in Spanish as *Las huellas en el desierto* by Roca Editorial de Libros, S.L. in Spain in 2014.

Cover design by Sophie Guët

978-1-4976-9039-4

Published in 2015 by Barcelona Digital Editions, S.L.
Av. Marquès de l'Argentera, 17 pral.
08003 Barcelona
www.barcelonaebooks.com

BARCELONA
EDITIONS

Distributed by Open Road Integrated Media, Inc.
345 Hudson Street
New York, NY 10014
www.openroadmedia.com

To my best friend and muse
My beloved and faithful Dougall.

FOOTPRINTS
in the
DESERT

1916

It's two years into World War I.

In Europe, on the Western front, trench warfare rages at the ongoing battles of Verdun and the Somme. On the Eastern front, Russia is at war with Germany and Austria-Hungary.

In Africa and in the Far East, the Triple Entente (Britain, France, and Russia) is fighting the Alliance (Germany, Austria-Hungary, and Italy) to keep their respective colonial possessions. There is also the war at sea, a race between Britain and Germany for naval supremacy.

And in the Middle Eastern theatre of war, the Ottoman Empire, allied with the Alliance, is fighting the British in its own territories: the Sinai, Palestine, Mesopotamia, Persia, North Africa, and Arabia, and the Russians in the Caucuses to the north east of Turkey.

CHAPTER ONE

May 1916

It was an unseasonably hot and humid spring in Izmir, western Turkey. The mercury rose to dizzying heights and the accompanying mugginess created a cloying cover, a miserable haze that even the sun couldn't burn through. The rumble of thunderclouds and flashes of lightning in the distance dangled hopes of a cooling rain, but it was only a tease. The clouds never came west. They roiled over the Bozdag mountain range, drenching villages and the valley beyond Mount Yamanlar, but never ventured towards the Aegean coast. The city was tense, like a volcano about to blow.

Just past seven in the evening on May 3, Salah Masri was staring out the large bay window of his small wood-paneled office that looked out onto Konak Square. It was swarming with Ottoman and German officers and soldiers. He noticed a new checkpoint at the north end of the square that led to the German military chief of staff's residence. He saw people rushing around, getting their evening errands done before the recent nightly curfew began. Country women, almost all of them dressed in black, their heads covered with the traditional black scarf, were being stopped as they entered the market just beyond the square with their produce, their baskets searched.

A loud commotion broke out on the street in front of one of the many coffee houses around the square. Salah couldn't quite make out what it was about, but policemen were taking a man away while two women on the ground held onto his legs, crying and screaming. "I've done nothing!" Salah thought he heard him say. "That's what you all say," and he watched as one of the policemen elbowed the man in the ribs, causing him to double over.

Salah took a deep breath and slowly released it. He walked back to his desk. Yes, the noose was tightening. But he was almost done. One more mission. That was it. He would have fulfilled his side of the bargain.

There was a knock on the door.

"Masri Pasha . . ." It was a young man who worked as an assistant.

"Yes."

"Sorry to bother you, but this telegram just arrived."

Salah slit open the envelope and pulled out a piece of paper.

THEY'RE ON TO YOU. GET OUT. DOCKS, 8 P.M. MN

Salah looked back down into the square. He saw four men in black suits and tarbush caps walking toward the building. In front of them was Colonel Omer Erdogan, who was rumored to be the new head of the Ottoman secret police. Salah's pulse rate picked up.

Damn!

He looked at his pocket watch. He had no more than five minutes before they reached his office. He hurriedly gathered the papers strewn across his desk and shoved some of them in an old, weathered cognac-colored leather pochette. The rest he inserted into a brown folder marked "Confidential" and threw it in a safe behind him. From the same safe, he pulled out an envelope and quickly thumbed through the lira notes before placing it in the breast pocket of his jacket. He also took out three passports and put them in along with the money. Finally, he opened the middle drawer of his desk. Inside a small locked compartment was a gun, a 9-millimeter German Luger. He checked the chamber to make sure it was loaded, unclicked and clicked the safety switch, and put it in the shoulder holster he had begun to wear. He got up, adjusted his jacket, and walked toward the door of his small office. Out of nowhere, a man appeared in the doorway.

"Colonel Erdogan!" Salah exclaimed.

The Ottoman officer crossed his arms across his chest and tried to puff himself up to Salah's height.

"You look a little flustered, Masri," he drawled.

"Just this damned heat," Salah replied, taking a handkerchief out of his pocket to wipe his brow.

Omer Erdogan stared at him for a moment through narrow, steely eyes.

"Where are your manners? You haven't offered me any coffee."

He placed two fingers on Salah's arm and moved him aside.

Salah allowed himself to be moved.

Born of a Lebanese father and an Egyptian mother, Salah was surprisingly tall. He was well over six feet, almost six foot three, and he was big: big body, big hands, big feet, big belly, big voice, big laugh. While he did not have movie-star good looks, Salah was attractive; his height and size and commanding voice creating a daunting presence. But his face suggested a different kind of person. His skin was pale olive, his eyes dark brown and lively, and his nose long and aquiline. A slender mouth, where a mischievous smile always danced around the edges, hid behind a cropped moustache and an equally cropped beard that looked more like two-day growth. He had short, dark wavy hair that he tried to tame with gel and water every morning, but it inevitably did as it pleased. All in all, Salah was a gentle giant of a man with a kind, expressive face.

Erdogan, on the other hand, at five feet ten, was by no means short, although next to Salah he seemed to be. He was muscular and lean and rather dashing, with prominent cheekbones and a chiseled jaw. His fair skin was sun tanned, his eyes icy blue, and he wore his thick dark blonde hair slicked back. He was wearing the Ottoman Army officer's uniform: a green jacket over grey pants tucked into black boots and a brown holster belt. On his head he wore a black fez.

"Nice office you've got here, Masri."

He strode in, his hands behind his back, as he surveyed the office. He ran a finger along the edges of Salah's desk before inspecting the large map on the wall of the Hejaz Railway that ran from Damascus to Medina, one of the many railway lines that crisscrossed the Ottoman Empire.

"You must be proud of this railway," Erdogan said, turning around and walking back to the desk. "I hear you had a lot to do with its completion."

"Look, Erdogan, I'm late for an appointment," Salah said.

Silence . . . broken by the sound of boots creaking on wooden floorboards.

"Erdogan, I don't mean to be rude, but . . ."

"You're to come to Damascus with me."

"Why? When?"

"Jemmal Pasha wants to see you."

"Why does the governor of Syria want to see me?"

"Aren't you one of the engineers for the Hejaz Railway?"

"Yes . . . but why me?"

"I have my orders."

"Erdogan, I'm a very busy man. I insist that if Jemmal Pasha needs any information, he should talk to the interior minister or his German advisor."

Erdogan shrugged, uncaring.

"I don't argue with Jemmal Pasha. We leave in the morning."

With that, the colonel swept by him, his saber clanging in its scabbard.

Halfway down the hallway, he turned. "By the way, Masri, your office looks unusually tidy for a busy man. I've noticed that most people sort out their affairs when they're planning on never coming back. You weren't thinking of leaving us now, were you?" Erdogan mock saluted Salah before walking away.

Son of a bitch.

—◦◦◦—

As soon as Omer Erdogan was out of sight, Salah turned and walked quickly down the five flights of creaking wooden stairs on the far side of the hallway, his mind whirring. *What do they know?* He stopped only once to wipe the sweat from his face and the back of his neck. He could feel his heart beating faster and he knew that the white shirt he wore under his navy blue pinstriped double-breasted suit jacket was drenched. In the lobby, he waved to the two guards on duty and stepped out onto the street.

Once outside, he stopped for a moment. He looked left and right. The street was empty, apart from a few people hurrying home, trying to escape the heat or potential trouble. Salah took a cigarette out of a rumpled packet, struck a match, and cocked his head as the flame lit the tobacco. And through the thin gray haze of smoke, he saw a couple of men come out of a café and walk over to the newspaper kiosk a few yards away in the middle of the square. *Erdogan's boys.* He was sure of it. Salah's heart pounded. *Stay calm.* Not wanting to let on that he knew who they were, he took a couple of puffs of his cigarette, adjusted his jacket, tucked his pochette firmly under his arm, and crossed the street toward the market.

The market in Alsancak, known for the produce that came from the countryside, was crowded. Housewives were shopping for the evening meal, arguing with vendors about their prices, while their bored husbands looked on, wishing they were sitting at the bar with their friends playing backgammon and enjoying a glass of wine.

Salah wound his way through the narrow aisles between rows of figs, pomegranates, melons, and peaches. Vegetable sellers shouted their prices, hoping to steal away their competition's customers by lowering them with every call. A plump old woman, her cheeks red from the sun and stained purple from burst spider veins, offered Salah some of Izmir's renowned Tulum cheese. He shook his head and moved on as she yelled at him for being so ungrateful. Every now and again he glanced back, but the two men were behind him, keeping a safe distance, their black tarbushes bobbing in and out of the crowd.

Up ahead, Salah saw Ilham, the olive oil seller, who was as slippery as the oil he sold.

"Brother Masri!" Ilham shouted and waved him over.

Salah did not reply. With his eyes he gestured over his shoulder to the two men who were following him. Ilham nodded and pointed to the tiny alley next to his stall. Salah quickly ducked in. Seconds later, he heard shouts and two consecutive thuds.

"You clumsy fool!" he heard a man yell. "What do you mean the jar slipped out of your hands? Look at us! We are covered in oil. And my friend here has a twisted ankle."

Salah scurried down the alley. At the end of it, he stopped. The main road was just ahead. He peeked around, quickly looking left and right. A couple of Erdogan's men were standing about a hundred yards to his right. Salah ducked back in. Taking a deep breath, he ventured out.

"There he is!" he heard one of the men shout. "Get him!"

Salah took off as fast as he could. He looked around as he sprinted down toward the sea. Erdogan's men were closing in. Salah reached the main road that ran along the coast. He saw a line of horse taxis waiting for a fare. He needed something faster. The Turks were almost on top of him. Just then, he saw a motorbike and a sidecar attached to it, sitting patiently next to a streetlight in front of a café. Two German officers were enjoying a coffee at one of the outdoor tables. Salah headed for the bike. He pushed down heavily on one of the pedals and the bike roared to life.

"Hey!" he heard someone yell behind him. "Halt! You! Halt! That belongs to the Germany Army!"

But Salah stepped on the accelerator, and drove off, headed straight for the port.

—⟋⟋⟍—

The Port of Izmir was bustling when Salah arrived. Freighters, cargo ships, passenger ships, and German war ships and U-boats—now part of the Ottoman navy—were getting ready to leave with the evening tide.

Salah abandoned the motorbike outside. Keeping his head down, he made his way to the customs house, a large stone building between two piers that also served as an immigration post for foreigners entering the empire. The quickest way to find who he was looking for in this mayhem was to ask the port captain, Mehmet Reza, a friend he didn't necessarily trust.

Mehmet was a diminutive man with a rotund head, exacerbated by a lack of hair, and a just as rotund body. He had small, beady black eyes, heavy jowls set beneath a lunar face, and a thin moustache above thin lips. His teeth were small and stained brown from coffee and cigarettes. He was writing at his desk, a monocle in his left eye, when Salah knocked on his door.

After a few minutes of greetings, a quick cup of Turkish coffee, a foul-smelling cheroot, and slaps on the back and promises to get together for a long dinner to catch up, Salah made his way to Quay 7.

"Come on, you lazy bastards!" a voice boomed, "we don't have all night. We have to unload this ship and reload and be out of here in twenty minutes! Now get a move on!"

"What I need to buy you is a whip," Salah addressed his old friend Musa Nusair's back.

There was a moment of silence.

"And if you did, I would use it," Musa replied, without turning around.

"Now listen carefully," Musa added, keeping his back to Salah. "Can you find your way to my office on the ship?"

"I guess so."

"I'll meet you there in ten minutes. Go quickly."

"Come on, you good for nothings! Get all those crates off the ship!"

Salah slipped away and made his way up the gangplank. There was no one on the ship. Everyone was on the quay.

There was a small office in the passageway toward the bridge. This was probably it. Salah opened the door. The air was scented with a mixture of pipe tobacco and cigars. On a small cabinet, a black cat lay fast asleep. Yes, this was Musa's office indeed. Salah sat down on a wood and leather chair that swiveled, and looked around while he waited. On the wall, there was a portrait of the Ottoman sultan, Abdul Hamid II, looking regal in his ceremonial turban, one hand on his sword and the other on his waist. There were a couple of empty nails next to the portrait and shadows on the wall indicating that, at one point, something had hung there. Musa probably changed the pictures around depending on the port he docked in. *That crafty Yemeni bugger.* The desk itself was a mess, papers of all kinds strewn everywhere, pencils, an inkpot, and a small gas lamp. Partially buried behind a piece of paper was a photograph of a woman surrounded by seven children. *Musa's wife, no doubt.*

Footsteps in the passageway. Salah jumped out of the chair and took a quick step toward the door and hid behind it, his hand on his gun, just in case it wasn't the ship's captain. Moments later, Musa Nusair walked into the office, sat down heavily in the chair Salah had vacated, took off his white captain's hat, and slammed it down on the desk, scattering the papers in all directions. He was a good-looking man. His black skin was smooth and relatively unlined. His face was round, his eyes were small and very dark, and he had thick lips and a big, toothy smile. Like Salah, he was tall, well over six feet, and large, his broad shoulders straining under the cotton strands of the white sweater he wore with black pants.

Salah stepped out from behind the door. Musa indicated that he close it.

"So what's going on?" Salah ventured.

Musa cradled his hands behind his head and took a deep breath, staring at the portrait of the Ottoman sultan. He exhaled slowly and sat forward, his elbows resting on his thighs, his hands clasped. "You've got to get out of here, brother."

"Yes, I know . . ."

"Tonight."

"Nusair, I've got one more thing . . . it's important."

Musa shook his head. "Masri, it's all over. The French ambassador's house in Beirut was raided. Apparently, Ahmad Jemmal has letters and correspondence between the Arabs and the British and the French, saying that the Arabs will revolt against the Ottomans with the support of the British and in return the British will recognize an independent Arab state."

Salah took a deep breath. "They have names?"

"Yes, Erdogan has already made several arrests in Beirut and Damascus."

"Wissam? Rafic?" Salah asked about his best friends.

"And Khaled too," Musa added sadly. "I just took him and wife back to Beirut a couple of weeks ago."

"To Beirut?" Salah shouted. "I told him you would get him out of Izmir, but why the hell did you take him to Beirut?"

"That's where he insisted on going. I tried to dissuade him, but he wouldn't listen. Something about his wife wanting to give birth in Beirut."

"His wife? Noura? Pregnant?"

"Yeah," Musa nodded. "So pregnant that she gave birth on my ship."

"Oh my God!" Salah exclaimed.

"Look, Masri, if they have your friends, you're next."

"But my name couldn't be on any piece of paper they may have found in the ambassador's house."

"You hope it isn't . . . but in any case, it doesn't matter. Jemmal won't need a piece of paper to throw you in jail."

"How much do they know about what I've been doing?"

"I don't know, but they know you're involved. Look, you have to disappear, tonight! You don't have any time. Once they arrest you, you'll rot in jail until they have their proof of treason."

Salah was silent

"Masri, Erdogan is on his way," Musa said, his tone urgent.

"He's already here. He came to my office just after your telegram arrived."

"As I said, you go with him and you're as good as dead."

The two men looked at each other. Musa raised his eyebrows questioningly.

"Musa, can you delay departure until midnight?"

"Are you crazy? How will I explain that to the port captain? And with this new curfew? They'll never agree to it. I'm a Yemeni freighter captain . . . a pirate for hire to the highest bidder. I have to get out by ten. That's the last departure slot they'll give me."

"Look, if I can arrange it, can we leave at midnight?"

"Why? What is more important than your life?"

"Musa, there is one more thing I need to do."

"Brother, you are going to get yourself executed."

"Nusair, it is the last and most valuable piece of the puzzle."

Musa looked at him silently.

"Just give me a few hours."

The captain sighed deeply.

Salah took his leave with a warm handshake. He ran down the gangplank and quickly walked to the customs house.

"Mehmet," he said, shutting the door.

"Salah! I wasn't expecting to have that dinner tonight . . . and I can't . . . my wife is expecting me . . ." Mehmet's fez sat askew on his big, bald, egg-shaped head.

"Mehmet," Salah put his hand up to stop him. "I need a favor . . . please."

It was close to nine o'clock when Salah left the customs house. In return for a sum of money, Mehmet had agreed to let the *Tree of Life* stay in port until midnight.

"But not a minute later, Salah," he warned. "I have to stamp the exit papers with today's date or else I will be hauled off for questioning. You know the rules. And then what will happen to my family if I am in prison . . . ?"

"Thank you, dear friend," Salah interrupted him.

—⁓—

The docks were still buzzing with activity. Voices mingled with ship horns as some of the vessels started to pull up anchor and move out of their berths. As Salah approached the guards at the entrance to the dock, he kept his gaze set on the street in front of him. He could feel them staring at him as he walked past. It was almost curfew and, in his suit, Salah didn't exactly look like a dockworker. And while he was a civil servant and had the right to be out past curfew, he was carrying a gun, a wad of cash, and several different identity papers. Getting stopped and searched was not ideal.

"Hey! You!" he heard behind him.

Salah froze.

Suddenly, a flash of lightning lit up the early night sky. Thunderclouds rumbled, only this time, they sounded closer than ever. In the split second that everyone's attention turned toward the sky and the long-awaited possibility of rain, Salah quickly slipped away amid the general chaos of horse carriages, donkey carts, passersby, and vendors.

Taking every shortcut he knew, he approached the small residential, cobblestone street just off Konak Square in the heart of the old city, where he lived on the top floor of an old townhouse that had been converted into apartments. He looked around cautiously before opening the main door, entering as quietly as he could. He didn't want his neighbors or the concierge or anyone to know he was back.

He stole across the courtyard and ran up the stairs to his apartment. The door was unlocked. Someone had been there. He padded into the darkened foyer, turned on the small gas lamp and glanced around quickly. Everything looked normal. He turned it off.

He hurried down the hall to his bedroom. He lit an oil lamp and waited for a moment, listening, just in case. But apart from the sound of the cicadas, there was silence. He grabbed a small satchel out of the closet. He opened the top drawer of his dressing table, pulled out a couple of shirts and a pair of pants and threw them in. He opened a second drawer and took out a diary, putting it in the satchel along with the wad of lira notes and three passports from his breast pocket and the papers from the leather pochette.

He stripped off his suit and hung it in his closet as he usually did, before tossing his shirt in a basket. Like his office, he wanted it to look as normal as possible. He pulled out a suitcase from under the bed. Inside was a khaki German lieutenant's uniform that he had quietly acquired the week before. It was a little tight on him, both the pants and the tunic straining at the waist, but it would have to do. He pulled on a pair of black boots, tucking the pants into them. He slipped into the standard leather holster that had several pockets around the belt, securing the Luger inside, and placed a brown officer's cap on his head.

A floorboard creaked. The sound seemed to be coming from the direction of the living room. He thought he could hear hushed voices. Moving quickly, he peeked through a crack in the curtain. The same two men who had followed him earlier were standing in the courtyard looking up at the apartment. The floorboards creaked again.

Salah's heart jumped. There *was* someone in the apartment. He quickly extinguished the lamp, slung the satchel over his shoulder and across his body, and went through his bathroom to the kitchen. Keeping close to the walls, he felt his way to the back door that led to a spiral staircase down to the garden. He found the doorknob and turned it, wincing at the loud whine of the hinges. He squeezed himself through the small door and locked it from outside with his key. The door wouldn't survive a good push, but it would give him a couple of extra minutes in case he needed them. He was almost at the bottom of the staircase when he looked up and saw the lights go on in his apartment. He saw shadowy figures dash from one room to the other and heard the sounds of furniture being overturned, closets being thrown open, and the sound of breaking glass.

Salah flew down the last few steps. He went quickly through the garden and out into the street through the back gate. It was a twenty-minute walk to the old Ministry of the Interior, an imposing early nineteenth-century building, now the seat of German military command. Salah knew the building like the back of his hand. It was where he first had his office when he began working at the Chemin de Fer Imperial in 1908.

It was a dark, silent night with the occasional rumble of thunder in the distance. Salah moved as quietly as possible, keeping to the darker corners and alleyways, avoiding the main roads and the streetlights. Sound traveled fast on nights like this. He had a couple of close calls along the way, almost colliding with a group of soldiers patrolling the area around the barracks.

As he neared the building, he veered off to the right. He walked under an arched bridge and stopped at an old rusted iron gate covered with clinging plants. He opened it and descended a short staircase into a narrow tunnel that went underneath the grounds of the building toward the back entrance of the Ministry. The Izmir Clock Tower rang out, telling Salah it was 10:15. He had an hour, maybe an hour and a quarter, but not much more.

Just as he came out of the tunnel near the back gates, they opened and a small convoy of cars pulled out, driving off into the night. The car in front was the dark blue Benz belonging to the military chief of staff himself. *Good! He's going home for the night.*

A high wrought-iron fence surrounded the compound. Salah knew that two guards were posted at the brightly lit main gate and the compound was patrolled by soldiers and German shepherds every fifteen minutes. Dropping down onto his belly, Salah cautiously approached the fence. There was another tunnel hidden in the embankment that surrounded the building that Salah knew would take him into the building. Once inside, all he had to do was get to the third floor and into the military chief of staff's office.

Digging in the earth near a stout old olive tree, Salah found the wooden gnarled door that led into the tunnel. The wood was rotted and the latch was completely rusted and initially refused to budge. Salah tried to coax it open but he couldn't. He didn't want to pull it, fearful of the noise it would make. He would have to wait until the next time the guards came by with the dogs and somehow get them to bark to mask the sound of him pulling open the door.

The clock tower struck 10:30. *They should be along anytime now.* Right on schedule, two guards with big German shepherds came walking along and stopped on the other side of the fence a few feet away from Salah. One of the dogs came to the fence and began to sniff. The other followed him. The guards lit up cigarettes. Salah rolled over on his back. His hand felt for a small rock and, saying a little prayer, he launched it.

"What was that?" one of the soldiers said. "It came from over there," he pointed to a dark corner.

"It's nothing . . . probably just a rat."

"Let's go take a look."

Just then, a cat came out of nowhere and ran across the compound. The two dogs began barking, baring their teeth, straining at their leashes as the cat squeezed through the iron bars.

"Hey, hey, hey!"

Salah heard them from inside the tunnel calming the dogs down: "It's only a little kitty cat." But the cat had done its job well. During the racket, Salah had used the butt of his gun to push the latch back.

The tunnel was pitch black. Once inside, Salah lit a match. The tunnel was dank, the sides black and green with mold. Salah went down the stairs. He was almost knee deep in dirty water and his head skimmed the ceiling. The tunnel was narrow enough that if he stretched his arms out, he could touch the sides. Rats scurried along the sides and God knows what else lurked in the filth beneath him. He knew he had roughly two hundred yards to go. Lighting match after match, he finally reached the short flight of stairs that led to another door. This one was behind a painted wooden panel in one of the hallways off the foyer on the main floor. Salah stuck his ear to the door and carefully pushed it. It wouldn't budge. *No!* He tried again. It wouldn't move. He put his ear to the door again, but he couldn't hear anything. Putting all his weight against the door, Salah shoved. The door gave a little. Hopeful that he could slowly get it to open, he shoved again and was about to give it another push when he heard a muffled voice.

"What was that?"

Salah held his breath.

"I didn't hear anything."

"It was like a groan."

"A groan . . . you're imagining things."

"I swear I heard it."

"Come on, this is an old building. Maybe they're ghosts."

"I probably just need some sleep."

Salah heard footsteps walking away from him. He heaved a huge sigh of relief. A couple more pushes and the door opened a crack, allowing him to peek in. But he had to move quickly . . . a crack in a wooden wall panel would be easily noticed.

Once in the foyer, Salah looked around. There was no one there. He cautiously took the staircase to the first floor, ran up the second, and was on the third when he heard footsteps behind him. He quickly ducked behind a heavy brocade curtain.

"Now, Captain Brandt, I need those reports typed up and on my desk within the hour."

Peeking through the slit in the corner he recognized General Otto Liman Von Sanders, the head of the German military mission. Salah moved into the shadows behind the curtain. *What the hell? So who was in his car?* All the information Salah was looking for was in Von Sanders' office.

The clock tower struck eleven.

"By the way, Brandt, why is the carpet on the stairs so dirty?" Von Sanders asked. "Actually, it looks like wet footprints. Find out who came up here with wet boots and get that cleaned, would you. It stinks."

"Yes, Sir," the younger army officer saluted smartly and went about his business.

Salah heard Von Sanders open the door to his office and then close it. *Now what?*

There wasn't much time left. He needed the information he'd come for. And, he had to get to the docks by midnight or else he was dead. Just as he was debating what to do, he heard the door to Von Sanders' office open. Through the slit in the curtain he watched him walk down the hall. *Where is he going? And for how long?*

Salah had to take the chance. He was about to step out when he stopped and pulled off his wet, smelly boots before padding across the hall. Cautiously, he went in and closed the door behind him. Boots in hand, he rushed over to the General's large mahogany partners desk, scanning the papers quickly. They were not what he needed. On the right, there was a wooden cabinet. Salah tried to pull the top drawer open, but it was locked. Outside he heard footsteps. He froze. They passed by and headed down the hallway. He looked around quickly to see where he could hide if he needed to. Behind the curtain of a tall French window was his only bet. Hurriedly, he hid his boots behind it.

Where would he keep the key to this damn drawer?

Salah looked around the desk. There they were, sitting in a little leather tray. He dove for them and quickly opened the drawer. Inside were files, all neatly labeled. This was it. Exactly what he'd come for. He began rifling through them. *Come on! Come on! Caucasus, Persia, Gallipoli, North Africa . . . Here! Arab Campaign . . . South Arabia Campaign, Sinai, Palestine, Mesopotamia.*

—⁂—

Salah opened the South Arabia file. There they were: maps of German-Ottoman military installations and key ammunition depots and reports of the latest troop concentrations from Damascus to Medina. He pulled out a small notebook and started scribbling madly. Suddenly, he heard Von Sanders' muffled voice coming down the hall. He was sweating. All he needed was five more minutes.

Von Sanders stopped outside his door. Salah saw the handle go down. He jumped up and quickly went behind the curtain. He stood there, his heart hammering against his rib cage.

"General! Please come with me to the war room!" he heard someone say.

"What is it?"

"We have received some very disturbing news from Jemmal Pasha in Damascus."

The clock tower struck 11:15.

Salah held his breath. From behind the curtain, he saw the door handle slowly go back up. "All right . . . Brandt, did you find out whose wet boots were on the stairs? Oh and Brandt . . . could you get me a little schnapps, *bitte* . . ."

Salah quickly went back and began copying down the information. He shut the files, placed them back exactly as he'd found them, and locked the drawer. Now all he had to do was get out. It was almost 11:30.

He was out of time. There was no way he was going to be able to get through the tunnel and to the docks in time.

Quickly, he opened the door to Von Sanders' office and slipped out out, pulling his boots on outside. The hallways were empty. Hopefully they were all in the war room. He got down to the ground floor and was wondering what to do when a door opened and he came face to face with Captain Brandt.

The two men stared at each other in silence.

"Lieutenant!" Brandt said, looking at the officer insignia on his sleeve.

"*Ya wohl!*" Salah stood to attention and saluted, looking straight ahead.

Brandt walked around Salah and came back and stood in front of him.

"Lieutenant, you stink? Where have you been?"

Salah looked down at his muddy boots.

"What are you waiting for, Lieutenant?" Brandt said loudly. "Get to your barracks and change. You cannot be in the war room with the general smelling like you've been in a sewer!"

Salah shook his head and smiled tightly.

"*Ja, mein Kommandant!*" he mumbled, trying to disguise his accent. He saluted the German officer again.

"Get this man to the barracks. He stinks!" Brandt said to the two guards who appeared.

"Go on, go on! What are you waiting for, you fool?" Captain Brandt flicked his hand shooing Salah away.

Salah walked backwards toward the front entrance and flew down the stairs to the courtyard and toward the gate. All he heard was the jeering laughter of the guards as he sailed through the gates on his way to the docks.

It was almost midnight. Carefully Salah entered the port. Thunderclouds rumbled and a flash of lightening lit up the sky. Salah ducked behind huge crates piled up at the entrance. He looked around for the guards but he didn't see them. Hiding in the shadows and behind dock equipment, boxes and anything that served as cover, Salah made his way to Quay 7. Suddenly, the wind picked up and thunder rolled again. He saw Musa Nusair pacing up and down the quay, smoking, his dark figure a stark contrast to his white cotton sweater and his white captain's hat that glowed yellow in the gaslight. He whistled softly to get the Yemeni's attention. Musa stubbed out his cigarette and whistled back. Lightening ripped open the sky and the crack of thunder this time was ominous.

"Quickly," Salah heard Musa say to his men who were standing by the gangplank. "Untie her and prepare to haul anchor. We leave now."

From where he was hidden, Salah saw Musa head toward the customs house, no doubt to get his exit papers stamped. Moments later he came out, holding his cap firmly across his brow as the wind twirled around him. He whistled again. Salah came out of the shadows and walked quickly toward the gangplank. Silently, both men boarded the ship.

Just as the *Tree of Life* pulled away from the quay, the Izmir Clock Tower struck midnight.

—◊—

A flash of lightning lit up the entire harbor, illuminating the man who sat quietly on a bench, looking out to sea. He took a long drag of his cigarette, crossed his legs and laid an arm across the back of the bench casually, as though he had all the time in the world. The gaslights of the harbor flickered as the wind picked up. The man looked first at his pocket watch and then up at the customs house. The light was still on in the office on the second floor. The wind and thunder died down, momentarily restoring the peaceful sound of water lapping around the wooden dock posts. Several minutes later, another man emerged from the now darkened customs house and came and sat down on the bench.

"So was our friend Mehmet amiable this evening?"

"The gold helped loosen his lips, Colonel Erdogan."

"Good."

"The boat is headed to Chania . . . in Crete."

Just then, there was a crack of lightening. Following a deafening roll of thunder, the rain came.

CHAPTER TWO

Leaning against the railing, watching Izmir recede into the horizon, Salah felt the first drops of cool rain hit his face. *Now what?*

He had turned thirty that spring. Eight years before, he had moved to Izmir after graduating from the American University of Beirut. His father had just died and his mother had decided to return to Cairo.

It was 1908 and the Young Turk Revolution, led mostly by young Turkish nationalists, had succeeded. A parliament had been restored in Constantinople and the Ottoman sultan had been forced to accept the changes that came with a constitutional monarchy.

A talented engineer and a congenial fellow, Salah had gotten a job quickly with the Chemin de Fer Imperial and was assigned to work on the Hejaz Railway, which was being built from Damascus to Medina in the Hejaz region of the Arabian Peninsula. The route was part of the Ottoman railway network and meant to link Constantinople, the capital of the empire and the seat of the Islamic caliphate, to the Hejaz, where the holy city of Mecca was located.

Salah was hired just as track construction reached Medina about two hundred miles short of Mecca. Hard work and dedication put him in good stead with his superiors and he was promoted to assistant chief engineer and finally to chief engineer for the narrow gauge railway line that began operating under his watchful eye. No one was prouder than Salah when he stood next to top Ottoman government officials at the ribbon-cutting ceremony at the Damascus Station in 1913. Salah had also suggested and spearheaded the construction of a branch that veered west to Haifa and the Mediterranean and had just begun track construction in Medina heading toward Mecca when World War I broke out.

He had certainly never meant to become a spy. He'd always envisaged a rather tame, conventional life for himself: a good job, a pretty girl, marriage by the time he was twenty-five, a family . . . that sort of thing. He'd fallen into the espionage game by accident exactly a year before in Damascus when he met Prince Faisal bin Hussein, the son of Hussein bin Ali, the sharif of Mecca.

—ɯ—

May 1915

There was a problem with the railway line between Kiswa and Deir Ali, just south of Damascus. The track gauge was too narrow and the heavier trains were derailing. Adding to the challenge was the terrain: it was mountainous and therefore rocky and unstable and Salah was in an office in the Interior Ministry in Damascus trying to find a solution.

"*Sayyidi*," a voice addressed Salah politely as he pored over a map, his eyebrows furrowed, a pencil stuck behind his ear.

"Hmmm?" Salah said absently without looking up.

"*Sayyidi*, it is almost eight o'clock," the voice said. "May I please have your permission to go home? I will be back first thing in the morning."

"Hmmm." Salah stood up, still frowning in concentration, pursing his lips.

"*Sayyidi?*"

Salah looked up and stared blankly at a man not much younger than himself.

"Ah, Rabih!" he finally said, recognizing the architect from his team. "I'm so glad you're here. Look, brother . . . I was thinking . . ." and he pulled the pencil out from behind his ear and pointed to a spot on the map. "If we can somehow go around this curve of the mountain, then I think we have a chance. The question is whether we can build a depot and a station in that spot. What do you think?"

"Sir," Rabih said apologetically. "Would it be possible to look at this tomorrow? It's just that I promised my family that I would be home for dinner."

"You'll get home for dinner," Salah replied. "It's only six o'clock."

"Actually, Sir, it's eight."

"What . . . ?" Salah said, taking his pocket watch out of his waistcoat, staring at it, shaking it around to make sure it was working. He shook his head. "Where does time go?" he muttered.

"Off you go, Rabih," he added. "I'll be right behind you. I have to run too."

Salah rolled up the map and put it back in a drawer before grabbing his jacket from the coat stand in the corner. He had half an hour to get home, change into black tie, and get to his friend Rafic Tabbara's home for a dinner party.

Salah walked out into a beautiful spring evening. The sun was just setting and the air was cool and refreshing after a day in the office. He breathed deeply, inhaling the fragrance of the jasmine bush he passed by. He was looking forward to seeing Rafic, Wissam, and Khaled, his three best friends from university. It had been a few years since he'd seen Rafic and Wissam, and despite Khaled having moved to Izmir to work on the Chemin de Fer Imperial as a lawyer, he had seen very little of him, mainly because of their respective schedules, the irregular hours Salah kept, and the frequent trips he had to take to the Hejaz. He had seen more of Khaled's wife, Noura. *Ah! Noura . . . her perfume, her hair, her eyes . . .* The last time he'd seen her, she'd come laden with fruit and cakes, claiming that Salah was not eating properly. They'd sat and had tea and talked and laughed. And he remembered the silence that followed after she'd left and how empty the apartment felt without her.

Stop it, Salah. She's married to your goddamn best friend.

It was almost nine o'clock when Salah rang the doorbell of Rafic's home in Bab Tuma, a neighborhood in the old city.

The door opened and a servant bowed respectfully. "*Masa al khair.*"

"*Masa an nour,*" Salah replied.

"*Sayyidi* is in the garden with the other guests. If you would follow me, please?"

Salah looked around as he walked through. It was a lovely old Damascene house that gave on to a courtyard open to the sky. A fountain in the middle spouted fresh spring water, and the surrounding gardens were filled with citrus trees and fragrant jasmine bushes. The archways, columns, and doors were intricately painted and the floors were tiled.

As he approached the courtyard, Salah saw four men standing in a circle talking, while waiters with trays of different kinds of juices and *mezze* stood off to the side waiting to be summoned. He knew all of them except for one who was dressed in typical Arab dress: a long white tunic, black cloak, and a white scarf on his head held in place with a black and gold braided rope. The three others, Rafic, Khaled, and Wissam, were, like him, in black tie.

Salah smiled when he saw his friends. Seeing them made him realize how much he'd missed them. Rafic was Syrian. He was short and had always been prone to being stout. He had curly black hair and dark, laughing eyes. He was an outgoing fellow with a sensitive nature and had, when they were at university, ambitions of being a poet, but had recently decided to become a cleric.

Wissam and Khaled, both Lebanese, were of average height. At five foot eight inches, Wissam was the best looking of them all, with a headful of blonde curls and sparkling blue eyes and a spirited, impassioned personality. For as long as Salah could remember, a long line of girls had always followed him around and when he finally married his wife, Samar, he'd left behind a train of broken hearts. He was a writer and ran a newspaper called *Al-Minbar* that had recently been shut down for its harsh views of the Ottoman treatment of the empire's Arab people and as a result, Wissam had spent some time in jail.

Khaled was surprisingly shy and reserved, given his vocation as a lawyer. Slender in physique, he had dark skin, and a brooding, serious face with fine black hair and dark eyes.

Salah grinned mischievously when his host turned to look at him.

"Well, well!" Rafic broke away from the group and came to greet Salah. "Brother Salah! You decided to join us. I'm so glad!"

"I am sorry for being late," Salah apologized, warmly shaking hands with his friend before enveloping him in a hug. "I was in the office and forgot the time."

"No matter," Rafic replied congenially. "Come! I think you know these two," he said, referring to the two men who came toward them.

Salah laughed heartily, enveloping each of them in his arms, ruffling their hair, and kissing them on the forehead. "Wissam! Khaled! So good to see you!"

"Good to see you too, brother!" Wissam playfully punched Salah on the arm.

"I was delighted to hear that the two of you were here," Salah said.

"Salah!" Rafic walked back over. "Let me introduce you to our guest of honor, Faisal, the son of Hussein, the sharif of Mecca," he said, taking him by the elbow to guide him to the middle of the courtyard.

"Salah Masri, this is Prince Faisal bin Hussein . . . Your Highness, *Jalaltak*, this is Salah Masri."

"*Jalaltak*." Salah put his hand on his heart and bowed reverently.

"Come, come." Prince Faisal came forward, his arms open to embrace Salah, kissing him three times on the cheek as was customary. "We are all brothers here."

"Thank you, Your Highness. You do me a great honor."

"Shall we sit down to dinner?" Rafic suggested, pointing toward a round table that had been set up in the garden just off the courtyard.

Conversation at dinner turned toward the war and the recent British land attack launched on the Gallipoli Peninsula in Turkey a few days earlier.

"What do you think of this latest British move, Masri?" Prince Faisal asked Salah, staring at him through narrowed eyes.

Salah put down his knife and fork and took a sip of wine, wiping his mouth with a starched white napkin before putting it back on his lap. "Well it was inevitable, I suppose, once the naval attack on the Dardanelles was repelled."

"Do you think they might actually reach Constantinople?"

Salah shrugged. "Hard to say, Your Highness, but I think the British are underestimating the fighting ability of the Ottoman soldiers. Besides, the terrain is rugged and there aren't many suitable landing beaches on the Peninsula. I think they may run into logistical difficulties in addition to being fired on by the Ottomans."

Prince Faisal did not reply. Expressionless, he nodded and turned his attention back to his plate.

"So you think they will lose?" he asked carefully.

"I'm not saying that," Salah replied. "I'm just saying that perhaps they are being a little overconfident."

"Yes . . ." Faisal closed his eyes and took a deep breath. "They can be that."

As the conversation continued around him, Salah looked at the Arab aristocrat: of average height and slender build, he looked quite fragile. He had a swarthy complexion. His face was long and egg-shaped, his nose shaped like a long slim beak of a bird, and he wore a perfectly trimmed goatee and moustache. He was a serious-looking man, with dark penetrating heavy-lidded, almost hooded eyes that were impossible to read. The heavy bags under them, which reached the top of his cheekbones, added to the look of worry that enveloped him.

Understandably, Salah thought. Things were not going well. The Turks had gone back on their word and promises of reform and greater local autonomy for the Arabs had disappeared into thin air. The Arabs were being "Turkified."

Constantinople had declared a *jihad* on Britain, France, and Russia, and urged Hussein, Faisal's father, whom the Arabs considered their true leader, to support the call with his troops. They looked toward the Arab *jihad* as essential in winning the war against the British. But Hussein refused to commit.

And now Hussein was in danger of being deposed, or even, so rumor had it, of being executed on trumped-up charges, in favor of his dispossessed cousin, whom the Ottomans thought more malleable.

As a counter move, Hussein now seriously contemplated an Arab revolt.

The idea had first arisen prior to the outbreak of the war when a secret dialogue began between the British and Hussein about mutual support in the face of Turkish aggression. Around the same time, Hussein had been approached by a small group of men, including Rafic, Wissam, and Khaled, who represented Al-Fatah and Al-Ahd, two of many Arab nationalist societies, to lead the Arabs in a revolt against the Ottoman Empire. At the time Hussein and his three sons, including Faisal, were skeptical about Arab unity and the strength of the Arab movement to fight the Ottomans.

But now, as the situation with the Turks worsened, the British

promised to support the revolt with money, arms, and officers and recognize and support an independent Arab state. In light of this development, Hussein changed his mind and sent Faisal to Damascus to revisit
the idea of an Arab revolt with the nationalists.

—⁓—

"Brother Masri." Prince Faisal came and sat down next to Salah as the
group of men enjoyed coffee and pastries in the garden. "It is very nice to
finally meet you. I have heard a lot about you from Rafic and the others."

"Thank you . . . and indeed it is an honor to meet you, Prince."

"Tell me, Masri, why is it that you have not joined your friends in
their adventures in Arab nationalism?"

"They tried their best to persuade me, Prince," Salah replied. "But
I am not political. I am a simple man who wants to live a simple life."

"Are you not proud of being an Arab?"

"Very much so, *Jalaltak*. But I'm not interested in going to meetings
to endlessly debate and discuss issues that I don't know much about."

Faisal did not reply.

"Prince, I will support Rafic and the others as their friend, but I . . . am
not an intellectual, or an ideologist," he said, weighing his words carefully.

"So you think that Arab nationalism is an ideology? That it does
not really exist? Or cannot exist?"

"Prince . . . the Arabs are a political mosaic. We are tribesmen, loyal
to the tribe or to our religion. We have a clan mentality and I think we
always will."

"Therefore a single unified Arab state that would extend from Aleppo
in Syria to Aden in the Yemen, is not something you can envision?"

"If it is your dream, Prince, then I pray it becomes a reality."

"You are a diplomatic man, Brother Masri," Prince Faisal said.

"Not really, Prince, just a practical one who likes to find real solu-
tions to real problems."

"There are many of us who think the situation of the Arabs under
the Turks is a real problem," Prince Faisal said. "And the real solution is
to get out from under the yoke of the Ottomans."

"Yes, Prince!" Salah laughed. "But I am an engineer who uses science, mathematics, and ingenuity to solve problems. If I could solve the Arab problem using science, I would!"

"You are right. Neither science nor mathematics can help us, but . . . ," he paused briefly. "We could use your ingenuity, Brother Masri," Prince Faisal said, staring at Salah from his expressionless hooded eyes.

"How so?" Salah asked.

"I understand you have full access to the Hejaz Railway . . . and count many Turks and Germans among your circle of acquaintances.

"Please . . . we need your help."

And that was how it had all begun. At first, Salah gave Faisal information about the railway, its strengths and weaknesses, and the scheduled military and civilian supply trains up and down the Hejaz. It was important information, all of which had either crossed his desk or he'd overheard during the course of a meeting with his superiors. But he had never done anything like he'd done tonight. It was something Faisal had asked him to do the last time he'd seen the prince in Mecca a couple of months before.

"My brothers and my father and I are planning the revolt, Salah," he'd said. "We need to know Turkish and German troop concentrations. Please . . . this is the last thing we will ask of you."

Salah leaned forward on the railing and pulled a cigarette out of his jacket. He lit it and took a deep drag. Slowly he let it out. He caught a whiff of a cigar. Seconds later, Musa Nusair came out and joined him. There were several minutes of silence as the two enjoyed their tobacco.

"Beautiful night," Musa remarked.

Salah nodded.

"That is why I love it out here . . . the stars, the open sky, the sound of water and the occasional dolphin. No matter what's happening out there," Musa pointed abstractly toward land, "out here, you can always find peace and tranquility."

"How did I end up here, Musa?" Salah asked. "I don't like uncertainty or living on the edge and I'm not fond of danger."

"You could have said 'no.'"

"How does one say 'no' to friends?" Salah rubbed his forehead with his thumb and forefinger. "I have known them since we were at university."

"They didn't ask you, Faisal did."

"Semantics, Musa," Salah said.

"Do you regret your decision to help?" Musa asked.

Salah took a deep breath. "I don't know." He flicked the cigarette butt overboard. "Not all Turks are bad. I liked my superior . . . and his wife. They were wonderful, warm, hospitable people. He took a chance on me, Musa. Without him believing in me, I would not have become the chief engineer." He sighed deeply. "There were many nights I fought with my conscience over what I was doing."

"Your loyalty is commendable, Masri."

"Yes, but I pay a high price."

"You think this Arab Revolt will work?"

Salah lit another cigarette. "Is there Arab unity? Is there an Arab identity? We will see if the sharif of Mecca's flag can accomplish that."

Musa puffed on his cigar, making the ash on the tip glow.

"You think the British will keep their word to Hussein?"

"There is only one of them I trust." Salah stared broodingly out at the dark sea. "Thomas Lawrence . . . he used to be an archaeologist."

"An archaeologist?"

"Yes." Salah nodded. "I met him just before the war in Izmir. He said he was headed toward the Negev Desert to do some research. After the war broke out, I received a letter from him saying that he was in Cairo and had been conscripted into the British Army.

"Anyhow, we stayed in touch and I recently heard he's lobbying the British general to become the liaison between Faisal and British Army."

"Why do you trust him?"

Salah shrugged. "He really believes in the Arab Revolt. He really believes the Arabs should have their freedom and he thinks he's going to be the one to give it to them."

"He's mad."

Salah nodded his agreement. "Yes, he is."

"Now listen, brother," Musa said, leaning on the railing. "Tomorrow, we dock at Chania, in Crete. I need to refuel, but more importantly, we need to know what is going on before we continue. I know a man who knows everything that happens in the empire as soon as it happens. After that, we will decide where you will go."

"I don't know, Musa," Salah said, worried. "As long as this war continues, I'll be looking over my shoulder."

"We'll get you somewhere where you can disappear." Musa glanced at Salah, a rare glint of worry momentarily apparent in his dark eyes. "Now get some rest. We've got a long day ahead."

—⁓—

The sun was shining brightly through the porthole when Salah woke up. He squinted, and rubbed his eyes, listening to the waves slapping gently against the side of the boat and the seagulls squealing as they skimmed the surface of the sea in search of a poor unsuspecting fish. He yawned and sat up, leaning on his elbows for a minute before swinging his legs over the side of the bunk. *Why are these fucking things so small?* He stretched and yawned again, his hands reaching the top of the small cabin. Despite having only slept a few short hours, he felt refreshed.

"Moor her in! Drop anchor!"

Good! We're here.

He washed quickly in the small basin and dressed in one of the shirts and a pair of pants he had brought with him. He hurried down the gangplank to join Musa on the quay.

"Good morning!"

"Good morning, Nusair!"

"Beautiful morning." The captain beamed a full smile, his teeth looking even whiter against his black skin. "So how does it feel to be in non-Ottoman lands?"

Salah smiled.

"It is a beautiful morning indeed, Nusair."

"Come on . . . let's go meet my old friend Sokratis."

"Is that really his name?"

"It's what I've always called him," Musa replied.

—ᴍ—

Despite the warm morning and the dazzling sunlight, the stone *taverna* was dark, cool, and empty, apart from an older man with white hair and a tanned, weathered face behind the bar cleaning glasses.

"Can I help you?" he said, his voice raspy and hoarse.

"I'm looking for Sokratis," Musa said.

"He's not here," the man replied without looking up and went back to cleaning glasses.

"We will wait."

The man shrugged.

Musa led the way to a darkened corner, away from the door and the windows and he and Salah sat down.

Moments later, a man walked in. He was average in height, with a muscular body and an angular face. He sported a thin, waxed moustache and was wearing a grey cotton cap. With his tanned skin, he could have passed for a fisherman, except that he was a little too well-dressed in a pair of fine navy trousers, a light blue cotton shirt with the sleeves rolled up, and a pair of dark blue suspenders. He was carrying a folded newspaper under his arm and went to sit at the bar. He ordered a glass of wine.

Salah looked at him over his shoulder. Something didn't feel right. He inclined his head toward the door, telling Musa that they should leave. Nonchalantly, both men got up and walked out, picking up the pace once they were outside.

"Who was that?" Musa asked as they made their way along the crowded cobblestone street toward the fish market.

"I couldn't be sure, but something felt wrong. He was too well-dressed to be in a taverna by the docks." Salah looked around. Over the heads of the crowd, he saw the well-dressed man come out of the café and look left and right before turning right just as they had done.

Damn!

"Nusair, we have to get out of here!" Salah ducked into a narrow street between the bright white buildings. "How can you get in touch with this Sokratis?"

"He's usually in that taverna," Musa said.

"Is there a back door to it?" Salah asked, squeezing his way through to the street that ran parallel to the one they were on.

"There must be."

"Let's go see if a few drachma will make the old man talk."

Just as they were approaching, they saw a man tiptoe out the back door of the taverna.

"That's Sokratis!" Musa hissed. "That bastard was in there the whole time!"

Quietly, they ran up behind the short, stocky bald man. Musa grabbed his right arm and Salah his left.

"Sokratis!" Musa whispered loudly. "How are you, you son of a bitch?"

"Ah! Nusair, my friend! I had no idea you were in Chania," Sokratis stuttered.

"Don't lie, Sokratis," Musa said.

"Aw, Musa! You are my brother . . . I would never lie to you."

Musa rolled his eyes. "Come back into the taverna. We need to talk to you."

"Musa . . . please . . . I am already in trouble with the local police, and if I am seen with you and your friend here," he said, pointing to Salah, "I will be in trouble with the Turkish boys also."

"I'm sure you have a secret room in the taverna where we can talk for a few minutes," Musa said as Salah and he hauled Sokratis up so that his feet dangled above the ground.

Inside, the taverna owner looked up briefly and, without so much as a raised eyebrow, went back to his glasses. Sokratis grabbed a bottle of wine from a rack, smiling tightly at the owner before opening a panel in a wall that lead down into the basement. It was dingy and musty and dark. There was a table and a couple of chairs and a small camp cot in the corner with some rumpled sheets and a pillow.

"So this is where you live?" Musa said, looking around. "Just like most vermin." He shook his head, looking disgusted.

"Now sit down!" Musa pushed him down on one of the chairs. "I really don't think friends should turn on friends," he said, his face coming very close to Sokratis. "What do you think, brother Salah?"

"Please, Musa." Sokratis' mouth trembled and he wrung his hands nervously. "I haven't said anything."

"You must have known the *Tree of Life* had docked at Chania." Musa shook his finger at Sokratis. "The port captain is your god-damned brother-in-law."

Sokratis looked embarrassed.

"So why avoid me?"

"It's because of him . . .," Sokratis said, pointing at Salah.

"Why?"

"Turkish secret police are looking for him. They arrived early this morning."

"What?" Musa spluttered. "We only left Izmir last night. What else do you know?"

"Nothing," Sokratis said.

"Salah, we have got to get you out of here," Musa said.

Sokratis nodded. "I don't think you have much time."

"We need to go now." Musa got up from the chair. "Sokratis, do you have a cap or something? Or even a tarbush?"

"No tarbush." Sokratis opened a filthy bag that sat in a corner. "But I have a couple of fishermen caps." He pulled out a dark blue and a brown one.

"Good! We'll take these." Musa grabbed them. Salah took the blue one and put it on, wrinkling his nose at the smell.

"Even with that cap, Masri, it's going to hard to disguise you," Musa said.

"What about you? You're the same height as me and black."

"Yes, but I'm better looking."

"Very funny, Nusair."

Sokratis pulled the cork off the bottle of wine and took a swig, wiping his mouth on the sleeve of his shirt.

"Thank you," Salah said to him as they went back up the stairs.

"Good luck to you, my friend."

Cautiously, Salah and Musa made their way back to the main street that led directly to the entrance of the port.

They walked quickly, keeping their heads down. Musa took off his white captain's hat and replaced it with one of Sokratis' fisherman caps so as to not stand out. Salah hunched, trying to make himself blend in with the other men who were all shorter than he was.

As they neared the port, Salah saw the same man from the bar. He was standing at the main entrance. Salah grabbed Musa's arm and inclined his head in the man's direction. Quickly, they hid behind a large plane tree. Salah looked around. A donkey cart filled with sacks of fruit piled high along the sides was slowly making its way to the harbor entrance.

"When that cart comes by, we get in the back," Salah whispered.

Musa nodded.

Salah and Musa crouched down in the cart, pulling jute bags of oranges, lemons, and limes over them. The cart slowed. "Come on, mules!" The cart driver whipped the animals. "What the hell is wrong with you two? I have to deliver this fruit or I won't get paid."

The cart made its way through the main entrance painfully slowly. Salah peeked out from underneath and saw the man looking the other way.

"Quickly," he whispered. "Let's get out."

They jumped off and disappeared in the crowd just past the entrance.

"You get on board," Musa told Salah. "I have to get the port captain to stamp my papers. "I'll meet you on the bridge in a couple of minutes."

Salah nodded and ran up the gangplank.

After several minutes, he looked at his pocket watch. Ten minutes. He paced up and down. Fifteen minutes. *What the hell is going on?* Suddenly, he saw about half a dozen men running through the entrance to the harbor toward the customs house. *Erdogan's men. Come on, Nusair!* Just as the men ran into the customs house from one side, Salah saw Musa come out from the other and walk hurriedly toward the quay. He ran up the gangplank followed by two of his crew who quickly hauled it on board. Seconds later, he came onto the bridge. He nodded silently to Salah.

"Hoist the anchor . . . and prepare to sail . . . immediately!" he said into the mouthpiece of a candlestick telephone that connected to the engine room.

It was only a couple of minutes, but to Salah, it felt like time had stopped. He kept his eyes on the customs house, watching for the Turks. *Come on! Come on!*

Just as they pulled away from the quay, the Turks came running out of the customs house. They stood on the dock, watching as the ship gathered momentum, her engine at full throttle, steam bursting out of her funnels in thick clouds. Salah watched as one of them took off his cap and threw it down in sheer frustration and stormed away. It was impossible to be sure, but Salah thought he looked like Omer Erdogan.

Salah lit a cigarette and heaved a big sigh of relief.

"That was a close call, Nusair."

"Yes, it was."

"Thank you, brother."

"Anytime, Masri," Musa said, steering the ship out into the Mediterranean. "So? Where are we going?"

"I'd like to go home," Salah said.

"I had a feeling you would say that."

—⚉—

"Ahmed Jemmal Pasha!" Colonel Erdogan saluted his superior.

The Ottoman governor of Syria was standing in front of his desk, his hands clasped behind his back. Fairly tall and on the stocky side, he was not a bad-looking man, in fact many thought he was quite handsome, but it was more the way he held himself and moved rather than his features. His skin was pale olive, his face oval. He had thick, black bushy eyebrows above dark eyes that looked cold and cruel. He had short black straight hair that was usually hidden beneath a fez, and a full beard and moustache, both of which were meticulously trimmed and waxed. He was wearing the dark brown uniform of the Ottoman Army, his pants tucked into black, shiny, knee-high boots.

"Tell me you have Masri in your custody," Ahmad Jemmal said in a low, sinister voice.

"I'm afraid not, Sir," Omer Erdogan replied.

Ahmad Jemmal snorted in frustration, pacing for a moment, his lips pursed tightly. He walked back to his desk and slammed it hard with his fist.

"What the hell happened?" he shouted.

"He slipped through our net, Pasha," Erdogan said apologetically.

"Where did you see him last?"

"Crete, Pasha. The port of Chania."

"Damn it!"

Ahmad Jemmal twirled the end of his moustache between his thumb and forefinger. He walked toward the tall French windows that looked upon the square below.

"Is everything ready for the execution of the traitors?"

"Yes, Pasha. It will be tomorrow at dawn."

"Masri is the only one I am missing," Ahmad Jemmal said.

"Except, Pasha, his name was not on the Damascus Protocol papers that we found in the French ambassador's house. We don't know that he was involved."

"He was involved . . ." Jemmal's eyes glinted. "I can feel it in my bones. How can he not be involved? His three friends were. He had to be."

"But we don't have proof, Sir . . ."

"We don't need proof!" Ahmad Jemmal exploded. "I am the governor of Syria and this is war, Erdogan! I will execute whom I please if I even sniff treason on them . . . and Masri reeks of it."

"Yes, Sir."

"Whose boat is he on?"

"It is Musa Nusair's, the *Tree of Life*, Pasha."

"Damned Yemeni!" Ahmad Jemmal snorted derisively.

"What did you get out of the port captain in Chania?"

"Nusair's exit papers show Benghazi as his next port."

"Libya?" Ahmad Jemmal said incredulously. "Nusair is going to take Masri to Libya? Impossible! The Italians are all over Libya. They'll arrest Masri for us. He won't even have time to spit on Libyan soil. I don't believe it! The Yemeni is lying."

"Perhaps we could send a couple of men . . . ," Omer Erdogan began to say.

"Shut up!" Ahmad Jemmal shouted. "Let me think . . ."

Omer Erdogan held his breath, not daring to breathe. The only sound in the room was that of Ahmad Jemmal's boots as he paced the stone floor.

"Nusair isn't going south west to Benghazi," Ahmad Jemmal finally said after staring at a map, a hint of a smile on his face. "He's going south east . . . to Alexandria or to Port Said. Masri's taking cover with the British. He's going home . . . to Cairo."

"What would you like me to do, Sir?"

"You leave for Cairo, now, Erdogan," Ahmad Jemmal ordered. "You throw a net so thick and wide that Masri will be caught in it the moment he steps foot in Egypt."

—⁓—

Salah breathed a sigh of relief as Port Said appeared on the horizon a couple of days after they left Chania. The seas around Crete had been rough and the journey had taken longer than expected.

"You can exhale now, brother," Musa said as he handed over the steering of the ship to his first officer.

Salah nodded.

"You should look happier."

"I should."

"You're thinking about Rafic, Khaled, and Wissam, aren't you?"

"Yes."

"I'm sure they're fine." Musa came and put his arm around Salah.

"I'm sure they're not." Salah bristled.

"When was the last time you heard from them?"

"Khaled was the last one I saw, a couple of weeks ago, when he told me he was going to try and escape and I told him to find you."

There was a moment of silence.

"What I don't understand is why the hell he asked you to take him and Noura to Beirut. That was crazy! He walked right into the lion's den."

"Perhaps he had a plan?"

Salah shrugged. "We'll never know."

"Come now, let's be optimistic."

"By the way," Salah said, "what did Noura have? A boy or a girl?"

"A girl."

Salah shook his head. "What has this war done to us? To make us not care about the things that really matter?"

"We are doing what we all need to survive, brother," Musa said.

"But still . . ." Salah put his hands in his pockets and paced angrily.

"Your mother will be surprised to see you." Musa changed the subject.

"Yes." Salah nodded. "I'll send her a telegram from Port Said."

"You think you'll be safe in Egypt?"

"I don't know about Egypt." Salah grinned. "But in my mother's house in the Khan el-Khalili, I think I'll be fine!"

"Yes, I don't think even Jemmal Pasha would have the gumption to cross your mother." Musa laughed.

—⁓—

When they docked, Salah went to the post office to send a telegram to his mother, letting her know of his imminent arrival. There, waiting in line, he read the headlines of the newspaper the man in front of him was reading. "May 6: A Bloody Day in Beirut and Damascus." His eyes fell to the line below it. "Ahmad Jemmal Pasha, Governor of Syria, Executes Arab Traitors."

Salah slumped, sadness darkening his face. His eyes scanned the list of names of those who had been hung at dawn, hoping his friends wouldn't be on it. But there they were: Khaled Shadid, Rafic Tabbara, and Wissam Jabbari. Salah took a deep breath, tears pricking the back of his eyes as he thought back to the four of them laughing and talking, lounging under a big magnolia tree between classes at the University of Beirut. He bit his lip, willing his tears back.

Suddenly, he no longer regretted the Turkish and German secrets he had stolen. He no longer felt guilty or torn. He would tell the British everything. Damn the Turks. He would see that the Arabs got their independence. And their country.

He closed his eyes to stop the tears from falling. But then they suddenly flew open.

Noura!

CHAPTER THREE

Noura bolted upright in bed. She was short of breath and her heart was racing. She ran a hand through her long, dark, disheveled hair, pushing it back and putting her hands over her face. She closed her eyes and tried to block the images of her dream, but it was no use. Her mind kept going to Khaled and the night he was arrested over a month before, shortly after they'd arrived in Beirut from Izmir . . . how he was hauled away by that Turkish soldier . . . his arms reaching out to her from behind the bars of the cart he was put into, telling her he loved her and that everything would be all right.

I never told him I loved him back . . . why? He needed to hear that from me. But I didn't tell him.

But she had been so shocked when they had accused him of treason, she hadn't known what to say or do.

Noura sobbed, her palms covering her eyes. *Dear God! Please don't let him have suffered.* As the anguish of the imagined pain suffered by her husband when they hung him in Burj Square overtook her, she curled up on the bed and buried her face into the pillow to muffle the sounds of her grief. *How could this have happened? And why?*

Her cries mixed with those of her newborn daughter, Siran, who was sleeping in a cot next to her and who had woken upon hearing her mother's distress.

Noura quickly jumped out of bed and picked up her daughter to soothe her. It was five o'clock in the morning and she didn't want to disturb Samar, her close friend and Wissam's wife, to whose home she and Khaled had come when they arrived in Beirut. Like Noura, Samar was distraught over Wissam's execution alongside Khaled, and Noura had held and consoled her until an hour before when she'd finally fallen asleep from sheer exhaustion.

Noura wished that she too could sink into the bliss of oblivion. But she couldn't. She had a little baby in her arms who was smiling and gurgling at her, fascinated with the gold medallion of the Virgin Mary that hung around her neck. Noura sat down in an armchair next to the window with Siran, staring out at the dark shapes of trees and bushes against the sky, which was beginning to lighten.

The next thing she knew, the sky was bright blue and the sound of cicadas had given way to birds. Noura looked down to see Siran cozily asleep in her arms, her little thumb in her mouth. Tears appeared in Noura's eyes. But she blinked them back, took a deep breath, and slowly got up, doing her best not to jostle her baby. She placed her carefully in the cot and covered her with a cotton blanket. She stood for a moment looking down at her, caressing her soft head. Four agonizing weeks had passed since Khaled's death. Now, her grief would have to wait. There were important decisions she needed to make: like where she and Siran were going to live . . . but more importantly, how and on what?

Noura was twenty-eight years old. Slim, but strong, at five feet six inches, she was tall for a Lebanese woman. She had an ample bosom and a small waist. And while she wasn't classically beautiful, she was considered pretty enough. She had an oval face with high cheekbones, and a thick mane of dark brown curly hair that was always tied back and rolled at the base of her neck. Her dark brown eyes, fringed with thick black eyelashes, drooped slightly downward, giving her a certain doll-like innocence. Her mouth was small, but her lips were sensual and rosy. Her two slightly crooked front teeth made her lips plumper and more alluring, even though she was always embarrassed about her smile. A round brown mole near her left eye drew attention to her eyes, which were always bright.

She washed up quickly, dressing in the long navy blue skirt, blue and white striped shirt, and sensible low-heeled shoes she had traveled in, and left Siran with Samar. She walked toward the port of Beirut, just east of the Saint George Bay, where Saint George is believed to have slain the dragon. She was going to a small pawnshop where Samar had told her she might have some luck selling her rings and pendant. While Samar had her parents to return to in the northern Bekaa valley, Noura had no one. Both her parents had passed away, her father dying just after she and Khaled were married. And she had no money. Khaled's salary was frozen and the house in Izmir belonged to the government.

She picked her way through the squalid streets until she arrived at a small square with a fountain in the middle. Shielding her eyes from the sun, she looked around, her small handbag clutched tightly in her hand. *Now where?* She took out the small piece of paper on which she had written the directions. "Opposite the fountain," Samar had told her. But there was nothing here. No shops of any kind, just a dusty square and small streets. She knew she was near the port. She could smell the salty air and hear the seagulls screeching loudly as they flew overhead. Disappointed, she turned back.

"Noura?" she heard someone call her name.

She knew that voice.

"Noura?" the male voice said again.

Noura whipped around. Her eyes grew large and a big smile broke out on her face when she saw Musa Nusair, the man who'd brought them to Beirut. She walked toward him while he quickly closed the gap between them, holding his arms out to her. Noura hugged him with all the strength she had. And though she didn't want to, she began to cry.

"I am so happy to see you, Captain." She finally looked up at him, trying to smile through her tears.

"Noura . . . I don't have the right words. I . . . I don't know what to say about . . ."

"Please," Noura interrupted quickly. "Not now."

"Come," he put his arm around her, "let us go and have some tea."

"Thank you." She fished out her handkerchief.

"How is my little Siran?" he asked.

Noura smiled, remembering her labor in Musa's cramped quarters. "She is fine. Healthy, happy, and innocent."

"I wish we could all be that way."

Minutes later, they were sitting at a quiet table in a corner near the window in a small harbor café, looking out at the hustle and bustle of the port. It was a beautiful and bright, warm morning.

But Noura's world was dark. She fought tears. Seeing Musa flooded her mind with memories of the morning she and Khaled had left Izmir: how they'd left the house under cover of night, how worried she'd been about giving birth on the way, how nervous Khaled had been. She remembered Khaled walking up to Musa on the quay, offering him a wad of bills. She remembered going into labor on the ship and how Musa had delivered Siran, and Khaled's face when he held their daughter for the first time. She clasped her hands together to try and stop them from trembling. She felt as though her heart was being squeezed and she couldn't breathe. She began taking quick, shallow breaths.

"Take your time, Noura."

Noura squeezed her eyes shut.

"He's gone, Captain," Noura said, her eyes moist again.

Musa nodded.

"I cannot imagine how you feel, Noura."

"The pain is unbearable," she whispered, hunched over, staring down at her hands.

Musa nodded silently.

"I don't what I am going to do," she added. "I have nothing . . . I have no money, nowhere to live . . . absolutely nothing."

"Please . . . let me help . . ."

"No!" Noura interrupted. "I mean, thank you," she graciously added, "but I will find a way. I have to. If not for my sake, then for Siran's."

"Well I am here to help you, Noura . . . all you have to do is ask."

"Captain . . . do you have any idea why Khaled brought us back to Beirut?" Noura asked. "If he was in trouble with the Turks, why not go somewhere where they couldn't touch him or us?"

"I can't answer that."

"And why didn't he tell me anything? I was his wife, for God's sake!"

She shook her head in anger and began to cry. Through her tears, she began rummaging around in her handbag for her handkerchief.

"Damn it!" she swore when she couldn't find one.

Musa took his and gave it to her.

"Thank you, Captain." Noura wiped her eyes and her nose. "I'm just so . . . I don't even know what to feel . . . I'm so angry . . . at Khaled, at the Turks, at the war . . . at everything. And I'm heartbroken and I'm sad and bereft. I don't know . . . I'm so confused."

Musa squeezed her hand.

"I have to leave Beirut. I can't stay here. There are too many bad memories . . . it's my hometown, it's where I was born . . . but I can't stay. I don't want to bring Siran up in a city run with this kind of cruelty."

"I can understand."

"But where do I go?" Noura looked out of the window pensively.

"What about your family?" the captain asked.

"All I have left is my great aunt in Cairo."

"Can you stay with her?"

Noura nodded. "She is elderly, but we can stay there for a while, I suppose. I will send her a telegram."

"Look, Noura, Cairo is a good idea," Musa said. "It's a British protectorate."

"How do I get there?"

"I have to go to the Yemen in a few days . . . but I will be back in about a month and then I will be going to Alexandria. I'd be happy to take you with me. Will you be all right until then?"

Noura nodded.

"But I have no money, Captain."

"You can pay me when you have the money," he reassured her.

"I can't take advantage of your generosity like that."

"Look upon it as a loan."

"Why don't I give you these in exchange?" She took out a small pouch and opened it revealing the rings and pendant.

"Don't be silly, Noura."

"Please, Captain! I insist," she said. "I don't like having debts."

"Keep them, Noura . . . give them to Siran."

"Thank you, Captain," Noura said. "This is the second time you have saved my life."

—❧—

At the end of July 1916, Noura boarded the *Tree of Life*, her daughter in one arm and her small, battered, brown suitcase in the other.

Despite all of Captain Nusair's assurances, she was nervous about the voyage. The naval war between Britain and Germany had escalated. The newspapers were filled with stories of German U-boats torpedoing and sinking merchant vessels even vaguely suspected of carrying military cargo for the British. After all, the sinking of the civilian *RMS Lusitania* off the coast of Ireland, which the Germans claimed was a military target a year before, was still very fresh in people's minds.

And here they were in the Eastern Mediterranean, which was swarming with German U-boats. Despite having spotted two of them shortly after they set out to sea, the journey passed without any mishaps and a couple of days later, Noura stood on deck, dressed in her navy skirt and white striped shirt, holding Siran in her arms as the ship approached the port in Alexandria.

The harbor was teeming with shipping vessels of all kinds: there were cargo ships, and passenger ships, but the majority were British warships and a few French ones. Noura took a deep breath when she saw the cannons, a reminder that while Egypt was a British protectorate, it was not a war-free zone. The British were using Egypt as a staging ground for all their military activities in the Middle East, while at the same time protecting the Suez Canal and the shortcut to India.

"Look, Siran," she said to the infant, "this is going to be our new home."

Siran cooed, gurgling and smiling.

We will have a fresh start here, insha'Allah.

Although Noura was trying to stay positive, she was nervous. She was in a country she didn't know, going to live in a city she'd only visited once years ago. She had very little money that Samar had given her, just enough to get her to Cairo . . . *What am I going to do here? I have to find a job. But what?* She hugged her daughter close, clutched the pendant around her neck and said a little prayer.

"So what does my little girl think of this country?" Captain Nusair took Siran from her mother.

"We still have to make it to Cairo," Noura said.

"I don't think that will be a problem," he said calmly, swinging the child up in the air.

"Captain . . ." Noura shook her finger at him playfully. "What do you have up your sleeve?"

"Who? Me?" he said, balancing Siran on his hip. "Nothing, Madame! Nothing at all!" He twirled around the deck with Siran, singing to her as he did.

—◊—

Noura watched the sailors from the *Tree of Life* lower the gangplank. As she walked down, her earlier anxiety returned. Worried about what the future was going to bring, she felt herself shaking, clinging to the ropes along the gangplank as she cautiously made her way down. Behind her came Captain Nusair carrying Siran in one arm and her suitcase in the other.

"Come, Noura, follow me," Captain Nusair said when they got to the bottom.

"Where are we going?"

"I've arranged for an official in the customs house to give you Egyptian papers."

"Honestly, Captain, I don't know how to thank you."

"Let us hurry," Musa urged.

Once inside, Musa began looking around before finally leading her to a small, empty, windowless office.

"Who are you looking for, Captain?" Noura asked, confused.

"Just a moment, Noura . . . wait here."

Noura looked around wondering what was going on. But Siran was starting to cry and she had to give the infant her complete attention.

"Noura," she heard the captain's voice.

"Yes." She turned to see Captain Nusair standing with a man as tall as himself, but bigger and broader. He was wearing a long white cotton tunic with thin dark red and saffron yellow stripes that sat snugly across his middle. His head was covered with a taupe-colored cotton fabric, wrapped around like a turban and drawn across his face, covering his eyes almost completely.

Noura looked at him. *Who is this man?* she wondered.

"*Sabah al-khair,* Madame," said a gruff, gravelly voice from behind the cloth.

Noura nodded, acknowledging him. She looked at Captain Nusair, her eyes questioning.

"Do you not recognize me?" the man continued.

Noura shook her head, smiling with embarrassment.

"My dear lady . . ." The man bent down and pulled the cloth from his face, revealing his eyes. They were brown and they twinkled. Suddenly, he winked.

Noura's eyes opened wide. She quickly handed Siran to the captain.

"Salah! Oh my God!" She threw herself into his arms.

Her mind flashed back to when Khaled had first introduced her to him. "Salah, this is the woman I'm going to marry," he'd said and Noura had looked at him, shocked, considering they were not even engaged at the time. "And, Noura, this is my best friend, Salah," he'd added. "We've known each other since we were ten years old." Noura remembered smiling shyly, still blushing from the last comment. "And don't worry about his bear-like appearance, he's really a pussy cat . . . who wears too much cologne!" Khaled had teased him.

Noura remembered that first evening with Salah and how well they had all gotten along, especially the instant connection she had felt with her husband's friend. Salah had her laughing all through dinner, insisting on showing her his dancing moves. "I promise to dance at the wedding!" He'd winked at her. "I've never seen Khaled like this before," he'd said to Noura when Khaled got up for a moment to go and get them more drinks. "He's had his share of girlfriends, but you're different." Noura had smiled shyly. "There will be a wedding soon . . . trust me."

Ever since, Salah had been in their lives. They would often meet for dinner, with Wissam and Samar sometimes joining in, and Rafic too when he was in town from Damascus. Salah was one of the three best men at the wedding. Shortly after, Khaled was offered a job as lawyer at the Chemin de Fer Imperial Office in Izmir. He had accepted immediately, knowing that Salah was already there.

And when they moved to Izmir, Salah helped them find a house that was close to his apartment and Noura often dropped by. Occasionally, Salah would come by and ask her to sew on a button or fix a tear in his pants or jacket. And Khaled was delighted to see the budding friendship between his wife and best friend.

Noura was so happy to see Salah that she wouldn't let go of him. He had to pry her hands from behind his neck and carefully put her down on the ground.

"I am so happy to see you, Noura," Salah said. "It has been too long. The last time I saw you was last year in September at that lovely birthday dinner you had for Khaled," he reminisced. "My God! It's been almost a year."

Noura looked down at the tips of her shoes; she pursed her lips in a tight line, holding back the tears that came with the images of that idyllic evening in their garden in Izmir. She remembered how that morning the doctor had confirmed her suspicions that she was pregnant. She remembered how excited and happy she was and how she was going to tell Khaled. She remembered waiting until all the guests had left and over a piece of cake and a glass of champagne, she had told him. She remembered the look on his face and how the initial shock had given way to a huge bright smile that lit up his whole face. He had taken her in his arms, hugging her, holding her, kissing her and he had told her how happy he was, how happy she made him and how much marrying her was the best thing he'd ever done. And he had told her he loved her. *Khaled! Where have you gone?*

Salah put his arm around her and hugged her. "Courage," he said.

Noura bit her lip, nodding, pushing back her tears.

"I can't believe you didn't immediately recognize my voice," Salah said quickly.

"Oh Salah, I am sorry. It's all so overwhelming."

"Yes . . . ," he said. "I know . . . look, Noura . . ."

"No Salah," she interrupted him, knowing he was going to say something about Khaled. "Not yet."

Salah nodded, respecting her wishes.

"Well now," Captain Nusair jumped in, "we need to get going. I have a very short turnaround time in this slip, only to unload and then I have to move on."

"Noura . . . ," Salah began. "I have to explain our plan to get you into Cairo safely."

Salah and Musa exchanged a conspiratorial look.

"What do you mean?" Noura looked at them suspiciously.

"I have a horse taxi waiting outside. The driver is one of my friends. He will take you to the station and get you and Siran on the train."

"What about you?"

"I will meet you in Cairo."

"I don't understand." Noura shook her head. "What happens when I get to the station in Cairo?"

"Another one of my boys will pick you up and take you to my mother's house."

"And I suppose that is where you will be?"

Salah nodded.

"Why the subterfuge?"

"The Turks are looking for me."

"Why?"

"Because Khaled, Wissam, and Rafic were my friends."

"Were you involved with them too?"

"Noura . . . it doesn't matter. They think I was."

"So why haven't they found you?" she asked.

"Once you see where my mother and I live, you will know why they have not been able to find me."

"Noura," Musa jumped in. "We don't want to take any chances. Egypt is filled with Turkish secret police. It is better for you not to be seen with Salah . . . for now."

"But what would they want with me? They already executed my husband!" Noura said hotly. "What do they think? That I am somehow involved?"

Neither Salah nor Musa said a word.

"Well, I don't care! Let them come after me! Let them try! The bastards," she cried.

"Noura, the Arab Revolt has begun. It began over a month ago on June 10 . . . they are fighting now to take Mecca," Salah tried to explain.

"The revolt be damned!" Noura cried. "It's what got my husband killed. I hope it fails! Let them all go to hell!"

Salah took a deep breath.

"Noura, this is all for your safety . . . and mine," Salah said. "I haven't left Cairo in weeks. I only came here today for you."

"Oh! This is just too much. I never thought we would have to go through such a charade. I hate this!" She exploded. "Why is this happening?"

"I know, Noura . . . I'm sorry," Salah said.

Siran began to whimper at the sound of her mother's angry voice.

"Oh Siran . . ." Noura walked around, rocking Siran gently. She took several breaths to control herself.

"Very well," she finally said in a calmer voice.

"Let's go then." Salah took her arm.

"I need a moment with the captain," Noura said, handing Siran to Salah.

"Captain . . . ," Noura started.

"Are you all right?" Musa asked.

"Yes . . . I'll be fine. I'm sorry I lost my temper."

Musa shrugged. "Don't worry, everything will be fine. I know the man Salah has chosen to accompany you. You will be well taken care of, I assure you."

"I know, Captain. I know Salah will never let any harm come to us. But I don't need anyone to come with me. I'll be fine. I think I can take a train on my own."

"I'm sure you can. But Salah organized all of this. Don't blame him. He's only looking out for you."

Noura bit her lip, nodding. "I'm sorry."

"It's all right. We understand."

"Oh! Before I forget, here are your papers. You and Siran are legal in Egypt."

Noura took Musa's hands in hers and looked up at him, her brown eyes shining with unshed tears.

"Thank you," she whispered, her voice cracking, "for everything you have done . . . for Khaled, Siran, and me."

"Noura . . . ," Musa interrupted.

She shook her head and put her finger to her lips, indicating he remain silent.

"I don't know how or if I will ever be able to repay you."

"You don't have to," Musa replied kindly.

Noura nodded, her chin was trembling. She looked down at her hands trying to control her emotions, but when she looked up at the captain, she couldn't hold back the tears. She put her arms around his neck and hugged him, crying softly into his neck.

"Thank you," she said again, once she'd regained control of herself. "I will never forget you."

And with that, Noura turned and walked to where Salah was standing with her daughter. She took Siran in her arms and turned to look back at the captain and blew him a kiss.

—⧓—

Later that afternoon, Colonel Erdogan was in his office in the outwardly unremarkable, but inwardly elegant house he'd rented for his sojourn in Cairo. He had arrived in Egypt nearly three months before, in early May. There was a knock on the door.

"Telegram, Sir."

Erdogan opened it.

NOURA SHADID IS HEADED TO CAIRO. AWAIT INSTRUCTIONS.

Interesting. Erdogan stroked his beard pensively. *This could work out well. She may well lead us to Masri.*

—⧓—

Salah's mother, Saydeh, lived on Zuqaq al-Hamra, a tiny cobblestone alleyway near the Al-Hussein Mosque in the Khan el-Khalili bazaar in Cairo's Islamic district. The El-Khalili bazaar was founded back in the fourteenth century, beginning as a stop on a caravan route that went through the city. As it grew, it became a tangle of lanes and tiny alleyways, a complicated and confusing labyrinth. It was the perfect place for Salah to disappear.

Saydeh's apartment stretched across the first and second floors of a four-story building that belonged to her and her late husband, Salah's father, and was close to one of the original gates of the bazaar. The ground floor was rented out to an antiques dealer who sold chandeliers and antique Berber jewelry. There was a smaller third floor that was filled with wooden boxes and old furniture covered with sheets, and an attic above filled with more boxes and old trunks that led onto the roof.

As promised, Salah stood behind his mother, smiling when Noura arrived.

"*Ahlan wa sahlan!*" Saydeh said, her arms extended toward Noura. "Welcome, *habibti*, welcome!"

Saydeh Masri was not, at first glance, a beautiful woman. She was about five feet three inches and rather plump, with a particularly large behind that shifted from side to side suggestively when she walked. Her round face looked even rounder by the way she wrapped the *hijab* around her head, covering her hair completely, emphasizing the jowls around her chin. Her dark brown eyebrows were thick and nicely shaped, shading her big eyes, which were light brown with amber highlights depending on the way the sun hit them. She had put a little kohl in them, but otherwise wore no makeup. Her olive skin was relatively smooth, except for the crow's feet around her eyes and the laugh lines around her mouth. She was wearing a long black *abaya*, but her hijab was a dusky pink that suited her complexion. Her beauty came from within . . . her laughter, her warmth, and her generosity overshadowed what she lacked in physical attributes.

"Come! Let us go upstairs," she said, leading the way. "You must be tired after your journey. I have some fresh, cold rosewater . . ." She chattered away as she climbed the stairs, holding onto the balustrade with one hand and her abaya with the other. "Please come in." She threw open the wooden double doors; a dark hallway led into a bright living room that was furnished with a divan, low stools, and large bright silk cushions. Sunlight poured in from the windows that gave onto the tiny street below.

"Hmmm!" Noura took a deep breath. "Something smells delicious."

"Would you like to wash before we sit down?" she offered. "My bedroom is through there." She pointed to another door along the hallway. "And next door is the bathroom. There is fresh water in the bucket."

"Yes, thank you," Noura replied. "I would like that."

"Off you go then . . . give me this sweet baby." Saydeh held out her arms. "What is her name?"

"Siran," Noura replied, handing the infant over.

"Siran." Saydeh fussed over the bundle in her arms.

She is so kind, Noura thought as she went into the bathroom. Upon entering there was a small sink and a table upon which was a wooden bucket filled with water. There was a mug and a small dish with a bar of green soap. Fresh linen towels hung on a rack next to the sink. The table with the bucket was placed against a small, waist-high wall behind which was a tiled area for bathing. A separate larger bucket sat neatly off to the side along with a small wooden stool.

On a shelf above the sink was an antique walnut shaving mirror and dresser that had undoubtedly belonged to Saydeh's husband. Noura tilted the mirror, changing the angle to get a better look at herself. Suddenly, tears filled her eyes and without warning began to spill down her cheeks. She tried desperately to hold them back but it was too late. She held onto the sink with both hands trying to stop the sobs, but one managed to escape. Quickly she grabbed a towel and buried her face in it. She didn't want Saydeh or Salah to hear her.

Why? She asked herself, looking at the torment reflected in the mirror. *Why? Why does it have to be so? Why do I have to be alone?* She railed against the image of herself, turning around, pacing up and down the bathroom, anger rising, her breathing labored, her face still covered with the linen cloth. She sat down on the stool in the corner and let herself cry, her shoulders heaving with the burden of her emotions. Slowly, the tide of sadness and anger that had risen without warning retreated and Noura began to relax, taking deep breaths to calm herself.

She heard Saydeh's voice outside the door, "Everything all right, Noura?"

"Yes," she managed to reply in what she hoped sounded like a normal voice.

"*Tayeb* . . . take your time," Saydeh said. "Come little one . . . ," she added and began to sing an old song to Siran as she shuffled away.

For some reason, the song brought a fresh round of tears to Noura's eyes. But this time, she managed to hold them back. She quickly washed her face with cold water, dabbing her eyes, hoping the redness and puffiness wouldn't show. Taking a deep breath, she squared her shoulders, and with one last look in the mirror went back to the living room.

"There you are." Saydeh looked up. A look of tacit understanding and compassion passed between them. Noura knew that the older woman knew she'd been crying.

"Where is Salah?" Noura asked.

"Someone was at the door. He'll be right back."

"*Imme!*" Salah's voice boomed from downstairs. "I'll be back in a few minutes." The door slammed.

"My boy . . . always busy. He can never sit still," Saydeh said. "Come, sit down and have something cold to drink." She indicated the cushion next to her on the low sofa.

Next to Saydeh, there was a tray with a large glass jug filled with pink rosewater, fresh rose petals, and lots of ice. Three glasses were placed around it. On the coffee table in the middle of the room was a very large, round tray filled with *mezze*, little appetizers of all kinds . . . *hummus,* a chick pea dip, *babaghanoush,* a roasted eggplant dip decorated with pomegranate seeds, a *tabbouleh* salad with parsley, small triangular spinach pies, round cheese pies, and small *falafel,* little balls of chick peas, spices, and parsley.

"This looks delicious," Noura exclaimed.

"I will go and get the bread," Saydeh said. "It is keeping warm in the kitchen."

"Let me go," Noura offered, feeling bad as the older woman fretted around her.

"Not at all," she ordered. "Sit down."

Noura smiled and looked in on Siran, who was fast asleep in a makeshift cot.

"So, Noura, where does your aunt live?" Saydeh bustled in.

"She lives in Old Cairo near the Church of Saint Sergius."

"That is quite far from here." Saydeh sat down. "And she is your mother's sister?"

"Actually, my grandmother's sister," Noura said.

"Ah, your great aunt. She must be quite elderly."

"She is," Noura replied, taking a sip of her drink. It was delicious . . . cold and sweet, just how she liked it.

"When was the last time you saw her?"

"It has been some time," Noura replied, "at least ten years, if not more."

Saydeh refilled Noura's glass and her own. She kept the conversation personable and light and Noura was grateful she didn't bring up what had happened in Beirut.

"I haven't been to Old Cairo in ages," she told Noura. "I rarely get out of El-Khalili. My life revolves around this souk. There is a fruit and vegetable market, everything I need I can find in one of these lanes downstairs . . . and all my friends live near here in the bazaar, so I have no need to leave. We get together every morning at Rania's Café after we finish the morning chores . . ."

"Do you know your way around the bazaar?" Noura asked. "It looks very complicated."

"Heavens, no! I only know my little places. Even those who spend a lifetime here don't know it well. There are very few people who do."

"Anyway, maybe you can come with me to Rania's Café one day?" Saydeh offered.

"Of course, I would love to," Noura replied. "As soon as I get settled."

"Good!" Saydeh bobbed her head from side to side, smiling broadly and rubbing her hands together.

Downstairs the door slammed. "Salah is home! You keep him company while I put the finishing touches on lunch."

"Let me at least help you clear the *mezze* dishes," Noura suggested.

"I absolutely refuse," Saydeh said, waddling off with the large tray in her hands. "You have just come from a long journey . . . make yourself comfortable."

"*Marhaba!*" Salah came in. "Sorry about disappearing like that." He untied his turban.

"Noura," Salah dropped his voice, "was the journey all right?" Noura nodded.

"Noura, please don't tell my mother that you traveled by yourself." "She doesn't know . . . anything?"

Salah shook his head.

"I understand. She's a lovely woman. She's been so hospitable."

"My mother is the queen of hospitality." Salah smiled.

"Salah . . . I'm sorry about my outburst in Alexandria this morning . . ." Noura began, playing nervously with the cuff of her sleeve.

When Salah didn't answer, she looked up. He was staring at her, a funny look on his face. Suddenly self-conscious, she turned and looked out the window, glancing at her reflection in the windowpane. The afternoon light brightened her face, her eyes and hair looked lighter and her skin luminous.

Noura looked back at Salah. She could feel the blood rising to her cheeks. She couldn't understand why the look on his face had flustered her.

"Noura . . . ," Salah began a little hesitantly.

She looked up at him, tilting her head.

"Lunch is ready!" Saydeh came bustling in before Salah had time to say anything. "*Yallah!* Before it gets cold," she added, urging them both to get up and herding them into the dining room on the other side of the hallway.

After lunch, they all sat enjoying a lazy afternoon in the living room with a relaxing cup of *café blanc*. Salah sat quietly and Saydeh sat with Siran in her lap. Noura stirred the orange-blossom flavored hot water in her cup. What was she going to do? How was she going to support them? *Khaled, why did you leave us like this? Tell me what to do. Help me!* Noura sighed inwardly. She didn't want to leave. She felt safe and cocooned here with Salah and Saydeh, who was so warm and generous. But she had to go. These people were not her family. She couldn't expect them to support her. As scared as she was about what lay ahead, she had to face it.

From beneath her eyelashes, she glanced at Salah's profile. Just then he turned to look at her. Embarrassed that he may have caught her staring at him, she quickly stood to take her leave.

"Now, *habibti*," Saydeh said, tearfully hugging Noura goodbye, "you keep in touch and if there is anything you need, all you have to do is ask."

"*Shukran*," Noura hugged her back. "And thank you for lunch. It really was wonderful."

"And Noura, I have not said anything about what has happened, because I wanted you to enjoy this afternoon and not have to think about the tragedy, but I want you to know how very sorry I am, *habibti*," Saydeh said.

Noura nodded her thanks.

"So if you want to talk, or you need a shoulder . . . ," Saydeh continued.

"*Imme!*" Salah jumped seeing how the expression on Noura's face had changed. "We have to go if Noura wants to be at her great aunt's by six."

"I hope you're going with her and not sending her in the carriage by herself." Saydeh folded her arms angrily in front of her.

"Of course I am, *imme*," Salah picked up the suitcase.

"You have a home here," Saydeh cried out after Noura. Noura turned and waved.

"Are you really coming with me?" Noura asked after Saydeh closed the door.

"No," Salah said. "You know I can't."

Noura felt deflated.

"But Nassim here will go with you." A young eighteen-year-old boy stepped up. Salah introduced them. "Nassim knows this souk like the back of his hand," he told Noura. "Every back alley, lane, every tunnel . . ."

"Thank you, Salah," Noura said.

"Come back whenever you want to." Salah held his hands out to her.

From beneath her eyelashes Noura could feel him staring at her. Shyly she put her hand in his.

"You will always have a home in the El-Khalili bazaar."

Suddenly, she felt terribly alone and tears pricked the back of her eyes. She didn't want to leave but she knew she had to go. Quickly, she withdrew her hand and without looking at Salah, she turned to follow Nassim toward the main square.

CHAPTER FOUR

A month later, on the last Friday of August, Salah was at his desk in his makeshift office in his mother's apartment. The desk and surrounding area were strewn with papers and maps. He had spent the morning reading reports of what was going on in the Hejaz.

The Arab Revolt had begun almost three months before at the beginning of June.

At Faisal's request, Salah had gone down to the Hejaz a month after he arrived in Cairo. Faisal asked Salah to run interference between the Arabs and the group of British and French officers who had arrived to assist with the revolt.

At the initial meeting, the English insisted that the Arab forces attack Medina as their first show of force. But Salah had argued against Medina based on the information he had taken from Von Sanders' office in Izmir . . . there were too many Ottoman troops and Fakhri Pasha, the Ottoman commander, was an aggressive man. "I would go to Mecca first, Prince," Salah urged. "Not only can we take the city, but it will help the sharif in terms of propaganda. It is, after all, Islam's holiest city." But Faisal went with the British opinion and Salah's advice was overlooked.

Nonetheless, Salah rode out with Faisal and his brother Ali at the head of the Arab troops to Medina, but as he had predicted, the Arabs were pushed back by an aggressive Turkish defense. Dismayed and embarrassed by their first setback, Faisal turned to Salah. Once again, Salah told him that the Arabs should begin with Mecca.

The Hashemite tribesmen attacked the Ottoman garrison in Mecca on June 10 and in an effort to wipe away the disaster of Medina, the sharif of Mecca proclaimed the Arab Revolt had officially begun. Mecca was taken by the Arabs at the beginning of July but had fallen back into Ottoman hands.

According to the report Salah was now reading, while the fresh battalion of Ottoman troops was outnumbered by the Arab tribesmen, the Ottomans were better armed and better trained and were defending the city well.

"Salah!" he heard Saydeh's shrill voice call out. "Salah . . . I'm going over to Rania's to meet the girls."

Salah looked up and rolled his eyes. "All right, *imme*."

"I'll be back in time for lunch."

"All right." Salah sighed.

"Are you going for Friday prayers?"

"Yes, *imme*, I always do."

"Such a good boy," he heard Saydeh mutter before the door closed.

Salah groaned inwardly. He, like his father, was anything but religious. In his new world, though, the house of God served a purpose: it was the perfect hub for espionage operations.

Salah looked at his pocket watch. *Damn!* He had to hurry if he was going to make midday prayers. Even though it was only a quarter past eleven and the Al-Hussein mosque was ten minutes away, Salah took a longer, different route every time he went. Magdi, the fruitseller, was one of the handful of people who lived and worked in the El-Khalili who knew all the alleyways, hidden lanes, and underground tunnels that crisscrossed the bazaar, and devised new routes for Salah to take to the mosque every Friday.

And it was Magdi who, along with his son, Hisham, had created a network of informants around the souk to warn Salah every time the Turks were in the bazaar. There had been a couple of difficult moments, but so far, Salah had managed to slip through their net.

Salah abandoned the report and finished writing something on a piece of paper, folded it, and put it in the pocket of a fresh tunic he was going to wear. He checked the gun in his shoulder holster before slipping into it. He put on the tunic that was cut to hide the holster, quickly tied his turban, and headed downstairs. Pulling the end of his turban across his face, he opened the door and looked around carefully, checking the rooftops, before stepping out into the narrow lane. Keeping to the corners and trying to blend in, Salah finally got to the Midan Al-Hussein, the large open square in front of the Mosque. This was the trickiest part.

Salah scanned the square. He looked at his watch. He still had a few minutes. He wanted to wait just in case any of Erdogan's boys showed up. As soon as the call to prayer sounded from the minaret, a group of men left a coffee house and came up the lane toward the mosque. Salah attached himself to the end, walking toward the mosque with them. Once inside the courtyard, Salah followed them, did his ablutions alongside them and went into the main mosque. He milled around for a few minutes, fingering his prayer beads, and when the imam called for everyone to take their places, Salah stood at the end of the first row and bowed his head. The young man next to him was another one of Magdi's sons. Salah took the note he had written earlier out of his pocket and handed it to the boy. In return, he received an envelope that he slipped into his tunic.

The prayers ended and in the general commotion that usually ensued at the end of Friday prayers, Salah slipped into a hallway that led to the back of the mosque and through a door that led to a street that looked more like a rabbit's warren. From here, there was a way home that took him across the rooftops of the bazaar's shops.

Back in his office at home, he pulled out the note that had been handed to him.

Urgent. Come to Mecca.

It was just past one o'clock in the afternoon. If he hurried, he could get the late afternoon train to the Gulf of Suez. Salah packed his small satchel and left a note for Saydeh saying that there was another problem with the railway in the Hejaz, similar to the one he'd had to deal with a few weeks before, and he had received orders from his bosses to go and take a look. *Sort of the truth.*

Outside, he made his way to the fruitsellers' lane near one of the old gates of the souk.

He slipped into a stall from the back entrance and sat on a small stool behind the seller, shielded by a screen made of reeds.

"*Marhaba*, brother," Salah said softly.

"Good afternoon, Salah," Magdi replied without turning around.

"Magdi . . . I have to get to Mecca. I'm taking the train to Suez. Can you arrange for transport to Jeddah?"

"I will send word to Nusair to meet you at Suez. A boat will be the quickest way there."

"That is what I was hoping. Where is Nusair?"

"He is not far. He's near Eilat. Hisham will send word to him now," Magdi replied.

"Thank you, Magdi."

Magdi nodded. "The Red Sea is safe. The British have cleared away all the Ottoman gunboats."

"One good thing they've done," Salah said.

"What is happening in Mecca?" Magdi asked. "How did the city fall back to the Ottomans?"

"I don't know, Magdi."

"Salah . . . ," Magdi said in a low whisper. "Word on the street is that the British are going back on their word."

"I have heard the same," Salah replied.

"Why promise us what they are not going to deliver?"

"I don't know that either. But trust me, Magdi, I will find out," Salah swore. "Because whoever is behind this, also betrayed my friends. If it turns out to be the English, they will pay for it."

"You can count on my help."

Salah took a deep breath. "Thank you, Magdi. I will send word from there."

"Very well. *Ma'asalame*."

LOST MASRI AT CAIRO TRAIN STATION.

Omer Erdogan slammed the telegram down on his desk.

"Why, in the name of God is it so hard to keep an eye on that giant?" Erdogan shouted at the team of agents standing in front of him. "How is it that you people keep losing him? Do you at least have an idea as to where he was going?"

"North? South? East? West?" Erdogan asked, his voice dripping with sarcasm.

—m—

It was midmorning. Noura was in her bedroom in her great aunt's house. She was exhausted. Siran had kept her up most of the night, having finally gone to sleep on Noura's shoulder only a few minutes before. Noura carefully set her down in her cot and sat next to her in a comfortable armchair, gently rocking her and humming softly.

As she did this, she looked around. It was a comfortable, large, bright and airy room with high ceilings and tall French windows at one end that looked out onto the small garden in the back. The windows were covered with creamy white cotton curtains. There was a big white wooden double bed made up with crisp white linens. At the bottom of the bed lay a red and white paisley-patterned cotton quilt. Next to it was the chair she sat in and Siran's cot. Near the window were a small sofa and coffee table and a small writing desk with a wooden chair that faced the windows. The walls were whitewashed and clean. There were no paintings, but there was a ceramic blue hand of Fatima that hung on the wall next to the window.

Noura got up and went to open the windows for some fresh air. She leaned on the small wrought iron railing in front of the window for a moment and took a deep breath.

Even though she'd only been in Cairo for a month, Noura felt as though it had been years. Time crawled. She had nothing to do, no one to talk to. Her great aunt, Hanan, suffered from dementia and sat in her room or the salon staring out into nothingness. The only other person in the house was Amira, Hanan's personal maid and longtime housekeeper.

There was a gentle knock on the door. Noura turned and ran to answer, hoping the noise wouldn't wake Siran. It was Amira with a tray of coffee and cookies.

Amira was a large, buxom woman who came across as Amazonian

and intimidating when in truth, she was gentle and kind. She was in her fifties, although she looked ten years younger. She had a perfectly round face, with beautiful, smooth, dark olive skin, and dark brown eyes that smiled sadly beneath bushy eyebrows. Her high cheekbones, thick, sensual lips, and short, squat nose made her look more African than Egyptian. She had a mass of sandy-gold, tightly curled long hair that she always kept in a tidy ponytail.

"The cookies just came out of the oven. You didn't eat much breakfast this morning, so I thought you would like some."

"Thank you, Amira," Noura said gratefully. "Siran kept me up all night. She's only just gone to sleep."

"Yes, I know . . . poor little thing. It was probably the heat."

"Did you hear her all the way at the other end of the house?" Noura asked, horrified.

Amira nodded.

"Oh my gosh! I hope she didn't disturb Aunt Hanan," Noura said, wringing her hands.

"Don't worry. Madame takes a sleeping pill before bed. She would not have heard the child."

Noura's shoulders sagged. As so often happened these days, tears appeared in her eyes. She willed them back, balling her hands into little fists at her sides.

Amira put the tray down on the coffee table.

"Would you like me to pour the coffee, Madame Noura?"

Noura shook her head.

"Madame Noura . . . ," Amira ventured timidly. "Is everything all right?"

Noura shook her head again, her gaze firmly on the floor as she fought back tears.

Without a word, Amira took Noura in her arms.

Noura began to shake. She buried her head in Amira's shoulder, sobbing silently so as to not wake Siran.

"I'm sorry, Amira," Noura finally said, wiping her tears with her handkerchief.

"No need for apologies," Amira said softly. "Come sit down, Madame. Have a glass of water."

Noura drank deeply. "Thank you, Amira."

Amira smiled.

"I'm so confused," Noura began, reaching for some more water. "I cannot come to grips with what happened. I don't understand why Khaled never shared anything with me. Why he did what he did? And why did he take us back to Beirut in the first place? It wasn't my idea to go to Beirut . . . it was his."

Amira took Noura's hand in hers. "I don't have answers to your questions, Madame."

"Oh Amira, sometimes I feel so terribly sad and alone and sometimes I just feel so angry . . . at Khaled for putting me in this situation and at the people who executed him who also put me here.

"What do I do, Amira? I have to do something. I have to make myself useful. I have to take my mind off of what has happened. I'm going mad just sitting around all day."

"What did you do in Izmir?"

"I had a husband to look after, I had a house to keep, I had friends, I had a life to plan . . . and now I have nothing. No husband, no home, no friends, nothing."

"You have your daughter, Madame, and she needs you."

"I know that," Noura looked over at Siran, "but I also need a life . . . I want my old life back," she lamented.

The two women sat silently.

"What is to become of Siran and me? Who will look after us?"

"Have faith, Madame Noura. God will help you. Now, have your coffee before it gets cold."

Noura smiled sadly. *God* . . . she was running very low on faith these days. She helped herself to the thick coffee and stirred it.

She wondered if Saydeh was at Rania's Café. She could see her sitting at a table enjoying a cup of coffee, laughing and talking about everything and nothing. Strangely, even though she didn't know Saydeh well, she missed her.

Noura sighed. And what would Salah be doing? Where would he be? She thought of Salah taking her hand in his, looking at her and smiling. She could see his eyes twinkling mischievously. She remembered all those times in Izmir when he would stop by on his way home. They would have tea and cake and he would make her laugh until her sides ached.

Suddenly, Noura realized what she was doing. *Stop it! Why am I thinking of him? What is wrong with me?* Salah was Khaled's friend, the best man at their wedding. Noura slammed her cup of coffee down on the saucer.

Siran whimpered. Repentant, Noura ran to the cot and took Siran in her arms, rocking her gently back to sleep.

—⚶—

It was Thursday and, for Saydeh, market day. On her way to the vegetable market, she wondered what she was going to make. Salah was away until God knows when . . . she could possibly host a lunch or a dinner . . . but it wasn't really opportune in the midst of the Arab Revolt, although you would never know it living in El-Khalili. The sun shone brightly in a cloudless blue sky, birds chirped here and there, and the morning sounds of the market mingled with the voices of vendors and made Saydeh feel safe and cocooned from the big bad world at war beyond

Standing at Amin's vegetable stand, Saydeh perused the mounds of eggplants, carrots, artichokes, and tomatoes.

"*Saba al-khair*, Madame Saydeh," Amin said cheerfully.

"Good morning, Amin," Saydeh replied.

"Can I help you pick something out this morning?"

"No, thank you. You are a rascal and you always give me the riper vegetables."

"Aw, Madame Saydeh." Amin held up his hands in protest. "I give you the best."

"I will pick myself."

Saydeh was deep in concentration, feeling the firm skins of the deep purple eggplants, rolling the tomatoes in her palms, turning the artichokes over to look for any spots.

"I need two pounds of eggplants, please," Saydeh heard someone say. "And two pounds of tomatoes, please."

Temporarily distracted, Saydeh looked up to see a man dressed in a dark suit standing next to her.

"These are beautiful vegetables," the man remarked.

He sounded Turkish. Saydeh's ears pricked up.

"Yes . . . all from Egypt," Amin said proudly. "How do you prepare eggplant?" he asked as he weighed the vegetables.

"I'm not sure," the man replied. "I am not a cook."

"Well, if I were you," Amin started, "I would . . ."

Saydeh rolled her eyes as Amin started to give the man a recipe.

"And finally, I would add onion . . ."

"What?" Saydeh interrupted. "Have you gone mad, Amin? That is the most ridiculous recipe for eggplant I have ever heard. Now, Sir." She turned to the man in the suit. "Do not listen to him. The recipe he gave you is terrible."

"Madame," the man tipped his tarbush hat to her, "I would be honored if you gave me your recipe."

Saydeh explained quickly.

"Thank you, Madame!" the man said. "We are simple Syrians from the countryside. We do not have the culinary skill you do."

Saydeh's brow knitted together. *Syrian? He's lying. Why would a Syrian peasant look as smart as this fellow? Besides, all Syrians are great cooks.*

"What are you doing in Cairo?"

"We are here on some business."

"I see."

"Yes, we are involved in the Hejaz Railway."

"Very interesting. What is a Syrian from the countryside doing working for the Hejaz Railway?"

"Many of us were recruited to work for the railway. In fact, I am looking for someone who also works on the railway . . . you might know him . . . Salah Masri?"

"Ohhh . . ." Amin opened his mouth, but quickly shut it when he saw Saydeh glare at him.

Saydeh turned toward the man. "Masri? No . . ." She pretended to think. "Why are you looking for him?"

"We need him to come with us to the Hejaz."

"Masri . . . No . . . doesn't ring a bell. Well now, I must be going."

Saydeh turned around and headed toward Zuqaq al-Hamra. Her heart was beating fast. *Why did he want to know where Salah was? And if he worked on the railway, wouldn't he know Salah was already in the Hejaz? So why did he lie? Something very fishy is going on. Is Salah up to something?* She looked over her shoulder. The man was paying Amin for the vegetables. Pulling her abaya close around her, Saydeh quickly disappeared into one of the labyrinthine lanes that led away from the vegetable sellers' square.

—⁓—

The port in Jeddah was chaos. British warships and seaplanes were crammed into every available dock space. Arab troops swarmed the quays, elated by having taken the Ottoman garrison a month before, at the end of July.

"There's the ship that won Jeddah for the Arabs," Musa Nusair pointed out as they anchored a couple of hundred yards at sea, waiting for one of the ships to pull out.

"It's a seaplane carrier," Salah said.

"Yes . . . the British pilots bombed the hell out of the garrison."

Salah leaned on the railing. He pulled a cigarette out of his pocket and lit it. *How did I get myself involved in this? I should be in Cairo with Noura.* "Nusair, I must get to Mecca."

"Let me see if one of my men can row you in, or I can lend you one of dinghies," Musa said. "Can you row?"

"I'll have to learn . . ." Salah smiled and climbed down into the little boat.

—⁓—

Salah rode by camel to Mecca and arrived at Faisal's camp just outside the holy city as the sun was setting. He saw Faisal's big white tent from a distance, glowing golden in the waning sun. The desert was beautiful at sunset. The dunes were all shades of chocolate and caramel and the sand looked like gold dust.

As soon as he arrived, he went to see the Hashemite prince.

"Salah!" Faisal's face brightened when he saw him.

"I came as quickly as I could. What is going on?"

"I don't understand, Salah," Faisal admitted. "There were only a hundred of them compared to five thousand of ours. The Holy City should have been ours after we captured the Ottoman government office. But the Turks refused to surrender. They are in the Turkish fort. Some of the tribesmen have gotten into the fort and there has been some street fighting, but we have not been able to overwhelm them."

"Prince, I am not a soldier. I do not know anything about military strategy. What are your military advisors telling you?"

"The British tell me this is a foolish strategy and I should go to Medina. But I did that before and it was a fiasco."

"Let us take a look at the Fort, Prince."

"We must do it tonight."

—✺—

As the sky turned a dark shade of purple, Salah and Faisal stole across the dunes toward the hill that overlooked the Turkish fort at the entrance to the Holy City. As they got to the top of the slope, they lay on their bellies, hiding as best they could behind a couple of dry desert shrubs. There were sentries watching the desert carefully, the lights from the fort brightening up a large perimeter around the building.

Carefully, Salah took out his binoculars, scanning the west side of the building.

"The fort is well built, Prince," Salah whispered. "The walls are thick. You will need British artillery to get in." He handed the binoculars to Faisal. "Take a look. The walls are not high. Your men are quick, but you will need every one of them to scale the walls and get to the top at the exact same time in order to storm the fort and take it. In the process, many will be killed."

"Yes," Faisal replied. "That is my worry."

"The other option is to lay siege."

Faisal shook his head. "The railway supplies them from the north end of the fort."

"What if we attack the train when it comes in?"

"We have tried," Faisal replied. "But they are smart. Sometimes, there is nothing in the cars. Sometimes, there is very little."

"Prince, your tribesmen, as brave as they are, will do you no good here. You need British artillery," Salah repeated. "That is the only way you will breach the walls of the fort."

"Yes, that is what I have started to think also. But what if the artillery damages the Holy Mosque?"

"You will have to take that risk, Prince."

"You don't care about the Holy Mosque? It is where all Muslims all over the world turn when they pray."

"I think God will understand."

Suddenly, Salah heard the crunch of pebbles behind him.

"Well, well! Who do we have here?"

Salah jumped, turning around and sitting up.

"Hey! Big boy . . . put your hands where I can see them."

Two Ottoman soldiers were pointing their rifles at Salah and Faisal.

"Who are you?" one of them asked.

"Arabs," Salah answered.

"We know that . . . why else would you be crawling on your bellies like desert snakes . . . your names?"

"Salah Masri," Salah answered.

"And you?" the soldier asked, pointing the barrel of his rifle at Faisal.

"I am Faisal ibn Hussein."

The Ottoman soldiers grew quiet for a moment.

"So, all I have to do is pull this trigger and there's no more Arab Revolt . . . ," one of them finally sneered.

"Don't worry, my brothers Ali and Abdallah will continue," Faisal said calmly.

Salah quickly surveyed the situation. Under his cloak, he could feel his Luger in the holster against his chest. He could take one of the soldiers. But the gunshot would no doubt bring out reinforcements. He had to work quickly, count on the surprise factor and get himself and Faisal over the hill.

While the two of them were focused on Faisal, Salah reached for his gun under his cloak. He pulled it out and shot. The soldier standing nearest to him crumpled to the ground. In the split second the other soldier looked at his partner go down, Faisal kicked the barrel of his rifle up in the air and fired a shot aimlessly. Salah got to his feet and with a couple of punches, knocked him out.

Meantime, the sound of the two gunshots attracted the attention of the sentries on top of the fort. Salah heard loud voices calling for help and reinforcements.

"Come, Prince, let us hurry."

Faisal looked at the two men on the ground.

"Prince, please . . . ," Salah urged. "They are coming up the hill."

But Faisal stood, temporarily frozen.

Shots were fired and a bullet whizzed six inches from Salah's head.

"Prince, you may want to die in the name of the revolt, but I do not!" He grabbed his arm and the two of them ran down the sandy dune to the safety of the Arab camp.

The next day, Prince Faisal asked his British advisors to join him. With Salah standing by his side, he asked for artillery to be brought to Mecca.

A few days later British-trained Egyptian troops and artillery pieces manned by Egyptian gunners arrived in Mecca. The walls of the Turkish fort were breached and the Ottomans finally capitulated after a long resistance.

Faisal and Salah rode into the fort on camels and amid the dust, debris, and sand flying everywhere, Faisal shook Salah's hand.

—⟨⟨⟨—

Noura stood in front of the small door of Saydeh's house on Zuqaq al-Hamra. She lifted the ornate doorknocker and rapped softly. When there was no response, she lifted it and let it strike the brass plate a little louder. She put her ear to the door, but heard nothing. She was about to walk away when the door opened.

"Noura!" Saydeh's face lit up when she saw her. "How lovely it is to see you! Come in, Come in!"

"*Tante* Saydeh," Noura said, respectfully addressing the older woman as "Aunt." "I'm sorry I didn't give you any advance notice."

"Not at all, not at all, *habibti*. Please," she stood aside for Noura to walk in.

Noura came in. Saydeh poked her head out and looked left and right, hurriedly closing the door and locking it.

"Is everything all right?" Noura asked.

"Oh yes!" Saydeh replied. "Everything is fine . . . now, what can I get you to eat and drink? And where is that beautiful little Siran?"

"She is with Amira, the lady who looks after my great aunt."

"Why didn't you bring her?"

"Oh, Tante Saydeh," Noura sighed. "I needed a break."

"Yes, I can understand. Now you just relax and tell me all about it." Saydeh hooked her arm in Noura's and the two of them walked up the stairs. "How long has it been since we saw you?"

"I saw you just as I arrived, so it's been almost two months."

"Too long," Saydeh said. "Much too long. You will have to give me all your news."

As soon as Noura walked through the door into the house, she let out a deep breath that she felt she'd been holding for a good long while. The house was bright and cheery. She felt immediately comfortable and at home.

"What will you have? Coffee, tea?" Saydeh asked, walking toward the kitchen "And you will eat something," she insisted. "I will make some fresh *manoushe*. It won't be as good as the one in Beirut, but I will do my best."

"Please, Tante Saydeh," Noura said. "Please don't go to any trouble."

Saydeh scoffed. "What trouble? It's none at all."

"Well then, at least let me help you," Noura offered.

"Come in then . . . ," Saydeh conceded.

The whitewashed kitchen was not big, nor was it small. It had a wood stove on the far side with a big bay window above it that gave out onto the courtyard below and the backs of the other houses. There was a small sink with a bucket of water under it and an all-purpose table along the side of the wall with a bench on either side. A big wooden bowl filled with fruit sat in the middle of the table and oregano, parsley, and basil plants occupied a small shelf above the sink. There was also a small glass cabinet in which Saydeh kept her plates and glasses and a wooden one for her pots and pans. Like the rest of the house, the kitchen was neat and tidy.

"So, how are you liking Old Cairo?" Saydeh asked.

"Well," Noura began, her eyebrows knitting together for a second while she thought about what to say, "it's fine, but it's a bit lonely. My great aunt is really very old," she finally admitted. "I don't think she even knows who I am.

"It's a nice house," she continued, "and there is Amira, a woman who is there all the time who looks after her, but . . . ," she paused briefly, "it's a little awkward."

"And she has no children, your great aunt?"

Noura shook her head.

"I haven't seen my great aunt since my grandmother died. And now, all of a sudden here I am."

Saydeh nodded.

"All I do all day is sit in my room and look after Siran. I am bored. I have no one to talk to. I feel so useless. And I think about Khaled all the time and I feel so angry.

"What is to become of us, Tante? Who is to take care of us?"

"Why you will, *habibti*, of course."

"But how?" Noura moaned.

"Why do you need someone else to do it? You have two hands and two feet," Saydeh assured her, "and you have a brain. You will find something. Noura, *habibti*, the worst thing you can do is feel sorry for yourself," Saydeh said gently.

Noura felt a little piqued.

"Can you blame me?"

"You are a mother now, Noura. You have a job to do."

Noura snorted in frustration.

"But that is all I do, Tante. There has to be more to life."

There was an awkward silence as Saydeh rolled out the dough.

Noura was upset. She'd expected Saydeh to be a little more understanding and compassionate. *What am I to do? Dear God! Give me something . . . a purpose.* Saydeh was right, she was a mother and, yes, Siran needed her. But Siran was an infant, not yet six months old. And what Noura had not admitted to Saydeh was that every time she looked at Siran, she was reminded of Khaled and the perfect life she'd planned.

"Please don't make too much," Noura said watching Saydeh put several pieces of *manoushe* in the oven.

"Don't worry," Saydeh smiled. "It will get eaten as soon as Salah comes downstairs."

Noura's heart skipped a beat. "Is he home?"

"Oh yes . . . he's locked up in his office. He's been doing some work on the Hejaz Railway. His bosses sent him back there recently. He only just came back a few days ago."

"Oh really?" Noura said. "His bosses from Izmir?"

"I assume so," Saydeh said. "Yes, they do rely on him . . . even though he took a leave of absence, they still ask him to go to the Hejaz."

"Does he go often?" Noura asked.

"Oh yes . . . he's been twice, or is it three times?" Saydeh said. "Help yourself to some fruit, dear."

Noura absently looked at the bowl of plums, green figs, and peaches. *What is Salah up to?*

"In fact, I'm a bit worried . . . the other day . . . ," Saydeh began, telling Noura about the man in the vegetable market. "And the man was definitely Turkish. Why did he lie to me? And if he was involved in the Hejaz Railway, he would know where Salah was . . ."

"Did you ask Salah?"

"Yes, and he told me not to worry," Saydeh replied. "He said that it was probably nothing."

"What do you think?"

"Noura!" Salah said, appearing suddenly in the doorway.

"Hello, Salah." Noura smiled.

"What a lovely surprise! We didn't know you were coming." He came and took both her hands in his and squeezed them.

Noura blushed.

"How have you been?"

"Settling in."

"Come, let's sit in the living room." Saydeh picked up a tray and bustled through. "Now make yourselves comfortable. I'll be right back," she added.

There was silence for a few moments after Saydeh left the room.

"How is Siran?" Salah asked.

"She's fine," Noura said. She was short and curt.

"Maybe you can bring her next time."

"Yes, yes, yes . . ." Noura got up from the sofa and walked to the window. "It's all Siran this and Siran that."

"Noura?" Salah started, hesitantly.

Noura turned on him, her eyes flashing. "It's all about Siran and her damned well-being. Well what about Noura? What about me? Nobody cares about what is happening to me, do they? All they can focus on is the child! And all everyone tells me to do is focus on her. Well, I am tired of focusing on her. I have done nothing but that since she was born. I want to focus on me. And I want people to focus on *me* and help *me*. Do you understand?"

Noura folded her arms across her chest to try and stop it from heaving. She stared out the window, trying to focus on the street below.

"I hate this life!" she paced up and down. "I hate not having my own home. I hate that Khaled is not with me. Why can't I turn back the clock and go back to Izmir? Why can't I have my husband back? Why can't I have my life back?"

Salah stayed silent.

"Obviously it was a bad idea to come here!" Noura said. "Please thank your mother for the coffee."

"Noura, I wish you would stay," Salah said. "Don't go like this."

"And you! What do you think you're doing, going back to the Hejaz?"

Salah looked surprised.

"Did you think I didn't know? Well I do! Your mother told me! What are you trying to do, Salah? Get yourself killed? Be a hero?"

Salah got up and went to Noura. He put his hands on her shoulders and gently pulled her toward him.

"No!" she said, tensing at his touch. "Leave me alone!"

But Salah took her in his arms. As soon as he did, Noura began to cry. "Why Salah? Why?"

Salah let her cry. He wiped her tears with his handkerchief and held it to her nose. "Blow," he said.

Noura shook her head. "I can't."

"Blow."

Noura did.

"Feel better?"

She nodded. Salah had always made her feel better. Even in Izmir when she and Khaled had a fight, Salah had always made her laugh.

"What did you say to Noura?" Saydeh walked in, going immediately to Noura and cradling her head on her chest.

"Nothing!" Salah said.

"He didn't do anything, Tante," Noura said, her voice gruff with tears. "It's my fault."

"But what prompted this?"

"Nothing, Tante . . . You were right. I was feeling sorry for myself."

"It's all right to feel sorry for oneself, *habibti*, so long as you put yourself to good use once you've stopped crying."

"I will, Tante. I promise."

"Good." Saydeh smiled and kissed Noura's forehead. Cocooned in his mother's embrace, Noura looked at Salah. He smiled and winked at her, his eyes glittering mischievously. Noura looked down. He wasn't angry at her as she thought he may have been after her outburst. She smiled back. "Thank you," she mouthed.

"Well, for now, how about coming with me to Rania's?" Saydeh suggested. "Perhaps the ladies there have some idea of what you can do?"

CHAPTER FIVE

Rania Assaf was behind the bar cleaning glasses, humming a tune. *Where is everyone?* she thought. She looked up at the huge clock on the wall. It was only ten o'clock in the morning. No wonder. She forgot that she had gotten up early today. Her eyes had shot open at six, and while she could normally force herself back to sleep, today she had gotten out of bed.

She came out from behind the bar and looked around, her hands on her hips as she took stock of the space. It was a decent size, with room enough for the old mahogany bar, behind which was a large mirror and glass shelves for glasses and cups. The plates and cutlery were kept under the bar. Her pride and joy, though, was the big, copper Belle Époque coffee machine. Both beautiful and functional, it ground coffee beans, made espresso, and heated and steamed milk. Along the bar were a few bar stools and the room was dotted with several small, round wooden tables with chairs. In the middle was a long farmhouse table with a bench on one side and chairs on the other. Directly over the table hung an antique wrought iron chandelier that she hardly ever used because the café closed at 6:30 p.m. But it was beautiful. She had placed another mirror directly across from the one behind the bar to make the room look bigger than it was. A painting of a vase of flowers and another of a bowl of fruit hung on the walls. Two large windows on either side of the front door flooded the café with bright sunlight. Off to the side of the bar, a small hallway led to the kitchen in the back.

The kitchen was just as bright. There, too, was a long narrow table in the middle of the room, over which Rania hung her pots, pans, and frying pans from a rack. In one corner was a round, dome-shaped wood-burning oven that Rania used for baking bread. Along the walls were shelves of all shapes and sizes where she kept bottles of spices and baskets of dried legumes and dried fruit. In a small cupboard in another corner she kept sacks of flour.

Both the café and kitchen were shabby and tired, the plaster and whitewash cracked and peeling. It was the same as when her husband, Adel, had inherited the small building where it was located, from his uncle. It was Adel's idea to turn the ground floor, which had been a general store run by his uncle, into a little café. Rania had been delighted. It was a new adventure setting up and running the café. She and Adel had been able to move out of his parents' home into a new apartment above the café, which, although small, was theirs, and she wouldn't have her nosy mother-in-law looking over her shoulder at all times of day and night. But then Adel had been called back into active duty and killed in the Suez Canal when Ahmed Jemmal Pasha attacked the British there just over a year before. So here she was, close to thirty and a widow. Tears came to her eyes as she thought of her dead husband. *Not now*, she thought, swallowing her sadness and quickly regaining her composure.

It could use some freshening up and some new clients would be nice too. But right now, money was tight. *Maybe next year . . .* she walked back to the kitchen to fire up the oven.

Rania was a beautiful woman, considered by many to be the most beautiful Christian woman in all of El-Khalili. She was tall, with thick black hair that waved and bounced with her every move. Most often, though, she kept it tied back in a ponytail or a messy chignon. Her huge dark eyes, accented by perfectly shaped, arched thick black eyebrows, were always heavily lined with black kohl, and she had a straight, long nose and full, sensual rosy lips. Her light olive complexion was smooth and unblemished. This morning she was wearing a long-sleeved, turquoise silk dress with large black and white polka dots covered by a big white cotton apron to prevent it getting stained. She wore stockings and sensible flat black shoes. The turquoise color suited her well and she looked particularly fetching.

She was standing in the kitchen, rolling out some bread, when she heard the little jingle of bells from the front door. *Someone's early*, she thought, wiping her flour-covered hands on her apron and going to investigate.

"Oh my God!" she cried.

A man lay slumped over the bar. He had a nasty wound on the side of his head, his clothes were torn, and blood and sweat poured off of him. His hair was matted to his head and his eyes were bloodshot. He looked like he'd been shot or stabbed or both.

Rania ran to him. "Who are you? What happened?"

"Please," the man groaned, "please help me. They're after me. They're going to kill me."

"Who?" Rania asked, trying to look at his wounds.

"Two men . . . ," the man managed to say before groaning in agony. "Please . . ."

Rania didn't know what to do. She looked at the man hesitantly and then quickly walked to the door to look outside. She saw two men in pinstripe suits coming up the alleyway. They certainly didn't look like they belonged in the El-Khalili. Stepping back inside, she shut the door and locked it. She only had light linen curtains covering the door and they were old and threadbare and didn't give much privacy.

"Can you walk?" she asked the man, who was still draped over the bar.

He shook his head.

"You have to. Come on," Rania said, gently taking one of his arms and putting it around her shoulders so she could support him.

The man winced in pain.

"I'm sorry," Rania said. "But we don't have much time. I fear the men who are looking for you will be here any moment. They must have seen you come in."

The man nodded and put most of his weight on Rania. As quickly as she could, she helped him toward the kitchen. At the back of the kitchen was a secret cellar, a cave like room that was unused. It was impossible to tell it was there because there was no door. To enter it, one had to push a particular brick and the wall swung open. When Rania first saw it, she had been astounded. When her husband had shown her, Rania had stood in front of it, eyes wide. "It's like Aladdin's cave," she'd said, walking in cautiously. "But what are all these bottles?"

As it turned out, her husband's uncle had a side business selling black market liquor. He kept whiskey, gin, and brandy that he bought from various smugglers, which was why the room was lined with shelving full of bottles. Rania had never known what to do with it, and so it had remained a cellar along with all the liquor they had inherited. She never told anyone about the liquor, using a little now and then to help calm some frayed nerves.

"Come on! Inside! Lie down," she told him, gently lowering him to the packed earthen floor.

Closing the wall, Rania rushed back to the bar, shedding her blood-stained apron along the way and stuffing it into a basket. She quickly grabbed another one and put it on. She pulled out a bucket of water and a mop from behind the bar, dipped a large cloth in the soapy water, and wiped down the bloodstained bar. She was mopping the floor when there was a knock on the door and she saw the two men through the curtains.

"Yes," she answered haughtily, standing in the doorway, mop in hand, looking the two men up and down. "The café is not open yet."

"We're not here for coffee, Madame," one of them said, as he tried to peer behind her.

"Madame," the second one said quietly but forcefully, holding the door open with his hand, "we would like to take a look inside."

"Why? This is a café. If you are not here for food or beverage, then you have no business entering this establishment."

"We are looking for someone," the man said, pushing the door open and moving Rania out of the way. "A man," he said, walking in and lighting a cigarette.

"As you can see, there is no one here," Rania said. "Only me. And now would you please leave, I have to finish cleaning the café before my customers arrive." And with that, she dipped the mop back into the bucket of water and purposely slapped it down on the floor so that some of the soapy liquid splashed onto the man's pants. Annoyed, he looked down at his pants and back up at her.

"And you have seen no one this morning?" he asked, looking at her through narrowed eyes.

"No," Rania said defiantly, holding his stare as she leaned her palms on the top of the mop.

The man pursed his lips and nodded.

"Nice machine," he said admiring the copper machine behind the bar.

"Thank you."

"Come," he said to his partner in Turkish, "we will get nothing from her."

"Thank you for your time, Madame," the man tipped his hat in salutation. He took a last drag of his cigarette and dropped it, stamping it into the wooden floor. "Oh!" he said, sarcastically. "So sorry about that."

And with that they both walked out.

"Bastard!" Rania muttered under her breath. She quickly finished cleaning the floor and took one last look at the bar to make sure she hadn't missed anything in case one of her regular customers came in early.

What on earth is going on? Who is this man in my cellar? And who are those men?

She ran up the stairs that led to the apartment above the café and pulled a couple of sheets from a closet, grabbed a cushion from her bed, and ran back downstairs. The man was exactly where she had left him, curled up in a ball. She knelt down next to him and lifted his head, placing it on the cushion. "I'll get you some water," she said and went to get a jug and a glass.

"Thank you," he said as he drank deeply, holding the glass out for more.

"You need a doctor to take a look at those wounds," Rania said, pouring some more cold water for him.

"No!" he cried. "No doctors."

"Well then at least you're going to have to clean them. I have some cotton wool and alcohol."

The man nodded.

"I'll go get you some. And please stay in here."

—⁓—

She was in the kitchen when the little bell on the door jingled.

"*Marhaba*, Rania!" she heard someone greet her.

"*Marhaba!*" she called back. She quickly looked at herself in a small compact mirror she kept in her apron pocket and walked back out to the café.

It was Fatmeh, a young Muslim woman who had recently gotten married and lived a couple of doors away. Her husband was in construction. Fatmeh was lovely in a petite, doll-like way. She was very fair with big dark eyes fringed with long, thick eyelashes, a small nose, and pink lips. On her upper lip, she had a small black mole that added a dash of sensuality to her otherwise innocent look. Today, as was usual, she was wearing a black *abaya* and *hijab*.

"*Sabah al-khair ya*, Fatmeh," Rania said, coming out to greet her, tying her apron properly behind her back.

"*Saba an nour*, Rania," Fatmeh said, clutching a small notebook in her hand. She sat down at the farmhouse table.

"What will you have this morning?"

"Do you have any fresh orange juice?" Fatmeh asked.

Rania nodded. "What are you writing today?"

"It's a poem," Fatmeh answered shyly.

The little bell jingled again.

A woman hidden behind yards of gold tulle and silk that she held between her plump arms walked in. Rania and Fatmeh looked at each other and smiled.

"*Marhaba*, Madame Yvonne!" Rania placed a glass of orange juice in front of Fatmeh. "Nice to see you. *Keefik l yom?*"

Madame Yvonne didn't reply immediately. She peeked out from behind the fabric to make sure she could see where she was going and gently laid the fabric on the farmhouse table, which she considered her regular spot. She hated sitting anywhere else. Sighing deeply, she set down a large bag she had slung over her shoulder. On top, she put the small purse she always carried to hold her keys, money, compact, and lipstick.

"How are you, Madame Yvonne?" Rania asked again.

"Oh *mneeha*, I suppose," she grumbled. "At least I'm alive and in decent health, my husband says."

Rania and Fatmeh exchanged a look. They both wondered about the fabric but didn't dare ask.

"What will you have this morning, Madame Yvonne?" Rania asked.

"Something to calm my nerves," Madame Yvonne replied, sitting down on the bench and trying to make sense of the fabric in front of her. "Coffee, I think . . . the special one today and a narghile."

Rania smiled.

"Add a little extra hashish today!" Fatmeh whispered, giggling softly.

Rania went back to the kitchen to prepare the narghile she made for Madame Yvonne every morning. While the coals were warming, she went back in front to make the coffee, adding a good swig of brandy before she put it down in front of Madame Yvonne.

Madame Yvonne was in her sixties. She was short and plump and had a large bosom. She was fair skinned, had smallish brown eyes, a long, hooked nose, and thin lips. Her forehead was large and age had given her jowls that made her face look bigger. She dyed her mousy light brown hair a darker shade of golden honey and teased it to make it look as though she had much more than she did. But all this really did was make her head look too big for her body. Together with her large head and large bosom, Madame Yvonne looked a little like a cartoon character. She liked long cotton dresses and was especially fond of wearing yellow.

"I compliment you, Rania!" Madame Yvonne took a sip of the coffee, nodding approvingly. "This is delicious today."

Rania put the narghile down in front of her. "Here you go! Let's see if this meets with your approval too." She grinned at Fatmeh.

Madame Yvonne put the coffee cup down and took a drag of the narghile. Rania waited expectantly. Madame Yvonne nodded. "Not bad, *habibti* . . . not bad at all."

Rania winked at Fatmeh and gave her the thumbs-up sign.

The little bell jingled again. A group of shopkeepers from south of the alleyway came in.

"*Marhaba*, Rania!" they greeted her cheerfully. "*Keefik?*"

"*Hamdellah!*" Rania replied and went to take their order. She was serving them their coffees when she realized that in the confusion of the morning, with the stranger showing up at her doorstep, she had completely forgotten about making fresh bread. *Damn!*

She ran back to the kitchen and quickly put some wood in the oven, fanning it with an old newspaper to light the flames. The doorbell jingled again. *No!* Rania sighed. *Now who is it?* She peeked around the wall and saw Saydeh walking in with a younger woman. *Who is that?* Rania wondered and quickly went back to rolling out the rounds of bread. Suddenly she heard a sound behind her. She whipped around.

"Please," the wounded man said softly, peeking out from behind the wall, holding out his jug for more water.

"What are you doing?" Rania hissed. "Get back inside!" she ordered. "I'll bring you some more water."

Rania quickly filled the jug. "Here," she said, handing it to him.

"Rania!" she heard behind her. She was so startled that she let go of the jug. Luckily, the man was holding it or it would have crashed to the floor.

"What's behind that?" Saydeh asked, taking a step toward her.

"Nothing." Rania smiled, pushing the wall shut and walking quickly toward the older woman.

"I didn't even know there was an opening there," she said, looking over Rania's shoulder. "It looks like the wall. What's behind it? Where does it lead?"

"Tante Saydeh!" Rania hugged her, trying to distract her. "You are just the person I need. I am so happy to see you!"

"But what is behind . . . ?"

"Tante Saydeh," Rania put her arm around her and herded her toward the middle of the kitchen, "listen, I completely overslept this morning," she lied, "and I forgot to make the *manoushe*. Please, can you help me?"

"Oh no! That is terrible, indeed. What can I do?" Saydeh said, immediately distracted.

"Can you quickly make the bread?"

"Yes, I will make it extra special."

"I'll be right back."

Saydeh nodded and began to roll out the dough.

Rania went out into the restaurant and then, remembering she had forgotten to check the wood in the oven, turned back to the kitchen. She saw Saydeh, her ear to pressed to the wall of the hidden cellar, gingerly touching the surface with her fingers, a puzzled look on her face.

"Tante Saydeh!" Rania exclaimed. "The bread! Please!"

"Oh!" Saydeh quickly waddled back to the oven. "Sorry."

In the meantime, Noura sat looking around her, taking in the new surroundings. Saydeh had introduced her briefly to Madame Yvonne and to Fatmeh, but then disappeared into the kitchen. She sat with her hands in her lap, playing with the little ruffle on the edge of the sleeves of her cotton dress. She wondered how Samar was doing at her parents' home in Douma. She had had no letters from Wissam's wife, but then, of course, the war was still going on. *Maybe I should have gone to Douma with her? I wonder if I did the right thing coming here by myself?*

Noura looked up from her musings and saw Fatmeh looking at her. Noura smiled. Fatmeh smiled back, shyly blushing. She seems sweet, Noura thought. She wanted to talk to her, but she was sitting next to Madame Yvonne at the other side of the table and felt it would be rude to get up and move.

"So . . . Beirut?" Madame Yvonne said, without looking at Noura. She was busy peering at a needle in her hands, trying to thread it. "Oh *haraam!*" she muttered, exasperated when she couldn't. She put her little wire-rimmed glasses back on and looked down at the magazine open in front of her. Suddenly one of the tables behind them exploded with laughter.

"What's wrong with these people?" Madame Yvonne turned around to give them a dirty look. "Why do they have to be so loud?"

"Madame Yvonne!" one of the men raised his hand to her, "you don't enjoy our jokes anymore?"

"No, you hooligans!" she responded, looking back and pursing her lips haughtily, "I don't."

"Come now, Madame Yvonne . . ." another one began teasing her.

"Don't!" she raised her hand without turning around, her gaze centered on the fabric in front of her. "Don't even think about talking to me today!"

"Can't they see that I'm trying to concentrate?" she rolled her eyes.

Madame Yvonne licked the thread and tried to thread her needle again. "You're from Beirut. Saydeh told us when you arrived a few weeks ago," she continued. "How do you like Cairo?"

"It's only been a few weeks," Noura replied politely.

"So, Yvonne," Saydeh came out and put her arm around Noura, "have you run Noura out of town yet?"

Fatmeh smothered a giggle.

"I heard that, Fatmeh," Madame Yvonne said, still focused on what she was doing.

Fatmeh looked at her, alarm spreading across her face.

"I have eyes in the back of my head," Madame Yvonne nodded proudly. "I see everything. Nothing escapes me."

Saydeh rolled her eyes.

"What are you doing anyway, Yvonne? Squinting away at that needle? What are you making?"

"It's a new project," Yvonne said proudly.

"*Ahlan wa sahlan!*" Rania smiled broadly, walking up to the table. "You must be Noura!"

"*Tsharrafna,*" Noura stood up. "I am pleased to meet you."

"Welcome to the café," Rania said enthusiastically.

"It's very nice," Noura said, looking around.

"Yes, it's unusually busy this morning. Normally it's just the ladies at this table and a few shopkeepers come for a coffee . . . but today has been a strange day." Rania's eyes darted worriedly to the kitchen.

Quickly, she regained her composure.

"What will you have? Some coffee?" She suggested to Noura. "Tante Saydeh?"

"I'll have another coffee," Yvonne piped in. Both Noura and Saydeh nodded.

"I'll be right back."

Saydeh turned back to Yvonne. "So what's the new project?"

"I have a wedding to go to," Yvonne announced.

"Really? Whose?" Saydeh immediately pounced. "This is the first I'm hearing of it."

"I don't have to tell you everything."

"You usually do," Saydeh said.

"I do not!"

"*Tayeb, tayeb*," Saydeh conceded. "So is this a dress for the wedding?" Yvonne looked at her over her glasses and nodded.

"And you're making it?" Saydeh asked.

"Why? You think I can't?"

Saydeh shook her head.

"*Khalas, bikaffe mesdames!*" Rania said, putting a tray down on the table. "Here's your coffee, Madame Yvonne, and for you, Noura and Tante Saydeh . . . and some more orange juice for you Fatmeh . . . even though you didn't ask for it."

"What kind of a dress are you making, Madame Yvonne?" Noura asked.

"This is the design." Yvonne handed her the magazine.

"This is quite elaborate," Noura said.

"Of course! It's French."

"It's very beautiful," Noura added quickly.

"Let's have a look," Saydeh peered over Noura's shoulder with Rania and Fatmeh.

"It is very nice, Madame Yvonne," Rania said, and Fatmeh nodded approvingly.

"You really think you're going to be able to make this?" Saydeh asked.

"Of course I will . . . you will all see."

"Madame Yvonne, may I take a look to see how you've cut the bodice?" Noura asked, looking closely at the pattern.

"Why?"

"Because this bodice is cut on a bias . . ."

"What do you know about dressmaking?"

Noura backed down.

"Where is Takla this morning?" Saydeh asked.

"I don't know," Rania answered. "I haven't seen her yet."

"Strange . . . Takla's always the first one here."

Just then, the door burst open and a woman came in, looking harassed and unkempt. She was wearing a knee-length green dress and had a white cotton shawl across her shoulders. She was an interesting-looking woman. Her long, dark, very curly hair had one strand of white running through it. Pulled back in a clip at the nape of her neck, loose strands fell around her face. Her cheeks were wet and her dark eyes were red and puffy.

"*Hamdellah a salame,*" Madame Yvonne commented sarcastically. "She's arrived."

As Takla approached, the expression on her face was one of fear and worry.

"Takla!" Saydeh jumped up. "What is the matter?"

Takla began crying as Saydeh hugged her and gently led her to the table.

"What has happened?"

"It's Nassim," she wailed. "My son . . . he's disappeared . . ."

"Now, now, Takla." Saydeh made her sit down, "Calm down. Rania, bring her something to drink."

Rania ran to the bar and poured a glass of cold sweet lime juice and water. She briefly wondered if she should mix in a little gin and decided that a little squirt would go undetected, wouldn't do Takla any harm, and would indeed calm her down.

"Now drink this and tell us what happened," Saydeh ordered.

"I don't know." Takla hiccupped. "I woke up this morning and as usual I went into the kitchen to make him breakfast. At nine o'clock, I called out to him like I always do. He didn't answer." Takla began to cry again.

"He's probably out with a girl . . . let him have a little fun . . . learn something about women," Yvonne butted in.

"What do you know?" Takla cried. "How would you feel if he were out with your daughter?"

"Enough, Yvonne," Saydeh said quietly. "Can't you see she's upset?"

"He'll come back," Yvonne insisted. "He's just being a boy."

"If only his father was still alive . . ." Takla wailed. "He doesn't listen to me anymore."

"Takla," Saydeh patted her hand, "I'm sure he's fine. Let's not start thinking the worst."

"But, Saydeh, I'm worried something terrible has happened to him," Takla said. "His bed hadn't even been slept in."

"Don't worry . . ."

"How can I not?" Takla cried, leaning her head on the table over her hands, the tears trickling sideways down her face across her nose. "Look what is going on around us. The British are everywhere . . . and the French and the Turks are still here. Who knows who has done what to my boy?"

"No one has touched a hair on the boy's head," Yvonne said, still trying to thread her needle, "except for a woman," she added, looking up at them.

Fatmeh's eyes were moist, her tears appearing in solidarity with Takla's. Rania looked worried, Saydeh annoyed, and Noura confused.

—ᨠᨠ—

The black telephone on Colonel Erdogan's dark walnut mahogany desk rang. The door opened and Erdogan strode in with a sheaf of papers in his hand. He grabbed the phone.

"Erdogan here," he answered. "Yes, Sir," he clicked his heels and stood at attention. "Sir, we have our best men here . . . I am working on it . . . I actually got close to his mother, but she didn't give me anything . . . yes, Sir . . . I have someone here now, one of Masri's boys . . . don't worry, Sir. . .we will make him talk . . . he will give us Masri."

Erdogan put the phone back on its receiver and pressed a button on a small box on his desk. "Captain Celik, come in please."

"Yes, Sir." The door opened a few seconds later.

"Where's the boy?"

"In the basement."

"Ahmad Pasha's orders. We're turning up the pressure. Make the boy sing, Celik."

—ᨠᨠ—

Salah was sitting in his office reading the newspaper. Half a world away on the Western Front, the Somme offensive was underway. Hundreds of thousands of lives had already been lost. Verdun was still going and Italy had declared war on Germany.

Suddenly, he heard the door knocker. Two quick short knocks, two long knocks, one short, two long, and one short . . . Morse for IMP . . . important. *What could it be?* He ran down quickly. Just as he got to the first floor landing, he saw a small envelope slide in under the door. It was a telegram. Quickly Salah tore it open.

THEY'RE CLOSING IN. WATCH YOUR BACK. RF.

Salah folded the paper and put it in his pocket. He climbed the stairs to his office. RF was Rabih Farhat, his architect. Salah knew the Turks were in Cairo, but how close were they? He'd been extremely careful, but could he have slipped up? He wrung his hands. He always knew that they would at some point tighten the noose.

I'd better go talk to Magdi. See if he or any of the boys have seen anyone suspicious in the souk.

"Salah!" he heard his mother's voice from the staircase. "Are you here, son?"

Salah rolled his eyes. Not now, he sighed. Taking a deep breath, stealing himself, "Yes, *imme*," he answered.

"Salah!" Saydeh came in huffing and puffing, her hand on her heart.

"What is it?" Salah put his hands on her arms.

"Salah . . . ," Saydeh started.

The door opened wide and Noura, with a supportive arm around Takla's shoulders, walked in.

"Tante Takla! Noura!" Salah said, surprised to see his mother's friend walk in with Noura.

"Come sit down, Takla," Saydeh went to take Takla's arm and help her to the sofa. "Noura, would you mind bringing some water?"

"What is the matter, Tante Takla?" Salah sat down next to her.

Takla began to cry. Salah looked questioningly at his mother.

"It's Nassim." Saydeh put her arm around Takla.

"What has happened to Nassim?" Salah asked. His heart began to beat faster.

"He's gone . . . ," Takla wailed.

"What do you mean 'gone?'" Salah asked.

"Apparently, this morning when Takla woke up, he was gone," Saydeh explained. "His bed had not been slept in."

"And you have no idea where he could be?" Salah asked, concerned.

Takla shook her head.

"I'm sure he's fine," Saydeh said.

Takla put her head on Saydeh's shoulder.

"What do you think, Salah?" Saydeh asked her son. "Isn't there anything we can do to help Takla? Do you have any idea where he could have gone?"

Salah's mind was racing. *Nassim wouldn't just disappear like that. He's too reliable, too responsible. If he's gone, it means the Turks have him. They'll start questioning him about what he knows . . . and they'll torture him.* Salah shuddered. He knew how merciless the Turks were when they wanted information.

"Salah?" his mother's voice penetrated his thoughts.

"*Eh, imme,*" he replied, looking at her with a blank look on his face.

"Can't you do anything?" Saydeh repeated.

Salah didn't know what to say to his mother. He felt responsible for Nassim. After all, it was Magdi and he who had brought the boy into this. He had to find out what had happened to him. If the Turks had Nassim, Salah didn't have much time. He might have to go even further underground. But he had to rescue Nassim first.

Salah looked at the clock on the wall. It was almost lunchtime. All the shops were getting ready to close. But he still had a few minutes. If he hurried, he could get to Magdi. Magdi's eldest son, Hisham, was a good friend of Nassim's and the two of them had organized a group of their friends who patrolled the souk. Hisham had to know something.

Salah got up and grabbed his headscarf.

"Where are you going?" Saydeh said. "It's almost lunchtime."

"I'll be back, *imme.*"

"But where are you going?"

"I'm going to Magdi's."

"The fruitseller?" Saydeh said, astonished. "Now?"

"Yes! I bought some figs and dates earlier and I forgot to pick them up," Salah told her.

"But you don't have to go now," Saydeh said, still taken aback. "You can go back later this afternoon."

"No!" Salah said a little too forcefully.

Saydeh looked taken aback and even Takla stopped crying for a moment.

"You never know with Magdi." Salah realized how hard he must have sounded. "He might sell my fruit to someone else."

Saydeh did another double take. "Even if he does, son, he has more."

"I have to go now," Salah repeated. He kissed his mother's forehead and quickly walked out.

Covering his head and face with a scarf, Salah rushed down the alley, causing many to shout and shake their fists at him. "Sorry! Sorry!" he kept saying, as he jostled his way through the crowd. "Look out!" Salah shouted at a baker who almost collided with him. "Watch it, you big oaf!" the baker cried as he tried to regain his balance. "You almost cost me my day's wages." Most people stood back or stepped off to the side when they saw Salah coming.

Finally he got to Magdi's fruit stand just as he was covering all the fruit with damp linen cloths to protect it from the afternoon heat.

"Magdi!" Salah shouted from the corner. "Magdi! Stop!"

The fruitseller turned to see Salah running toward him.

"Magdi! I need some figs!" Salah said for the benefit of the other fruitsellers. "My mother is beside herself!"

"Did you think I was going to run out of figs?"

"Magdi," Salah's voice dropped to a whisper. "Where's your son?"

"Which one, brother? I have five."

"Hisham."

"He should be at home." Magdi shrugged. "It is almost time for lunch."

"I need to know where Hisham is now!" Salah came very close to Magdi's face, their noses almost touching.

"*Tayeb, tayeb!*" Magdi replied. "Calm down! What is the matter with you?"

Salah stood back and adjusted his long *galabiyya* and his headscarf. "Look, Magdi, it's important. I need to talk to him."

"*Shoo? Khair?* What is the matter?" Magdi asked, retying his own headscarf.

"It's Nassim," Salah whispered.

"What about Nassim?"

"He has disappeared."

Magdi nodded, understanding. "Come," he said, pointing to the back of the stall. He quickly looked around to make sure the street was empty and pulled down the reed shutters. He walked back to the wall and felt under a couple of bricks until he found a lever that he pulled. The wall swung open. Salah had no idea this hidden passageway existed. Magdi walked in and picked up a small oil lantern. He lit it and indicated that Salah follow him. They walked down a long dark corridor, finally coming to what looked like a dead end. But it wasn't. Again, Magdi felt for a lever that released a door with a big puff of dust. Behind it was a secret room with only two small narrow windows that gave out on to the street above. It was clearly underground and was completely bare except for a straw mattress on the floor and a small table with a lantern and a cup of water.

"We are underneath my house," Magdi informed him. "Wait here. I will get Hisham. I don't want his mother to know anything."

Salah nodded. Several minutes later Magdi came back with Hisham in tow.

"*Marhaba,* Salah," Hisham said.

"Where is Nassim, boy?"

Hisham took a deep breath.

"We were at the Queen of the Nile last night," the eighteen-year-old boy began.

"The nightclub?" Salah said.

Hisham nodded. "Dalida, you know . . . the belly dancer, was performing."

Magdi slapped the back of his son's head. "Just wait until your mother hears about this."

Hisham grimaced, scratching his head.

"Although I have heard she's very good," Magdi interjected.

"She was."

"Shut up!" Salah growled. "Both of you. Go on Hisham . . ."

"There were two men there and they didn't look like they were from here," Hisham said. "Nassim told me he thought they were Turkish, but we weren't sure. We tried to get near them, but couldn't. The room was too full. After Dalida finished, he said he wanted to follow them . . . said he had a funny feeling about them. I told him I would go with him, but he told me not to. He said he would be back."

"Go on."

"But I insisted, and walked with Nassim outside the club, where I heard them speaking in Turkish. They were talking about you, Salah, and someone else, but I didn't catch the name. They began walking toward the south gate of the souk and Nassim went after them. I followed them at a distance, then I don't know what happened. Suddenly, they all disappeared; and I felt a hand around my mouth and someone was twisting my arms around me. I think one of them must have hit me. I felt a pain in my head and I don't know . . . when I opened my eyes I was still on the street. So I made my way back here."

Hisham looked at his shoes.

Salah nodded. The Turks were one step behind him.

"I'm sorry, Salah." Hisham looked at him expectantly.

"You should have said something immediately," Magdi admonished him.

"What's done is done. We have to find Nassim and we *all* need to be careful," Salah warned.

"What about Nassim?" Hisham asked, tearfully.

"We will find him," Salah assured him. "Now, I have to get back or else my mother will be out looking for me." Salah draped his scarf around him. "And I would sooner face the Turks than my angry mother.

"How do I get back to my house?" Salah turned to Magdi. "Safely . . . ," he added.

"You'll have to duck and weave a bit, but if you go out the back door of my house, you can take the small alleyways that will take you to the back of Rania's Café," Magdi told him. "There is a tunnel under her kitchen that leads straight into the chandelier shop on the ground floor of your mother's house. You should still be able to use it."

Salah nodded, draping his scarf over his head. "Thank Allah this souk is filled with tunnels. Thank you, brother."

Magdi nodded. "*Ma'as-salame.*"

CHAPTER SIX

Just past two o'clock, Rania saw the last customer out and locked the door behind him. She turned the little panel on the door that read "closed until 4:30 p.m.," before peeking through the curtains to see if there were any strangers lurking around, but the street was empty.

What's this? She noticed a little black notebook on the floor. She picked it up and opened it. It was Fatmeh's, Rania realized as she leafed through the pages. *All these poems . . . they're all about love. Oh, they are beautiful. She's so lovely . . . so quiet and unassuming. I'm so happy she's in love with her husband.* Rania smiled to herself and put the notebook in her apron pocket for safekeeping and went back to the task at hand.

It had been an incredibly busy morning, what with the regulars, the ladies, not to mention the stranger in the cellar. *Well, it's time he left,* Rania thought, wiping her hands on her apron. *This is a perfect time for him to go, there's no one in the streets,* she thought as she slowly walked to the back of the kitchen. *Who is he? A thief? A killer? What sort of trouble is he in? And what about those wounds? He really needs to see a doctor. Why would he refuse to see one? And who were those men? Clearly they'd been looking for him.* She stared at the brick wall for a moment. *I'm crazy to have let him stay here. I should have kicked him out after those two men left.*

Rania pushed on a brick and the wall creaked open.

"Excuse me!" Rania called out before going in.

When he didn't reply, she pushed the wall and stuck her head in. He was lying on the floor, wrapped up in the sheets and fast asleep. Gently, she tiptoed over, looking down at him. His head was resting in the crook of his shoulder and his features were relaxed. He was still sweating and his face, hair, and beard were caked with streams of blood. Cleaned up, he was probably a good-looking man. He had short, dark, wavy hair and a dark beard and moustache. The shirt he was wearing was torn. He had broad shoulders and well-defined arms. His skin looked tanned. The white-ribbed vest he wore under his shirt was terribly stained with dirt and blood, as were his khaki pants. He was still wearing black shoes that looked well worn. She knelt next to him. The alcohol and cotton wool sat untouched but the jug of water was empty. Rania didn't know what to do. She picked up the jug to get some more water.

Suddenly, his eyes opened. Startled, Rania took a short, sharp breath and leaned backwards, almost losing her balance. The stranger's hand immediately shot out to grab her. But Rania regained her balance and sat back on her heels. The stranger put his hand back under his head. They looked at each other in silence.

Rania looked down at her fingers, unable to hold the man's frank and openly appreciative gaze. She could feel the color rising to her cheeks. "I will get you some more water," she said hurriedly and got to her feet. She heard him groan when she walked away. When she came back, he was sitting with his back to the wall.

"Are you hungry?" she asked.

He nodded. "I have not eaten in a few days."

"I will make you something. There is no one in the café, so you can come outside. Can you stand?"

Slowly, the man tried to get to his feet, but his strength kept failing. He looked at Rania and smiled, embarrassed to ask for her help.

"Come," she said, "lean on me." She crouched and put an arm around his waist and he placed his right arm, the least injured of the two, around her shoulders. Slowly, Rania stood up. The man's face contorted with pain. "I'm sorry," she said.

He shook his head, telling her silently that it wasn't she who was hurting him. It was a strange sensation for Rania as she helped him walk. She was, for all intents and purposes, in the arms of a complete stranger, albeit one who was injured and needed help. It had been some time since she had felt strong male arms around her. The man smelled of sweat, blood, and war. Rania breathed through her mouth as they slowly walked through the door into the kitchen, where she helped him sit at the table. As soon as she let him go, he slumped forward with a short, sharp cry, holding his bloody, bruised side.

"Would you rather lie down?" she asked.

"No, no," he replied. "Just give me a moment."

"You probably have a broken rib," Rania said.

"Or several." He tried to smile through the pain.

Rania went about preparing a simple lunch, all the while keeping an eye on him. She poured him a glass of sweet lime juice. "Drink this . . . the sugar will give you a little strength." Quickly, she warmed up a chicken stew she had made the night before and fresh bread straight from the brick oven.

While he ate, she cleaned the morning dishes, trying to find ways to look at him, occasionally glancing at him from underneath her eyelashes. He didn't look like a thug, she thought. He seemed polite and considerate.

"So who are you?" Rania asked.

"I suppose I owe you an explanation."

"You do." Rania looked at him. Her heart began beating faster. He had olive brown eyes that smiled and twinkled.

"Where are you from?"

"Beirut," the stranger answered.

"Your name?"

"Rabih."

"What are you doing in Cairo?"

"I . . . uh . . . was in the Hejaz," Rabih stammered.

"The Hejaz is a big place. What were you doing there?"

"I was . . . ," Rabih started and then stopped. "I, uh . . . was doing a little work."

"What kind of work?"

"I am an architect."

"What do you build?" she asked. "Houses?"

Rabih nodded.

"So what were you building in the Hejaz?" Rania asked innocently. "Surely not houses . . . it's the middle of the desert."

He shrugged.

"Those two men who came in this morning spoke Turkish. Why were they after you?"

"They probably wanted to talk to me," Rabih said carefully.

"Talk? Do you really think they wanted to 'talk' to you? You must take me for a fool!" she exploded. "You come in here, half dead, beaten up, bloody, falling over my bar, and a few minutes later these thugs show up looking for you and you want me to believe they wanted to 'talk' to you?"

Rabih sat silently. "Well if you won't give me an explanation, then get out . . . right now!" she ordered, standing up and pointing at the door. "I don't need the headache of harboring a criminal in my café. I have enough problems as it is."

"I am not a criminal," Rabih said quietly.

"Well then how did you get this way? You are seriously wounded and Allah knows how it happened, but you won't even see a doctor . . ."

Suddenly, there was a loud knock on the back door.

Rania's heart jumped. Rabih looked at her anxiously.

"Quickly! Can you get to the cellar by yourself?" she whispered. "*Meen*? Who is it?" she shouted, running to the door.

"Rania!" a muffled male voice sounded through the wooden door.

Rabih stumbled as he got up, crashing to the floor with a big thud.

"Rania! Are you in there?" the voice sounded.

"Hurry!" Rania quickly helped him up and he shuffled and hopped as quickly as he could, weaving his way through the kitchen back to his hiding place.

"Coming!" she said. "*Meen?*" she asked again, once she saw Rabih entering the cellar.

"Rania, it me! Salah! Open up!"

Rania quickly fixed her hair, smoothed down her dress and apron, and opened the door.

"*Marhaba*, Salah!" she said, smiling brightly. "Your mother went home a while ago for lunch."

"I'm not looking for my mother," Salah said. "I need to get home."

Rania looked at him questioningly.

"Rania . . . it's a long story," Salah began, "that I will explain to you someday, but right now I need to get home."

"Of course," Rania reached for the key ring she kept in her apron pocket. "I'll let you out the front door."

"No!" Salah said and caught her arm.

Rania looked at his hand gripping her arm and back up at him.

"I'm sorry," Salah apologized immediately.

"Look, Rania, I'm in a bit of trouble," Salah admitted. "I can't use the streets. Magdi tells me there's a tunnel under this kitchen . . ."

"What tunnel?" Rania looked astonished.

"Under this kitchen . . . ," Salah repeated.

"I don't know of any tunnel."

"Rania, there has to be," Salah insisted. "Magdi knows the tunnels of this souk like the back of his hand. Perhaps the entrance is in the café?"

"Salah, there is no tunnel either here or in the café," Rania insisted.

Salah began to look around the kitchen. He looked on the floor, bending down to touch around the stones. He went to the wall where Rania kept spices and began to touch some of the bricks. He approached the back wall that opened to the cellar where Rabih was hiding.

"Salah! What are you doing?" Rania quickly went and stood in front of him.

Salah gently moved her out of the way. "There has to be a way . . ." He continued to touch the wall. "What is behind this?" he asked.

"Nothing."

"Rania . . ." Salah raised his eyebrows.

"Nothing really," Rania lied, "just an old cellar."

"That's where the tunnel must be," Salah said. "How do you get in?"

Rania didn't know what to do. She knew Salah, of course. His mother came to the café every day. But she didn't know how he would react to seeing a wounded man on the floor of her cellar.

Suddenly, the brick wall opened slightly. Salah jumped back. A pair of hands pulled the wall back exposing the cellar. Rabih stood in the archway.

"*Ahlan,* Boss!" he said to Salah. "Good to see you!"

"What the . . . ?" Salah's eyes widened.

"Can't mistake that voice," Rabih said.

Salah took a step toward Rabih and hugged him, leaving Rania looking shocked. Rabih grimaced with pain.

"Salah . . . be careful! He's hurt."

Salah and Rabih turned to her, their arms around each other's shoulders. Salah was smiling, whereas Rabih tried to smile.

"*Shoo hayda*? What's going on here?" Rania exclaimed. "You two know each other?

"My friend!" Salah pointed a finger at Rabih.

"My boss!" Rabih pointed a finger at Salah.

"What?" Salah looked at him. "I'm not your friend anymore?" he joked.

Rabih smiled shyly and looked down at his shoes. "Boss and friend," he conceded, before Salah engulfed him in another bear hug.

"Ohhhh!" Rabih groaned in his arms.

"I am glad to see you alive, brother." Salah gave Rabih a gentle punch in the arm.

"And I you." Rabih sighed, holding his side.

Rania turned, shaking her head. "I don't understand what is going on."

"Rania, Rania!" Salah said, leaving Rabih and walking over to put a soothing arm around her shoulders.

Rania continued shaking her head. "This is all too much for me. Rabih shows up this morning, bleeding, injured, looking like he's been shot or stabbed or something, then these two other men show up looking for him . . . now you, looking for a tunnel . . ." She looked worried. "And then it turns out that you two know each other."

"Wait!" Salah stopped her. "What do you mean, two other men?"

"I mean what I said," Rania looked at him. "Two men came in this morning looking for Rabih just after he stumbled in here. Turks."

"Ahmed Jemmal's men," Salah muttered under his breath.

Suddenly, Rabih groaned loudly, crying in pain as he slid down the wall, falling on the ground and holding his left side.

Salah immediately ran to him.

"Let me take a look," he said to Rabih. "Rania, put his head in your lap." Rania obeyed, sitting down on her heels and gently taking Rabih's head and placing it on her thighs. Rabih looked up at her gratefully before his eyes rolled back in his head. Rania began to caress his head trying to calm the pain. Salah tore off Rabih's vest to look at his chest. There was a wound, crusted with blood, on his left side and huge bruises everywhere. Salah touched around the bruises and Rabih screamed with pain.

"He's wounded here too," Salah said, looking at the tear in his pants. "By Allah! This is a bullet wound!"

"We have to get him help!" Rania said.

Salah nodded, sitting back on his haunches.

"Salah!" Rania insisted. "We have to get him a doctor!"

"We can't take him to a doctor," Salah replied, his forehead creasing with worry.

"Why not?" Rania shouted, incredulous.

"Because how will we explain these wounds without attracting the attention of the local Egyptian authorities?" Salah asked.

"What we need is an English military doctor," he said. "Problem is, how do we get him to the English barracks? The Turks are probably watching us."

"But there's no one outside," Rania said.

"You might not see them, Rania," Salah told her, "but you can be sure they are watching."

"What are we going to do?" Rania asked.

Salah stroked his chin.

Rania looked down at Rabih. His face was contorted with pain and he was moaning softly. "It's going to be all right," she whispered tenderly.

"At the very least, we need to clean him up," Salah said. "We need to put him in a bed. We can't leave him on the floor."

"Take him upstairs," Rania said. "We can put him in the small bedroom next to mine. There is a single bed in there."

"Come on, brother." Salah gently took Rabih in his arms. Rabih groaned.

Slowly Salah lifted him off the floor and put his arm around his waist, hoisting him up. Rabih winced. "I know, brother," Salah muttered. "*A'afwan.* I know you have a couple of broken ribs."

Suddenly, there was a soft knocking on the front door of the café. "Now what?" Rania rolled her eyes. "Can't they read the 'Closed' sign?"

"You'd better go deal with that," Salah said as he began to climb the stairs with Rabih.

Rania looked through the multicolored striped linen curtain that covered the glass panel of the door. It was Fatmeh.

"*Marhaba,* Rania," Fatmeh said.

"*Ahlan, habibti!*" Rania replied. "*Khair?* Is everything all right?"

"Yes, yes," Fatmeh replied.

There were a few moments of silence while Rania waited for Fatmeh to say something.

"Did you need anything?" Rania asked.

"Yes . . . actually, I was wondering if you found my notebook," Fatmeh stuttered.

"Yes!" Rania said. "I did! When I was clearing up after lunch, I found it on the floor." *Now, what did I do with it?* she asked herself as she walked back into the café.

"Rania . . ." Fatmeh hesitated.

Rania stopped and looked round.

"Did you open the notebook?"

"I did," Rania said, "because I didn't know who it belonged to." "Then you read some of it?"

"Well . . . I did, but very little," Rania assured her. "You're very talented, Fatmeh."

"I . . . uh . . . thank you, but . . ."

The sound of an abrupt, loud thud followed by a long, muffled cry sounded throughout the café.

Rania looked up toward the ceiling. Fatmeh did too, but didn't say anything. Moments later came the sound of another groan and heavy footsteps on the floor above.

Rania noticed the spatter of blood near the stairs. She looked up and saw Fatmeh look at the same spatter.

"Is everything all right here?" Fatmeh asked gently.

"What? Yes, yes! Everything is fine," Rania replied.

"Can I help? My father is a doctor and I studied to be a nurse."

"Really?" Rania said. She went to the bottom of the stairs. "Salah!" she called out.

"Salah?" Fatmeh asked, surprised. "Salah Masri? What is he doing upstairs?"

"Salah! It's only Fatmeh! Come downstairs!" Rania shouted.

Salah came downstairs holding his forehead.

"What happened?" Rania asked.

"I hit my head against the doorframe," Salah admitted, dropping his hand from his forehead.

"Good afternoon, Fatmeh."

The younger woman returned his greeting with a shy smile.

"Salah, Fatmeh is a nurse," Rania quickly explained.

"Well, I'm not really a nurse," Fatmeh said, "I was studying to be a nurse, but then I got married . . . and my husband, well, he didn't want me to continue."

"That's enough for me," Salah said. "Listen, Fatmeh, a friend of mine is hurt . . . he's upstairs . . . he really needs to see a doctor, but for now he can't move. Can you help him, please?" he pleaded.

"I . . ." Fatmeh took a step back. "I don't know. How badly is he hurt?"

"Rania, please show Fatmeh upstairs and I'm really sorry but I have to go. Fatmeh, I'm sorry . . . thank you . . . I'll explain it all to you."

Fatmeh nodded. "But what about that bruise above your eye?" she asked. "It's turning purple."

"I'll live." Salah smiled. "Please do what you can for Rabih." He walked to the cellar and into the tunnel Magdi had told him about and headed home.

—⁂—

The small, windowless room was dark and stuffy and stank of sweat and animal waste. The walls were dirty, as was the straw on the mud floor. The only sound was that of rats and vermin scurrying around trying to find food or shelter. The door opened and light from the hallway revealed a body lying in a corner.

"Wake him up, Sergeant Celik!" Colonel Omer Erdogan snapped.

While Erdogan stood in the doorway, the sergeant walked in with a bucket of water and emptied it over the figure. "Get up!" He kicked the soaking body.

The figure groaned and turned over. Sergeant Celik kicked again. "Get . . . up!" he said again, enunciating his words.

The figure still didn't move. Sergeant Celik looked at his superior. Erdogan nodded. The Sergeant walked out and came back with another bucket of water and doused the figure again. He left the room again and returned with a small wooden chair. He pulled the limp body off the floor and sat it in the chair, tying the hands at the back and the feet to the chair legs. He adjusted a gaslight strung up on a rope just above the figure's head and lit it. The light revealed the bruised, beaten face of Nassim Alamuddin.

"Where is Salah Masri?" Captain Omer Erdogan hovered over the boy's face.

Nassim's head hung to one side.

"Douse the little bastard."

The sergeant overturned another bucket of water. Nassim began coughing and spluttering. Slowly, he opened one eye; the other one was black and purple and so swollen that he couldn't open it.

"Give me Masri, boy!" Erdogan said. "Where is he hiding?"

Nassim looked around in a daze at the two men in front of him.

"Salah Masri!" the captain brought his face down to Nassim's. "Rabih Farhat?"

"Who?" Nassim murmured.

"Don't lie to me! You know who they are!"

"I don't," Nassim groaned.

"But I know you know Masri."

"Please . . ."

"You live in the El-Khalili souk, don't you?" Erdogan said, pacing with a riding crop in his hand.

Nassim nodded.

"Then you must know him, Mr. Alamuddin," Erdogan insisted. "Masri is not someone you forget."

Nassim shook his head. "There are many people in the souk."

"You are a filthy swine and a liar!" Erdogan shouted and cracked the riding crop across the boy's chest.

Nassim whimpered in pain.

"You were twice seen talking to him."

Nassim's head hung to his side again.

"Now, once and for all, tell me where he is or you will pay for it with your life!"

Nassim remained silent, saliva dripping from the side of his mouth.

"Tell me!" Erdogan said ominously. And suddenly, without warning, he took out his pistol and a shot rang out. Nassim screamed with pain. Erdogan had put a bullet in his leg.

"Stop screaming!" Erdogan aimed his gun at the young boy again. Nassim began to whimper.

"Bring the needles!" he ordered. "I'm tired of waiting."

Sergeant Celik left the room.

"Now . . . you will tell me where Salah Masri is, or I will lift your fingernails off one by one. Your fingers will be left raw."

Nassim groaned in agony.

The sergeant came back with a box.

"Stick him," Erdogan ordered his subordinate.

Sergeant Celik opened the box and took out a long, slim, steel needle. He forcefully pried one of Nassim's fingers from the chair's arm and stuck the needle under his finger, pushing it into the nail bed. Nassim screamed from the pain and fainted.

"I don't think we'll get any more from him right now, Sir." Sergeant Celik looked up at Erdogan.

Omer Erdogan snorted. He struck his riding crop against the wall. "Son of a bitch!" he swore and spat. "Masri has the luck of the devil."

Erdogan swept past Sergeant Celik and walked down a hallway and up a flight of stairs to his office. He took off his black fez and threw it down on the desk. Pulling off his gloves, he flung them along with his riding crop on the chair. He put his sword on the chair and the pistol on his desk. He loosened the top buttons of his green Army jacket and his belt and sat down at the desk.

He pulled out a sheet of paper and quickly scribbled a note:

> *Put café under round-the-clock surveillance.*
> *Woman to be watched very carefully.*

He put it in an envelope and sealed it. He pressed a button on his desk and moments later Sergeant Celik appeared.

"Sir!"

"Get this to our man in the El-Khalili immediately."

—m—

Salah made his way back to his house through the tunnel that ran below all the houses in the alley. *I wonder why our house is linked to Rania's Café*, he thought, as he slowly made his way through, matches in hand, picking his way through the puddles and mud and the rats that scampered off squealing when he approached. *God I hate rats!* He scrunched up his nose as he saw their tails disappearing into holes in the walls on either side. Suddenly, the tunnel ended. *Now what?* Salah thought. He looked up, feeling the ceiling just above his head.

A few inches away, a small rusted iron ring stuck out from the ceiling. He reached over and pulled on it and felt something give. He pulled a little harder and the ceiling felt like it was going to give way. Finally, with one big tug, a trap door came down and Salah was staring into the chandelier shop. Luckily it was lunchtime and the shop was empty or he would have had a lot of explaining to do. He heaved himself into the shop and walked toward the back where he knew a staircase led up to his mother's apartment. But he also knew it was locked. There was a big iron lock on the inside that his mother had put on ever since she had rented the ground floor to the chandelier merchant. He had no other choice but to knock and have his mother open up.

Crouching, he waited until he heard someone walk by and gently knocked. The footsteps stopped and came back and stopped in front of the door. Salah knocked again.

"*Meen?*" It was Noura's voice.

Salah heaved a sigh of relief.

"Noura . . . it's me, Salah."

"Salah? Where are you?"

"Behind the door."

"What are you doing behind the door?" she asked.

"I can explain, but can you open it?"

"There's a huge lock on it," she told him.

"I know," Salah nodded. "My mother has the key, although I don't know where she keeps it."

"Your mother took Tante Takla home," Noura told him. "She's not even here."

"Noura, can you look in the kitchen? Or in her bedroom?"

"Wait! There's a key hanging here on the wall. Maybe this is it?"

Salah heard the lock click open a few minutes later and Noura opened the door to let him in.

"What on earth is going on, Salah?" Noura said. "You told your mother you were going to buy fruit!"

"Well, I did go to the fruitseller . . ."

"But that was at least an hour ago."

"I know," Salah said.

There was silence between them.

"*Ya Allah!* Salah!" Noura said softly. "You're still involved aren't you?"

Salah was silent.

"How could you, Salah?" Noura cried angrily, the color rising in her face. "After what happened to Khaled and Wissam and Rafic . . . you're still helping those goddamn foreigners."

"Noura, please try and understand . . . ," Salah began.

"You bastard!" Noura shouted. "They're the ones who murdered your friends . . . they betrayed them all . . . they hung because of that betrayal."

"I know, Noura."

"Tell me why the French ambassador would leave town and leave behind only the correspondence between him and Rafic? Why?" Noura cried. "He took everything else, destroyed everything else, yet left those letters . . ."

Salah was silent.

"And still you go on?"

"They would have wanted me to," Salah said. "They would want me to continue the struggle."

"What you want, Salah, what you all wanted is nothing but a dream," Noura said vehemently. "Do you really think the Arabs will be allowed to govern themselves? Not a chance . . . these Westerners lie to get us to help them, and in the end, they will help only themselves because they are arrogant enough to think they are better than us and that we are ignorant natives who know nothing. They will never understand this part of the world. It is too complex."

"I can't get out now, Noura," Salah said.

"You are just as much of a traitor as the French!" Noura stepped back from Salah, her eyes blazing. "You do not mourn your friends . . . you never have. You continue to plot with their murderers."

"Noura, they died for a cause they believed in," Salah tried to explain. "They are martyrs . . ."

"Oh spare me your pathetic explanations!" she sneered. "I don't want martyrs! I just want my husband back."

Salah didn't know what to say to calm her.

"We had plans, Salah," she continued, her slender hands balled into fists at her side. "Plans for a life, a home, another child, maybe two. We had plans to grow old together . . . and now what? Now what do I have? I'm a widow, a single mother stuck with an infant, living on my great aunt's charity! I have absolutely no one to turn to, no one to ask for help . . ."

"You have me, Noura," Salah said gently. "And you have my mother . . . we will help you. You should consider this your home and come here . . ."

"Oh stop it!" Noura said. "Don't patronize me!"

"Noura," Salah began softly.

"I'm angry, Salah. I don't want this life."

"But Noura, you have Siran," Salah said. "You have to think about her."

"Think about Siran! Why does everyone always say that? Are you all parrots repeating the same thing? Of course I think about her, Salah! Do you really think I'm that selfish? But I also need a life. I can't live for a daughter who will one day go away and have her own life."

She paused briefly.

"I have to go," she said. "If I'm going to live on someone's charity, it might as well be my own family's."

Salah tried to take one of her hands in his. But this time, Noura held them rigidly by her side.

"Endings are inevitable, Noura," Salah began hesitantly. "An ending can be the end of a year, the end of a summer, the end of a war, or the death of someone we loved. Whatever they are, endings always make us feel sad. But we move on. And the people we have lost along the way are the small clear voices in our heads that will be with us always.

"I am here for you, Noura," he said before he walked through the door.

CHAPTER SEVEN

"Meet at mosque . . . urgent" was the message Salah encrypted into a newspaper article.

He handed it to Hisham. "Get this to Major Thomas Lawrence at the British Army barracks. Wait for an answer."

"Tomorrow. Evening prayers," came the response.

—~~—

Salah zigzagged his way through the bazaar. He was even more careful than usual. Close to the mosque, he noticed a couple of men in red tarbushes a few feet behind him. He quickly ducked into a spice shop, watching, waiting. But the two tarbushes walked casually by. Salah came out of the shop and looked left and right. All the way to the mosque he kept looking over his shoulder. Near the mosque, he saw a couple of men leaning casually against a lamppost, smoking. Salah quickly turned on his heel and took another street to the mosque. As he got closer, he saw a man reading a newspaper. As Salah walked by, the man lowered the newspaper and made eye contact with him. Salah nodded a greeting and kept going. His heart started beating faster. He wondered if he'd made a mistake acknowledging the man. He looked behind him, but the man was still in the same place reading his paper. He breathed a sigh of relief.

Finally, he arrived at the Midan Al-Hussein just as the *adhan* sounded from the minaret, calling the faithful to prayer. He quickly crossed the square to the mosque and went in, removing his sandals at the entrance and placing them in a small cubicle and performing his ablutions at the fountain with everyone else before going inside to pray. He stopped quickly at the shrine of Hussein, a huge engraved silver casket that sat on a slab of pure white marble, and said a quick prayer for his friends who, in his eyes, like Hussein, were martyrs.

In the enormous prayer hall, Salah looked around surreptitiously. He was looking for the Turks and the Englishman. But no one stood out. Everyone looked the same in their long white tunics, prayer caps, and long white scarves. Slowly they all shuffled into place and the imam came and took his place. "*Allah u Akbar!*" he began the evening prayer.

"I have heard the gardens in the back courtyard of the mosque are pleasantly cool this time of year," a voice whispered next to him.

"I believe they are."

"Perhaps you would join me in an exploratory stroll?"

Salah arrived first and sat down on a marble bench under the cool archway that bordered the rose beds in the middle. He breathed in the scent of the flowers. It was so beautiful and peaceful, with nothing but the sound of a few bees and the gentle trickle of water flowing from the fountain into the small streams that fed the roses.

"Good evening, Salah!"

"Lawrence!" Salah acknowledged the Englishman who emerged from behind one of the pink Egyptian marble pillars.

The Englishman was not a tall man; in fact, he was rather short. At five feet and five inches, he came up to Salah's chest. He was handsome, with piercing blue eyes, fair skin tanned from hours in the sun, bushy eyebrows, a long, plump nose, and thin lips. Despite his adherence to all things Arabic, he was clean-shaven. His thin, wiry frame was also quite a contrast to Salah. He was wearing a white Arab cloak over his military uniform and a white scarf covered his head, hiding his short, light brown hair.

"Salah . . . haven't seen you in ages. I'm very sorry about your friends."

"Thank you. But right now, I need a favor," Salah said.

"Of course."

"A young boy, Nassim Alamuddin, has disappeared," Salah said. "He's eighteen years old and he has been my ears and eyes in the bazaar, keeping me informed about strangers . . . watching my back."

Lawrence nodded.

"I know the Turks have him," Salah said. "I need to find him before they kill him. They're after me, Lawrence, and this boy's gotten caught in the crossfire. I have to help him, even if I have to turn myself in."

"You'll hang if they find you."

"I know, but I couldn't live with myself if they kill Nassim."

"If he's in Cairo, we'll find him."

—–⁓—–

Back at the café, Rania led Fatmeh upstairs to tend to Rabih's wounds.

"Come!" Rania said. "He's in here."

Rania gently pushed the door open.

Rabih was lying on his back on a small single bed. His arms lay at his sides. His head was turned to one side, exposing the wound on his head. His eyes were closed and his breathing was shallow. His torn shirt was open, revealing the shredded and soiled vest he wore underneath. His chest was gleaming with blood and sweat. Rania wasn't sure if he was asleep or just resting. She turned to Fatmeh.

"Bring me hot water, boiling water," Fatmeh said calmly. "And as many towels as you can. And rubbing alcohol."

Rania nodded as Fatmeh picked up a small wooden stool and set it down next to Rabih. She touched his forehead. He didn't move. She pursed her lips. His skin was burning.

Rania came back in with a small pile of towels and a bottle. "The water is boiling. How is he?"

"He has a very high fever . . . What is his name?" Fatmeh asked.

"Rabih," Rania answered quickly.

"And he's a friend of Salah's?"

Rania nodded.

"How did this happen to him?"

"I don't know."

"I need some kind of antiseptic." Fatmeh looked back at Rabih, peering at his wounds.

"Is alcohol not enough?"

Fatmeh shook her head. "What he needs is carbolic acid or

hydrogen peroxide, but we can only get that in a hospital or in a doctor's office."

Rabih turned his head slightly and groaned. Fatmeh and Rania looked at him.

"Lemons," Fatmeh said suddenly, her face lighting up. "Lemons and honey. That, with the alcohol, will do. Where's the alcohol?"

"Here."

"Is this all you have?" Fatmeh asked, looking at the green bottle that was barely half full.

Rania nodded.

"He's going to need a lot more than this."

"I don't have any more."

"Bring me one of those bottles you keep behind the bar," Fatmeh said calmly, "the clear liquid."

"You mean gin? But that is for drinking."

"It has alcohol in it." Fatmeh turned to Rabih who was starting to get agitated. "Go! Quickly!" she ordered.

Fatmeh put her hand again on Rabih's forehead.

"Rania," he moaned, turning his head.

"Please don't move," Fatmeh said softly, reassuring him with the touch of her hand. "You've lost quite a lot of blood. I'm going to try and stop that."

Rabih groaned, turning his head back to the other side. *Hurry, Rania,* Fatmeh thought, wishing she had access to the bottles in her father's dispensary. She took what little alcohol there was left in the bottle and soaked one of the small towels. She needed hot water, but this was going to have to do until Rania returned. She looked at the bloodied man in front of her. He had all kinds of knife wounds, not to mention a bullet in his leg that was going to have to be surgically removed.

"This is going to sting," she warned Rabih before she began, softly and deftly cleaning the congealed gash on the side of his head.

Rabih gave a sharp cry of pain. "I know," Fatmeh said soothingly. "Stay strong . . . please."

Rania came back a few minutes later, clutching a heavy bucket of boiling water with both hands. Breathlessly, she put it down next to

Fatmeh, spilling a few drops on the stone floor. "I'll go get the gin and the lemons. I couldn't carry everything."

"I'm going to need more hot water too."

"I'll put some more on to boil," Rania said, walking out the door.

"Rania . . . we're going to need some kind of linen or cotton to bind these wounds," Fatmeh said.

"I don't have anything . . . a few pieces of linen, maybe."

Fatmeh continued to clean Rabih's wound as Rania looked on.

"I know." Fatmeh put down the alcohol-soaked cloth for a moment. She got up and started to unbutton her abaya.

"Fatmeh!" Rania said, shocked. "What are you doing?"

"We will use this for his wounds," Fatmeh declared. "Bring scissors too."

"Fatmeh, please, you will get into such trouble," Rania pleaded.

"We will cross that bridge when we come to it," she said. "Now go, get the scissors. I need you here as my assistant."

Rania turned to go back downstairs.

"He was asking for you," Fatmeh said behind her as she continued to work on Rabih's head.

Rania stopped, her hair swinging behind her as she did.

"I'll be right back," she promised in a tone of voice that Fatmeh knew was meant for Rabih, not for her.

—⁓—

It was early evening when Salah and Lawrence left the mosque. The sun was slowly dipping into the horizon in front of them. Lawrence stood in the alleyway behind the mosque and looked left and right. Quickly and carefully, they made their way across the square into the bazaar. Back on familiar ground, Salah heaved a sigh of relief.

"Don't get too comfortable," Lawrence said suddenly.

"Oh no!" Salah said, immediately understanding. "Turks?"

Lawrence nodded.

"Did they have to come after us today?" Salah groaned.

"Yes." Lawrence sighed, putting his hand on the gun he was carrying around his waist. "Unfortunate, really."

"Damnation, Salah!" Lawrence glanced behind him. "You're really done for if they recognize me . . . I mean, not that you've got it any easier now . . . but if they recognize me, Ahmed Jemmal will happily shoot you himself."

Salah hurried down the alleyway. "What if we split up?"

"There's two of them," Lawrence said. "And they're closing in.

"Any ideas, Salah?" Lawrence said after a few moments. "This is much more your turf than mine. I have no idea where we're going."

"Turn right!" Salah said suddenly, swerving into a barely visible narrow alley. He began to run. "Follow me!"

"Do you know where you're going?" Lawrence hissed behind him.

"Don't worry! We'll manage!" Salah said over his shoulder.

"That's what a camel driver once told me!"

Both men ran down the alleyway, turning left at the next lane.

"Are they still on our tail?" Salah asked.

"Yes!"

Salah ducked into another tiny alley, crossing another lane, and going down the next one. At the end of it, he stopped.

Lawrence looked around them quickly. He went to the corner and peeked out. The next lane looked clear. "We have to keep moving."

"Come on!" Salah dragged Lawrence by the sleeve of his *thawb*. Crisscrossing a couple of lanes and a few more alleys, they emerged across from Rania's Café. The "Closed" sign was still on the door. Rania had not opened after lunch.

"It's closed, Salah."

"No! I know she's in there."

"But how do we get in?"

"This way!" Salah said, moving quickly. They walked behind the building. Navigating another smaller maze of alleyways, some of which Salah had to squeeze himself through, they finally came to a door. Salah knocked.

Rania's face peeked through the curtain that covered the back door of the café. She looked at Salah and shook her head in indignation.

"Now what?" she said, opening the door.

Salah strode in. "Thank you!"

"Again?" Rania stood with her hands on her hips. "Can't you use the front door like normal people?"

"Rania, this is my English friend, Lawrence . . . Thomas Edward Lawrence." Salah ignored her, making introductions instead.

"Lawrence," Salah pushed the short Englishman in front of him. "Say hello to Rania."

"Good evening," Lawrence said politely.

Rania nodded, still indignantly staring at Salah.

"Say something nice again." Salah poked Lawrence.

"I'm very pleased to meet you." Lawrence bowed.

"Salah!" Rania punched him gently. "What in God's name is going on?"

"Rania!" Fatmeh's voice sounded at the top of the staircase. "Please! I need your help."

"Don't think you've gotten away with this," Rania said, shaking her finger at Salah. "I'll be back." She ran up the stairs.

"Phew!" Salah wiped the sweat from his brow.

"Who is upstairs?" Lawrence asked, sitting down on a small bench.

"Rabih Farhat," Salah said, "my old colleague."

"When did he get here?"

"I don't know. He was in Rania's cellar. Speaking of Rania's cellar, I think I am going to enjoy a glass of whiskey."

"I thought you were a Muslim."

"Only when it suits me."

"Why does Rania keep whiskey in her cellar?" Lawrence remarked, astonished.

"Well," Salah took a bottle out from behind the bar, "she inherited it from her husband's uncle. I think he was a smuggler of some kind."

"I see," Lawrence said, as Salah took a bottle out from under the bar.

"You sure you don't want just a sip?" Salah held up a bottle of single malt.

"I suppose I could . . ."

"Just to calm the nerves."

—⁓—

"Salah!" Rania called out. "We need you up here, please."

"Would you excuse me, please?" Salah said to Lawrence.

"Of course." Lawrence smiled, raising his glass.

"Fatmeh is going to try and extract the bullet from Rabih's leg," Lawrence heard Rania tell Salah when he reached the top of the stairs. "You're going to have to hold him."

Lawrence stared into his whiskey. *I should have stuck to archaeology and history and not gotten involved in the war business.* A loud shriek of pain filled the house, followed by grunts, undoubtedly Salah's, as he tried to hold his friend down. *Oh Lord help him!* Lawrence thought. Another scream echoed from above. *This is unbearable.* Lawrence gulped down the last of his whiskey and reached for what was left of Salah's. *I should be used to this by now.* Shaking his head, he walked through the kitchen to the café in the front. He peeked through a sliver of an opening between the curtains on the door and saw the two Turks who had been following them walking by. He immediately crouched down on the floor and slowly came back up, looking through the same sliver with one eye.

"Where the hell did they go?" he heard one of them say.

"Isn't this the same café that we went into looking for Farhat?" the other said.

"I don't know," the other said in an annoyed voice. "All these goddamned coffee houses and lanes look the same."

"Don't worry. We'll get them."

"The big one was Masri, I am sure of it. But who was he with?"

"I couldn't tell, Sir, except that he was short."

"We're not going to find them now. It's getting too dark."

"Why don't we ask around, Sir . . . just in case?"

"I don't think we'll get anywhere . . . it seems as if they're all protecting him. But why?"

"Perhaps he's paying them, Sir?"

"Don't be stupid! How can he be paying the whole bloody souk?"

"Perhaps we should just look inside this café, Sir?"

Bloody hell! Lawrence crouched back down.

When he didn't hear anyone at the door, he looked back out and saw the Turks walk to the next alleyway, looking into all the open shops along the way, occasionally saying something to the shop owners, almost all of whom shook their heads and shrugged.

Suddenly, Lawrence had an idea. He tried the front door. It was locked. Unwilling to disturb Salah or Rania, he looked at the windows that gave onto the street. They were a bit small, but if he held his breath, he'd be able to squeeze through. Slipping through, he walked quickly up the street. He planned to catch up to the Turks and follow them. He was positive they would lead him to their hideout, which is where they were probably holding Nassim.

Lawrence drew his headscarf across his face to cover everything but his eyes and drew his cloak around him to hide his British military uniform. He walked quickly to keep up with the Turks, ducking into a fabric shop when he saw them fifty yards ahead.

"*Ahlan!*" the shopkeeper smiled broadly when he saw the Englishman enter.

Lawrence, who was keeping a close eye on the Turks, didn't reply at first.

"May I help you?" The man approached Lawrence.

"*Shoo?*" Lawrence turned, suddenly realizing the shopkeeper was addressing him.

"What can I do for you today?" the shopkeeper rubbed his hands together excitedly at the prospect of a sale.

"*Ana* . . . uh . . . ," Lawrence muttered, one leg outside the shop, his eyes on the Turks up ahead.

"A turban, perhaps?" the shopkeeper pointed to the oversized turbans that were in fashion. "A tarbush?" he said, grabbing a few in different colors and showing them proudly to Lawrence.

"No . . . really," Lawrence muttered, his attention elsewhere.

"Come on, brother!" the shopkeeper continued. "Or this beautiful cloth for your wife?"

"No . . . I'm not married."

"Ah! Then your mother! I'm sure your mother would appreciate it."

"Uh, no . . . thank you," Lawrence replied, still watching the Turks who had stopped up ahead and were talking animatedly among themselves.

"Perhaps for your sister?" the shopkeeper opened another bolt of fabric.

"Perhaps another time?"

"This turban is perfect for you, brother," The shopkeeper plonked a large white one on Lawrence's head. But it was too small. The shop-keeper looked puzzled and tried to pull it down further.

"My head is larger than you think," Lawrence said, a bit embar-rassed.

"This is the next size." The shopkeeper put it on Lawrence's head.

"Look . . . I'm really not looking for anything."

"Then why did you come into my shop?" the shopkeeper asked, annoyed.

Lawrence looked at him and let out an exasperated sigh. "Fine! How much is this?"

"For you, a special price . . . one pound." The shopkeeper grinned, knowing he had a buyer.

"What?" Lawrence cried.

"Fifty piastres." The shopkeeper bobbed his head, his hands together in hope.

Just then the Turks started to move. Lawrence quickly reached into his pocket and handed the man a coin.

"*Shukran*, brother! *Shukran!*"

"Yes, yes . . . ," Lawrence muttered, settling the turban properly on his head.

As he approached the open square in front of the Al-Hussein Mosque, Lawrence was grateful for the turban, which allowed him to blend in completely with the rest of the men milling around. He continued trailing the Turks past the mosque and was careful not to lose them in the lanes around the Al-Azhar University. Just past the university, the two men turned into a small compound. Lawrence made a mental note of the address and the lush mango tree in the driveway that led up to the main door. Luckily there were lots of bushes and trees, allowing Lawrence to carefully approach the house without being seen. Tip-toeing around the back of the house, he saw a light in the basement. He got down on all fours and crawled on his belly to the narrow window, which was slightly ajar to let in some air.

"On your feet, boy!" Lawrence heard a male voice. "Hold him up, Celik!"

"Yes, Sir."

Lawrence heard someone whimper. *That's Nassim. It must be.*

He heard the click of the safety switch of a gun. "Why the hell are you so loyal to him? What has he ever done for you?" he heard someone say.

"Sir," another male voice said. "What if we use this boy as bait and lure Masri out?"

"That is what we are doing, you idiot."

"Sorry, Sir."

"Are our boys keeping a close eye on the café and the woman?"

"Yes, Sir."

"And they haven't seen Masri in there or Rabih?"

"No."

"And what about the woman? Has she gone out?"

"Only to do her shopping at the market."

"Rabih is in there, Celik. And Masri too. I am sure of it. Goddamn it."

"We need to storm the café, Sir."

"We can't do that. The British cannot know we're here. If the woman calls the police, we're done for. We're not supposed to even be in Egypt."

"But, Sir . . ."

"Celik . . . we are Turks operating in a British protectorate. Do I need to remind you that our government is at war with theirs? They'll throw us straight in jail. Actually worse . . . as military men, we'll be prisoners of war. No. We have to be smarter."

Lawrence had heard enough. He had to move quickly.

Slowly Rabih opened one eye. The other one remained closed under a swathe of soft cotton wool. He looked up at the ceiling. The whitewash looked dull and the plaster needed repair. From the periphery, he could see Rania sitting on a chair next to him, her arms crossed across her middle, her head lolling on her chest. She looked as though she was asleep. He turned his head to look at her and a bolt of pain shot through his head. He winced, whimpering, the pain so sharp that he had to close his one eye again until it passed. When he opened it again, she wasn't there. He stared back up at the ceiling. His entire body ached. He was cold, but could feel himself sweating at the same time. His thigh throbbed, his rib cage pounded dully, and his head felt like it had been hit with a hammer. His tongue felt as dry as the desert. There was a jug of water and a glass sitting on a small stool next to him. He tried to sit up to reach it, but he couldn't lift himself. He stretched out his arm, but couldn't hold the jug properly. Exhausted with the effort, he lay back and closed his eye.

When he came to, Rania was sitting in the chair next to him. Seeing him awake, she immediately came to the bed and knelt by his side, sitting on her heels.

"Don't try to move," she told him. "Would you like some water?"

He nodded weakly.

Very gently, she placed her hand under his shoulders, cradling his head against her breast and brought the glass to his lips. Rabih could hear her heart beating faster.

"Now, you need to rest," she said.

"Where is the nurse?" he asked weakly.

"Fatmeh? She'll be here in just a while. It's lunchtime now."

"How long have I been asleep?"

"For many hours. But you need to rest more."

Rabih looked at her. She was wearing another dress. This one had a pink and orange paisley pattern with ruffles along the neckline and the sleeves. Over it, she wore a white cotton crocheted shawl that she let fall over one shoulder, exposing her neck and décolleté. The dress suited her perfectly, he thought. It showed off her curvaceous figure. He noticed the swell of her breast, her small waist, and the way the dress clung to her hips, rustling seductively when she walked.

"You look very nice," he remarked, his voice barely a whisper.

"Thank you." She smiled graciously.

He smiled. His eyes closed again, his mind filled with Rania, the gentle touch of her hand, the scent of her skin, her plush hair, her eyes, her smile . . . he fell asleep.

—⋙—

Downstairs, Rania heard the back door open. She wrapped the shawl around her.

"Rania?" she heard Fatmeh's soft voice.

"*Marhaba, habibti!*" Rania said, coming down the stairs.

Fatmeh turned and smiled. "You look lovely today."

"Thank you," Rania said. "I'm sure you too would look lovely in a dress and some kohl."

"Perhaps one day." Fatmeh smiled woefully. "But for the moment, I'm stuck in this." She pointed to the abaya.

"I went to my father's dispensary and got a few things." Fatmeh opened her satchel and pulled out a bale of cotton wool, a large bottle of rubbing alcohol, proper linen bandages, and a few other implements.

"What are these for?" Rania picked up a small leather case filled with needles.

"He needs stitches, Rania," Fatmeh said sympathetically as Rania visibly squirmed. "I was able to take the bullet out, because otherwise he would have lost his leg, but now I have to put him back together."

Rania swallowed, hugging herself.

"And this, *habibti*, is rubbing alcohol." Fatmeh laughed. "I don't think I'll ever be able to drink gin again."

"What do you mean, again?" Rania looked at her, shocked. "Have you ever drunk it?"

"I tried a little sip one day of Madame Yvonne's lime juice," Fatmeh admitted.

"*Yallah!* He's asleep, so you can work on him."

"I also have a tranquilizer that I will give him so he sleeps through the stitches."

"You realize it is going to take him some time to heal," Fatmeh whispered as they approached the bedroom.

"You'll have to look after him, Rania," she added. "I can't be here all the time."

Rania nodded, blushing. Fatmeh noticed immediately.

"But I'm not a nurse, like you," Rania said quickly.

"No, but you're kind and caring . . . and loving," Fatmeh ventured, "and that's all nursing is."

Rania looked away.

"He's very handsome." She smiled and put her arm in Rania's.

"Stop it!" Rania giggled. "I don't even know him."

"No, but sometimes you don't have to," she said. "Sometimes you just know."

"Shhh!" Rania put her finger to her lips. "What if he's awake and heard you?"

"Somehow I don't think he would mind."

"I must be mad!" Rania admitted.

"You're not mad at all, *habibti* . . . just smitten. And it was about time."

—᙭᙭—

Salah slipped into the El Fishawy café.

"Today's newspaper, brother?" one of the waiters offered him.

"Thank you." Salah took it.

Inside was a note:

Café being watched. Rania in danger. Get Rabih out immediately. Nassim found. Extraction set. Details shortly.

Lawrence had better hurry. I don't want to hand Nassim's body to his mother. Salah looked around quickly to make sure no one had seen anything. He left a few coins on the table and left.

Just as Salah turned the corner, he saw two men wearing red tarbushes walking down the lane. They stopped for a second when they saw him. Salah took off, zigzagging around the alleyways. Despite his size, he was moving quickly. At the end of the alleyway was the fruit-sellers' square. Salah quickly ducked behind Magdi's stall. He crouched down. Seconds later, the two men appeared, breathless, looking around. They ran to one of the sellers at the far end and pulled the poor man off his stool, shouting at him and asking whether he had seen a large man come through the square. The fruitseller indignantly shook them off. As they turned their backs to walk away, he ran up behind them and pelted them with an overripe watermelon, cracking it open over their heads. All the fruitsellers began laughing. Salah chuckled and disappeared into the tunnel behind Magdi's stand.

—m—

Rabih opened his eyes.

"*Sabah al-khair*," Rania said softly.

"Good morning," Rabih replied, turning his head to look directly at her.

"How are you feeling today?"

His eyes smiled with appreciation. "Much better."

"Would you like some breakfast?"

"But don't you have to open the café?" he asked.

"I have an hour or so."

He remained silent, staring at her, drinking in how she always had to push back that one lock of rebellious hair. She tilted her head to one side and looked down, elongating the long, swan-like neck that he dreamed of caressing, kissing, and breathing in its scent, her scent.

"I don't know how to repay your kindness, but I will."

"It's not necessary," she said.

"Yes, it is," he replied. "After all, who am I to you? A stranger who walked in the door."

"First you get well," she said, standing up, "then we will discuss it."

He nodded in agreement.

"Now, what about your breakfast?"

Rania got up. He grabbed her hand. She drew in a quick, surprised breath and looked down at him, her eyes nervous.

"Will you at least eat with me?" he asked her.

Rania smiled. She pulled her hand from his. "I might," she said and swung her hair around as she left the room.

As Rania busied herself preparing breakfast for Rabih, there was a soft knock on the back door. It was Salah.

"Where is Rabih?"

"Well good morning to you too!" Rania said.

"Rania, listen, I have to move Rabih."

"What? What is going on?"

"I'll explain later," Salah promised. "But for now, I've got to get him out."

"But, Salah," Rania argued, "I don't think he's well enough . . . besides, Fatmeh is monitoring him."

"Rania . . . please don't argue. I have to get him to a safe place."

Rania's eyebrows knitted together in a frown.

"Look, instead of upstairs, why don't I set up the cellar? You can help me put a mattress in there," she suggested. "I'll clean it up and we can move him there."

Salah looked at her. *They'll both still be in danger, but it's not a bad idea.*

"All right, but we have to do it now. Before you open."

"Give me half an hour."

"And Rania, you have to be careful."

Rania turned to look at him.

"What does that mean?"

"Rania, I swear to you that I will explain what is going on, but please, just keep your wits about you. Don't go out, and if you have to go to the market, send Fatmeh."

While Rania went upstairs to get some sheets and pillows, Salah walked into the main café. He peeked through the curtains. Across the way, he saw a couple of men idling, smoking. At the end of the lane, there was another one. The Turks were definitely here.

CHAPTER EIGHT

Omer Erdogan sat at his desk in his office, tapping his fingers in frustration.

Goddammit! Why is it so difficult to get Masri? How does he manage to give me the slip every time I get near him?

"Come in!" he said, responding to a knock on the door.

"You asked to see me, Sir?" Sergeant Celik stood at attention.

"Have you gotten anything out of the boy?"

"No, Sir . . . he's still recovering from the shot to his leg."

Erdogan growled in irritation. "It's only a bullet for God's sake! No balls . . . none of these people have any balls. Tighten the net, Celik. I want you to double the teams in the bazaar."

"Yes, Sir."

"Actually, you know what Sergeant," Erdogan stroked his chin, "we're not doing this the right way. We need to go for the jugular." Erdogan got up from his desk. "Let's bring the woman . . . the café owner, in for questioning. She will tell us where Rabih is."

"The woman, Sir?"

"Yes, Celik! The woman."

The sergeant nodded.

"And let's get Masri's mother."

"His mother?"

"Are you a parrot, Celik?"

"No, Sir."

"Have you found out where they live?"

"We think we are close to it, Sir."

"Someone has to want Turkish gold. Find someone who will tell you."

"We know it is near the café, Sir."

"Of course it's near the damned café, Celik . . . that's obvious."

The sergeant looked embarrassed. "What do we do when we find his mother, Sir?"

"Kidnap her, Celik." Erdogan looked at him, astonished. "Bring her here. I will make her tell me where her son is."

Erdogan's icy blue eyes narrowed and he smiled at his own brilliance. The sound of voices outside his door made him shake his head with irritation when he realized Celik had not properly closed his door. He growled, got up and slammed the door shut.

—⧖—

"Sergeant Celik!"

"What is it?"

"Sir, the widow of Khaled Shadid is in the El-Khalili bazaar."

"Are you quite sure?"

"I'm almost positive, Sir! I remember her from Izmir."

"Who did she go see?"

"I'm not sure. I lost her near the mosque."

"You lost her?" Celik said, looking nervously toward the colonel's office. "Find her . . . I would bet that she's in touch with Masri. And when you find her, make sure you keep a close eye on her. I want to know everything Noura Shadid does from the moment her eyes open in the morning," he ordered.

"Yes, Sir."

"Go. Well done. I will tell Colonel Erdogan at once. And send a couple of our men into the café. Let's see who's in there. Tell them to keep an eye on the café owner."

—⧖—

Rania came to the cellar carefully carrying a tray laden with breakfast. Rabih was sitting up, his back to the wall. He had made a remarkable recovery in such a short time. She grinned when she saw his eyes light up at the sight of the pastries.

"What can I tempt you with this morning?" she asked, surveying the tray in front of her.

When he didn't reply, she looked up and saw him staring at her. The expression in his eyes was so intense that she had to look away. Without saying more, she handed him a plate, her fingers brushing his lightly. Rania sat down in the little wooden chair next to his bed. She reached for her cup of coffee and held it with both hands to stop herself from trembling.

She looked at him from under her eyelashes. He was still looking at her. She tried to move her chair backwards in an effort to stop being pulled closer to him. But it was useless. It was almost as if there was a magnetic field around him that was drawing her in.

Unable to look at his face, she looked at his chest, watching it rise and fall as he breathed. She focused on the dark chest hair peeking out from under the bandages, but that only made her want to run her fingers over it. She wanted to touch his neck, rest her head on his shoulder, and feel his arms around her. She wanted to touch his lips with her fingers . . . Rania jumped up from the chair. She had to leave the room. The suddenness of her action broke the tension.

"Uh . . . ," she stuttered. "I'm sorry . . . I have to open up."

Rabih nodded.

As she turned to walk out, he caught her wrist. She stopped, looking straight ahead of her, not daring to meet his eyes. Slowly, he caressed her wrist, running his thumb over her throbbing pulse. She turned her head to look down at his hand and hesitantly turned to face him, her gaze downcast. Slowly, her eyes traveled from his hand on her wrist up his arm, his neck, until she finally allowed herself to look at him. Without letting go of her wrist, he tried to sit up, grimacing from the effort. Immediately, she fell to her knees to try to help him, adjusting the pillow he had put behind his back against the wall. He still did not let go of her wrist and she didn't want him to.

"Rania," he said softly, "please look at me." He placed his thumb under her chin and tilted her face up. "Please."

Slowly, she lifted her eyes and looked into his. His lips came towards her. When he covered her lips with his, moving them sensuously, gently entering her mouth with his tongue, she closed her eyes. He placed his free hand around her neck, drawing her closer, his thumb caressing her cheek, his fingers running through her thick hair. Their tongues fenced, their kiss deepened . . . She lifted her free hand and gently placed it on his shoulder, sliding it behind his back, running it up and down over the bandages. She brought it up and placed it behind his head, pressing it toward hers.

Suddenly, Rabih pushed her back. She looked at him, her eyes questioning him, their hands and arms still intertwined.

"Rania," he said hoarsely. "I . . . uh . . ." He smiled shyly and, without meaning to, he looked down at the crotch of his pants. It was clearly bulging.

Rania quickly looked away, smiling bashfully. "I have to open the café," she said, still grinning.

"Yes," Rabih said, unable to look at her out of embarrassment.

"I'll leave you with the pastries."

In the kitchen she giggled, hugging herself with excitement. She twirled around, doing a little dance and, without meaning to, she let out a little whoop of delight. "Dear God!" she turned her face to the ceiling. "Thank you!" she kissed the cross she wore around her neck.

A loud knock interrupted Rania from her reverie. Quickly, she pulled her hair back, twirling it around in a bun, smoothed her dress and apron, and walked to the door. She pulled back the little curtain and saw Madame Yvonne holding a large swathe of fabric and tulle in her arms. Rania turned the key and opened the door to let the older woman in.

"Madame Yvonne!" Rania exclaimed. "You are early." She turned the little sign on the door to say "Open."

"Actually, no," Madame Yvonne shook her finger. "You are late."

"I am not," Rania said, taken aback.

"Oh yes you are," Madame Yvonne insisted, standing defiantly with her hands on her hips.

"Madame Yvonne . . . ," Rania started.

"Look at the clock." Madame Yvonne pointed at the wall. "Your clock," she emphasized.

Rania turned to look. Madame Yvonne was right. It was 11:15.

"I am sorry, Madame Yvonne. The morning got away from me."

The little bell on the door jingled and Fatmeh walked in.

"I cannot believe you left me standing outside like that," Madame Yvonne complained. "What on earth were you doing? I kept knocking and knocking . . ."

Fatmeh raised her eyebrows at Rania. Rania rolled her eyes.

"But of course there was no answer," Madame Yvonne continued her rant. "I even walked around to see if you were in the kitchen, but I couldn't see a damn thing. Where were you?"

Fatmeh's eyes opened wide as she sat down and immediately opened her notebook.

"I was upstairs," Rania replied. "What would you like to drink?" she added, quickly trying to get Madame Yvonne off the topic of her tardiness.

But Madame Yvonne ignored her. "Upstairs? What happened?" she probed. "Sleep late?"

"No . . . ," Rania said and went back around the bar to pour some fresh juice for Fatmeh.

"Pomegranate, please, Rania," Fatmeh interjected timidly.

"Then what happened?" Madame Yvonne insisted. "Why were you still upstairs at eleven?"

Fatmeh giggled. Rania glared at her.

"What are you laughing about?" Madame Yvonne turned on Fatmeh. "You wouldn't be laughing if you'd been standing outside, your arms laden with heavy bags!"

Fatmeh's eyes widened again, this time with fright.

The doorbell jingled again and Saydeh walked in with Noura in tow.

"*Sabah al-khair!*" Saydeh wished them all good morning.

Rania welcomed them warmly. "*Ahlan*, Tante Saydeh, *Marhaba*, Noura."

"What's going on here?" Saydeh waddled over to the table. "What are you so angry about today, Yvonne?"

"Rania didn't open on time." Yvonne pouted.

"So?" Saydeh shrugged.

"She claims she was upstairs."

"And?" Saydeh asked.

"She left me waiting outside for fifteen minutes."

Saydeh looked around at the other women.

"Well, I was carrying a heavy load," Yvonne whined.

Saydeh sighed, shaking her head.

"Rania, why were you late this morning?" Saydeh asked. "I'm asking you only because if you don't tell her, we'll be here all day listening to her wail about it."

They all looked at Rania, except for Fatmeh, who buried her face in her notebook.

"The time got away from me this morning," Rania replied.

"You know, come to think of it," Saydeh knit her eyebrows together, "you are a little distracted lately. *Shoo? Khair?*"

"Everything is fine," Rania replied.

"I agree." Yvonne nodded her head vigorously. "She doesn't even open in the afternoons anymore. I have to make my own coffee and buy mammoul at the bakery."

"Why don't you make your own mammoul?" Rania asked.

"Because she's too damn lazy." Saydeh turned to Yvonne.

"What do you mean, lazy?" Yvonne shot back.

"Then why don't you make your own mammoul?" Saydeh retorted.

"Ladies, ladies!" Rania quickly went and stood in the middle of the two older women. "There will be no shouting in here, please. Keep your voices down."

"What?" Yvonne shouted. "It's not as if you have a baby sleeping upstairs that we all have to keep our voices down."

"No . . . I don't have a child," Rania agreed.

Fatmeh spluttered and everyone turned to look at her. "Sorry," she said, "it went down the wrong pipe."

"Now, what will everyone have?" Rania asked, going behind the bar to start the coffee machine.

"Lime juice?" Rania offered. "Madame Yvonne?"

"Oh very well," she conceded.

"What can I get you, Tante Saydeh?" Rania asked. "Noura? Coffee?"

"Yes, please," Noura replied.

"You look very nice today, Noura." Rania came out from behind the bar with a tray.

"Thank you!" Noura said, helping herself to a mammoul cookie.

"That's a very pretty dress," Rania remarked.

"I was just about to say that," Fatmeh chimed in. "I wish I could wear dresses like that."

"Thanks . . . I made it," Noura replied.

"Really?" Rania said, coming to sit next to her to take a closer look.

"Yes . . . I learned how to sew when we were in Izmir," she told them. "I had plenty of time on my hands before Siran came."

"Well you certainly have a talent for it," Rania remarked.

"I also alter things . . . ," Noura added.

"Maybe Yvonne here could use your eyes and hands," Saydeh suggested.

Yvonne looked up at her over her glasses and gave her a filthy look.

"What? Don't look at me like that!" Saydeh shot back. "You look like you're making a complete mess of it."

"What do you know?"

"You can't even thread a needle!"

Yvonne scoffed.

"And you'd better hurry up or you'll be crying and complaining that you have nothing new to wear to the wedding."

"When is the wedding?" Rania asked.

"It's coming up," Yvonne replied.

"Tante Saydeh is right, Madame Yvonne," Rania said kindly. "Why not let Noura look at it?"

Yvonne looked down at her handiwork and over at Noura. "Have you made dresses for weddings before?" she asked.

"No, not for weddings specifically," Noura replied.

"Then what makes you qualified to make this dress?"

"Nothing really, Madame Yvonne . . . ," she admitted.

"*Ya haraam*, Yvonne!" Saydeh cried. "Let her take a look! What does it matter?"

Reluctantly, Yvonne put her scissors down and sat back.

Noura looked hesitant.

"Go on!" Saydeh urged her on with a gesture of her hand.

Everyone watched as Noura went over to inspect the dress, looking from the pattern Madame Yvonne was following to the various pieces of fabric.

Suddenly, the little bell on the door jingled and Takla walked in, dressed in a black dress with a black cotton shawl over her head.

"Takla!" Saydeh cried.

"Tante Takla!" Rania ran to her. "Please come in!" she put her arm around the slight woman's shoulders and guided her to the table. Takla looked like she'd aged ten years overnight. She had deep, dark bags under her eyes. Her cheekbones looked sunken. Even her hair looked greyer.

"I'm so happy you came," Saydeh said, sitting down next to her. "It'll do you good to be here with us. You can't lock yourself up in your house forever."

Takla said nothing but sniffed, taking a big handkerchief from a pocket in her dress. Rania immediately went to get her a glass of water. Fatmeh came and sat on the other side of Takla and held her hand. Takla put her head on the younger woman's shoulder and began to cry. "Thank you," she reached her other hand out to Rania, "I don't know what I would do without all of you . . . even you, Yvonne," she added.

"Have some water, Tante," Rania urged. "And let me make you something to eat. I'm sure you haven't had anything substantial in a while."

Takla smiled gratefully.

"Some nice hummus, a little eggplant, some falafel?"

Takla nodded eagerly.

"I wouldn't mind some too," said Yvonne.

"Me too!" Saydeh put her hand up.

The door jingled again and a couple of strangers walked in. Rania's heart skipped a beat. Were they the same men who'd come looking for Rabih? They were both well dressed in suits and tarbushes and sat down at a table in a corner, from where they could see the brick wall that opened into the cellar. The curtain separating the café from the kitchen was not wide enough.

"Can I help you?" Rania walked over.

"Two coffees, please."

"Anything else?" She peered at them but they were not the same men who'd come in the day Rabih arrived.

"No."

Rania went into the kitchen to calm her nerves. She peeked through the curtains. There were four men outside, two standing across the lane opposite the café's entrance, and two at the end of the lane. Her heart started beating faster. Up until then, Rania had only occasionally seen a couple of them. But now there were six of them and they were coming into the café. *I have to warn Salah and Rabih.* She couldn't go into the cellar without them seeing her. And she couldn't leave the café to find Salah. They would surely follow her. *What should I do? What if they try to kidnap me, as Salah warned? No . . . they won't do anything with all the ladies here. They are just trying to scare me,* she told herself. She took several deep breaths to regain her composure before walking back out with a tray of food.

—◦◦◦—

Noura bent her head and spread the fabric out on the table. This is a disaster. She turned it around, thinking that perhaps she was looking at it the wrong way. *Where is the neckline? The armholes? Also, this pattern is not going to suit her at all. It's completely wrong for her figure. She needs something more flowing and free, not cut on a bias.* But how was she going to tell Madame Yvonne? And worse, how was she going to tell Madame Yvonne that she had made a complete mess of the dress and the only way to make it right was to buy some more fabric and start again?

"Madame Yvonne," Noura started, "may I make a suggestion?"

"Why?" Yvonne snapped.

"Because . . ."

"I knew it! You can't fix it!" Yvonne slammed her glass down on the table.

"Madame Yvonne, it's not that," Noura said. "It's just that this pattern is cut on a bias and you've already cut the cloth, so in order for it to look like this," Noura held up the pattern, "I will have to sew all these pieces together . . . which I can do," she continued, "but you will be able to see all the seams, so the skirt won't look as smooth as this pattern."

"You stupid girl!" Yvonne shouted. "Those pieces are for the bodice."

"But Madame Yvonne," Noura said patiently, "these pieces are not enough for the bodice."

"You can cover them with the tulle."

Noura sighed and took a deep breath.

"Madame Yvonne, if you do that, then it will definitely not match this pattern."

"So there's nothing you can do?"

"Madame Yvonne, if you want this pattern," Noura explained, pointing at the sheet of paper, "then we will have to buy more fabric . . ."

"I can't buy more fabric! Do you know how much that cost? It is pure silk!"

"Madame Yvonne," Noura stood her ground, "I can make you a dress from this, but it will not be the pattern you picked. It will still look beautiful and I think it will be more flattering to your figure."

"Of course, it'll probably look better on her than that design she picked," Saydeh piped in.

"What do you know about dresses and how they look?" Yvonne shot back. "All you ever wear are those horrible house dresses."

"At least I don't try to look twenty years younger."

"Are you suggesting that I do?"

"Of course! Look at this dress you want to wear. It's for an eighteen year old who weighs at least seventy pounds less than you."

Yvonne scoffed.

"And look at your hair color, Yvonne!" Saydeh continued. "It's blonde! And you're not a natural blonde. Have you ever heard of growing old gracefully?"

"Pshaw!" Yvonne grunted. "Speaking of hair . . . what about yours?"

"I color my hair too, but it's much more natural."

"Who can tell with that stupid scarf you always wear around you head?" Yvonne taunted her. "You could be bald for all we know."

"I've had it with you, Yvonne! I can't understand how your husband can stand being around you . . ."

"Don't bring him into this . . ."

"You only care about yourself," Saydeh shouted. "All this poor girl is doing is trying to help you . . ."

—◊◊◊—

In the midst of all this, the two strangers got up and left. But a few minutes later, another two came and sat down at the same table. Rania muttered an excuse and went into the kitchen. She peeked through the back door, hoping that Salah would miraculously appear. But the alleyway was empty.

Meanwhile, Fatmeh walked through the curtain.

"Rania, can I go upstairs? I have to prepare a few things for Rabih that you can give him later."

"Yes, of course."

"Everything all right?" she asked.

"I don't know."

"Tell me."

"I don't know what to tell you except that I have a bad feeling about the strangers who just walked in."

"Should we call the police?"

"And say what? They haven't done anything. And this is a café. They are allowed to come in and have coffee."

"Don't worry, Rania. I'm sure its fine."

"Yes, you are probably right," Rania replied. "Salah and Rabih have made me paranoid."

—◊◊◊—

Inside the cellar, Rabih sat up when Salah emerged through the tunnel.

"We've got trouble, brother," Salah took a deep breath.

Rabih's brow furrowed.

"Ahmed Jemmal's men . . . ," Salah began. "They have Nassim, one of my boys who was my ears and eyes in the souk."

Rabih nodded, worried. "Do they know I'm here?"

Salah shrugged. "They know you're in Cairo . . . and they think you're here. At any rate, they're watching the café and keeping a very close eye on Rania."

"*Ya Allah!*" Rabih rubbed his forehead. "I need to get out of here. I'll never forgive myself if something happens to her."

"I'm worried they might snatch Rania, just like Nassim, in order to get to us."

"Do you know where Nassim is?"

Salah nodded. "Lawrence found him. I'm waiting for him to tell me when we can go in and get him. He'd better be getting him out soon, or I will go in there myself."

"How is it going in the Hejaz?"

"Slow." Salah was disgusted and annoyed, not to mention weary. "The British are not advising Faisal well."

"Why doesn't Lawrence become the liaison?"

"That may well be on the cards."

—⁂—

"Tante Saydeh! Please, both of you, not another word," Rania pleaded. "Now we are going to fix this issue with the dress right now, all right? *Khalas!* I've had enough."

She turned to Noura.

"Noura, what is the story with the dress? Can it be fixed?"

"*Akeed!* Of course!" Noura said. "But it will not look like the pattern Madame Yvonne originally chose. It will still be beautiful and it will look lovely."

"And if she wants this pattern?" Rania asked.

"Then we have to buy more cloth and start again."

"So what would you like, Madame Yvonne?" Rania asked.

"She should have gone to a dressmaker in the first place instead of pretending to know everything about everything," Saydeh remarked.

"Tante Saydeh! Please!" Rania put a hand on her shoulder to stop her from confronting Madame Yvonne again.

"Why do you have to be such a know-it-all?" Saydeh jabbed again.

"Why do you have to be such a nosy pain in the ass?" Yvonne hooked back.

"Ladies!" Rania cried in exasperation. "Stop it . . . seriously, or I will ban you from coming here."

The women fell silent.

"Now, Madame Yvonne," Rania turned to her first, "why don't you let Noura work on this dress and make something for you? And if, when you have tried it, you don't like it, then we will try and find another solution . . . but give her a chance."

"Why don't we just put her in a burlap sack," Saydeh muttered, "and throw her in the Nile?"

Rania glared at Saydeh.

"Now, is that an acceptable solution?"

Madame Yvonne nodded.

"Good!" Rania let out a deep breath.

In the meantime, the second pair of men had gotten up and walked away.

Rania went over to their table and began clearing away the empty cups and plates. She happened to look outside and her heart jumped into her throat. On the other side of the alley, she saw two men, wearing black pinstriped suits and black Fedora-style hats. Both were smoking and looking over at the café and the floor above it. They were the same men who had come in the day Rabih stumbled through the front door. She watched as they stubbed out their cigarettes and began to walk over, hands in their pant pockets.

Before she had time to do anything, the bell on the door jingled. The two men sat down at the table she'd just cleared.

"*Sabah al-khair,*" Rania said, wishing them a chilly good morning. "Can I help you?"

"You know, we were so saddened when your café was closed the last time we were here, that we decided to come back," one said to Rania.

Rania stared at them, her expression blank.

"Yes, your café seems very popular with the locals," the other added.

"What do you want?" Rania hissed.

"We would like two coffees and two narghiles."

They definitely looked and sounded Turkish. Even though their Arabic was perfect, they still had traces of an accent.

While she was putting fresh water in the narghiles and preparing the tobacco, Yvonne came into the kitchen. "I would like a narghile as well," she told Rania.

"Very well," Rania said quickly. "Why don't you go back into the café, Madame Yvonne." She took the older woman's arm and steered her toward the curtain that separated the kitchen from the café. "I'll bring the narghile out to you with the other two." Rania didn't want Yvonne in the kitchen, just in case.

But Yvonne was not to be maneuvered. She turned around and sat down on a stool. "Who are all these strange men who've been coming in all morning? I've never seen them here before."

"No . . . ," Rania said, while she formed three tobacco patties.

"They are well dressed." Yvonne nodded approvingly. "Give me a little more hashish in my tobacco," she added, looking over Rania's shoulder.

"You really want more?" Rania asked.

Yvonne nodded.

Rania pretended to put some more of the resinous cannabis in Madame Yvonne's narghile, but when the older woman wasn't looking, she put it back in the terracotta jar. She'd already had two glasses of lime juice well laced with gin.

Suddenly, the curtain was drawn aside and the two men walked in. Rania took in a sharp breath.

"We were wondering what was taking so long?" one of them said as the other walked around the kitchen, looking at everything, picking up spice bottles, touching the copper pots, running his fingers over a bowl of fresh fruit.

Yvonne looked at him quizzically. "What is he doing?" she asked out loud.

"Would you please go back into the café?" Rania said, slightly breathless. "I do not allow my customers in the kitchen. I will be right out with the narghiles," she said, wiping her hands on a dishtowel.

"But she's a customer." One of them pointed to Yvonne.

"Madame Yvonne is my friend, not a customer."

Yvonne puffed with pride at her special privileges. "Yes!" she said. "Besides, what's your hurry?" She jumped up, standing in front of the one who was standing next to Rania. "Narghiles take a long time.

You have to heat the coal, prepare the tobacco, make sure the water is fresh . . . Now go back out there . . . *Shoo! Shoo!*" She gestured as though she were sweeping away a stray cat.

"Yes, yes, we know how narghile is made, old woman," he said in a nasty tone.

Yvonne drew herself up to her full height and puffed out her already large chest. "Who are you calling old?"

The man sniggered.

"How dare you?" Yvonne raised her voice. "Just who do you think you are?" She poked her finger in his chest.

"What's happening here?" Saydeh came rushing in. "*Ya Allah!* What's everyone doing in the kitchen? Rania?"

Rania bit her lip.

"What's through here?" one of the men asked when he saw the staircase beyond the slim archway.

"That is private." Rania went and stood in front of him.

"Come on, Sir! He must be upstairs."

Upstairs there were sounds of footsteps and the creaking of furniture.

"Come, Sir!" the other man said. "I hear him. He's upstairs."

He pushed Rania out of the way and tore up the stairs with his superior close behind.

"You can't go up there! That is my home!" Rania shot up behind them.

"What are they doing?" Saydeh put her hands on her face incredulously. "Who are those men? Who do they think is up there?"

Yvonne shrugged.

Suddenly, they heard a loud scream and saw the two men come barreling down the staircase barely able to keep their balance.

"Get out of here!" the women heard Fatmeh shout. "How dare you come into my room? Wait until I tell the police . . . that you were harassing me!" Fatmeh was holding a broom, standing at the top of the stairs.

Saydeh and Yvonne looked up at the top of the stairs curiously, while the two men began picking themselves off the kitchen floor, wincing and moaning from their fall down the staircase.

"I wasn't feeling well, so I was lying down," Fatmeh said. "And suddenly these two men kicked the door down. Can you imagine what would happen to them if my husband finds out?"

"Those bastards!" Yvonne swore. "Throw me that broom," she told Fatmeh.

Rania appeared from behind Fatmeh and came down the stairs with the broom and handed it to Yvonne.

"Get up!" Yvonne hit the Turks with the straw end of the broom. "You cowards! Get up and get out immediately! How dare you come in here and harass us women. We've done nothing to you." She swished the broom against them as if she was trying to sweep them out of the kitchen.

Saydeh took a bucket of water and threw it on them. "Take that, you cads! That'll cool you down. Now out with you . . . both of you! Whatever it is you're looking for is not here. So don't come back or else we will call the police."

"Don't worry! We'll be back," one of them said.

"Take your threats somewhere else!" Yvonne swept their feet, pushing them toward the door as the two of them danced around, trying to avoid the broom. "Come on! Out!"

Finally, with a big push, Saydeh and Yvonne shoved them out the front door. A cheer went up from the table of shopkeepers. Yvonne and Saydeh looked at each other and started laughing.

"Good work, Yvonne!" Saydeh put her hand out.

"That was good, with the water," Yvonne acknowledged and shook Saydeh's hand.

"Who were they anyway?" Saydeh asked as they walked back, arm in arm, to the table.

"Allah knows," Yvonne replied.

"Where's Rania?" Saydeh asked, looking around.

"Probably upstairs with Fatmeh. Poor Fatmeh," Yvonne said, shaking her head, "what a fright she must have had seeing those two men."

Saydeh nodded her agreement.

"But what was she doing upstairs lying down in the middle of the day?" Yvonne asked.

There was silence for a moment before Saydeh broke into a big smile.

"*Shoo?*" Yvonne said.

"She must be pregnant."

"You think so?"

"Of course!" Saydeh said. "She doesn't talk much about her husband, but she is relatively newly wed."

"I don't know . . ."

"Why else would she be lying down on Rania's bed?"

"Yes . . . well, I suppose . . ."

While Saydeh and Yvonne speculated about whether or not Fatmeh was pregnant, Rania and Fatmeh were laughing uncontrollably.

"You are incredible, Fatmeh!" Rania said. "That was hilarious! Did you see the look on that man's face when you went after him with the broom?"

"It was all I could find up here."

"And then Madame Yvonne and Tante Saydeh literally swept them out of the café . . . that was too much." Rania was holding her sides with laughter.

"Lucky I was up here."

CHAPTER NINE

Omer Erdogan paced his office.

What happened at the café is unacceptable! I have idiots on my team! How could they have let a couple of old women get the better of them? He had been in Cairo for months and Masri continued to slip through his fingers. How was that possible? He had the best team of agents with him from Constantinople and his men here knew the city like the back of their hand.

"Sergeant Celik!" Erdogan called out.

"Yes, Sir!"

"I am getting tired of this cat and mouse game with Masri."

"Sir?"

"Bomb the El-Khalili bazaar."

"Sir? The whole bazaar?"

"Yes," Erdogan replied without blinking. "As much of it as we can."

"Sir, this is a British protectorate."

"Yes, Celik, I am well aware. But do I need to remind you that we are in the middle of a war? In any case, I want to make it look as if the British did it. That will drive a nice wedge between them and the Arabs."

"What about civilian casualties, Sir?"

"I don't care about collateral damage."

"If you say so, Sir."

"Find cases of British dynamite. Buy it, steal it . . . I don't care how you get it. And make sure you keep the crates that have 'British Army' burned on them. We will leave those lying around for the Arabs to find."

"I want bundles of dynamite placed directly around the café and within a one-mile radius. I want to be positive that we get Masri and Farhat."

"It will take us a couple of days to get all of that into place, Sir."

"And I want them all attached to one fuse . . . so we have one massive explosion."

"Very well, Sir. I will get working on it."

"Let me know when the preparations have been made. I want to give the order to detonate myself."

Celik saluted and left.

Erdogan stroked his chin. *Why didn't I think of this before? I'll just blow them all sky high. How dare they all insult me? They will know who they are dealing with.* Smiling, he congratulated himself on his plan.

—⁓—

Carrying Madame Yvonne's half-made dress in a linen bag, Noura wove her way along the cobblestoned lane, heading toward Rania's. She'd worked on the dress with the sewing machine at home, but she needed Madame Yvonne to try the bodice before she finalized it. She'd asked Amira to look after Siran and she took a tram to the Al-Hussein mosque. Sitting on the tram, looking out at the city, Noura smiled. She was really looking forward to seeing all the women in the café.

As she entered the souk, she was unsure of the way to the café, even though she'd written it down. Somehow, she got lost and walked round and around in circles. An hour later and just about to give up, she came to a small square that she thought she recognized. She went down a narrow lane at the end of which she saw the small alley at the back of Rania's Café.

As she approached, she saw a man kneeling on the ground at the back door of the café. He looked like he was digging. Suddenly, he got up. Noura quickly hid behind a doorway. The man looked around, adjusted his jacket and fixed the knot in his tie, and walked away. A few houses away from the café, he fell to his knees and did the same thing. He took something out of a satchel he was carrying on his shoulder. It looked like a cable. He got up and walked to the end of the lane, unwinding it from a spool as he moved. Hidden in the doorway, Noura watched him until he finished. After he turned the corner, she waited a few minutes before she went to investigate.

And there, carefully hidden under a small stack of rocks outside the back door of Rania's Café was a bundle of dynamite. Noura's heart started to beat faster. She ran to the next doorway where she'd seen the man kneeling and there, too, she found the same. Following the cable the man had camouflaged under leaves, she found the next bundle. Noura walked all around the block and down the lane and there were bundles of dynamite every hundred yards. *Oh my God! I've got to warn Rania . . . the shopkeepers . . . everyone . . .*

Noura banged on the back door of the café.

"Rania!" Noura shouted. "Rania! Open up! It's me, Noura!"

"Noura . . . !" Rania said, surprised.

"Rania, you've got to get out of here! We've all got to get out of here!"

"Why? What has happened?"

"There's dynamite outside this café and all down the lane. And there may be more!""

"What? Where?"

"Behind the back door to the café and all around the block until the end of the lane," Noura said, pointing toward the square she had come from.

"Oh my God! Look, can you get Salah?"

"There's no time. We don't know when it's going to blow."

"Noura, listen . . . there's a friend of Salah's hiding in the café. He's hurt and he can't move quickly."

Noura shook her head in anger. "Why the hell is he involving you?"

"Involving me in what?" Rania asked.

"Never mind, I'll explain later. For now, give me a sharp knife."

"What are you going to do?"

"I've got to try and stop this."

"But how, Noura?"

"Don't worry about me. You go find Salah."

Noura rushed out. She dug up the dirt the man had covered the electric cable with and pulled at the cable, but it was wedged in the bundle of dynamite. Gently, she cut it. She followed the cable and cut the second fuse.

Sweating, Noura methodically went around, following the cable, and began to cut it where she couldn't pull it out. Suddenly, she heard a short hissing sound. She froze and held her breath. But then it stopped.

Her heart pounding and shaking with nerves, Noura continued. At the end of the lane, the cable disappeared. Noura looked around. *Where was it?* She turned right, but there was nothing there. Cautiously she double backed. Several hundred yards ahead, she saw two men unfurling cable from a large wooden spool. Noura ran along and found several more bundles of dynamite placed along buildings on either side of the lane. Working quickly, she was able to cut the cables until she reached the edge of the fruitsellers' square. She could hear the cries of the sellers trying to attract customers.

Looking left and right, Noura saw no one. And then out of sheer luck, one of the reed coverings on an empty fruit stand lifted up with the wind and Noura saw the same two men kneeling behind the stand. They were attaching the cable to the detonation box. There was a third man standing in the shadows. Noura panicked. She didn't know what to do.

"Shall we detonate, Sir?" one of them asked the man in shadow.

"Blow them all up."

"Yes, Sir . . . take cover, Sir."

The second man pushed forcefully down on the lever of the box. A hissing sound began. Noura looked around. She had to hide. She saw a little wooden shed in the alley. She quickly ran and crouched down behind it. She covered her ears with her hands and closed her eyes tightly. Several seconds passed. But nothing happened. Suddenly, there was a small muted explosion. *That wasn't loud. It sounded more like a firecracker.* Slowly and carefully, Noura peeked out from behind the shed. She saw shadows moving behind the reed covering. She strained her ears to hear what they were saying. One of the men was shouting.

"Idiots! Bloody idiots!" she heard one of them shout. "This is a fiasco. You are not fit to call yourself soldiers."

There was a brief pause.

"Clean this up immediately and meet me back at the house. And hurry. The police will be here soon. And make sure you don't screw that up and get yourselves thrown in jail," commanded the same angry voice.

Noura quickly crouched down as the man pulled the reed shutter open and came storming toward the alley where she was hidden. She got a quick look at him as he walked by. He looked familiar, but she couldn't place him. He was dressed like one of the strangers who came into Rania's Café. *Could it be the same man?* As he buttoned his jacket, she caught a glimpse of a gun he was carrying. Noura put her hand to her mouth to stop herself from making any sounds.

She stayed hidden until she was sure the man had gone and then came out.

Bewildered, she made her way back to Rania's Café. She stopped just short of the small square near the café and looked around.

Stepping carefully, she made her way to the back door. Still dazed, she walked in and sat down at the table in the kitchen, the knife still in her hands. *What could have happened? What happened to all that dynamite?* Suddenly, the brick wall opened and Salah burst in.

"Noura! Oh my God, Noura!" He took her in his arms and held her for several moments. Finally he pulled back and looked at her, tipping her chin so that she was looking up at him.

"Are you all right?"

Noura nodded. But she was shaking.

"What happened?"

"The Turks . . . ," Noura whispered. "They were going to blow up the souk."

Salah took a deep breath and let it out slowly. "You saw them?"

Noura nodded. "I cut the cables of all the dynamite bundles I could find," she said, her voice shaking. "I don't know how many there were. But I only heard one small explosion."

"There was only one," Salah said. "It was near an empty stall on the edge of the fruitsellers' square. It wasn't very big."

"Was anyone hurt?"

"I don't think so."

"Did I manage to cut the cables of all the bundles?"

"You must have." Salah took her hands in his. "My brave, brave Noura. Thank God you are all right. I would never have forgiven myself if something had happened to you."

Noura nodded.

"The local police have arrived. It's in their hands now."

"Salah," Noura said quietly. "I know you're still involved."

Salah nodded.

"I cannot lose you too," she said.

—◊◊—

Salah paced up and down the hallway of his mother's apartment. He was worried. The Turks were breathing down his neck. They had tried to get to everyone close to him to smoke him out. The dynamite at Rania's was the closest they had gotten. He'd been waiting all morning for a note from Lawrence about when they were going to rescue Nassim. But nothing had arrived. *This is taking too long. Nassim could be dead by now. I'm going to have to get him out myself.*

Salah looked out the window, his mind whirring. He saw his mother coming up the lane, her basket laden with fruits and vegetables. She stopped to talk to someone . . . it was a man. But from this angle, Salah couldn't tell who it was. What if it was the same Turk his mother had told him about at the vegetable stand? *No!* Just as Salah was about to run into the street, his mother began walking toward the house. But she didn't stop at the front door. She kept going and disappeared at the end of the lane. Salah was confused. *Where did she go?* Moments later, he heard someone in the kitchen. Carefully, he padded through the dining room and stood next to the door that led to the kitchen. He heard drawers being opened, the sound of water running, and someone humming. When he peeked around, it was Saydeh putting away her fruits and vegetables.

"*Imme?*" he said, astonished. "How did you get here?"

"I live here, son."

"I know, but I saw you in the lane below the living room."

"I took the back way."

"There's a back way?"

"Of course, isn't there always?"

Salah was flabbergasted.

"Who was that man talking to you?"

"He wanted to know where I bought this fruit."

"Fruit? That's it?"

"Yes, why? You're very nervous today, Salah. Are you feeling well? Besides, why aren't you at El Fishawy?"

"I'm just going."

—⟋⟍—

Damn it! Salah pulled the scarf angrily across his face and headed to El Fishawy. He was fed up with the whole situation and very worried about Noura and his mother and that the Turks were using them to get to him, not to mention Nassim. *God only knows what condition he's in.*

He ducked around the smallest alleyways following the little maps that Magdi devised every week.

El Fishawy was not terribly crowded and most of the customers were sitting at tables that were closer to the street. Salah went straight to the back, where he sat down in a dark corner. He ordered a narghile and enquired if there was a special edition of the morning's paper. He was told there wasn't. *Still nothing from Lawrence.* Salah growled and hid behind a newspaper.

—⟋⟍—

A sinister-looking man in a black and red striped cotton galabiyya and a dark red turban sat several tables away, behind a plant, occasionally glancing toward Salah's corner. He had very brown skin and wore an eye patch over his right eye. His left eye was lined with kohl. He had dark wavy hair that reached his shoulders. His closely trimmed beard looked more like a five o'clock shadow and he had a slim, perfectly trimmed moustache. Silver rings adorned almost all his fingers and he wore a black bracelet on his left wrist. His hand bore a tattoo of a snake and another tattoo just below his Adam's apple said "Allah" in Arabic calligraphy. Around his waist he wore a brown leather belt from which hung a scabbard that housed a Persian dagger with an ivory handle. Sitting on his lap was a small monkey wearing a red fez and a little red jacket, to whom the man occasionally fed some nuts.

—⟋⟍—

"Hello, Salah, you old bastard."

The voice sounded familiar.

Very slowly, Salah lowered the newspaper and peeked over the top of it.

"Nusair!" he cried, jumping up and hugging the Yemeni warmly. "What in the world are you doing here?"

"Just passing through." Nusair smiled, his white teeth gleaming against his black skin. As usual, he was wearing black pants, a white cotton sweater, and his classic white captain's hat.

The two men hugged and shook hands vigorously.

"Come, sit down." Salah dragged a chair from another table. "I am damn glad to see you. You've made my day."

Musa smiled.

"How did you know I was here?"

"I saw your mother in the bazaar," Musa replied, ordering a glass of mango juice from a passing waiter. "And she mentioned that at this time of day, you would probably be here."

Salah rolled his eyes. "So it was you she was taking to!"

"I told her not to tell you because I wanted to surprise you."

"Well you certainly did. So where are you headed?"

"Aqaba. I've got a shipment for the Turks garrisoned there."

"Oh Nusair! Where's your loyalty?"

"You know it's to you, brother," Musa said, "but I have to live and eat and feed my wife and my seven children back in the Yemen. So I take work where I can get it. I don't care if it's English money or Turkish money or French money . . . if it's honest money and I can make it relatively honestly, I don't care."

"But don't you care about what's in the shipments?"

Musa leaned forward. "We're in the middle of a war, brother. I have a ship and I'm its captain. I don't take sides in wars. My ship is for sale to the highest bidder."

"I'm so fed up with this damn war, Nusair," Salah said.

"You're lucky to be alive, my friend."

"Yes, but do you know how hard it is to stay alive? Look at me, Nusair . . . I don't exactly blend in. I'm several inches taller than the average man who walks around this souk, I even stick out in the mosque at prayers . . ."

Musa laughed. "Those Turks must be really stupid if they haven't caught you yet."

"I'm tired of hiding, of looking over my shoulder . . . I just hope in the end that it will have been worth it. That we get what we want . . . that my friends have not died for nothing."

Musa nodded. "What are you doing here?"

"I'm waiting for a message from Lawrence."

"What's going on?"

Salah told him quickly about Nassim. "But it's taking too damn long . . . I've got to get him out, Nusair. If anything happens to that boy, I will never forgive myself."

"So what do you want to do?"

Suddenly, an idea dawned on Salah. "Listen, Nusair . . ."

Musa sighed. "Now what?"

"I want you to find Lawrence at the British Army headquarters," Salah said. "Get him to tell you where the Turks are holding Nassim."

"Then what?"

"Then you and I will go and get him. Lawrence is taking too long."

"You and me against the Turkish Secret Police? Have you gone mad?"

"Fine! I will go by myself!" Salah said.

"Masri . . . look, we have to think this through, don't be rash."

"I'm done waiting, Nusair!" Salah exploded. "This is my boy. He's in trouble because of me. I am going in there and getting him out."

"Do you have a plan?"

"I will," Salah said. "By the time you get back with the information."

"All right," Musa conceded. "I'll go."

Salah and Musa Nusair walked out of El Fishawy.

At the same time, the man in the red and black galabiyya also got up, threw a couple of coins down on the table, and walked out behind them, his monkey sitting on his shoulders. The man tore off his eye patch, smiled at his little pet, and walked down the lane. When he looked up, Salah and Nusair had disappeared. Pursing his lips in annoyance, he looked at the monkey, who screeched and pointed to the alley on the right. The man ducked into it just as Salah and Nusair turned left at the next lane. Quickly, the man sprinted down and turned left, following them. The monkey screeched again, pointing as they turned right. The man hurried behind them. At the end of the alley, the man looked left and right. Salah and Nusair were nowhere to be seen. The man looked up at his monkey, who was also looking around perplexed. Suddenly, the monkey screeched and pointed in front of them and the man caught a glimpse of Salah disappearing down an alleyway. The man took off, running in the same direction. As he did, he reached down to hold the dagger in place at his waist. The man was catching up to Salah. But where was the other man who was with him?

Suddenly, someone came up from behind him and grabbed him around the neck. The monkey screeched and jumped down, scampering away into the alley. The man immediately reacted and broke free, throwing his assailant over his head so that he lay on the ground in front of him, groaning. It was the black man who had been with Salah. The man wiped the spit from his mouth on the sleeve of his tunic. He whistled and the monkey came running back and leapt up onto the man's arm and sat back down on his shoulders. The man unsheathed his dagger.

"Where is Masri?" the man asked Musa, who slowly got to his feet.

"No one's been able to do that to me in quite a while, brother," Musa said, grimacing as he tasted blood in his mouth.

"Where is Masri?" the man repeated.

"He's gone," Musa said, wiping his mouth with a handkerchief.

"Look, I'm not looking for a fight with you, I'm looking for Masri."

"What do you want with Salah?" Musa asked.

The man in the galabiyya looked at Musa through narrowed eyes. He looked around quickly. He knew Salah was around somewhere. He could sense it.

The monkey screamed and the man whirled around just in time to see Salah lunge for him. Terrified, the monkey scampered off again. The lone man now faced both Musa and Salah. Salah lurched for him again and tried to get his arms around his back while Musa came with a frontal assault. But the man was trained. He kicked Salah in the shins and despite his height and weight, spun him around so that Salah and Musa knocked each other out, both of them on the alley cobblestones groaning in pain, holding their heads, which they had butted when they collided. The man whistled and his monkey came running back. He took a fig out of his pocket and gave it to the animal, who began munching on it. The man stood over the two men and slowly sheathed his dagger.

"Salah Masri," he said.

Salah looked up. The man was offering him a hand to help him stand up. Dazed and confused, Salah took it.

"My name is Charles . . . Charlie Hackett," the man announced in a perfect English accent. "I bear regards and best wishes from Lieutenant Lawrence . . ."

"Couldn't he have sent a telegram or a card?" Musa said, still lying on his back.

"Sorry, Sir." Hackett offered his hand to Musa.

"If this is Lawrence's way of sending regards, I'd hate to think what he might do if he didn't like you." Musa adjusted his captain's hat and brushed off the dirt.

"Why were you following me?"

"Oh, I wasn't really following you, Sir," Hackett replied.

"Then?" Salah looked puzzled.

"I've been assigned to you, Sir," he said.

"Assigned to me."

"Yes, Sir, to protect you."

"What?" Salah said, shocked.

"Well yes, Sir," Hackett explained. "I'm part of British Special Forces."

"Well there you go, brother!" Musa gave Salah a friendly punch in the arm. "And here you were complaining Lawrence had abandoned you. Instead, he's sent you your own personal bodyguard."

"And, judging by your accent, you're English, right?" Salah asked Hackett.

"English father, British Army officer, Lebanese mother, born in Beirut, Sir. Educated in London.

"I also have a message from Lieutenant Lawrence . . . We meet at 2100 hours at the north east corner of the mosque."

Just as twilight spread across the Cairene sky, Salah walked through the souk to the main square in front of the mosque.

On the northern side of the square toward Al-Azhar University, Salah thought he saw some shadows moving. The sky was not inky blue, but stars had started to twinkle and the half yellow moon was beginning to rise. He walked toward the shadows, spotting Lawrence as he got closer.

"I am going in to get my boy out," Salah said as they stole across the street, headed toward the university.

Lawrence nodded. "Fair enough. Let's go."

Silently, they arrived at the street where the Turks were holding Nassim. Lawrence handed Salah a pistol and bullets and let his men know that he and Salah were leading the raid.

"Ready?" he looked at all of them.

Everyone gave him the thumbs-up sign.

They all headed to the small house, which was dark, except for one room. Directly inside the front gate were two Turks. The English soldiers pounced on them before they could sound the alert and held chloroform-filled cloths to their noses until they passed out on the ground.

Six men fanned out across the small garden, two stayed at the front gate, and another four went around the back.

Another four of Lawrence's men approached the front door ahead of Lawrence and Salah and cautiously cracked it open. A dim light revealed a large, shadow-filled foyer. A brighter light was shining under one of the doors off the foyer. Salah indicated he was going into that room. Slowly he opened the door, his gun poised in front of him. It was an office and it was empty. Salah softly closed the door and turned around, indicating to the others that there was no one inside. Suddenly, a couple of men appeared at the top of the stairs.

"Hey!" one of them shouted. "Who are you?"

Salah aimed and fired. He caught the man in the shoulder and he collapsed on the staircase. The other turned and ran.

Suddenly, lights went on in the house, and doors on the first floor above them began to open as men poured out. Salah, Lawrence, and the four soldiers began firing at them, taking cover behind the round foyer table. Another group of men came running down another hallway off the entrance.

"I'll take them," Salah shouted to Lawrence over the gunfire.

"I'll come with you."

"You two! Come with us," Salah told a couple of the soldiers.

The front door burst open and the four Englishmen from the garden came in and joined in the gunfight. Lawrence ordered them to cover the men in the foyer.

Salah, Lawrence, and their group faced off with the men in the hallway. Slowly, they made headway and Salah reached a staircase that led downstairs to the basement.

"Cover me," he said to Lawrence, as he moved to run downstairs. Just then, the door at the bottom of the staircase opened and Omer Erdogan and Sergeant Celik emerged.

"Masri! You bastard!" Erdogan swore and took a shot at Salah. The bullet grazed Salah's arm as he quickly dove behind the banister. The Turks came running up the stairs firing. The English returned fire. Salah aimed and shot. He got Sergeant Celik in the leg, who doubled up and collapsed. But Erdogan kept coming. He killed a couple of the English before he aimed at Salah. He pointed directly and shot. His gun clicked. He was out of bullets. Erdogan looked shocked. He rustled around trying to find another weapon. He dove for one of the dead men's guns, but Salah got there first.

"Not your day, Erdogan," he said. "Cuff him," Salah ordered.

Salah ran down the stairs, Lawrence close on his heels. In the basement, they discovered crates of dynamite stamped with the British Army insignia on it.

"What the hell . . . ?" Lawrence stopped on the stairs. "This is all the British ammunition that was stolen from the depots a few days ago. This is what they used to bomb the El-Khalili."

"Right now, I don't care, Lawrence! Where the hell is Nassim?" Salah swore.

"Through there!" Lawrence pointed to a smaller door.

Salah burst in and there on a pile of hay was the bloodied, battered body of Nassim. Salah ran to him and took him in his arms. Nassim's entire face was swollen, his lips cut, his eyes were shut, and there was dried and fresh blood everywhere on his body.

"Come on, son . . . we're going home," Salah said gently.

CHAPTER TEN

Carefully, Noura took a perfectly folded dress out of a bag and placed it on the table in the middle of Rania's Café. Saydeh, Fatmeh, Takla, and Rania all sat around the table, holding their breath in anticipation. She opened it and held it up.

They all stared at the dress.

Noura's brow furrowed with fear when no one said anything.

"Well," she started hesitantly, "what do you all think?" She looked around at the group. Fatmeh's mouth dropped open and Saydeh and Takla's eyes opened wide.

"You made that?" Rania asked incredulously.

Noura nodded.

"Noura . . ." Rania ran her fingers over the silky skirt, "this is absolutely spectacular. It's so elegant. And you put the tulle underneath."

"Thank you." Noura smiled, letting out a huge sigh of relief. "Yes, this shape will be much more flattering on Madame Yvonne's figure."

"I knew it! I knew you could do it!" Saydeh went and hugged her.

Takla nodded approvingly. "She's going to look so much better in that."

Noura looked at Fatmeh, waiting for her reaction.

"I'm speechless, Noura," Fatmeh said. "I just wish I could wear a dress like that."

The doorbell jingled and Yvonne walked in. Noura gasped, grabbed the dress and ran into the kitchen.

"What?" Yvonne asked. "What has happened? Why does everyone look so scared?"

"No, no, Madame Yvonne!" Rania jumped up. "Nothing has happened. Let me get you some coffee."

Yvonne sat down, placing her purse next to her. She looked up to see Takla, Fatmeh, and Saydeh all staring at her.

"Why are all of you looking at me like that?" she cried. "Do I have something on my face?" She reached for her little compact mirror.

"Madame Yvonne," Noura approached hesitantly, with a brown paper packet in her hand, "this is for you." She placed it in front of Yvonne.

Yvonne didn't say a word. She opened the packet and lifted the dress that Noura had re-folded.

Everyone watched as Yvonne twirled the dress this way and that, inspecting it closely.

"Well, Madame Yvonne?" Noura bit her lip nervously.

"You put all the tulle under the skirt," she said, lifting the hem.

"Yes, Madame Yvonne," Noura said, "it gives a little volume and lift to the skirt so it can hide any imperfections . . . you know . . ."

"Imperfections . . . ? Are you suggesting that my figure is imperfect?"

"Yvonne!" Saydeh clicked her tongue. "We all have imperfections . . . look at my big behind."

Yvonne glared.

Rania came out from behind the bar with the coffee.

"So, Madame Yvonne, do you like it?"

"Of course, I have to try it on," she said.

Noura nodded. "Naturally, and I can make any adjustments that you wish."

"You should be a seamstress, Noura," Rania suggested.

Noura smiled shyly.

"In all seriousness, though, I think you could do quite well," Rania said.

"I've never trained as a seamstress."

"That doesn't mean anything," Rania said. "I never trained as a cook, and here I am with my own café."

"But what would I do?" Noura asked, looking around helplessly. "Would I have to open a shop?"

"Look, I don't think there is a seamstress in this alley or around here . . . so we all sort of do our own repairs," Rania said, "and not everyone can sew."

Yvonne raised an eyebrow and pursed her lips.

"Madame Yvonne, please," Rania put her hand up before the older woman could say anything. She turned back to Noura. "You can do repairs, alterations, or create new patterns . . . and not just clothes, maybe you could make curtains . . . anything to do with sewing. You clearly have the talent."

Noura nodded. Her great aunt had a sewing machine. She had used it to make Madame Yvonne's dress. "Yes, I suppose I could take it all to Old Cairo."

Rania shook her finger and her head. "No," she said. "If you are going to work for people here, you have to be here. What do you think Tante Saydeh?"

Saydeh nodded. "Rania is right, *habibti*. You would need to be here."

"But how can I do that, Tante Saydeh?" Noura said. "I live in Old Cairo."

"You have a home right here in El-Khalili," Saydeh said, tilting her head in the direction of her house down the street.

"Tante Saydeh," Noura answered, "I don't want to be ungrateful, you and Salah have already done so much for me, but I can't take advantage of you like that."

"Don't be silly, Noura!" Saydeh said. "It would be a pleasure to have you and the baby. Remember I have the third floor free. Salah is supposedly on the second floor, but he's not; he's always in my apartment on the first floor."

Noura wrestled with the idea, wringing her hands. What would that mean? She would have to move out of Old Cairo. Would her great aunt be offended, even though she was not completely aware mentally? Would she even realize Noura had gone? *And what about here? Living in the same house with Salah, the floor just above him? Oh Khaled . . . how would you feel about this? Would it be awkward? Would Tante Saydeh think it untoward? But then again, she wouldn't have offered if she thought anything of it. Is it what I should do? Please, Khaled, tell me what you think.*

It wasn't the thought of working that bothered her. It was living in such close quarters with a man toward whom she had feelings . . . feelings she realized were going further than just friendship.

"And you could put your sewing machine in the attic . . . ," Saydeh began. "And that way, you would have a place to live and a place to work. Yes," she nodded, agreeing with what she had just said, "it is always better to not live where you work, even if only one step separates you."

"But, Tante Saydeh, that is just too generous and I cannot in all good conscience . . ."

"Why don't you pay Saydeh rent if you feel so badly?" Yvonne jumped in.

Taken aback, Noura turned to look at her.

"Well?" Yvonne spread her hands. "It seems like a logical idea, doesn't it? Saydeh has the space, you need the space; she wants you there and would give it to you for free, but you feel badly. So instead of feeling obligated to her, pay her rent."

"Which," Takla suddenly interjected, "is a very good thing because then you won't feel as though you are a permanent guest in Saydeh's home. It will be yours too."

"It is her home . . . now, even though she won't admit it," Saydeh added.

But Noura's brain was whirring. Yes, paying Tante Saydeh rent would also make her feel independent and much better about herself. She didn't want to accept anyone's charity.

"You can pay her with the money you earn from the sewing," Yvonne advised her. "Obviously don't give her everything! Keep some for you and your daughter."

Noura nodded. It really wasn't such a bad idea. And this way, she could come here to live and work in the El-Khalili just like all these women around her. She had to admit that she was much happier here. It was so much more lively and dramatic. Old Cairo was lonely. *Besides Salah was here.* Noura's heart skipped a beat when she thought of him. *Stop it, Noura!*

"So?" Rania leaned her hands on the table. "Are you going to come here?"

"I would love to have you," Saydeh added. "And I know Salah would agree with me."

Noura looked at her.

"Why the hesitation?" Yvonne asked. "Why not just say yes?"

Rania nodded enthusiastically "I agree, Noura. Take the chance.

I don't think you'll be disappointed. Change is always good, and it's scary at first but it is always for the better. You'll be happy here."

Noura looked around the table. They were all waiting expectantly for her to say something. Yes, she liked all these women. Despite the fights and the arguments, they supported each other.

"Yes, I think I will be happier here too," she finally said.

"So you'll come?" Saydeh asked, hopeful.

Noura bit her bottom lip. And quickly before she lost her nerve and found an excuse to change her mind, she nodded.

—⁂—

Ahmad Jemmal was at his desk in the Grand Serail Palace in Damascus when he was told about the arrest of Erdogan and his men in Cairo.

"Bloody idiot!" he swore loudly. "What the hell was he thinking?"

His secretary stood calmly in front of him. "Would you like me to do anything, Pasha?"

"Get me the military governor on the phone. I have to get Erdogan out of the hands of the British."

"Yes, Pasha."

"And in the meantime, send in another team to Cairo to watch Masri."

"Yes, Sir. Anyone in particular?"

Ahmad Jemmal glowered at his secretary.

"Someone competent."

—⁂—

Salah and Lawrence were at the British High Command in Cairo going over the details of a shipment to Faisal.

Faisal had recently put Salah in charge of liaising with the British to make sure that he received everything as promised and on time. As luck would have it, Lawrence was the man the British general had put in charge of organizing British supplies to the Arabs.

"It's going to be easier to get supplies and troops to Faisal now that he controls the Red Sea ports," Lawrence remarked as they walked toward a warehouse on the British Army cantonment.

"Yes, but it's been such slow going, Lawrence."

"Look, those tribesmen are struggling against fifteen thousand well-armed and trained Ottoman troops that were just moved to the Hejaz . . . it's not easy."

"No, I suppose not."

"Come on ol' boy . . . chin up," Lawrence said as they walked into the warehouse. "Now, what have we here?"

"Twenty thousand pounds of gold for the tribesmen, ten thousand guns," Lawrence read off his sheet.

"And where is the artillery coming from this time?" Salah asked.

"Three pieces of artillery are coming from the Sudan."

"With Egyptian gunners?"

"Yes . . . the boys will ship out on a seaplane carrier from Suez," Lawrence said.

Salah began inspecting the crates filled with ammunition.

"So are you breathing a little easier now that Erdogan is in jail?" Lawrence glanced up at him.

"I suppose I am," Salah replied. "But they got very close Lawrence . . . my mother, Rania, Nassim, Noura."

"Yes, but it's all over and done with. And now you've got Charlie looking over your shoulder."

"You know, Lawrence, I've said this often enough, but I never signed up for it and now I'm up to my neck in it," Salah said.

"Indeed you are. Perhaps one day you will tell your grandchildren about it."

Salah glared at him.

"I must be off. Thank you, Lawrence." Salah shook his hand. "I'll be at Suez to take charge of the consignment."

"Who's taking you to Jeddah?"

"Nusair."

Salah left the British Army barracks and headed to Rania's Café. He knocked at the back door. When there was no answer, he opened it and went in. The café was full. Salah heard Rania taking orders. He tiptoed through the kitchen and went directly to the cellar.

"How are you feeling, brother?" Salah asked Rabih, who was sitting up.

"Much, much better."

"Rabih, listen, I'm heading to the Hejaz with some supplies for Faisal and Abdallah's army. I want you to come with me."

"Count on it, Salah. When do we go?"

"Tomorrow all right with you? Charlie's going to come with us and Lawrence will meet us in Jeddah."

"I'll be ready."

"And when we come back, you're moving in to my mother's house," Salah told him. "You can't live in Rania's cellar."

"I was going to talk to you about that," Rabih said.

—⁓—

Just outside the brick wall in the kitchen, Rania was talking to Fatmeh about a similar topic.

"So?" Fatmeh asked, smiling mischievously. "How's it going with Rabih?"

"Well . . ."

"That doesn't sound good. You were over the moon the last time we talked."

"I was," Rania said. "And I like him . . . I just . . . don't know."

"What do you mean?"

"I've been thinking, and I think I need to slow down, Fatmeh. I just feel that it's all going a little too quickly. After all, Adel's only been gone a year."

"I understand. But Rabih is a good man, Rania, and men like him don't come around that often."

"I know. I just don't want to jump in with both feet," Rania said. "I'm only just starting to come to terms with being on my own. And it's taken a while. I want to be a whole person before I start anything with anyone else . . . not the broken one I was after Adel died."

"Maybe you are right."

"I spoke to Salah. He will move in with him and Saydeh."

"Well he won't be too far away."

—∭—

A few days later, Salah, Rabih, and Charlie, along with a small group of British soldiers, boarded the train to Suez, riding in the same car as the crates of ammunition, food, and medicines that were going to Faisal's army.

Nusair was at the port of Suez waiting to receive the cargo, and as soon as they loaded up, they pushed off down the Gulf of Suez toward Sharm el-Sheikh and Cape Mohammad.

—∭—

MASRI, FARHAT, AND BRITISH AMMUNITION
ON YEMENI BOAT HEADED FOR JEDDAH.

Ahmad Jemmal smiled sadistically as he read the communiqué. This time Masri was not going to escape.

"Shall I tell German naval command to blow up the ship, Sir?"

"They could do," Ahmed Jemmal said, "since they are carrying British ammunition . . . but no . . . I want Masri and Farhat alive.

"Tell German naval command to intercept the *Tree of Life*," he instructed his secretary. "They are to arrest Masri and Farhat and deliver them to me. After that, they can blow the ship out of the Red Sea if they want."

—∭—

Salah was away when Noura arrived at the Khan el-Khalili bazaar. Her daughter was in her arms and her battered brown suitcase and the black case that held her great aunt's sewing machine were next to her on the pavement when Saydeh opened the door.

"Noura! *Habibti!*" She opened her arms when she saw her, waddling over to hug her and Siran.

"It's good to see you." Noura kissed the old woman.

"Come! Let's get you upstairs and we can have a nice coffee after you've settled in," Saydeh said as she led the way up to the first floor. "Now, I have cleaned the third floor and the attic, and I had Salah re-organize some furniture before he left, but you will see how you want to set it up."

"Thank you, Tante . . . I am very grateful. But where is Salah?"

"Oh . . . that boy. He's off again. This time, he took Rabih to the desert."

Noura was disappointed. Not only had she been looking forward to seeing Salah, she wanted to apologize for her last outburst . . . she also wanted to apologize for her behavior in general over the past several months. She'd taken her anger and frustration out on Salah, including blaming him for Khaled's death, and that was not fair. But now she would have to wait until he returned.

"He'll be back soon," Saydeh assured her.

The third floor of Saydeh's house was small, but open and airy. There was a narrow entrance area just off the landing that led into a room with two tall French doors that gave onto a side alley below. There was a low, off-white divan against the wall, a small rug, and a wooden table on which stood a shiny copper jug filled with a huge bouquet of creamy roses. On either side of the divan stood two ornately carved wooden Syrian armchairs painted silver. There were light white cotton curtains on the windows to keep out the glare, but not the bright sunlight. Down a narrow corridor was a wooden double door to a small bedroom and next to that, a bit further down, was a tiny bathroom with just about enough room to wash. There was no kitchen. The only one in the house was in Saydeh's apartment.

Noura looked around. The wooden floors were clean and there was no sign of dust anywhere.

"How beautiful!" Noura said as she bent over to smell the roses. "Thank you, Tante."

"So what do you think, Siran?" Noura walked around the room, stopping at the French doors to look out on the street. "What do you think of our new home?"

The infant gurgled, smiling up at her mother.

"Yes . . . I think we'll be very happy here." Noura set her down in a small cot.

"I have another little surprise," Saydeh said.

"What is it?" Noura smiled with excitement.

"Follow me!" Saydeh took the lead up the spiral staircase to the attic. Noura followed her. In the attic, Saydeh turned and smiled and made a wide gesture with her hands. Noura's mouth dropped open as she took in the scene in front of her. Some old furniture had been tidied away in a corner and covered with sheets, as had some trunks and small wooden crates, creating a space that led directly out onto a terrace and was incredibly bright, with sunlight streaming in through the skylights in the pitched roof.

Against the wall, next to the terrace door, was a wooden table on which Noura's great aunt's Singer sewing machine could sit proudly. Directly above the table there were shelves within arm's reach that could be used for keeping spools of thread, boxes of pins, notepads, pencils, chalk, and other tools Noura might need. There were also a couple of bigger shelves a little further away for bales of cloth. Next to the desk was an old tailor's mannequin and around its neck hung a measuring tape. In a corner was a cast iron for ironing clothes. In the middle of the room directly under one of the skylights was a square wooden table that could be used for cutting fabric.

Noura couldn't believe it. It was a little tailor's atelier. She looked at Saydeh, speechless.

"Do you like it?" Saydeh asked tentatively.

"Like it?" she cried. "I love it."

Saydeh came forward with a small brown paper packet wrapped with string.

"For me?" Noura's eyes filled with tears as she held the packet to her chest.

"Open it," Saydeh urged.

Inside was a navy blue velvet pouch in the shape of an envelope. Noura opened the flap and gasped. There were two pairs of brand new scissors in different sizes, a couple of thimbles, a pretty purple pincushion, and some new needles.

"I don't know what to say," She choked back tears.

"It was Salah's idea," Saydeh said. "And the roses downstairs . . . ," she reminded Noura.

Suddenly, the tears that Noura had been holding back spilled out without warning. She turned toward the wall and reached quickly for her handkerchief. She didn't want Saydeh to see her sob. She was overwhelmed . . . her great aunt's kindness over the past six months and now Saydeh's warm welcome and generosity . . . it was all too much and Noura's shoulders started to shake. Her mind turned yet again, as it had done so many times in the recent past, to Khaled. "I am so proud of you," she heard him say. "You must move on, Noura. I will always love you. But you have to live another life now."

"Come, child," Saydeh put her hands on her shoulder and turned her around to take in her arms. "Hush now, there is nothing to cry about," she consoled.

Saydeh held Noura until she stopped crying and the sobs turned into little hiccups.

"I'm sorry, Tante," she said, wiping her eyes. "I feel like such a child."

"It's all right," Saydeh whispered.

"Now I have to work hard and make sure I have enough money to pay you the rent."

"Don't worry about that, *habibti* . . . if you don't make it," Saydeh said reassuringly, "I won't throw you out."

"No, Tante Saydeh," Noura said firmly. "I will pay you the rent every month."

"*Insha'Allah*, everything will work out, child . . . now how about some coffee and something sweet to make these salty tears disappear?"

—m—

Captain Nusair was on the bridge. It was particularly rough going around Cape Mohammad today and the ship was heavy. He peered into the distance. He grabbed his binoculars and tried to focus on the dark shadow just under the surface of the water.

"How's it going?" Charlie interrupted.

"Here look, what do you think that is?" he handed him the binoculars and pointed out in the distance.

Charlie took the binoculars.

"Holy shit, Nusair . . . we have to move! That's a fucking U-Boat!"

"What?"

"Move this ship, Captain," Charlie said. "If they know we're carrying ammunition and guns, we're done for. We'll be a military target and the Germans will blow us out of the water."

"What the hell are the Germans doing in the Red Sea?" Musa grabbed the ship's wheel. "Give me everything you have!" he said to the men down in the engine room.

"What's going on?" Salah came running in, with Rabih just behind him.

"Germans."

"Shit!" Salah swore. "We must hide the guns."

"Where are you going to hide five thousand guns?" Charlie asked.

"Nusair?" Salah said. "Don't tell me you don't have a secret hold on this ship."

"There's a hold under the main hold," Nusair said, handing Salah a key. "There's a secret door through the kitchen galleys."

"Come on!" Salah said and Charlie and Rabih rushed out with him.

"You don't have much time!" Musa yelled. "I've just spotted another U-Boat . . . Come on! Come on! Give me a little more steam! Put that boiler on full!" he shouted into the receiver to the engine room.

But the *Tree of Life* was no match for the Germans.

"Stop your engines!"

Musa looked around at his crew on the bridge. He picked up the receiver and gave the order to the engine room. "Go find Salah," he told one of his men. "Tell him the Germans are coming onboard and to stay hidden."

"*Guten tag, mein Kapitan*," the tall, blonde German naval officer haughtily addressed Musa. "We have received a communiqué that you are carrying military cargo."

"I am not," Musa replied.

"Really? Then you would not mind if we searched the ship?"

"Not at all."

"*Komm! Gehen wir!*" the German said to his men. "Look into every nook and cranny of this ship."

Musa's heart was beating hard. There was no way Salah had moved all those crates in time.

The German sailors fanned out.

Musa sat down, the German commander paced. Everyone waited. An hour later, a German lieutenant returned.

"Nothing, *mein Kommandant*," he reported to his Captain.

"What do you mean, nothing? Impossible!"

"I assure you, Sir, we have looked everywhere."

The German commander turned to Musa. "Where is your cargo?"

"In the cargo hold," Musa replied, "where I normally keep it."

"What is your cargo?"

"Food and medicine."

"Is he telling the truth?" the German turned to his first officer.

"Yes."

Suddenly, shouts came from outside. "We have him! We have him!"

The Germans rushed outside, with Musa following closely behind. It was Charlie, standing with his hands tied behind his back.

"Where is Salah Masri?" the German asked him.

"I don't know," Charlie said calmly.

The German came up very close to Charlie.

"Get him out of my sight!" He ordered. "Take him onboard! Let us see how he feels when he is standing in front of Jemmal Pasha in Damascus."

He whipped around to face Musa. "You're lucky we didn't find any contraband on your boat, Yemeni. I would love nothing more than to torpedo you out of the water."

Musa shrugged.

"You be careful, Yemeni. We're going to keep a close eye on you."

Charlie was pushed into a small dinghy, his hands still tied. Musa and his crew watched as the dinghy and the Germans pulled away. Charlie looked up at Musa and winked. Musa put two fingers to his captain's hat and saluted him. The Germans hurriedly disembarked, rowing towards the U-Boat.

When they were half way to the German submarine, a trap door on the deck opened and Salah and Rabih came through, hiding behind the crowd of sailors. They all stood quietly watching as the submarine's motors started up and the gigantic steel vessel dove deep into the waters of the Red Sea.

When the submarine had completely disappeared, the crew went back to their posts. Musa, Salah, and Rabih were left standing at the railing of the deck.

"He'll be all right," Salah said, his voice gruffer than usual. "This is what Charlie is trained for."

No one said anything. Salah and Rabih lit up cigarettes and Musa his pipe.

"How am I going to tell Lawrence?" Salah muttered.

No one answered.

"Do you think they're going to blow up the ship?"Rabih finally asked.

"They didn't find any cause," Salah said.

Musa rolled his eyes. "They don't need cause. If they want, they can blow us up and invent a cause."

Rabih and Salah exchanged a glance before looking out at the water.

After a while, Musa looked at them, nodded and went back up to the bridge.

—◊◊◊—

"What does this mean?" Ahmed Jemmal shouted at the German officer who presented him with a note from the German naval commander that said neither ammunition nor Masri or Farhat were on board the *Tree of Life*. "You people are bloody idiots! Get out! Get out of my sight!"

"Would you still like for us to destroy the Yemeni freighter, *mein* Pasha?" the young German asked, his gaze squarely on the window behind the Turkish commander.

"Didn't I order you to get out of my sight?" Ahmed Jemmal snarled.

The German saluted, clicked his heels and walked out.

Ahmed Jemmal tapped his fingers on his desk, his nostrils flaring in anger.

—◊◊◊—

A harrowing few days followed. U-Boats hovered around the *Tree of Life*, some even fired a torpedo or two, but they were mostly meant as scare tactics because none came close enough to do any damage.

The *Tree of Life* docked at Jeddah a couple of days later.

"Salah!" Lawrence greeted him as he walked down the gangplank.

"Lawrence, listen," Salah put an arm around him. "I have some difficult news."

"What?"

"I'm afraid it's about Charlie."

"What has happened?"

"Well . . . we had a run-in with a U-Boat around Cape Mohammad . . ."

"Hello, Salah!" a familiar voice said, before he could continue.

Salah whipped around and came face to face with Charlie.

"Oh thank God!" Salah grabbed him and engulfed him in his arms. "I thought we'd lost you."

"Careful, Salah . . . I survived the Germans, but I may not survive you!" Charlie laughed.

"Hackett, you old bastard!" Musa Nusair came up and hugged him.

"You are a cat with nine lives!" Rabih shook Charlie's hand warmly.

"I cannot tell you how pleased I am to see you." Salah let him go. "What happened?"

"Well, it was not all fun and games, but the U-Boat got stuck on the ocean floor near Aqaba. While everyone was busy trying to get us out of the mess, they left a young engine room boy to watch me. Poor kid, he was scared. I managed to break free, disarmed him, which wasn't hard, and attached myself to the divers who were going out to fix the problem. I don't know how, but I managed to swim away, got to shore, and took your Hejaz Railway all the way down here."

"Well I hope it was comfortable!" Salah laughed.

Charlie punched him affectionately.

"All right, let's get these cases off the boat!" Salah ordered. "Then we can celebrate before we head out to Mecca tonight! Lawrence here is buying!"

"I am?"

"The British Army can pay!"

CHAPTER ELEVEN

In Mecca, the Arabs were preparing to attack Medina. Despite the disaster in June four months earlier, Faisal's British military advisors were pushing for a second assault.

"Prince," Salah began, "with all due respect, I disagree."

"I think it's a sound idea," Faisal retorted.

"Sir, the Ottomans have their best men in Medina. They want to show that even though they lost Mecca, they are not going to give up on Medina."

"We need Medina," Faisal said. "My father is in agreement with the British. The Ottomans are desecrating one of Islam's holiest cities . . . we can use that against them to further justify the revolt."

"Prince, please reconsider," Salah pleaded.

Faisal shook his head. "We attack Medina this week. The sharif has given his blessing. Will you ride with me, Salah?"

Salah took a deep breath and let it out slowly. "I don't have a choice, do I?"

Faisal smiled. "No, you don't. What's the matter, Salah? Why so mistrusting of the British?"

"There are stories, Prince, rumors."

"About what?" Faisal stroked his beard.

"That British strategy has nothing to do with the Arab strategy . . . or your dream of an Arab nation. They are using us to tie the Ottomans down, nothing more. If there was no Arab Revolt, the Ottomans would either deploy their forces to Western Europe or use them to attack the Suez Canal, which would be a huge problem for the British," Salah argued.

"Instead, the British are using us to fight the Ottomans for them here in Arabia, while they focus on Western Europe and keeping India safe."

"I don't believe it."

"I do not believe they will ultimately give us what you want."

"Salah, we cannot turn back. We must go forward."

"And what will we have in the end?"

"We will have our pride."

"Prince, look, if there is even a remote chance of your getting what you want, there is only one Englishman whose word I trust and whom I would like you to meet."

"Why?"

"Because this one really believes in your cause," Salah said. "He believes that the Arabs should be free and have their own land and he thinks that he is the one who will give it to them."

"I have noticed, Brother Salah, that you never refer to the cause as 'our cause.'"

"Prince, I have never hidden the fact that I'm a reluctant revolutionary . . . I have gotten involved out of loyalty to you and perhaps a misplaced sense of duty to finish what my friends began."

"And for that, I thank you," Faisal said. "Now, who is this Englishman you trust."

"His name is T.E. Lawrence. Until now, he has been in charge of the supplies the British Army is sending us. If anybody can get you Arab independence, he can."

"Well then we should meet him."

As Salah predicted, the second Arab attack on Medina was a disaster. The Arab forces were pushed back in a bloody counter attack that led to many of the tribesmen renouncing their allegiance to the revolt.

"What the hell happened?" Prince Faisal fumed at the English officers in his tent. "This was a surefire bet."

"I'm not sure . . ." Colonel Cyril Wilson hesitated. "The Ottomans are fighting on the defensive. They are well supplied."

"I don't care how they are fighting! And I too have supplies . . . yours! I want answers, Colonel!" Faisal exploded. "This is a catastrophe in every way. We have lost men, allies, not to mention the propaganda war."

The British officers remained quiet. Prince Faisal paced his tent.

"Prince . . . ," Salah said, "I have an idea."

"Well . . . spit it out, Masri."

"We have to get to the Ottoman supply line," Salah began. "If we can slow it down or break it, I think we can make some inroads."

"What do you propose?"

"Guerilla warfare, Prince," Salah said. "Attack the Ottoman supply lines so that they would be constantly engaged in repairing or protecting it."

Faisal stared at him for a minute as the idea took root.

"You think it could work?"

Salah nodded. "It doesn't hurt to try."

"Where do we start?" Faisal said.

Salah turned to Rabih as they all pored over a map of the Hejaz. "Do you remember the details of the railway line just east of Aqaba near Yiza?"

Rabih nodded.

"Let's start there."

Slowly a plan began to emerge. Salah and Rabih were to strategize the attacks and Lawrence was to execute them.

In late November, Salah and Rabih returned to Cairo. Charlie asked for a few days off and went back with them. Lawrence, who was fast becoming Faisal's confidante, stayed behind in the desert.

—⁂—

Rania inserted her key into the front door of the café and walked in. She was glad it was empty. She wanted to be by herself and didn't want to have to smile or speak, if only for a few minutes before she knew she had to open. This anniversary was a tough one. The trip to the cemetery brought back all the memories of loss and tragedy she had tried to drown. She draped her shawl around a chair and looked around. She was so thankful to have this place. No matter how shabby, it was hers. It had given her a roof over her head and it had given her independence and confidence, and a means of supporting herself. And for that, she had to thank her dead husband.

She went to turn the little sign on the door to read "Open." She cleared away her shawl behind the bar and put her apron over her black dress.

"Rania!" The doorbell jingled. "Where have you been? We came by earlier . . ." Saydeh's voice sounded behind her.

Rania turned and smiled, smoothing her apron down over her dress.

"Oh!" Saydeh stopped, her hand going to her mouth as soon as she saw the black dress. "Oh *habibti!* I'm so sorry. I forgot the day. It slipped my mind." She went over and hugged Rania.

"Thank you, Tante Saydeh," Rania bent down to embrace her. "But there's no reason for you to remember."

"I'm a bit disoriented these days," Saydeh said, "with everything going on."

"Noura has officially moved in." She turned to Noura who was standing politely behind her. "So she is now part of the neighborhood."

"*Ahlan wa sahlan,* Noura," Rania smiled. "I'm so happy you are here."

"Today is a sad day for Rania," Saydeh explained to Noura. "It is the day she received news that she had lost her husband."

"I am so sorry, Rania," Noura said, her own grief rising as Khaled came to her mind. "I can understand."

"If anyone can, it is Noura," Saydeh squeezed her hand. "She lost her husband in May. He was one of the men Ahmad Jemmal executed."

"Oh no! I am so sorry, Noura."

"Thank you. And I am sorry for you, Rania."

Rania nodded her thanks.

"Are you happy you came here?" Rania changed the subject.

Noura nodded eagerly.

"I am," she said. "Now, of course, I also have to see how to get my business going."

"That will happen . . . ," Saydeh said.

"What if . . . ," Rania began. "What if, well, I'm not sure how it would work, but you know there are announcements in the newspapers?"

"Announcements?" Saydeh said.

"Maybe we can put one in the newspaper?" Rania suggested.

"People in the souk don't read the newspaper . . . it's word of mouth . . . it's been like that since this souk began," Saydeh said.

"You are right," Rania said. "In that case, why don't we tell the lady next door? Her sons are in the Expeditionary Force. They are home for a couple of weeks and have to go back to the Sinai. I bet they have repair work on their uniforms."

"Wait! Military uniforms . . . ," Saydeh said excitedly. "That's a great idea. There are a few people I can tell, too . . ."

—*m*—

As they sat pondering other ideas on how to best spread the word about Noura, the doorbell jingled and Yvonne walked in wearing a long black abaya, followed by Takla a few minutes later. Holding her abaya tightly around her, she walked to the long table in the middle.

"*Marhaba*, Madame Yvonne," Rania welcomed her from behind the bar.

Yvonne waved at her.

"*Marhaba*, ladies," Yvonne cheerily greeted her friends. "How is everyone this morning?"

No one knew quite how to respond to Yvonne's sudden cheerfulness or her abaya.

"What happened to you this morning?" Saydeh asked, guardedly.

"What do you mean?" Yvonne immediately shot back.

"I mean why are you being so pleasant? And why are you dressed in an abaya? Did you convert?"

"Very funny." Yvonne made a little face at Saydeh.

"Maybe she got lucky," Takla suggested sarcastically, looking around at the little group. "And a little *hammimi* went on this morning!" she added.

"You should be ashamed of yourself talking like that!" Yvonne admonished. "You sound like an eighteen-year-old boy."

"Oh for goodness' sake . . ."

"It's not as if you have any luck . . . ," Yvonne started.

"That's because I am a widow," Takla retorted.

"Ladies!" Rania intervened before it deteriorated into a fight. "Enough!"

"Madame Yvonne, I'll be right back to take your order." She swept past with a tray of coffee and small plates piled high with baklava.

"So, Yvonne . . . ," Saydeh looked her up and down, "did you really convert to Islam?"

"What?" Yvonne frowned in irritation.

"You're completely covered up," Saydeh said.

"Yes!" Takla interjected. "What's with the abaya?"

"*Yih!*" Yvonne's angry expression cleared and she broke into a small smile. "This is what I came in to show you." She took off the abaya and twirled around. She was wearing the new dress Noura had made for her. Fatmeh's mouth fell open. Takla and Saydeh stared wide-eyed at Yvonne and Noura smiled happily. She'd been right. The dress looked perfect on Yvonne. It was simple with lines that suited her figure and flattered it. Even the dusky gold color looked much better on her than Noura had thought.

Noura looked around her. *Yes, everything is going to be all right.* For the first time since Khaled's death, she felt she could breathe.

—⟪⟫—

Suddenly, the door flung open and Fatmeh came in, panting and out of breath. "Rania!" she cried. "Where's Rania?"

"In the kitchen . . ."

"Fatmeh!" Rania said, surprised when she saw the young woman stumble into the kitchen. "Fatmeh, what's wrong?"

"Rania," Fatmeh gasped. "He's going to kill me."

"Who?" Rania put her arms on Fatmeh's shoulders.

"Walid . . . my husband."

"But . . . but why?"

"He found my notebook of love poems." Fatmeh was terrified. "And he is convinced I am having an affair." She began crying.

"I told him that the poems were about him, but he didn't believe me," she sobbed. "He claims that I cannot possibly write about love without having firsthand experience," she declared.

"Well, you are recently married . . . ," Rania said.

"But the man I write about in my poems is not my husband, Rania." Fatmeh collapsed on a chair. "And he knows I don't write about him. He knows the way he treats me . . ."

"Oh God, Fatmeh . . . you're having an affair?"

Fatmeh didn't answer.

"Rania . . . please help me . . . I'm so scared," Fatmeh's tears began again. "He's probably looking for me right now. He was so angry when I ran out of the house."

"Did he hurt you, Fatmeh?" Rania crouched down on her heels and looked at Fatmeh in the eye.

"He tried to choke me," Fatmeh took off her headscarf.

Rania drew in a sharp, short breath when she saw the purple bruise marks on her neck.

"Where is she?" a man's angry voice rang out in the café. "Where is that whore I have the misfortune to have married?"

"Quickly, Fatmeh!" Rania pushed her. "Into the cellar!" she ordered.

"She has to be here!" He strode around. "Where's the owner?"

"Are you looking for me?" Rania drew the curtain and stepped out into the café.

"Where is my wife?" Walid stood with his hands across his belly, his face contorted with anger. "Where are you hiding her?"

God certainly missed this one, Rania thought as she confronted him.

Indeed, Walid El Askar had not been blessed with looks or brains. He clearly enjoyed being domineering and listening to the sound of his own voice. He was not a tall man and was very round . . . everywhere. Without his tunic, he probably looked like a ball stuck on two sticks.

"She is not here." Rania faced him defiantly.

"Come on, brother!" one of the shopkeepers said. "A little respect."

"Shut up! Don't talk to me about respect!" Walid turned on the shopkeeper.

"Where is she? Where is that two-timing little bitch?"

"Would you stop talking like that?" the shopkeeper stood up and faced Walid. "There are ladies present."

"Ladies?" Walid sneered. "You call these ladies?"

The rest of the shopkeepers got up.

"It's time you left, brother." One of the men squared up to Walid.

"Not until I find my wife."

"Well she's not here."

"Yeah! We haven't seen Madame Fatmeh in days."

"Don't you dare take Fatmeh's name, you filthy pig!" Walid lunged at the man.

"Are you calling me a pig?" the shopkeeper said, angrily pointing to himself.

He was the only shopkeeper who was still sitting and suddenly he got up. He was big. He came menacingly close to Walid.

"Come on!" The burly shopkeeper gestured for Walid to come closer. "Take your best shot! Come on, you coward!"

Walid attacked him first, swiping at him, hitting him on his chin. Caught off guard, the shopkeeper fell backwards on a chair that collapsed in pieces. Reaching for a stool that one of the other men had just vacated, he swung it at Walid. He missed and the stool crashed on the floor. Meanwhile, Walid picked up a chair and tried to hit the shopkeeper with it. The shopkeeper ducked and Walid slammed the chair into one of the tables, causing it to break in half. Coffee cups and plates smashed into smithereens on the stone floor. The other men joined in the fray. More tables and chairs broke as the fight broadened and tempers flared even hotter.

"*Ya Allah!* They are going to destroy my café!" Rania cried, her hands covering her ears. "Tante Takla . . . please, can you go get Salah?"

Takla nodded and ran out.

"Oh!" Yvonne's hand went to her heaving chest as a saucer went flying over her head.

"Come, Yvonne!" Saydeh held out her hand and the two women ducked and wove their way to the bar, crouching down behind it just as one of the men came flying across the room, his fall broken by the bar itself.

"Allah! My furniture!" Rania cried, wringing her hands.

She stepped in.

"Stop it!" she shouted as loudly as she could, standing on the farmhouse table in the middle. "*Khalas!* Stop it you animals!"

Suddenly, they all stopped and stared at her.

"What is wrong with all of you?" she shouted. "If you want to kill each other, do it outside, in the street . . . but not in here. This is my café, my home. So either you behave like human beings or don't ever come back here again.

"And you!" she went up to Walid. "You are a revolting man . . . you have a foul tongue and a filthy temper."

Rania breathed heavily, the anger and adrenaline coursing through her veins.

"Get out now and don't you ever come back here," she told Walid in a low voice. "Because if you do, I will call the police and I will have you arrested."

Walid stared at her in anger.

"You have no respect for anyone . . . Get out!" Rania screamed.

Walid stuck his chin out belligerently, but finally left.

"And the rest of you, go on! *Khalas!* Out."

"Sorry, Madame Rania." The shopkeepers started walking out in single file, each one looking guilty, staring down at their shoes, unable to look her in the eye. "*Be'tezeer,* Madame Rania."

After they had all left, Rania turned and sat down on the bench, her head in her hands. She was shaking.

Slowly, Saydeh and Madame Yvonne emerged from behind the bar.

"Well, no wonder Fatmeh never talked about her husband," Saydeh said, crawling out.

"I have to get back to make lunch, but tomorrow I want to hear all the details of Fatmeh's story," Saydeh said.

Rania nodded.

"See you tomorrow." Madame Yvonne took her leave as well.

"Fatmeh . . .?" Rania opened the cellar.

Fatmeh came out. Her hand went to her mouth. "Rania, I am so sorry. Look at this place! I will pay for the damage . . . somehow, I will pay it all back to you."

"They didn't destroy the whole place . . . luckily." Rania looked around. "It's only a couple of chairs and a table and some crockery."

"I'm just so sorry," Fatmeh repeated.

"Now, you want to tell me what's really going on?"

"I don't know where to begin." Fatmeh played with the sleeve of her abaya.

Rania waited patiently. While Fatmeh gathered herself, she got up and got a couple of glasses of sweet lime juice.

"So," she said, sitting back down on the bench next to Fatmeh, "are you going to tell me or not?"

"Rania . . . please don't judge me or think ill of me," Fatmeh began.

"Fatmeh," Rania put her hand over Fatmeh's, "that is God's job, not mine."

"But I don't want you to think I am a whore."

"I know you're not."

"I'm in love with a man who is not my husband."

"Yes, well I thought so," Rania said gently. "Who is he?"

"Rania," Fatmeh hesitated, "he's . . . well . . . he's a foreigner."

"What?" Rania's eyes opened wide. "Who?"

"Well, half a foreigner." Fatmeh let out an embarrassed giggle.

"Who is he? And how on earth did you meet a foreigner?"

"Right here in the souk."

"But . . . how?" Rania scratched her head.

"I had just bought some fruit from Magdi and I was walking home," Fatmeh began. "And in front of Tante Saydeh's house, down the alley here," Fatmeh pointed south, "I slipped on one of the cobblestones and fell and my basket went flying.

"I looked around quickly to see if anyone had seen me," she continued. "I was so embarrassed. Anyway, I didn't even see him. I don't know where he came from, but as I tried to get to my feet, trying to gather this abaya that had ballooned out, I saw a hand. I didn't dare look at him, but I accepted his help and he heaved me up."

—⁓—

As she told Rania what happened, Fatmeh's mind wandered back to that day a few weeks prior.

"Are you hurt, Madame?" he asked.

Fatmeh shook her head.

"I am sorry for your fall," he said. "Some of these stones can be slippery."

Fatmeh tried to glance at him from under her lowered eyelashes. But she couldn't see past his knees. All she could tell was that he was wearing a red and white striped galabiyya and smart black leather shoes.

"Here you go, Madame." He handed her the basket. "I tried to recover all the fruit I could, but I'm afraid you might have lost a few plums."

Fatmeh felt herself blushing.

"Thank you," she managed.

"Now, are you quite sure you're not hurt?" he asked again.

Fatmeh nodded. She looked up only when she saw him walking away. He was tall, and at least from behind looked like he had broad shoulders.

"A couple of days later," Fatmeh continued her tale, "I went to my father's dispensary to pick up some bandages and ointments for Rabih. When I went in, there was a man in the waiting room. I remember getting the feeling that I knew him from somewhere. My father was busy with an emergency and asked me to help out until his nurse arrived. I did. I put on a nurse's apron and went out into the waiting room and asked the man if I could help him.

"I came to get some aspirin, please," he said.

"Of course. Please come this way," Fatmeh said, leading the way into the office.

"What do you need this for?" she asked as she measured out the tablets.

"A headache," he replied.

Fatmeh nodded, wrote out a label, and put it on a small glass vial. "Now remember," she looked up at him, "take two every six hours and no more than four per day."

"Yes, Madame," the man replied, "thank you."

His voice sounds so familiar, she thought. *But who is he?* Fatmeh wracked her brain trying to remember where she might have seen him. He was really quite handsome. Tall and well built, he had very tanned skin, deep, brown eyes, dark hair, and a trim beard and moustache.

Fatmeh shrugged, but she couldn't shake the feeling that she knew him from somewhere.

"Have you been to the dispensary before?" she asked him, handing him the vial.

"No," he replied.

"*Tayeb* . . . now if the headache gets worse, then come back and we can prescribe something stronger," she told him and came out from behind the desk, looking him up and down.

Suddenly, she stopped. He was wearing the same smart black leather shoes. She took in a short, sharp breath.

"It's you!" she stared wide-eyed.

He smiled.

"Isn't it?" Fatmeh said. "You're the one who helped me the other day, when I fell?"

"Yes." He nodded, smiling.

No wonder he looked familiar. Fatmeh was suddenly overcome by shyness.

"There were no repercussions of your fall?" he asked politely.

Fatmeh shook her head.

"And after that, I kept bumping into him, Rania," Fatmeh continued. "Everywhere I went, he was there . . . I would go to Magdi's and somehow he would appear, or at the vegetable man . . . or the general store."

"You said he was a foreigner, though," Rania said.

"He's half English and half Lebanese. He works for the British Army."

"Fatmeh . . ." Rania began cautiously. "Has anything happened between the two of you? Anything intimate?"

"Not yet," Fatmeh sighed wistfully. "He knows I am married and he is always very polite and courteous."

"How do you know you're in love with him and he with you?"

"I know, Rania . . . I just know," Fatmeh replied, "the look in his eyes, the tenderness, the kindness . . ."

"What do you do? Where do you meet?"

"We've only met a few times . . . in my father's dispensary. Some-how he always knows when I'm there and he has come in to ask for some aspirin and we've begun to talk.

"Just being with him makes me feel alive," Fatmeh continued. "The other day his hand brushed mine and I felt as though my hand was on fire."

Rania smiled.

"I am dying for him to touch me, but I am so scared of betraying my husband," Fatmeh said. "At least for the moment, while I feel guilty, I can still truthfully say that I have not been with another man."

Rania put her hand over Fatmeh's and squeezed it.

"He makes me feel like a woman, he makes me feel as though I matter," Fatmeh said. "He makes me feel beautiful, Rania . . . can you understand?"

"More than you know."

"Oh I knew you would understand, Rania!" Fatmeh squeezed Rania's hands.

"But the question now is, of course, what do you do?" Rania said.

"I don't know," Fatmeh said sadly.

"You will stay here, with me," Rania said. "And we'll figure it out. But you have to get out of your house. I won't let you go back there, not after what happened here."

"I thank you, *habibti*," Fatmeh began, "but I can't . . . where will I sleep? You have no room."

"In the small room next to mine," Rania said.

"Oh by the way, what was a British Army officer doing loitering around these parts . . . ? I mean it's not the most obvious part of El-Khalili to attract foreigners," Rania said, clearing away their glasses of lime juice.

"He mentioned he was a friend of Salah's."

Rania stopped.

"Another friend of Salah's!"

Fatmeh laughed.

"Come, let's go upstairs and you can wash up," Rania said. "And maybe you'll get rid of that horrible tent you wear and dress a bit more comfortably and sensibly.

"Maybe you'll even wear a dress of mine . . . ," Rania suggested.

"And maybe Noura will make a dress for me?" Fatmeh grinned.

Rania left Fatmeh resting upstairs and went back down. Suddenly, she realized how hungry she was, she fixed a small plate of mezze for herself and sat down at the kitchen table to eat, reflecting on Fatmeh's situation.

No wonder she never talked much about her husband. He's a monster. How did she survive even a day with him? Well, she'll have to stay here temporarily. I can't very well throw her out. And we'll have to figure out what she's going to do.

After she finished eating, Rania cleared up and went to the front door to make sure it was locked. She was about to turn around when she thought she saw a monkey in a red jacket disappear around the corner. How strange, she thought, furrowing her brow. She turned around to look again and saw a red and white striped galabiyya billowing around the corner.

—⁓—

"Masri and Farhat back in Cairo. Shadid widow has moved to El-Khalili," read the telegram.

Omer Erdogan was back in Damascus, Ahmad Jemmal having pulled every string imaginable to extricate him from prison in Cairo. *What is Masri plotting now?*

"Sergeant Celik, get us on a boat to Alexandria. We're going back to Cairo. I have an idea . . ."

CHAPTER TWELVE

Noura was up in her atelier. She had one of the military tunics laid out on her tailor's table and was going over it with a fine-tooth comb. She had repaired the most obvious rips and lost buttons, but was now looking for the most minor tears she could fix, meticulously making notes in a little notebook. Suddenly, she stood up. *Wouldn't it be nice to wash the uniforms and iron them before sending them back?* And she could do it out on the terrace and hang the clothes out to dry in the sun. She filled a wooden basin with water and carried it out to the terrace. She came back inside and grabbed a big bar of soap, a brush, and the washboard and went outside again. While she left the uniform soaking in the soapy water, she made sure the small clothes line she had rigged up on the terrace would take the weight of the uniforms. As she began scrubbing the uniform, she thought she heard someone call her name.

"Noura!" she heard as she clattered down the stairs.

"Coming, Tante!" she cried out from the third-floor landing.

"Here I am, Tante Saydeh," she said, walking into the kitchen.

"Ah! Come to the salon!" Saydeh said, leading the way.

In the salon were three bags filled with clothes.

"Military uniforms," Saydeh said proudly. "From all the mothers in the area, whose boys are home on leave."

"Tante Saydeh!" Noura said excitedly. "This is enough to keep me busy for weeks."

"Yes, well, you only have two," Saydeh told her, "that's all the leave they get."

"Then I better get started." Noura smiled.

"Each bag is labeled with the house it comes from . . ."

"*Mneeh ktiir*, Tante," Noura said, piling the bags in her arms.

—⁓—

Noura's tailoring business was growing. And the closer it got to Christmas, the more bags of uniforms arrived at the little house on Zuqlaq al-Hamra as more boys came home on leave.

"Here's another one." Salah, who was just back from his most recent trip to the Hejaz, put a bag down in the attic where Noura was busy organizing the uniforms that were coming in.

"*Shukran ya*, Salah," Noura said, pushing her hair off her forehead. She stood still for a moment and took a deep breath, looking around her, her hands on her hips.

"I'm very proud of you," Salah said.

Noura blushed. Her heart beat faster. She daren't look at Salah.

"Noura . . . it's a beautiful day," Salah said, "which means it's going to be a beautiful evening."

"Yes . . ."

"I'd like to show you one of my favorite places in Cairo."

"And it's not your office?" Noura asked.

Salah laughed. "Why? Am I spending too much time in there?"

"Yes."

"Come on! Let me show you one of the most beautiful places on earth." Salah deftly evaded further explanations.

"Salah . . . whatever it is that you're doing, please tell me it is not dangerous."

"Don't worry." Salah put his hands on her arms.

Noura gave him a skeptical look.

"So . . . what about this evening?" he asked.

She took a deep breath.

Inwardly she shut her eyes and dove in. "All right."

"Really?" Salah asked, looking mildly shocked.

"Yes, why not?"

"I . . . uh . . . I just wasn't expecting you to say yes, that's all."

"So, what time?"

"I'll see you at the front door at six o'clock," Salah said.

—∞—

Shortly before six o'clock, Noura buttoned a creamy silk shirt with a ruffled neckline she had recently made for herself, pairing it with her old navy blue skirt and short bolero jacket. She pulled on the jacket and peered at herself in the small mirror. She stepped back and nodded approvingly at her reflection. *That's not bad at all*, she thought. *I didn't think it would suit me, but it does.* She rubbed some cream blush onto her cheeks, brushed her eyebrows and decided on a very thin line of kohl on her top lid close to her eyelashes. Somehow the traditional style of heavily lined eyes had never suited Noura. Her features were delicate, and too much makeup drowned her eyes rather than enhanced them. She brushed her eyelashes with a little kohl, pinched her cheeks, and bit her lips for a little more color. Finally, she dabbed a little bit of rose essence behind her ears.

Her thick long hair was pinned up and held with a clip. She had tied a piece of navy blue silk around her head like a headband and let some of the tendrils curl and wave around her face. She pinned a brooch on her jacket, grabbed a small velvet bag and a shawl in case it got chilly, and slipped into sensible low-heel black shoes, the only dressy ones she had.

She was waiting at the downstairs door when Salah appeared on the first floor landing, ten minutes late.

"Noura!" he called out.

She turned and looked up as he hurried down the already creaky stairs that groaned under his weight.

"I'm sorry I'm late," Salah said, short of breath.

"It's all right," Noura said, putting her hand in the arm he offered her. "I haven't been waiting long."

"I was reading something and forgot the time."

"So . . . where are we going?" Noura asked.

"Can't tell you."

"Why not?"

"Patience, *habibti*." Salah patted her hand. "It is a virtue and it is almost always rewarded." He winked.

Noura laughed and glanced at him from the corner of her eye. She felt her heart beating faster. She wondered if he could hear it. She felt guilty. She wondered if she should allow herself to feel this way.

"Noura . . . ," Salah started to say, a little hesitantly. "I want you to meet someone."

"Who? Now?"

Salah nodded.

"Why?"

"Because he has to take us to where we're going."

Noura opened her mouth to say something.

"Please, Noura . . . I am involved in the revolt. I won't lie to you. And the Turks are still after me. And after the dynamite at Rania's, we need to be careful . . . so please meet Charlie Hackett . . ."

Charlie was outside the door when Salah opened it.

"Charlie is British Special Forces and he's got my back . . . our back now."

Noura conceded. "Hello, Charlie."

"Let's go," Charlie said.

They took a circuitous route to the Midan Al-Hussein, where Charlie ushered them into a car and jumped in the front.

"You're taking a real risk, aren't you?" Noura whispered as they drove toward the new center of Cairo.

"Yes."

"Just for me?"

"Yes."

"Salah!" Noura shot up in her seat. "Look! The river! My goodness! It's the Nile," she exclaimed with excitement.

Salah smiled.

Noura suddenly felt self-conscious. "What?" she looked back at him.

"You look very beautiful this evening. I'm sorry I forgot to tell you . . . I got so flustered because I was late . . ."

"We're here, Salah." Charlie turned around. "I'll wait here for a bit and then I'll follow behind . . . at a safe distance, of course."

"Come," Salah said and held out his hand. Together they walked toward a bridge.

"This is the Qasr al-Nil bridge that connects Cairo to Gezira Island. You see, all this, beyond the bridge, is Gezira Island."

"And what are those?" Noura pointed at two large lion stone statues that flanked the bridge's entrance.

"They were made by a French sculptor, Henri Alfred Jacquemart."

"They're beautiful," Noura said.

They walked to the middle of the bridge, stopped, and leaned over the edge to look down into the blue-gray water, staring at their reflection in the gentle undulations of the great river. Noura saw the two of them together and how they looked. She continued to stare at Salah's reflection in the water as he looked pensively out toward the shores of Gezira Island. She saw the way his turban sat proudly on his head, saw the kindness in his face and the generosity in his heart. She turned to focus on a group of water lilies as they floated by. *I feel so at ease with him*, she thought as she looked at the flowers. *I feel as if I can tell him anything, as if he will always be there for me no matter what . . . he makes me feel safe . . . as though when I'm with him, nothing bad will ever happen . . . that he will protect me, always.*

Noura's gaze shifted to her own reflection. Ya Allah! *What am I doing? What kind of a widow am I? Khaled hasn't even been gone a year, and here I am allowing myself to be seduced by another man . . . and not just any other man, but his best friend. Am I insane?*

It's your fault, Khaled, she began a conversation in her mind. *If you hadn't left me none of this would be happening. We would both be living in that pretty little house near the Hamidiyyeh Clock Tower and Siran would probably have a little sister or brother on the way. Instead, here I am, a seamstress repairing uniforms and paying rent to Tante Saydeh and allowing myself to fall in love with Salah.*

How can this be? Is it possible to forget someone you love that quickly? she mused.

I loved you, she told Khaled in her mind. *I loved you very, very much. And I will always love you. And I will cherish your memory and remember you. And I have not forgotten you, nor will I. And I will tell Siran about her father and the hero he was and how he died for what he believed.*

But crying and mourning you for years won't bring you back. It will only make me bitter and cynical and I will be a horrible mother to Siran, not the pillar of strength she's going to need in this chaotic, crazy world we live in.

And I think you would want me to be happy too, wouldn't you? You wouldn't want me to be miserable. Please, Khaled, she prayed, *let me let you go in peace and with grace and dignity.*

"Noura!" Salah's voice penetrated her thoughts. "Come on or you'll miss it."

Noura looked up to see Salah standing at the end of the bridge. "*Yallah!*" he gestured for her to come over. Noura skipped and ran along to catch up with him. Salah held out his hand and Noura put hers in it.

"It is so lovely here," Noura said. "I am so pleased that I let you talk me into it."

"Everyone needs a break, Noura, and I know you've been working hard."

"It's only because I want this little business to succeed," Noura said, putting her head on Salah's arm, "but let's not talk about that just now. Let's enjoy the evening."

"Good!" Salah rubbed his hands happily. "If you are enjoying this time, then my mission has been accomplished."

"So where are we going, exactly?"

"We're almost there." Salah tucked her hand into the crook of his arm. Noura took a deep breath. *Just walking with Salah feels right.*

They crossed over to Gezira Island and followed a curvy path south, surrounded by trees and plants that led into a deeper wooded area.

"This used to be called the Jardin des Plantes under the Khedive," Salah explained as they walked. "He had a huge collection of exotic plants shipped here from all over the world and had a French landscape designer named De la Chevalerie design the island's landscape and plan the gardens and the nurseries. That's Gezira Palace." Salah pointed to the Khedive's u-shaped summer mansion. "It was built in 1869 and it was first used by the Khedive to host his guests who came for the opening of the Suez Canal."

Noura took a deep breath. *It is so green and fresh here . . . so otherworldly and so perfect.*

"There's another palace being built on the other side of the island for Prince Amr Ibrahim," Salah said. "And that's the Gezira Sporting Club." Salah indicated an imposing colonial building with his head.

"We're almost there . . . now close your eyes and let me guide you," Salah said.

Noura did as she was told. Step by step, Salah led her, finally making her sit down. Noura felt around. It felt like a stone bench.

"You can open them now."

Slowly, Noura opened her eyes. She was sitting on a stone bench in a little garden that ran down to the water's edge. The garden was a clearing in the middle of the woods. The view of the Nile in front was spectacular and beyond, on the other bank, was Cairo and the Citadel of Saladin on a hill overlooking the city.

"Saladin built the citadel in the twelfth century to protect the old city of Cairo from the European Crusaders," Salah said. "Now look over here." He got up and Noura followed him. In between the trees was a natural grotto that was fed by a freshwater stream on the island.

Noura drew her breath. "Salah! Look at that red fish!" She pointed, running to the edge.

"It's a rare collection of African fish," Salah told her.

"Oh Salah! They're gorgeous!" Noura gazed up at Salah, giving him a big, beautiful smile.

"So this," Salah said as they sat back down on the bench, "is my favorite place in Cairo."

"But why isn't there anyone else here?" Noura asked.

"Yes, it's curious. It seems as though I'm the only one who knows about it. Whenever I come here, I'm always all alone."

"Salah, it's like heaven. It's breathtaking."

"Wait," he smiled. "It gets even better."

"What?"

"The view."

"How do you mean?"

"Shhh," Salah said.

They sat together in silence, listening to the sounds of the river lapping gently at the edge of the garden. Occasionally a *felucca* would sail by. Every so often the cry of a bird would add to the tranquility of the place, not break it. The cries of the sailors on the *felucca* would sometimes reach them, their voices carrying across on the gentle breeze that skimmed the river.

Gradually the sky changed color as the sun started to dip into the Nile. The sky in the east changed from light to cobalt blue, slowly turning to purple and orange in the west. A flock of birds suddenly chirped overhead and the sound of cicadas started up in the bushes, the sounds of night slowly taking over from the day.

Twilight fell and the sky began to fill with stars. The garden filled with the intoxicating smell of jasmine and queen of the night. Noura inhaled deeply.

"Salah," Noura whispered, reluctant to break the spell. "I don't think I've ever been as happy and content in my whole life as I am now."

Salah remained quiet.

"And I need to thank you," Noura continued, "for everything. You are the most honorable man I know. If it wasn't for you, I don't know what I would have done here. You've given me so much, Salah, and I don't know how I can ever repay you."

"You don't have to repay me . . . ," Salah began.

But Noura put her finger on his lips. "No, let me continue. And I've just been so brusque and nasty to you at times . . ."

Salah tried to protest but she silenced him.

"I came back to El-Khalili because I knew you were there," Noura said.

She took a deep breath. Tears had filled her eyes and her chin was trembling. She was glad darkness had fallen and her face was in shadow.

"I think you know that I have always felt a special connection to you," Noura began. "Ever since the day Khaled first introduced me to you, something clicked and I just knew we were going to be friends. And when we all went to Izmir, I couldn't have been happier because

I knew I was going to have a friend there. And I was really quite sad when you started traveling so much . . . after the first couple of months, you were hardly ever in Izmir. And I missed you. I missed talking to you, laughing with you . . . I missed our friendship. When I first realized I was pregnant, you were the first one I wanted to tell . . . strange isn't it? Even before Khaled, I wanted to tell you."

She paused and looked out at the river before looking back down at her hands.

"And when I found you again, here in Cairo . . . oh! It gladdened my heart, Salah . . . just to see you. And now, every day, I look forward to seeing your face, listening to your voice, watching you look after Siran . . . It's because of you, your patience, your kindness to me, that I have been able to move on from Khaled.

"I just don't know what I would do without you, Salah . . . I need you in my life."

Noura's voice cracked.

"Oh Noura . . ." Salah gathered her in his arms and kissed her forehead, caressing her hair. "Do you know why I was always traveling?"

"No," Noura shook her head against his chest.

Salah sighed. "I went away, Noura, because I had to. Because to be so close to you and not hold you, not tell you how beautiful you are to me, not be able to look after you as I wanted, was more than I could bear. And I knew it was impossible. You were Khaled's wife and he was my best friend and I would never, could never, betray him. But it was torture every time I had to come to dinner, it was agony when you came over to my house and helped me decorate and cooked for me . . ."

"Salah . . . ," Noura whispered. "I never knew."

"And I couldn't tell you . . . at least not until now."

Noura took his hands in hers and kissed both of them.

"You know I hadn't planned on making this speech tonight," Salah admitted.

"I'm glad you did."

"Look at those stars." Salah looked up still cradling Noura in his arms. "It's magical, isn't it . . . the sky at night? What do you think is up there?"

"I don't know . . . God, Allah, Saint Peter . . . who knows?"

"If Khaled is up there, do you think he's watching us?"

"Probably." Noura shrugged.

"Were you happy with him?"

"Yes," Noura replied. "I was. It was a different kind of happiness to the one I feel now. For some reason, this feels more complete."

"Do you miss him?" he asked.

"I did . . . very, very much in the beginning," Noura admitted. "And I still do. But the waves of sadness have receded and I feel as though I can remember him now without breaking down."

"Khaled was one of the smartest men I knew," Salah said. "He was a serious fellow and he didn't have a trail of girls chasing after him."

"You mean he wasn't like Wissam." Noura smiled forlornly.

"No," Salah confirmed. "Wissam, he was not. And he didn't take love frivolously. He didn't fall in and out of it like some of us did back then. He always said that when he found the right girl, he would marry her and love her forever."

Tears welled up in Noura's eyes.

"And that's what happened with you." Salah took Noura's hand in his. "He fell in love with you and he married you and it was going to be forever. In fact, I remember when he started to talk about you: it was always Noura this and Noura that . . . but it was the way he talked about you . . . it just felt different . . . special. And then one day I came out and asked him.

"'I think I quite like her, Salah,' he said in that serious way of his. And I knew that he had fallen. Khaled always took a long time committing to something because he always thought everything through ten times, looking at it from every angle possible. He was not spontaneous, but once he committed, he usually stuck with it through to the end.

"And . . . he was the most faithful and loyal man I knew . . . to his friends, to his family . . . you could always count on Khaled."

Salah wiped a tear from his eye.

"That is why I could never show my feelings for you, Noura," Salah continued. "I could never have betrayed Khaled. I would have let you go before I betrayed him."

"You loved him very much, didn't you?" Noura said.

"I did." Salah's voice broke for a moment before he regained his composure. "He was my best friend, my brother . . ."

"Some part of me will always love him, Salah," Noura said in the dark.

"I know that."

Noura sat forward and put her hands together on her knees and closed her eyes.

Salah makes me happy, Khaled . . . just like you once did. And if there was anyone you would entrust Siran and me to, it would be to Salah. I know you would.

"Think he's angry?" Salah chuckled in the darkness. "That his wife and his best friend are together?"

"No. I think he's smiling and giving us his blessing," Noura replied.

"Good! Because I am now going to do something that I've wanted to do for a long time," Salah said. He bent down and placed his lips on Noura's in a gentle, soft, and loving kiss.

"Mr. Masri," Noura said when they pulled away. "That was quite a cheeky thing to do."

"Well, Mrs. Shadid, it was thoroughly enjoyable."

"Yes it was . . . Salah . . . ," Noura began.

"I love you, Noura," Salah whispered against her forehead. "Always have. Always will."

Noura adjusted her abaya and headscarf in the mirror in the hallway on the first floor. While she was not a Muslim, it provided the perfect cover. It had been Salah's idea, and while she had balked at it in the beginning, insisting that no one would come after her, she had finally given in. She pulled her veil across her mouth and nose, hoisted her bag of clean uniforms on her shoulder, and opened the door. She looked right and left and walked out. As she approached the top of the lane she saw a man leaning against a wall smoking a cigarette.

He looked at her carefully. Noura held his gaze boldly and continued on her way. As she made her way through the cloth sellers' lane, she occasionally stopped to touch a bolt or two. She glanced back. The man was there. And from the way he was dressed, he was definitely Turkish. Should she try and give him the slip? *Or what if I confront him? Let's see what he does.*

Noura turned and walked toward the Turk. When he saw her coming, he stood up straight. He looked uncomfortable. Noura kept walking toward him. Suddenly, the man turned and fled in the opposite direction.

—⚭—

"So, Celik, where is Noura Shadid?" Colonel Erdogan asked.

"She is definitely in the El-Khalili. But we think she is dressing in an abaya, so we have not been able to ascertain that the woman we think is her is, indeed, her."

"So tear off the veil," Erdogan said.

"You want me to tear off the veil of a Muslim woman in the El-Khalili, Sir?"

"Well, do something! I don't care how you find out!" Erdogan said. "I want to be sure of it. I don't want a case of mistaken identity."

"What do we do with her, Sir?"

"What do you think, Celik? Kidnap her, of course. Masri will come to rescue her and we will get him then."

—⚭—

Christmas 1916 came and went. In Europe, the two biggest and bloodiest battles of Verdun and Somme were finally over. Over a million men were lost during the Somme offensives, and close to the same at Verdun. No one knew what the New Year would bring in the West, but there was talk of the United States entering the war on the side of the Allies.

In Cairo, the British Military Command was planning the Palestine and Mesopotamia Campaigns. T.E. Lawrence was now completely ensconced in the Arab Revolt and Salah was deep into planning the attacks on the Hejaz Railway that were about to come into play.

Shortly after the New Year of 1917, Salah, Lawrence, Rabih, and Charlie were in the inner courtyard of the Al-Hussein Mosque.

"Wejh . . . here on the coast," Salah pointed to a place on the map, "will be the base of attacks on the Hejaz Railway."

"Why?" Lawrence asked.

"It is the midway point of the railway, so we can go north or south," Salah said. "Also, I think Faisal should base himself at Wejh. It is a short march from there into Ottoman Syria."

"He's about to begin the march north."

"He should take the coastal route," Salah said.

"Yes," Lawrence agreed. "That is what I have told him."

"What are his two brothers doing?" Rabih asked.

"Ali is launching nightly raids into Medina and Abdullah has begun raiding Ottoman military depots," Charlie said. "He just captured a convoy in the desert. I think he got twenty thousand pounds' worth of gold coins."

"So, as soon as Faisal starts north, the guerilla forces will start blowing up tracks of the unguarded sections of the railway."

"Very well," Lawrence said. "I'm looking forward to lighting up Ottoman skies. I'll send the orders to my 'irregulars' to launch the attacks on the tracks, and Charlie and I will leave in a couple of weeks. I need to square away some monies from my bosses."

Siran's birthday was still three months away in April, but Saydeh was in a tizzy.

"Noura!" she shouted up the stairs.

"There's my mother." Salah was upstairs in Noura's atelier.

"Noura!"

"I think you're in trouble."

"Why?"

"My mother wants to talk to you about Siran's first birthday party."

"What? But it's months away."

"How would you feel celebrating it a little early?"

"Why?"

"Because we could make a little announcement of our own before I have to go back to the Hejaz."

"I don't want you to go, Salah. Why do you have to go? Why don't you send them the information?"

"I have to go," Salah insisted.

Noura pulled away from Salah. "I hate this."

"Noura . . . let me finish what I started."

Noura wrung her hands. "I don't even know what to say. Nothing is going to change your mind, is it?"

Salah smiled wanly.

"So," he tried, "why don't we have a party and celebrate Siran's birthday and announce our engagement?"

"Why the rush?" Noura asked. "Are you planning on not coming back?"

"Noura," Salah soothingly took her hand in his, "no rush, just feels right. Besides I want to do this more often and not feel guilty." With that, he bent his head and kissed her tenderly.

—⁓—

"Tante!" Noura called as she came down the stairs.

"In the salon, *habibti*," she heard Saydeh's voice.

"Tante Saydeh, I am so sorry, I didn't hear you," Noura came into the salon and sat down. "I have several uniforms to get through before the end of the day."

Saydeh clicked her tongue. "We have more important things to discuss . . . it's much too depressing to talk about military uniforms because it just reminds me how many of our boys are out there fighting with the British."

"Yes," Noura agreed. Saydeh was indeed right. Every time Noura repaired a uniform, she would embroider the name of the soldier on the inner pocket. They were only names, but there were men behind those names. Who were they? She would wonder as she sat bent over her work. Were they married? Did they have a families? Wives? Children? Would they come back safe and sound to them? Often, when she ironed the uniform before sending it back to its owner, she always said a little prayer over it, hoping that the new uniform would bring the soldier luck.

"Anyway!" Saydeh brightened up. "Let the men deal with the war . . . and let's you and I look after our families and friends, which is much more important."

"Yes!" Noura sat forward on the low divan.

"Now . . . I know it's only January, but I wanted to talk to you about celebrating Siran's first birthday early in February before Salah has to go back to the Hejaz."

Noura nodded. "Tante Saydeh," she added. "I was thinking . . . how would you feel if we had the party at Rania's?"

"Why? Isn't it going to be just us?"

"Well . . . ," Noura started, "I thought it would be nice to invite Madame Yvonne and Tante Takla . . . and, of course, Fatmeh and Rania . . . and maybe even Magdi and his sons, and, you know, open it up a bit."

"But why?" Saydeh looked at Noura quizzically.

Haraam! Noura thought. *She knows what Salah and I want to do. But how would she know?*

"It's only because . . . well . . . ," Noura searched for a plausible excuse, "because I now feel part of this community and I would like to thank everyone properly for welcoming me in and being so good to me . . ."

CHAPTER THIRTEEN

Sergeant Mehmet Celik and a young captain peeked in through one of the side windows of Rania's Café.

It looked wonderfully festive. The lanterns gave off a lovely soft glow, their colored panes throwing shades of pink and green and red around where they hung. The colored tablecloths had been starched and ironed and all the tables had little posies of flowers and small candles. The farmhouse table in the middle groaned with the weight of all the dishes Saydeh had piled on top, and the bar was filled with drinks of all kinds. Everything looked beautiful.

"This is perfect," Celik whispered. "Captain Demir, go now to Colonel Erdogan. Tell him there is an event at the café. I'll start placing the dynamite."

"Yes, Sir."

"Hurry, Demir. Ask him if he wants to come or if we should go ahead without him."

—⚊—

The party was in full swing. The little quartet of musicians, which included a violinist, an oud player, a tambourine player, and a bongo player, had set up in a corner and filled the room with the sounds of popular folk songs.

Everyone was there, including Magdi, the fruitseller, with his wife, Hala, and their sons. Rania looked beautiful in a dark red dress that suited her complexion and set off her hair. Fatmeh was still in her abaya, but had let Rania line her eyes with kohl that made her fair skin look even brighter. Takla had given up her usual black for an olive green dress and tied her thick, curly, salt-and-pepper hair back in a neat bun, making her long neck even more swanlike. Yvonne wore the dusky gold silk-satin dress Noura had made for her.

"This is a birthday party, Yvonne, not a wedding," Takla remarked when Yvonne swanned in, cooling herself with a little gold fan.

"I think she looks very elegant," Rania said.

"I do too," Fatmeh chimed in.

Yvonne smiled at them, gave Takla a haughty look, and helped herself to a glass of her special lime juice.

"Where are the birthday girl and her mother?" Yvonne looked around.

"If you don't see them, they're obviously still not here," Takla said.

"Tante Takla, today is a happy day . . . ," Rania reminded her. "So, please, perhaps we could all join in the gaiety?"

Takla sighed heavily in acquiescence.

"*Marhaba*, everyone!" Saydeh came out from the kitchen. She was wearing a turquoise and green printed long loose tunic and a matching hijab. And since they were all *en famille*, she had decided not to wear her abaya. "Besides, who's going to look at me," she had told Rania earlier. "I'm past the age of cat calls!"

"You look lovely, Saydeh," Takla remarked. "Nice change from the black."

"I think she looks beautiful." Rania put her arm around her.

"She does." Fatmeh put her arm around her other shoulder, the two younger women flanking her.

"She looks like a proud mother," Fatmeh said.

"And grandmother." Rabih approached the group, his eyes on Rania.

"Come here!" Saydeh extricated herself from Rania and Fatmeh and gestured for Rabih to come over. "Look how handsome you look today!" she exclaimed, holding him to her bosom. "Indeed, today I am a proud mother . . . with my new family."

The shrill ring of the doorbell broke the spell. Rania looked up to see a burly black man walk in.

Saydeh screeched with delight. "Captain Nusair!" she went toward him to greet him with a big hug, kissing him on either cheek.

"I was in the neighborhood," he smiled down at Saydeh. "I hope you don't mind me crashing the party."

"I would have been insulted had you not come," Saydeh said.

"I was actually just at your house and Salah told me to come over here . . . that he would be right over."

"Is he on his way?" Saydeh asked.

"Yes . . . I think he was waiting for Noura and Siran. She was still upstairs."

Saydeh nodded. "In the meantime, come, what can I offer you to eat or drink?"

—⁓—

With all the music, conversation, and people moving around and help-ing themselves to the buffet of food, no one saw Sergeant Mehmet Celik lurking around outside placing sticks of dynamite outside the café. *Where the hell is Demir? He should have been back by now.*

When he finished, he stood up to survey the work when suddenly, out of nowhere, someone punched him in the face. Celik was momen-tarily disoriented. His attacker grabbed him from behind, coiling his right arm around his neck. Slowly he squeezed. Celik lost conscious-ness and fell to the ground.

"Sergeant! Sergeant!" A young man came running down the lane. He knelt by the sergeant and felt for his pulse.

He felt a sharp blow on the back of his neck and fell on top of the sergeant.

—⁓—

Inside the café, silence fell on the room. Everyone turned to the door-way. There stood Salah, with his arm around Noura, who held Siran in her arms.

"*Marhaba*, everyone!" Salah said in his deep, grave voice. Noura looked around the room and smiled. She was wearing a simple, long, off-white dress accented with red roses. Siran was in a new white cotton dress with pink and white gingham piping that her mother had made for her. On her feet were little white socks and white shoes.

Salah walked in first and went around the room, hugging and kissing and shaking hands with everyone. Noura walked toward her group of friends, who all looked at her questioningly, but didn't say anything. There was a mildly awkward silence for a moment as they all waited for Noura to say something.

When Noura didn't say anything, Fatmeh began cooing over Siran. "She looks like a little doll."

"I can't believe it's been a year," Noura said. "Or almost a year."

After a few minutes of catching up on the daily goings on, Noura went to the bar to get something to drink. She helped herself to a glass of pomegranate juice.

"Hello, Noura," she heard a male voice behind her.

She put the glass down and turned, her eyes tightly shut.

"Please tell me it is you, Captain Nusair," she said, putting her hands on his arms, smiling as she felt the thick cotton of his white sweater.

"It is, dear girl."

Slowly, she opened her eyes and looked up, scared that someone was playing a joke on her and it wasn't really the Yemeni captain. But the moment she looked into his broad, black face and his shining white smile, she threw her arms around him, her eyes filling with tears of happiness. Musa Nusair lifted her up off the floor, holding her tightly to him.

"I can't believe it's you," she said. "Thank you for coming."

"I wasn't going to miss my little girl's first birthday, was I?" he said, putting Noura back down on the floor.

"But why didn't you send word?" Noura asked.

"I wanted it to be a surprise," Captain Nusair told her. "Anyhow, I came by the house earlier, but you were still upstairs and Salah told me to come here."

"I am very happy to see you."

"You look very well, Noura." Musa Nusair looked down into her face. "You look very happy."

"I am," Noura admitted.

"You made a good decision coming here. Cairo suits you."

"Actually, the best decision I made was to come here to El-Khalili."

"Yes, Salah told me briefly about your huge success as a seamstress."

"Well . . . it's all relative, Captain." Noura blushed at Salah's praise. "At the moment I'm only repairing military uniforms."

"Yes, but one step at a time, Noura," Captain Nusair told her. "Look at how much you've already achieved in this past year . . . and how you've dealt with everything that happened . . . and how gracefully you've borne the pressure. Anyone else would have buckled under."

"Thank you," Noura replied.

"You're a courageous woman, Noura . . . really courageous."

Both turned to see Salah walking over to them.

"Having a nice time, brother?" Salah put his arm around Musa Nusair.

"How can I not?" the Captain replied.

"What do you think, Musa?" Salah winked at him. "Shall we do this?"

Musa Nusair stepped out in the middle of the café.

"*Ahlan wa sahlan*, everyone! Thank you all for coming to this party."

"What's going on?" Fatmeh whispered to Rania.

"What's all this, Saydeh?" Yvonne gestured to Captain Nusair.

"I don't know." Saydeh shook her head.

"You didn't orchestrate this?" Yvonne asked.

"No! I swear I didn't!" She looked at Yvonne. "Really!" She looked back and forth from Yvonne to Takla, while Rania winked knowingly at Fatmeh.

"My name is Musa Nusair, and I am a sea captain," Captain Nusair started off, telling the group how he knew both Salah and Noura and how he had been the one to bring Siran into the world. "As a matter of fact, where is my little goddaughter?"

"Here you go." Salah handed her to him.

"And now here she is, growing up before our very eyes. She's going to be a very special girl, given how special her mother is and how special Salah and Saydeh are." Musa Nusair looked down at Siran, who was in the crook of his arm, looking from him to the crowd around her curiously, occasionally trying to reach up to grab Musa's nose.

"*Ya, Allah!*" Saydeh squealed, placing her hand to her heaving bosom, tears forming in her eyes.

"And so we are here today to celebrate the birth of this very special little girl, but also something else . . ."

"And that is the engagement of my best friend, Salah Masri, to Noura," the captain announced.

Everyone started clapping and whooping with joy and the musical band began playing a jolly tune usually reserved for weddings. Shouts of "*Mabrook*, brother" went up as everyone began crowding around Salah, slapping him on the back and shaking his hand. Noura looked around and saw Rania coming toward her smiling, her arms open. Fatmeh came too, "*Mabrook!* Noura, I am so happy for you!"

"Where's Tante Saydeh?" Noura asked, trying to look for her in the crowd.

"I don't know, but I thought she was right behind us," Fatmeh said.

As they made their way through the little throng, they found Yvonne and Takla on the floor fanning Saydeh, who had fallen off the bench in excitement.

"Tante Saydeh!" Noura immediately ran to her, falling to her knees, holding her hand. "What happened?"

"She fell off her chair when the captain announced your engagement," Yvonne said.

"My dear child," Saydeh said, smiling broadly, "my dear little *habibti*." She caressed Noura's head from her horizontal position on the floor. "I am so very happy for you both." She pulled Noura down to her chest and hugged her.

And that is how Salah found them, having dashed over when someone told him his mother had fallen on the floor and couldn't get up.

"*Imme!*" he was by her side. "What's wrong? What's the matter?"

"Nothing, *ibne*," she caressed his cheek, "nothing at all."

"But have you hurt yourself?" he asked, concerned, putting his hand under her head.

"No . . ."

"But, then, why are you still on the floor? And why are you crying?"

"I'm just enjoying the moment," Saydeh said.

"Come on, *imme*," Salah heaved her up. "You're being a little dramatic!"

Together the three of them walked over to the center of the café and stood with Musa Nusair as cheers went up and another round of congratulations was heaped on Saydeh and Noura.

—⟶⟵—

Outside, Charlie handed over the still-unconscious Sergeant Celik and Captain Demir to the British Army police. "Take them away. Keep an eye on this one," Charlie said, pointing to Sergeant Celik. "He's a slippery bugger."

—⟶⟵—

Salah and Rabih were deep in concentration, playing backgammon in Saydeh's kitchen. Suddenly, they heard the sound of females giggling, followed by soft footsteps, whispers, more giggling, and warnings to be quiet coming from Noura's atelier. Salah looked at Rabih, who shrugged. Salah looked in on Siran in her bassinet. She was quiet. The two men went back to their game. Suddenly, from the corner of his eye, Salah saw movement. He looked up and saw three huddled women trying to walk very softly along the corridor, looking over their shoulders.

"*Masa al-khair*, ladies," Salah said in his deepest voice.

There was a sharp cry and all three jumped and hid behind the door.

Noura was the first to recover. "Salah!" She walked over and punched him playfully in the chest. "What are you trying to do? Have us all drop dead from fear?"

"But what are you hiding from?" he asked.

"Your mother . . . she'll ask too many questions," Noura replied.

"About?"

"Fatmeh . . . come on out," Noura said.

"She's too nervous," Rania's voice came from behind the door.

Rabih, who had been lounging on the diwan, shot up when he heard her voice.

Rania poked her head from around the corner, "Noura . . ." She glared at her. "A little help please."

"*Marhaba*, Rania," Rabih said.

"*Marhaba ya*, Rabih," she replied quickly before disappearing around the corner.

"Excuse me, gentlemen," Noura said.

Salah cocked his ear, trying to hear what was being said.

"They sound like crickets."

"Let them be," Rabih said.

"Women! I swear, brother, for as long as I live I will never understand them."

"Come, let us continue with the game," Rabih suggested.

"Your move, Rabih!" Salah laughed. "Ha ha ha! I'm clobbering you, brother." Suddenly, he did a double take. There at the entrance of the salon was a woman, flanked by Rania and Noura. Rabih's mouth fell open and he dropped the backgammon piece. Salah was so flustered that he mistakenly hit the backgammon board with his knee and the pieces went flying everywhere, raining down over the salon.

"Praise be to Allah!" Salah quickly got to his feet. "*Ahlan*, Madame!" he said, looking around for his turban. "Please . . . come in . . . ," he said, flustered. "I apologize. It's a bit messy . . . Rabih! Get up, for God's sake and help me tidy up . . ."

"Salah . . . ," Noura said.

"Perhaps . . . uh," he ignored her, "you'd like to wait just a moment in the dining room. My mother should be here soon. I'm not sure where she went . . . ," he continued to stammer.

"Salah!" Noura said in a louder voice.

Salah stopped and looked at her.

"This, my darling fiancé, is Fatmeh."

Salah's mouth fell open and his eyes opened wide. Rabih was equally shocked.

"That . . . that's Fatmeh?" he pointed at her, but looked at Noura in disbelief.

Noura and Rania nodded, both women smiling broadly.

"Our Fatmeh?"

They nodded, while Fatmeh blushed and looked down at her shoes.

"From Rania's Café?" Salah approached her and walked around her.

"She's not a camel, Salah!" Rania hit him on the arm.

"I . . . I know . . . it's just that I don't know what to say . . . I'm shocked," Salah said. "What do you say, Rabih?"

Rabih was still staring at Fatmeh.

"I really am Fatmeh," Fatmeh finally said, smiling at their reaction.

Noura clapped her hands in excitement, as did Rania, and the two of them hugged each other, delighted they had accomplished their task.

Fatmeh looked spectacular. Her dress was long, simple, and elegant. It was deep crimson silk satin that was soft and flowing, and gathered just above the waist in Grecian folds. The skirt billowed around her elegantly while the bodice was simple with a square neckline and sweet lace ruffles bordering it. The sleeves were long and bell shaped, with the same lace ruffle on the cuff. Noura had cut an extra swathe of crimson lace for Fatmeh to use as a wrap. She carried a small velvet pouch as a purse and wore Noura's kitten-heel black shoes.

Her face glowed. Rania had lined her eyes with kohl, brushed her thick, arched eyebrows, plucking off a few stray hairs to give them a better shape, and curled her already thick, long eyelashes. She'd used only the faintest dab of a translucent powder to get rid of the shine on her nose, pinched her cheeks for some color, and put some Vaseline on her lips to make them glisten. Her hair was brushed and shiny. Rania had curled it and put it up, letting the curls and ringlets fall naturally from her crown, and tied a thin scarf around her head to keep the hairdo in place.

"Is it possible to ask where you're going?" Salah asked, still shocked.

"She's going out," Noura said.

"Well someone needs to escort her. She can't walk out like that by herself," Salah said.

"We have a plan," Rania told him. "We are all going to wear the abaya and we will both walk with her and wait until . . ."

"Until what?" Salah asked.

"Until she's ready to leave."

"Leave for what?"

"Oh Salah," Noura said. "Don't you get it? Fatmeh has a rendezvous tonight."

"Right, come on, Noura! We have to go or Fatmeh will be late," Rania said.

Without any further ado, the three women stole through the alleyways and lanes.

"I feel like we're a group of thieves," Fatmeh whispered as they hurried toward the Midan Al-Hussein. When they arrived at the archway that led to the square and main road ahead, they stopped.

"Oh my God!" Fatmeh clutched Noura and Rania's hands. "There he is!"

All three of them looked over to see Charlie standing next to a shiny black car.

"Now, let's take a last look at you." Noura inspected her, while Rania fiddled with the hijab around her head, untying it and fluffing her hairdo, which had flattened a little.

"Now, hand me the abaya and off you go," Noura said. "And remember, we want all the details tomorrow morning."

Fatmeh looked at the two women. "I don't know what to say."

"Then don't say anything," Noura said.

Quickly Fatmeh hugged them both. She stepped out onto the square and walked quickly to where a car was waiting.

"She looks beautiful," Noura remarked as they all hid under the archway and peeked behind the wall.

"She does," Rania agreed.

—◊◊◊—

As Fatmeh ran across the open square to Charlie, two shadowy figures watched her.

"Follow them," Colonel Erdogan said, throwing his cigarette butt on the ground. "I want the man who put Celik and Demir in jail."

"What about the woman with him?"

"Kill them both. She's dispensable."

"Yes, Sir. What about the other two women?"

"Leave them to me. I have other plans for them."

—w—

"Where are we going?" Fatmeh asked shyly.

"I thought we would enjoy this lovely evening and go for a drive," Charlie said.

"Yes." Fatmeh smiled.

"And perhaps if you'd like to have a nice cool drink . . . ?" he suggested cautiously. "But it's entirely up to you," he added quickly.

He knew what a huge risk Fatmeh was taking coming out this evening. No matter the circumstances, she was still married and he had to respect that. It wouldn't do for them to be seen together. That was why when she agreed to come out he had agonized over what to do and where to take her. He would have loved to have taken her to the British Officer's Club for dinner, but he had no idea if it was something she would enjoy, and, given how shy she was, she would probably be much too intimidated by such a public place. So after much thought, he finally decided on a drive and a walk around the gardens of the Gezira Sporting Club.

Fatmeh sat on the edge of the car seat with her two hands on the window looking out at the wide, tree-lined avenues and the Belle-Époque architecture of the apartment buildings of Wust el Balad. Well-dressed people were strolling in the twilight, looking in shop windows, occasionally stopping to greet acquaintances and friends before moving on, walking into brightly-lit cafés to quench their thirst. The women were all dressed in western outfits; long, elegant dresses and big, bold hats with ribbons and feathers and bows that looked more like pieces of art than something one would put on one's head.

"Different, isn't it?" Charles moved over and sat next to her, his chin almost resting on her shoulder.

"Yes . . . it is," she laughed. "I've never seen anything like it."

"It's a very Europeanized section of Cairo," he said, pointing out buildings that were replicas of their original counterparts in Paris.

"People live in those buildings?" Fatmeh asked, sticking her head out of the window to get a better look. "But they are so big."

"Yes . . . and the apartments they live in are very big, too. Some of them live on an entire floor, for example."

"Really?"

Charles sat back and smiled. She was so wonderfully innocent, so unlike some of his recent girlfriends; English girls, daughters of some of his commanding officers, who were spoiled and bratty and demanding. Fatmeh was so different. Perhaps it was because she didn't know this other world. She had told him she had never ventured far from the souk and even her nursing skills had been learned directly from her father. So naturally, coming here would be like going to another country.

But it wasn't just her innocence that appealed to him. It was her manner. She was gentle and kind. Being around her soothed him, made him calmer, somehow made life look much less brutal and chaotic.

And she was beautiful and didn't know it. Those eyes, which tonight shone with excitement, the wonder of a new discovery, were captivating.

"Here we are!" he announced and got out of the car. He came around to open her door.

Timidly, she took his hand and placed a foot on the ground and got out. But she was not used to the little heeled shoes she was wearing and stepped on a large stone and lost her balance. She let out a short cry and tried to daintily regain her balance. But she couldn't. She fell. Charles, who had been holding her left hand, was immediately by her side, catching her in his arms. Dazed, she instinctively put her hands around his neck. Holding him tightly, she leaned against him, while he held her, his arms firmly around her waist.

"Fatmeh! My God! Are you all right?" he searched her face anxiously.

"Uh . . . ," she murmured. "Yes . . . yes I think so."

"Can you stand? Are you sure you haven't broken anything?"

"Really . . . I'm fine."

"A sprain then?" he asked.

"No, no."

Fatmeh took a couple of steps. A sharp pain shot through her foot when she put pressure on it, but she didn't say anything, unwilling to spoil the moment.

"Very well!" Charles said. "Shall we go?" he offered her his arm, which she took.

Slowly, they walked across the Qasr-al Nil Bridge. Charles pointed out all kinds of rare birds that flew past in the early evening, exotic plants that grew along the riverbank, the colorful flowers, and the tall majestic magnolias that created a natural arbor, covering the pebbled path they took that wound down and around until they reached a tall hedge that prevented any views of the other side.

Fatmeh looked questioningly at Charles. He patted her hand reassuringly and pointed to a small, rusty wrought iron gate hidden by creeping green plants that had grown over it. Fatmeh smiled, excited. Charles tried to push the gate open but it wouldn't give. He tried shoving it with his shoulder, but it didn't move. He stood back and looked at the gate, wondering what to do.

"Charles, look!" Fatmeh pointed at a small lock that had been placed in the bolt inside.

"Dash it!" he muttered. From his breast pocket he pulled out a small leather pouch from which he took out what looked to Fatmeh like a crotchet needle. Charles put his arms through the bars of gate, held the lock in one hand and with the instrument poked around until he heard a click. He pulled off the lock, slid back the bolt, and the gate creaked loudly on unoiled hinges. With a little help from Charles, it finally swung open.

"Oh!" Fatmeh said as she stepped across the threshold. A lush green lawn surrounded by woods stretched out toward a lake, which was fed by a stream that emerged from the earth. Off to the right, tucked away on the top of a small hill, was a small ancient Egyptian temple in white stone that was barely visible, hidden behind the rich foliage of the palm trees that stood like sentinels surrounding it.

Charles smiled at Fatmeh's expression of awe. He offered his hand and drew her to him.

"Charles!" Fatmeh pointed at a couple of peacocks that emerged from the woods to come drink at the lake. "Oh! They are beautiful."

"And there . . . scarlet ibis," Charles pointed out.

"Charles, where are we?" Fatmeh asked.

"These are part of the gardens of the Gezira Sporting Club," he told her. "And this is known as the exotic lake . . . shall we stroll around? You never know what else you might see."

And indeed they did. Pink flamingoes stood on one leg around the lake, mingling with the ibis and the peacocks, while multicolored parrots of all shapes and sizes cawed from the trees.

Slowly they made their way around the lake, walking up a small pathway that led through the woods to the temple. Charles squeezed Fatmeh's hand and smiled excitedly at her. He still had his big surprise and he was hoping she would enjoy it. They came to a clearing and there, sitting in the middle, was the small temple they had seen, with its own little earth-fed freshwater pond and two stone sphinxes guarding the temple entrance, along with two obelisks decorated with gold hieroglyphics on either side.

Off to one side of the temple, there was a small red and white striped desert tent, billowing gently in the breeze.

"What?" Fatmeh exclaimed, shocked.

"This way, please, Madame," Charles said, smiling.

Forgetting about her foot, Fatmeh took a step and winced with the pain.

"Fatmeh!" Charles said. "What's the matter?"

"Nothing . . . really." She smiled, tears of pain filling her eyes.

"It's your foot, isn't it," Charles said. "I knew it wasn't right."

"I'm fine . . . it's nothing but a little muscle pull . . . I am sure of it," she reassured him. "Now show me what's inside the tent," she urged, trying to take his mind off her foot.

"All right," he agreed, reluctantly.

The tent was an oasis of color. It was lined in pink and orange and red silk and velvet hangings with gold tasseled fringes. Old Moorish lamps lit the interior softly, throwing shadows on the cornucopia of cushions in all shapes and sizes that were strewn all over the tent. A colorful handmade carpet covered the floor. In the middle was a low table, laden with food. Off to the side was a silver ice bucket that had a bottle of wine sticking out from beneath a white starched linen napkin.

"This is exquisite!" Fatmeh gasped. "I feel like I'm in the middle of *One Thousand and One Nights.*"

While Charles struggled with the cork on the wine bottle, Fatmeh pulled her dress just over her ankle and gulped. Clearly she had done much more than twist her foot when she fell. Her ankle was completely swollen and Fatmeh knew that if she took off her shoe, she would never get it back on. Reclining comfortably as she was, it wasn't doing more than throbbing, with the occasional twinge of pain if she moved in a certain way. Quickly, she covered it up just as Charles sat down in front of her.

"Surprised?" he asked.

Fatmeh smiled shyly in response.

"A walk in those gardens," she pointed to the outside, "would have been more than enough."

"Well . . . I wanted to take you out for dinner, too."

"Thank you."

He gazed at her, searching her face that glowed softly in the candle-light. He noticed her eyes, her mouth, her hair, her neck . . .

"Fatmeh," he whispered, "you've never been more beautiful to me than you are now in this moment."

Fatmeh's heart began to pound. She didn't know how to respond or what to say. She smiled and put her hand over his, holding it tightly.

"Well . . ." He cleared his throat and poured himself a glass of wine. "Would you like to try some? It's quite delicious."

"I've never had any," she admitted.

"Of course, if you feel awkward . . ."

"No, no, I'd like to try. Madame Yvonne always has a little gin in her lime juice, and God hasn't rained his wrath down on her," she joked.

Slowly, Fatmeh put the wine glass to her lips and took a sip.

Charles stared at her. "Well?"

Fatmeh smiled. "Mmmm, it's very good!"

He smiled back, pleased.

Suddenly, there was a scuffling noise outside. Fatmeh stopped, her heart in her mouth. Charles started to his feet. There was more scuffling. Charles put his index finger to his lips. "Don't move," he whispered.

"No! Charles! Don't go!" she caught his hand. "We don't know who they are or how many . . . they could kill you."

"Fatmeh, I'll go take a quick look. I'll be right back," he caressed the side of her face. "Don't worry."

"Charles! What if it's my husband? What if he followed us?"

"Let me go and look," he deftly unwound her fingers from his wrist. He knelt and kissed her forehead. He took his gun out of its holster.

Fatmeh sat back. She was petrified.

Suddenly, a series of loud gunshots cracked through the tranquility of the garden, followed by the sound of physical fighting.

Fatmeh covered her ears, her heart pounding.

The flap of the tent opened. Charles appeared, his suit muddied and dusty, his hair ruffled, his face covered in dirt and a small cut near his lip.

"Charles!"

"We need to leave immediately."

Fatmeh hobbled to her feet. Charles pulled a knife out of the waist of his pants and ripped an opening in the side of the tent. With Fatmeh in his arms, he ran all the way back to the car.

He put Fatmeh in the passenger seat and jumped in. In the rear-view mirror he saw two figures come running across the bridge and jump onto motorcycles.

Charles slammed the car in gear and stepped on the accelerator.

"Hold on, Fatmeh."

The car screeched around the corner and they sped along the wide boulevard of the new French quarter, zigzagging between the slower horse carriages and other traffic.

Charles switched gears and revved the engine, pushing the car to go faster. The motorcycles kept up.

As they went over a small bridge, Charles swerved into a tiny parallel lane and screeched to a halt. Looking up, they both saw the two motorcycles pass them, disappearing down the road.

"Fatmeh . . . are you all right?" He took her hand in his. "I'm so sorry."

Fatmeh nodded but she looked scared and her eyes filled with tears.

"I'll take you home," Charles said gently.

CHAPTER FOURTEEN

It was just past eight o'clock in the morning when Fatmeh heard the back door in the kitchen open with a small click. *Rabih?* She wondered. It was awfully early for him to be here. Usually he didn't come in until 9:30 or so. She got up with some difficulty, reached for her crutches, and hobbled to the kitchen. She pulled the curtain apart with one crutch and saw Rabih taking all of his paint boxes and tools out of a cupboard.

"Rabih!" Fatmeh called to him. "*Sabah al-khair!*"

Rabih whipped around when he heard her.

"*Marhaba ya*, Fatmeh!" he greeted her with a shy smile. "What are you doing up so early?"

Fatmeh limped in so he could see her crutches and her bandaged foot.

"*Ya Allah*, Fatmeh!" he cried, coming over immediately. "*Shoo hayda?* What's all this?"

"Remember the night Rania and Noura escorted me to the Midan Al-Hussein?"

Rabih nodded.

"I was getting out of a car that night and slipped," she told him.

"Come on now! You shouldn't be on your feet. You need to keep this foot elevated." He took her arm and helped her into the kitchen.

"What are you doing here so early?" she asked him, as he helped her sit down in a chair.

"Couldn't sleep," he replied.

"Neither could I," Fatmeh said, "but that's because I'm in pain. So I decided to come down here and write. It's quiet this time of morning. Even the birds are quiet, it seems."

Rabih smiled.

"What's your excuse?" she asked.

He shrugged.

"So is the foot broken?" he asked, changing the subject.

"No, thank Allah, just a bad sprain."

"So how long do you have to be on crutches?"

"Oh, about six weeks my father says."

"Does your father know yet that you have moved out?" Rabih asked.

"I had to tell him," Fatmeh nodded. "He wondered why Walid was not with me when I went to get my foot bandaged."

"How did he take it?"

"Better than I expected," Fatmeh sighed. "He's, of course, hoping that I will go back to Walid in a few weeks . . ."

"And you?"

"I don't know, Rabih." Fatmeh took a deep breath. "It's all so confusing."

Rabih nodded.

"I've got a lot of thinking to do."

"So do I," he admitted.

There was a momentary pause in the conversation.

"It's to do with Rania, isn't it?" Fatmeh asked.

Rabih nodded.

"Can I help?" Fatmeh asked.

"I don't know what happened, Fatmeh," Rabih said, putting his head on his hands. "It's as if she can't make up her mind . . . one minute she's smiling at me and the next pretending as though I don't exist."

"I think she got scared," Fatmeh said.

"Scared . . ." Rabih frowned. "Of what?"

"Not of you, Rabih," Fatmeh explained, "of herself and the feelings she has for you."

"I don't understand."

"Rania's confused," Fatmeh said. "She had the rug pulled out from under her not that long ago and she's had to build herself back up, and do it alone . . . it's not that easy.

"She's still in that awkward place between life's stages . . . she's not in the old one and she's still struggling to get to the new one . . . but she will get there, of that I am sure."

There was a pause.

"Give it time, Rabih," she advised him. "That's all." She squeezed his hand reassuringly.

Rabih shrugged.

"Just time," Fatmeh repeated, "she'll come around."

"I hope so."

"And a little patience," she added quickly.

Upstairs the floorboards creaked.

"Rania's awake," Fatmeh said. "She'll be down soon. It probably wouldn't be the best idea for her to see us gossiping."

"No, probably not." Rabih drained his coffee cup.

"Rabih," Fatmeh said, catching his wrist as he got up, "stay in Cairo."

—⁂—

It was a beautiful day in March, yet Salah and Rabih were sitting in one of the darkened back rooms at El Fishawy. A waiter came in with fresh narghiles, glasses of hot, sweet mint tea, and plates of almonds and dates. After he left, Salah opened a map of the Hejaz and Rabih began to make a few notes.

Salah was just about to help himself to a juicy date, his hand hovering over a small bowl of the dried fruit, when a small furry creature jumped on the table, snatched the date, and ran off screeching with delight.

"You little minx!" Salah swore.

"Sorry about that, Salah." Charlie appeared out of nowhere. "George, give Salah his date back."

The monkey ambled back, looking ashamed, and handed the date to Salah.

"The monkey has a name?"

"Yes . . ."

"You gave a monkey a name?"

"He deserves one," Charles said, handing the monkey a few nuts to munch on. George beamed at Charles, showed him all his teeth, and scampered away.

"Where's Lawrence?"

"He should be here any minute."

"Here I am!" Lawrence announced. "Good afternoon, gentlemen. How is everyone today on these ides of March?"

"How are our guerillas doing?" Salah asked.

"Excellent!" Lawrence replied enthusiastically. "We've only just begun, but we're tying the Ottomans up nicely. They're expending an enormous amount of resources and sending more of their troops down to the Hejaz to defend the railway, which means they won't be able to send as many to the Western Front to help the Germans, or attack the Suez Canal."

"Is that the British strategy?" Rabih asked.

Lawrence nodded.

"So . . . it is as I have suspected all along," Salah started.

"What do you mean?"

"What you are saying is the British don't care about Arab indepen-dence at all . . . all they care about is defending the Suez and winning the war in Western Europe."

"Salah," Charlie said. "If the British and the Allies win, the Arabs will have their independence."

"You're sure about that?"

"Of course!" Lawrence said.

"I don't know, Lawrence," Salah said. "Something tells me that the Arabs will get buggered in the end. Even if the British win, they will not give Faisal an Arab state."

"What makes you say that?"

"Word on the street is that the British and French have already signed an agreement to split Arab land between themselves . . . they've promised the same piece of land twice, to the Arabs and to themselves," Salah said. "I've heard it's called the Asia Minor agreement."

"Salah, don't be silly," Lawrence said. "We've given our word. We won't go back on it."

"Please don't take me for a fool, Lawrence," Salah said. "If the British have not gone back on their word, then why and how did my friends all die?" Salah leaned forward.

"Salah . . . what happened to your friends was horrible . . ." Lawrence started.

"My friends were betrayed," Salah interrupted. "By the British and the French. Their heads were handed to Jemmal on a platter."

"Salah, please, I assure you that the Arabs will have their state."

"What makes you so sure?"

"Because I will give it to them."

Salah snorted and sat back in his chair, looking at Lawrence through narrowed eyes.

"Very well, Lawrence," Salah said. "Let's see you prove it. If I hear one word from Faisal that British gold or supplies are not getting to him, I swear, Lawrence, I will find you and you will answer for it."

"I will, Salah," Lawrence replied. "Now look, I have a plan. In addition to the guerilla attacks, I think we should attack Aqaba."

"The village?" Rabih said, surprised. "Why?"

"Because it's another port and while my 'irregulars' are doing a good job, the Turks are getting smarter about blocking supply routes to Faisal, and we need those to be open. Our intelligence sources say that the Turks may try and take back the ports of Jeddah and Yenbu."

"But how are you planning on taking it? The Germans must have U-boats in the gulf around Aqaba," Salah said.

"I'm going to go over land."

"You want to cross the Nefud Desert?" Rabih was incredulous. "You are mad indeed."

"I've got seasoned tribes with me. But, it's going to take me some time to convince the British command here to let me go with Aqaba."

"In the meantime, we need to keep distracting the Turks?" Charlie asked.

"Yes, we do."

"What if you make the Turks believe that you're headed straight up to Damascus?" Salah suggested. "They will start concentrating troops further north in Syria, which means troop concentration in Aqaba will be slim."

Charlie nodded his approval. Lawrence's frown turned to a smile.

"We need to start attacking the railway further north than we have been doing?" Rabih chimed in.

"That's it," Salah said.

"So, we need to look at the railway near Ma'an." Rabih pointed on the map.

"Lawrence, we can leave the guerilla tribesmen in the Hejaz and we can ride north to Syria to throw the Ottomans off," Charlie said. "And as soon as we get the go-ahead from General Murray for Aqaba, the tribesmen can start blowing up the railway in conjunction with the attack on Aqaba."

"But for now, we should do a little damage to the railway north, in Palestine, to throw the Turks off the scent of Aqaba," Salah said.

They all nodded.

"And, Lawrence, you need to turn up the volume," Salah said. "Why blow up just the tracks? Blow up the goddamn trains themselves."

"All right . . . with pleasure."

Salah sat back in his chair and took a puff of his narghile.

"Will you come with us, Salah? Rabih?" Lawrence asked.

"I'm in," Rabih said.

"Very well," Salah agreed, after a long pause.

—⁘—

Yvonne and Saydeh were deep in conversation, Fatmeh was writing, the usual shopkeepers were enjoying their morning coffee, and Rania was behind the bar when Takla flew into the café; she was shaking with anger.

"Where is that son of yours?" she barked at Saydeh, her eyes glinting with anger.

The café went quiet as everyone turned around to look at her.

"Calm down, Takla." Yvonne put a hand on her wrist.

But Takla yanked it away.

"I don't know where Salah is," Saydeh replied, her forehead knitting with worry at Takla's distress. "What's the matter? Maybe I can help?"

"No!" Takla turned on her. "You can't help!"

"But at least tell us what is the matter," Yvonne tried.

Rania silently put a glass of orange juice in front of Takla.

"Have a seat, Tante Takla," Rania urged softly. "Whatever it is, we'll work it out."

"No . . . this cannot be worked out," Takla said sadly, her shoulders sagging, tears filling her eyes.

"My Nassim is going to fight this war," Takla said, her voice breaking. "And it's all Salah's fault. He put all these nonsensical ideas about Arab freedom into his head and now he's leaving me and he's going . . ."

Silence fell on the farmhouse table. No one knew what to say.

"And he and Hisham are leaving . . . I don't know when . . . maybe even this week . . . with Salah and Rabih in a few days," Takla sobbed.

"Takla, take a deep breath," Yvonne encouraged.

Takla took several.

"Now tell us what is going on."

"Where are Salah and Rabih taking Nassim and Hisham?" Rania asked.

"I don't know . . . somewhere in the Hejaz," Takla sobbed.

"The Hejaz . . ."

"Why did Salah do this? What did I ever do to him to deserve his taking my only son away from me?"

No one knew what to say.

"Who is he to meddle in my life and Nassim's?" Takla shook her head sadly, tears forming rivulets down her cheeks. "He knows Nassim has no father . . . he has manipulated my son and filled him with all these crazy ideas. Isn't it enough that I lost my husband? Do I also have to lose my son?"

There was another long silence.

Rania went back to the kitchen. Rabih was in the back alley mixing whitewash to spruce up the inside and outside of the café. She crossed her arms and stood in the doorway and watched him for a few minutes. He stood up and was about to pick up the bucket when he saw her.

She was wearing a white cotton dress with multicolored polka dots. A piece of the same fabric was wrapped around her head to keep it out of her face as she worked. Her hair was tied in a loose, messy chignon.

"When were you going to tell me?" she asked.

He cocked his head to one side and put his hand in his pockets. "Tell you what?" he replied a bit sheepishly.

"That you were leaving," she snapped.

He remained silent.

"And on top of that . . . not just leaving, but leaving to go into the middle of a war."

Rabih shrugged.

"So when were you going to tell me?" she said.

"Today," Rabih muttered.

"When today? And you didn't think I would find out?" Rania said angrily. "This kind of news travels fast in the souk."

Rabih said nothing.

"When did you decide this?"

"Yesterday."

Rania didn't know why she felt so angry. After all, it was she who had decided to cool things off between them, so she really had no right to feel the way she did . . . but she couldn't help it.

"How can you just leave like this?" she cried. "You're going to leave the café half finished!" she accused him.

"No," he answered. "I am almost done. It will be finished before I go."

"Are you planning on coming back?" she asked, almost spitefully.

"I don't know when."

"I see," she said, tears of anger filled her eyes. "Fine!" She jutted out her chin, her head held proudly high.

"I need to get on with my work," Rabih said and picked up his bucket.

Rania stood aside and let him pass. As she watched him go through the kitchen, his shoulder muscles rippling as he balanced the heavy bucket, she wanted him to stop, turn around, and come back and take her in his arms and tell her everything was going to be all right. But he didn't and the tears she had been holding back spilled out, filling her eyes like big dark pools of salty water. Rania stepped out in the alley-way, her chest heaving from breathing heavily in an effort to push the tears back. She paced up and down, hoping the exercise would alleviate the heaviness she felt in her heart. But the heaviness only became stronger until it dropped like a cannon ball into the pit of her stomach. She let out a little cry and bit her own hand to stop herself from giving in to the big, huge sobs that she knew were roiling inside her. This damned war was taking him away. *God!* She looked up at the sky. *Why is this happening to me again?*

—⁓—

Fatmeh wrung her hands nervously as she sat in the kitchen waiting. In front of her was a telegram Charles had sent earlier that evening. She read it for the hundredth time. "*Need to see you. Important. Tonight at the café.*" Fatmeh had been sick with worry ever since she'd received it, wondering what was so important, going round and around in circles, creating all kinds of scenarios in her head, scaring herself half to death.

There was a gentle rap on the window. Fatmeh got up and hopped to the door on her crutches.

"How's the foot?" he asked.

"Healing," she replied.

"I really am sorry."

"About what?" Fatmeh smiled. "It wasn't your fault. It was mine."

Charles looked tense.

"Where is Rania?" he looked around.

"She is consoling the mother of a young boy who's decided to go join the Arab Revolt."

Charles rolled his eyes. "Nassim or Hisham?"

"Nassim," Fatmeh confirmed.

"What can I get you to drink?" Fatmeh offered, turning slowly to go through to the café.

"Let me help you."

She looked up at him and smiled. He put his arm around her waist and she draped hers around his neck.

"It's good to see you again," she ventured timidly.

"Yes," he murmured.

"So what is so urgent?" Fatmeh asked.

"Fatmeh . . . I'm being shipped out . . . to the Hejaz."

"To the war?"

"I am a soldier." He smiled.

"For how long?"

"I don't know."

"Charles . . .," her eyes filled with tears.

"I know . . ." He caressed her cheek. "I don't want to go, believe me. But I have to."

Fatmeh sank down onto the bench.

"I wanted to come here tonight and tell you myself," he added. "I was looking forward to seeing you, if only for a moment."

He took her hand in his and stared at it, caressing the soft mound of her palm with his thumb. She waited expectantly.

"Just . . . please wait for me." He looked into her eyes.

Noura's sewing business was booming. It had been only five months since she'd moved in with Saydeh the previous November, but word had spread quickly and she was now fixing, mending, and repairing the uniforms of the British Army soldiers. They loved her work, and especially appreciated her washing and ironing the uniforms before sending them back. Twice a week, Noura went to British Army headquarters and dropped off and picked up bags of work. The British captain in charge of uniforms had suggested that Noura come to work at the barracks, an offer that she was considering and had been trying to find a moment to talk to Salah about.

Noura was sitting at her sewing machine in her attic atelier, rethreading the needle on her machine. She was so deep in concentration that she jumped when she felt hands on her shoulders. She took off her wire-rimmed glasses and turned around to see Salah looking down at her.

"Salah!"

"Hello, my beautiful Noura," he said, bending down to give her a gentle kiss on her lips. "Come sit with me in the living room."

"What's the matter?" Noura asked.

"I have to talk to you," he said over his shoulder as he went down the spiral staircase. Noura followed him down, her eyebrows knitted.

Salah took her hands in his when they sat down on the sofa.

"This is going to be bad," Noura said.

"Noura, I'm going back out to the Hejaz with Lawrence and Charlie and Rabih."

"Why?"

"Why? You're asking me why?"

"Yes, I am," Noura said sarcastically.

"Noura, I have to go. Lawrence and I have a new plan that we think will propel the Arab Army further up into Palestine."

"I don't care! And what am I supposed to do? Wait here and wonder every day if you're going to come back to me or not?"

"Of course I'm going to come back."

"Salah, there is a very good chance that you will not come back."

Salah clicked his tongue. "Of course I will."

"No!" Noura yanked her hands back. "I will not let you go. I cannot lose the man I love . . . not a second time."

"I have to finish this. I have to see it through."

"I hate this revolt," Noura steamed. "It has taken everything and everyone from me."

"Noura, I don't like it either," Salah said. "I never wanted to be involved. I have gotten dragged into it."

"Fine! Then if you're going, so am I."

"Don't be silly!"

"I am not. If you are going to fight for the idea of an Arab state, which is what Khaled also wanted, then I will go with you."

"Noura . . ."

"No, Salah! Don't patronize me," Noura said.

"Noura, I cannot, in all good conscience, take you out into the desert and have you fight."

"I'm sure there are other things for me to do."

"No."

"I will not sit here in this atelier and sew military uniforms while you are out in the desert fighting."

"Noura, you cannot come with me. I will never forgive myself if something happens to you."

"I am not going to sit by idly."

Salah remained quiet.

"Salah, this is not fair."

"Noura . . . this is a war I am going into."

"Salah, need I remind you that it was I who cut the cables from the dynamite bundles around Rania's? I am not scared."

"Have you not thought about your daughter?"

"Siran will be fine here with your mother."

"And if something should happen to you?"

"She will be fine here with your mother," Noura repeated.

"Noura, what you are suggesting is crazy . . ."

"Then go! Get out! Go to hell, Salah!" Noura shouted. "I don't need you. I can look after myself and Siran just like I have been doing."

Salah got up and walked to the staircase.

"This is the end of our engagement," Noura said.

Salah stopped.

"If you go to the Hejaz on this damned foolish scheme, I will not be here when you come back."

Salah looked at Noura, whose chin jutted out defiantly.

"Noura . . . aren't you being a little dramatic?"

"You choose, Salah . . . it's me or the revolt that you claim was never something you wanted to get involved in," she said bitterly.

Silently, Salah turned and walked down the stairs. *She'll come around. She will. She has to.*

Fatmeh walked out of Rania's Café and looked left and right. She knew Walid was having her watched. She'd caught too many glimpses of his thug friends in the past few days for it to be a coincidence. She was on her way to the mosque. She wanted to speak to the imam.

It was a particularly windy day, with unexpected gusts blowing through the alleys and lanes of the souk. Fatmeh pulled her abaya close around her as she hurried up Zuqaq al-Hamra toward the main artery of the souk, which would take her to Midan Al-Hussein. As she turned a corner, a man stepped out in front of her. Startled, she took in a sharp breath. *"A'afwan,"* she muttered as she tried to skirt by. But he stepped in front of her again. Fatmeh tried again, but he wouldn't let her go by.

"Look out!" she suddenly shouted, and when he looked up, Fatmeh slipped by him and tried to run. But even though he'd been momentarily distracted, he was fast. He caught her by the folds of the abaya that billowed behind her. He held her arms behind her back, pinning her to him.

"*Shoo baddak?*" she asked, nervously. "What do you want?"

"A word to the wise, Madame Fatmeh," he growled in her ear. "Don't do anything you're going to be sorry for."

He twisted her arm behind her back, causing her to cringe in pain.

"No more flirting with the enemy," he said harshly.

"I . . . uh . . . let me go!" she cried.

"Do you hear me, Madame Fatmeh?" He shook her.

"Please, you're hurting my arm," she grimaced, as he twisted it even more tightly behind her.

"I would stay away from men with monkeys, if I were you," he sneered. "And no more secret car drives . . . we wouldn't want you to do worse than sprain an ankle."

"Let me go!" she cried louder.

"Did you hear me, Madame Fatmeh?" he said gruffly, his tone threatening. "Otherwise, this is what you'll see . . ."

And catching both of her hands in one of his, he drew out a jeweled dagger and swiped it from left to right in front of her neck.

Fatmeh swallowed, petrified. *Ya Allah*, she prayed. *Please save me. Do not let me die here today at the hands of this scoundrel.* Suddenly, in the distance she saw Rania walking up the lane.

"Rania!" she cried with all her might. "Help me!"

Suddenly, the man's hand was on her mouth, muffling her screams. She tried to fight and bit his hand as he dragged her away into another, even smaller, alleyway. *I'm going to die*, Fatmeh thought. *Or worse, he will rape me and then kill me.*

Fatmeh fought as hard as she could. But he was too strong for her. Tears welled in her eyes.

He dragged her down and put his hairy forearm on her chest and mouth, pinning her to the ground, preventing her from screaming. He pulled up her abaya, but there was too much material. He pulled out his dagger and ripped it open. Using his free hand he began to pull up the tunic she wore underneath.

She felt his hand on her inner thigh. She tried to scream but her voice stuck in her throat. As he fumbled with his pants, his forearm slipped and moved off Fatmeh's mouth. She let out a blood-curdling scream before bringing her teeth down to bite him with all her strength.

The man screamed in agony and rolled off her. Fatmeh somehow got to her feet and grabbed his dagger, holding it to his neck.

"It seems as if the game has changed," she said, drawing on every last ounce of courage she had, her eyes glinting.

"Don't you ever dare come near me again," Fatmeh heard herself say in a voice, which, when she thought back on the incident, didn't sound like her own.

"I want you to take a message to my husband . . . You tell him to watch his back. And you . . . ," she spat, "next time I will do worse than just bite you."

And with that, she kicked the man in his groin. The man groaned, rolling on the ground. Fatmeh walked away, her fingers wrapped tightly around his dagger. Her heart was still pounding and she shook from the adrenaline coursing through her.

"Fatmeh!" Rania came running around the corner. "Oh, thank Allah!" she muttered, taking her in her arms. Fatmeh stood, her arms limply by her side, as all the energy drained out of her. If it hadn't been for Rania's arms, she would have fallen to the ground in shock.

"Where is he?" Rania looked around, but the man had disappeared. "What happened?" she looked at her.

Fatmeh stared blankly in front of her. Slowly, Rania took the dagger from her.

"Fatmeh!" Rania shook her, realizing she was in shock. "Fatmeh!" she shouted.

Finally, Fatmeh looked up at her. Recognizing Rania, her eyes filled with tears and she clung to her.

"It's all right." Rania soothed her. "Whatever happened, it's all right. Did he hurt you?"

Fatmeh said nothing.

"But he tried?"

She nodded.

"You're all right, apart from the fright he gave you?"

She nodded again.

Rania inhaled deeply before letting it out, her shoulders sagging with relief.

"Come . . . I'm going to take you home. Can you walk?"

"Yes."

But when Fatmeh took a step, her legs gave way and she stumbled. Quickly Rania put her arm around her, holding her close.

"Rania . . . ," Fatmeh began, "Walid knows about Charles. He sent this man to threaten me. I was on my way to see the imam this morning . . ."

"Why?"

"I want a divorce."

CHAPTER FIFTEEN

A month after the meeting at El Fishawy, in mid-April 1917, Charles, Salah, Rabih, Nassim, and Hisham all boarded a train, along with a handful of other men from Charles' Special Forces unit and a platoon of soldiers who were headed toward Gaza. All the windows in the train car were open, but the heat was nonetheless stifling. The train was carrying ammunition, food, water, and other supplies for the expeditionary forces under General Archibald Murray, who was waging the Mesopotamia and Palestine campaigns against the Ottomans. So far, the British had fared well in Mesopotamia, wresting Baghdad from the Turks, but in Palestine, they suffered great losses in the first and second battles of Gaza and fell back. The British were currently regrouping near Beersheba.

"Forty winks," Charles announced and pulled his cap's visor down over his nose, crossed his arms, leaned his head against the window, and went to sleep.

"God! It's really hot!" Hisham complained, his face already drenched in sweat, the handkerchief he wore around his neck soaking. "How can he sleep in this heat?"

"Better get used to it," Nassim said.

"You can't get used to heat," Hisham scoffed.

"Of course you can," Nassim argued.

Hisham looked to Salah for help.

"Actually, he's right," Salah said.

They all felt silent, swaying with the movement of the train as it chugged along.

"I kind of like this uniform," Hisham said as he smoothed down the jacket of his new khaki brown military uniform. "Tante Noura sewed my name inside," he added, proudly. "I wonder why that is."

"So in case you die, they'll know who you are and can tell your family," Nassim said.

"That's a rather morbid explanation," Charles commented from under his cap.

"But isn't it true?" Nassim asked.

"Sort of, I suppose," Charles continued, still pretending to nap.

"But what happens if my uniform gets torn and I borrow Rabih's," Hisham said, "and I get killed, then whoever finds me will think I'm Rabih and will tell his family he's dead."

"And that has happened," Charles confirmed. "They try to be very careful about it, but in a war like this, it's inevitable."

"But that's terrible," Nassim said.

"So, Charles, I bet the girls love a man in uniform . . . ," Hisham interjected.

Charles grinned, his cap still on his eyes.

"They do, eh!" Hisham said excitedly. "Heh, heh! What do you think of that, brother?" he gently punched Nassim in the arm.

"You have such a one-track mind." Nassim turned to him and went back to poring over the small leather notebook he was writing in.

"What is that?" Hisham asked, admiring the reflection of his uniform in the window.

"A diary."

"Since when did you start keeping a diary?"

"I've just started."

Hisham raised his eyebrows.

"I might keep one too," he added.

Silence fell in the car. Apart from the voices of a couple of soldiers, everyone, it seemed, was dozing or napping.

"How far is it to Suez?" Hisham asked.

"About eighty-seven miles," Rabih said.

"What do we do after that?"

"After that, we cross the Sinai by camel." Charles sat up and adjusted his cap.

"All these guys will come with us?" Hisham asked.

"No . . . ," Charles clarified. "The soldiers stay in Suez, but my men come with us to Aqaba."

"What does your group do?" Rabih asked.

"We're all part of the British Army, but we're trained to do special operations . . ."

"What happens to the soldiers in Suez?" Nassim asked.

"They won't stay in Suez," Charles said. "They'll go north to Beersheba in Palestine and hook up with Murray."

"It's been tough going for Murray in the Sinai, hasn't it?" Rabih said.

"It has," Charles agreed. "He's tried to take Gaza twice now, but hasn't been able to . . . yet. I've heard they may bring Allenby in."

Charles excused himself and left to go talk to his colleagues. Salah dozed. Rabih moved next to the window and leaned against it, idly staring out at the countryside that whizzed by in a screen of steam that rose from the bottom of the locomotive. Hisham crossed his arms across his chest and leaned his head back against the back of the bench, staring at the ceiling. And Nassim continued poring over his map, making copious notes in his notebook.

A couple of hours later, the train chugged noisily into the city of Suez. Nassim stuck his head out of the window as they approached the station, the train whistling as it pulled up along the crowded platform.

"This is it, boys!" Charles said. He hoisted his backpack over his shoulder and climbed down from the train. Outside on the platform, he waved to a small, wiry man dressed in Bedouin robes.

"Gentlemen, this is Hammoudi, our guide," he announced, after giving the man a big hug. "He knows the Sinai like no one."

"Do you think he'll teach us to ride a camel?" Hisham whispered to Nassim as they followed him out the station.

"Have you really never ridden a camel before?" Nassim hissed.

"No!" Hisham said. "I've lived in El-Khalili all my life. Where would I have ridden a camel?"

"There are camels in the souk."

"And they belong to the people who come to the souk, do their business, and leave," Hisham retorted. "They don't exactly rent their camels out for rides like at a fairground."

"Come on!" Nassim clapped him on the back. "You'll learn. It's not hard."

Hisham made a face at his friend's back, rushing after the little group when he realized he would be left behind if he didn't keep up.

—⁓—

"All right, everyone here knows the drill!" Charles addressed his team at the military barracks in Suez. "We travel by night. We rest by day. We leave tonight. Any questions? Good! Platoon dismissed!" Charles stood at ease. "Everyone back here in three hours. We have to be mounted and ready to move out before the sun dips.

"Now, Nassim and Hisham," he said, approaching them. "Hammoudi here is going to give you a quick lesson in camel riding."

"What? Now?" Hisham looked terrified.

Hisham looked up at the sky and put his hands together. "Dear God!"

"Come on, Hisham!" Salah put his arm congenially around the younger man. "Camels are not that bad."

"Yeah . . . they bite people!"

"Look, Hisham," Salah said, "before we go any further, I need to know that you're ready. This is not a game and it is not about how many women you get wearing a uniform."

He took a deep breath.

"This is war. It's serious. I can't guarantee that you won't get hurt. I can't guarantee that you'll come back alive."

Hisham looked embarrassed.

"If you're doing this because Nassim is," Salah said, "that is not enough of a reason to go to Aqaba."

"I'm not," Hisham said, studying his toes.

"Look boy, when you fight for something, when you commit to giving your life for it, you have to believe it. It would be a waste of your life to throw it away on something you don't feel really matters to you," Charles added.

Hisham remained silent.

"Do you believe in the Arab Revolt?" Charles asked.

Hisham nodded.

"And you know what it stands for?"

"Yes."

"And you feel strongly enough about a free Arab nation to go out and maybe have to give your life for the cause."

"Yes."

"Good, then buck up, stop whining, and go do it. Dismissed, soldier."

That evening, just when the sun started to set, a caravan set out across the desert. A total of a dozen camels in single file padded over the dunes, starting the hundred-and-fifty-mile trek to the Gulf of Aqaba.

Salah looked back at Hisham.

"Are you all right?" he cried out, giving him the thumbs-up sign, uncertain that he had heard him. Hisham returned the thumbs-up.

Salah looked out at the scenery. It took his breath away. The desert stretched out like a wavy, sandy sea in front of him. Behind him, the sun was setting, its fading light changing the colors of the dunes from sandy blonde to deep chocolate and orange. There were occasional rocks and a few limestone hills dotting the landscape, but nothing else. Above, the sky was still blue with a few stray clouds.

"How long until we get to Eilat?" Salah asked Charles when they stopped in the early hours of the morning near a well for a short break.

"In a week, maybe a bit more." Charles came and joined him on the sand around the fire that Hammoudi had started to keep away the chill of the desert night.

"It's beautiful out here, isn't it?" Charles looked up into the star-covered sky, taking a sip from a small flask.

"Yes," Salah agreed, taking a drag of a cigarette he had just lit.

"The desert can't be claimed or owned," Charles said. "Here you don't belong to anyone or to any country. You become one with the desert. It's a place that demands your complete faith because you disappear into it and it can keep you alive or destroy you."

"Whiskey?" Charles offered his flask to Salah.

"I don't mind if I do."

"Things going to be okay with Noura?"

"She was pretty angry."

"But you know that you are right. This is no place for a woman," Charles reassured him.

"Noura's tough."

"I know, but still. It's harsh out here. And it's going to get harsher once we start north."

"She'll calm down."

"What about Fatmeh?" Salah added. "How did she take the news?"

"I'm a soldier, Salah. This is my job."

—⁓—

While Salah and Charles sat chatting around the fire, Rabih was sitting at the top of a sand dune, looking up at the stars, calmly smoking a cigarette.

"*Ya Allah!*" he heard Hisham's voice.

Rabih rolled his eyes. He wanted to be alone with his thoughts.

"Rabih!" Hisham said, surprised to see him. "What are you doing here?"

"I came up here to look at the stars." Rabih took a deep drag of his cigarette.

Hisham sat down heavily next to Rabih. "My ass hurts," he said. "Does yours?"

Rabih shook his head.

"You're thinking about Tante Rania, aren't you?" Hisham asked.

Rabih continued to smoke silently.

"Why are women so weird?" he mused.

Rabih turned his head to look at him and stared back up at the sky.

"Why do they play these silly games?" Hisham continued. "They say 'no' when they mean 'yes,' they say 'yes,' when they mean 'maybe,' and they say 'maybe' when they mean 'no.' Why can't they say what they mean?"

"You really think that?" Rabih asked him, breaking into a smile.

"Yeah, I do. Why can't they be straightforward like us? It would just be so much easier."

Rabih chuckled.

"Can I have a cigarette?" Hisham asked.

"You sure you want one?" Rabih asked, pulling out a packet from his breast pocket.

Hisham nodded.

They sat together silently smoking.

"Rabih, what does it mean when you can't see the stars anymore?" Hisham was lying on his side, his head propped up on his hand.

"What do you mean?"

"See over there." Hisham pointed towards the horizon. "There are no stars there."

Rabih sat up and peered into the distance. Suddenly, he jumped up. "God help us!"

"What? What's wrong?" Hisham stood up.

"Hisham . . . run!" Rabih said urgently. "Come on!"

"What?"

The two ran down the sand dune, sinking into the sand, tumbling down to the bottom. Rabih ran toward the little group sitting around the fire near the well.

"Sandstorm!" he screamed.

For a split second, no one moved.

"Move!" Rabih shouted. "Cover the well! Take cover!"

"Rabih!" Charles said loudly. "Take care of Nassim and Hisham. Salah and I will help Hammoudi with the animals."

"Where do we shelter, Rabih?" Nassim asked, his voice shaking.

Rabih looked around. There was nothing. "Cover your faces," he ordered. "Now look, I am going to tie us all together and we have to keep moving. We can't stop. If you do, the sand will build up around us and lock us in. We will all suffocate."

"What are the others going to do?" Hisham asked.

"I don't know," Rabih tied Hisham's hands to Nassim's.

"And the camels?"

"Camels are used to it . . . I'm sure Hammoudi has been through this and knows how to handle them."

"Now, be careful . . . don't open your mouths," Rabih told them, just before the sand rolled in.

Suddenly and without warning, the storm was upon them. The sound of the wind was deafening. Columns of sand whirled around like individual tornadoes, and more sand flowed along the ground like a rising river. It felt as though the entire surface of the earth was rising. Pebbles struck their knees, their ankles, their faces. Grains of fine sand found their way into their clothes. The sky was completely invisible and they couldn't even see their own hands in front of them.

"How long is this going to go on?" Hisham screamed, trying to make himself heard. But he couldn't say anymore. His throat filled immediately with sand and he began to cough violently. He tried to swallow but he couldn't. He tried to spit, but he just got more sand in his mouth. Suddenly, he felt he couldn't breathe. He couldn't get any oxygen. Every time he tried, it was sand.

"Nassim! Nassim!" he thought he heard Rabih's voice in the wind. "I can't hold you."

Hisham was starting to lose consciousness when he felt hands around his neck and a leather water skin was pressed to his lips. "Drink and spit," he heard a voice say. Hisham tried, but he couldn't. He was suffocating. He began to feel weaker and weaker until everything went black.

—𝔪—

The sun was high in the sky when Rabih opened his eyes. He shut them again quickly when a few grains of sand got in. He used his headscarf to clean his face as best he could. He looked around. He saw a mound covered by sand to his left and quickly scrambled over. It was Nassim. *Oh God!* Rabih sank back on his heels, tears smarting his eyes. *Hisham . . . where's Hisham? Please . . . I can't have lost both of them.*

Rabih walked around under the hot sun. Every time he saw an embankment or a small hill, he ran to it and started digging with his hands. He prayed silently. But Rabih couldn't find him. The sun was slowly moving toward midday. The sand would soon be scorching.

He had to somehow find Charles and the rest of the party. *I'll just sit down here for a minute*, Rabih thought. His head was spinning. His eyesight was getting blurry. He blinked but he still couldn't focus. He started to feel nauseous and weak. His heart was beating furiously and he felt his entire body break out in sweat. He couldn't see, even though he knew his eyes were open. Suddenly, as the blood drained from his head, he fell on his knees and, before he could do anything about it, he lost consciousness.

—⁓—

Slowly, Rabih opened his eyes. He was able to make out shapes hovering over him, but he could not make out what they were. He heard sounds, but they were unintelligible, ranging from whispers to screams. They didn't even sound human. Rabih floated back into oblivion.

When he next opened his eyes, there were no shapes or sounds. He groaned and tried to move. Suddenly, the shapes were back.

"Rabih!" he heard his name, but it sounded like an echo in a large, empty room. "Can you open your eyes?"

Rabih tried to open his eyes wide.

"Rabih do you know who you are?" a voice sounded.

Rabih nodded.

"He's all right," the voice pronounced. "He's coming around."

Rabih felt cold liquid wetting his lips and he slowly licked them. He felt water trickle into his mouth. It felt good as it spread across his tongue, moistening it, making it come alive again. Slowly, the shapes in front of Rabih's eyes began to take a form. It was Hammoudi. Rabih tried to lift his head, but the Bedouin forced him back down. Rabih watched as he took a small glass vial out of the inside of his robes, popped it open and put it to Rabih's lips. "Drink," he ordered. Rabih didn't have the strength to argue. Whatever the mixture was, it tasted vile, but in moments, he could feel his blood circulating again, the oxygen rushing to nourish his brain.

"He will sleep now," Rabih heard Hammoudi say. "When he comes to, he will be fine."

Rabih's eyes closed again.

When he opened them again, Salah was sitting next to him.

"What happened?"

"Severe dehydration and near suffocation."

Rabih closed his eyes and reopened them, relieved.

"Where are we?"

"Near an oasis due north of Saint Catherine's Monastery."

"Did we lose any time?"

"No," Salah shook his head. "We carried you on a stretcher hoisted between two camels. We'll be in Eilat in two days."

Rabih nodded.

"Salah . . . I lost them. Both of them."

"Yes."

Rabih tried to sit up, but immediately felt dizzy.

"Easy now, brother."

"There was nothing you or anyone could have done. A sandstorm is a sandstorm."

"I could have held onto them . . ."

"You can't blame yourself . . ."

"What a waste of young lives," Rabih turned away in dismay. He lay back down on the camp cot and stared up at the roof of the striped tent.

"I'm sorry, Salah,' Rabih put his head in his hands. "I am so sorry."

—⁓—

The following afternoon, just before reaching Eilat, a port on the northernmost tip of the Gulf of Aqaba, they came across a small encampment of Bedouin tents next to an inland oasis where Charles halted the caravan and dismounted.

"Well, well, well!" A man dressed in Bedouin, desert robes came out of one of the tents and stood smiling, his arms across his chest. He wore a big white headdress held in place with a black, braided agal around the crown, a long white tunic, and a white linen cloak. A sword and dagger hung from a belt at his waist.

"Hello, boys!" Lawrence walked toward Charles, Salah, and Rabih. "Come on in. How was the trip?"

"Long. We ran into a sandstorm just after we left Suez."

"To start a journey in a sandstorm is good luck, you know," Lawrence said.

"Not this time, Lawrence," Salah said sadly. "We lost Nassim, and Hisham . . . one of my boys from the El-Khalili."

"Oh dear." Lawrence bit his bottom lip. "I'm sorry."

"So what's the plan, Sir?" Charles asked.

"We're going to give the Turks a taste of their own medicine." Lawrence rubbed his hands with glee. "We'll plant a few tulips and light up the skies over Ottoman Syria. You all ready to leave?"

They nodded.

"We leave at 2300 hours." Lawrence opened the flap of the tent. "In the meantime, let me introduce you to Auda Abu Tayi."

—⁂—

Auda abu Tayi was a formidable man. He was short, standing no more than five feet six inches tall, but muscular and very strong. Despite his height, he had a huge presence and charisma. He was dark-skinned, had curly black hair that was always covered with a white headscarf, and sported a slim moustache and a beard that was trimmed razor thin along his very angular jaw line. But the most intimidating thing about Auda was his stare. He had a pair of piercing blue eyes that glinted like steel and forced even the toughest of men to look away. He was a skilled swordsman, quick with his dagger, and an accomplished camel rider. When he fought, he was cold and fearless and had earned a reputation of being the most formidable warrior in the Hejaz. He'd been married twenty-eight times.

It was just past the evening prayers and Auda was in his tent. It was simple and didn't have much inside, apart from a carpet, a few cushions, a couple of small, colorful leather stools and a low table. On a small brass table next to him was a tray that held a terracotta jug and several small cups. Relaxing, leaning back against the cushions, Auda was smoking a narghile, his blue eyes staring at the water bubbling at the bottom of the pipe. He was wearing a white tunic, tied at the waist with a thick, multicolored cummerbund, in which he carried a dagger. He wore a short brown sleeveless jacket over his tunic, across which he wore two crisscrossing leather bullet holders.

"May I, Sheikh?" Lawrence pulled up the flap of the tent and stuck his head inside.

Auda's face brightened. "Tell me something good."

"I have someone for you to meet," Lawrence said.

"If it's not a woman with blonde hair and blue eyes, I'm not interested! It's just not that easy to meet a beautiful woman anymore," Auda complained with a mischievous grin, "especially not here in the Hejaz."

Auda turned his intense blue gaze on Rabih and Salah.

"Allow me to introduce Salah Masri and Rabih Farhat, Sheikh. Salah was the chief engineer for the Hejaz Railway and Rabih was his architect. They are going to help you continue harassing the Turks."

"Yes indeed . . ." Auda took a long drag of his narghile. "It is one of my favorite pastimes. Come in, come in!" Auda got up and warmly greeted Salah and Rabih. "Let's get you some nice cold water to drink."

While Auda was being hospitable, Lawrence opened a map of the Hejaz and smoothed it out on the carpet.

"Sheikh, I'm sorry to interrupt, but we need to get to work."

"Rush, rush, rush!" Auda teased. "You're always rushing, Lawrence. Let us humor the Englishman, shall we, brothers?"

They all sat down in front of the map.

"Right, now here we are," Salah began. "And here, between Mudawarra and Ma'an, Sheikh." Salah made a little circle on the map with his index finger.

Auda rubbed his chin.

"This building . . . ," Salah said, pointing on the map, "is where the Turks keep ammunitions and supplies as a backup for Aqaba . . . and these tracks here are rounded . . ."

Auda listened carefully as Salah and Rabih laid out the plan for him.

—◊—

"What are our orders, Sir?" Charles asked Lawrence as they saddled up the camels.

"Auda is going to gather the tribes here, and while we await the official green light for Aqaba, we want to make the Turks believe that the Arab Army and the British forces are headed to Syria now and that we are targeting Damascus or Aleppo instead of Aqaba."

"And is that what we are going to do, Sir?" Charles mounted his camel.

"Yes . . . besides being a reconnaissance mission."

"It will be a good way to find out if the troop concentrations and supply lines have remained somewhat similar to the information I stole a year ago," Salah added, strapping the belt tightly around his camel's belly.

"Agreed. Besides, Faisal also wants to know how many of the tribes further north he can count on," Lawrence said.

"So if I understand you correctly, if the Turks believe that the Arabs and British are going north, it will make them reinforce their troops in the Syrian province and will leave the Hejaz lean?" Rabih asked.

"That's right." Charles nodded.

"Is there a garrison at Aqaba?" Rabih asked.

"Not really." Charlie shrugged. "It's a small village as you know. But the Turks keep a three-hundred-man garrison at the mouth of the Wadi Itm just in case there's an attack from the Sinai."

"Although didn't the British Navy shell Aqaba?" Salah asked.

Lawrence nodded. "And," he added, "last year, they landed a marine platoon ashore, but I think they decided that a sea attack was impossible."

"There are no beaches there to land the ships," Charlie interjected. "No harbor."

"Now . . . ," Lawrence said, changing the subject, "how do we drop our first hint to the Turks about Damascus being our next target?"

Riding on the back of one of his camels and with another in tow, Hammoudi approached the Turkish garrison at Wadi Itm, a shattered chasm of red and black rock on the outskirts of Aqaba, facing the desert. A group of soldiers was sitting around a campfire.

Hammoudi whispered to his camel and she made a low-pitched "*nuuuuur*" sound and spat.

"Have you no manners, spitting like that?" Hammoudi slapped her rump.

"Hey! Who's there?" One of the soldiers around the fire got up and came toward the camels.

"Hold your fire." Hammoudi raised his hands.

"Dismount the camel . . . slowly." The soldier aimed his rifle at Hammoudi.

"Who are you?" the Turkish soldier shouted.

"Hammoudi."

"That doesn't mean anything to me. What are you doing here?"

"I live here."

"What do you mean?"

"I live in the desert."

"This is the Turkish garrison. You have no business being here."

"Sorry. I was trying to avoid Auda Abu Tayi's camp. There was a lot of commotion there."

"Really? What's that wily Arab up to?"

"He and that Englishman, the one they call Lawrence of Arabia, are planning a big attack with the Arab and British Army on Damascus."

"What?" the Turkish soldier choked. "Damascus?"

"Or maybe Aleppo."

"Are you sure?" the Turk said, wide-eyed.

Hammoudi nodded.

"You!" the Turkish soldier pointed at one of the others sitting around the fire. "You take over here. I have to deliver this news to the camp."

—m—

Much later that night, in the early hours of the morning, four camels set out in single file from Auda's camp, padding softly on the sand dunes, heading north into the Negev Desert.

May in the Negev was almost unbearable. As much as they could, they traveled by night and rested by day.

"It's lucky you know the wells and oases in the area," Rabih said when they stopped on the first night next to a small pool of water.

"Yes, it does come in handy." Lawrence chuckled, taking off his headscarf. "Charles!" he called out. "Anything?"

"I think our little trick worked." Charles came and sat down, taking a long drink of the cool water that was fed from somewhere deep inside the earth.

"Are they following?"

"Someone is," Charles confirmed. "They're about three hours behind us."

"Do you know who they are?" Rabih asked, taking a piece of bread out of the backpack he was carrying.

"Bedouins probably," Charles said.

"Why wouldn't they send their own?" Rabih asked.

"Because no one, apart from the people who live in the desert, are really prepared for it," Lawrence told him.

"Besides, the Turks still have a few Bedouins on their payroll," Charles added.

"Think they'll be a problem?" Rabih took a bite of bread.

"I shouldn't think so," Lawrence said.

"They might try harassing us, but won't do much more than that," Charles said.

Charles was right. They had a couple of minor skirmishes with the Bedouins following them, but they were no more than scare tactics to put them on edge and, a few days later, they reached Gaza.

"We're still several days from Damascus," Charles commented. They were sitting in Matouk, a small restaurant popular with the soldiers.

"I was thinking the same," Lawrence agreed.

"It doesn't matter," Salah said, "the more time we take, the more convinced they'll be that Damascus is the real target."

"Well, well, well," they heard a voice behind them.

All four turned around to see Musa Nusair smiling down at them. Salah jumped up first. "What are you doing here?"

"*Marhaba*, brothers!"

"Sit down, please! Pull up a chair!" Salah beckoned him. "Waiter! We have one more in our party."

"What are you doing here?" Charlie asked.

"I'm on my usual rounds." Musa stuffed his pipe with tobacco. "I've got some cargo I need to get to Ahmed Pasha in Beirut."

"Are you sailing to Beirut?" Salah suddenly sat upright in his chair.

"Yes, tomorrow morning," Musa replied. "Why?"

"Can you take us?"

"What?" Musa asked.

"Us . . . the four of us?"

"Why do you want to go to Beirut?" Musa said loudly. "Sorry . . . ," he said, immediately looking around to see if there were any unsavory characters lurking.

"Beirut first and then on to Damascus," Salah's voice boomed loudly.

Musa looked at him oddly. "Aren't you supposed to be in the Hejaz with Faisal?" he whispered.

"Diversionary tactic." Charles winked. "We want the Turks to think that we're the advance team for Faisal's army marching into Syria. We want them to take their eyes off Aqaba."

"But won't they arrest you as soon as you get in?" Musa asked.

"Not if they can't actually find us."

"You want to go into Turkish Syria? Have you lost it? How do you expect to get in and out?"

"Very, very carefully!"

Charlie winked, grinning.

CHAPTER SIXTEEN

Noura came downstairs to the first floor, her daughter in the crook of one arm and a bag on her shoulder.

"Tante Saydeh, would you mind looking after Siran for a little while?"

"Not at all."

"I'm going to be working at the British Army barracks today."

"I wish you would reconsider." Saydeh sniffed, taking the baby from Noura. "I don't think it's proper for you to be working there in the middle of all those men."

"Tante, I'm enjoying what I'm doing. And they are paying me very well."

"Were you not happy with the work we were getting for you from the souk?"

"I was, Tante," Noura said. "And please, I am very grateful. And I'm still doing it. But I don't think there's any harm in expanding the business."

Saydeh shrugged.

"Who knows where this will take me?" Noura said. "Perhaps one of the officers' wives will have me make something for her?"

Saydeh pursed her lips disapprovingly.

"Well, I had best get going or I will be late."

Noura looked at herself in the mirror as she put on her headscarf. She put on an abaya, but then with a defiant lift of her chin took it off and left it on the chair. She was wearing a new skirt and shirt she had made for herself and she wanted to show it off.

Outside, she walked briskly toward the Al-Hussein Mosque, where she took the tram that dropped her off at the entrance to Gezira Island. It was an easy walk from there to the British Army barracks on Zemalek.

She slipped into a bench on the tram and slid down toward the window. It was a cloudy day, but she still loved looking at the wide, tree-lined boulevards. Two men got on at the next stop. Noura glanced at them and then turned her attention back to the road. One of them came and sat down next to her. And from the corner of her eye, she saw the other one sit directly behind her. The man next to her was carrying a box wrapped in brown paper and tied with string that he held under his arm.

At the next stop, the same two men got off the train. Noura thought it odd, but shrugged it off. A couple of stops later, she gathered her bag and got up to leave. Her foot accidentally hit something. She looked down. It was the same brown paper package that the man sitting next to her had been holding. She bent down to pick it up. There was no name on it. She turned it around, wondering what it was. *It's probably a book or a box.* As they approached her stop, she handed it to the conductor and told him that it belonged to a man who'd been sitting next to her and that he'd gotten off a couple of stops before.

The tram slowed. Noura waited on the exit step until it came to a complete halt. Just as she stepped onto the street, she heard an odd hissing sound. She turned around. Suddenly, there was a huge explosion and Noura felt herself thrown to the ground. Fire, smoke, and debris engulfed her. She tried to keep her wits about her, but she couldn't. The last thing she remembered was the pain that shot through her entire body.

—⚬—

COME TO CAIRO IMMEDIATELY. NOURA BADLY HURT.

—⚬—

The *Tree of Life* left Gaza as soon as Salah received the telegram. It was decided that Lawrence, Charlie, and Rabih would continue on to Beirut and wait there for Salah.

Salah was ashen when they pulled into port at Suez.

"Courage, brother." Musa squeezed Salah's shoulder.

"It's all my fault, Nusair." Salah covered his face with his hands. "They went after her because of what I'm doing. First my friends, my mother, and now the woman I love. This is too close, Nusair."

"Come . . . let's get to the train station."

—⁂—

At the British Army hospital, Salah was immediately escorted to Noura's bed.

"What happened, Doctor?"

"A bomb exploded on a tram."

Salah's heart dropped into his stomach. "How bad is it?"

"She was getting off the tram but she was caught in the peripheral blast," the doctor said.

Salah clenched his jaw in anger.

"She broke two ribs and her right arm, and her right hand was crushed by someone who fell on top of her. There were burns on her face and body. She was badly bruised from the fall and there is a nasty gash near her spine that we are monitoring. We don't know how deep it is yet. I'm hoping there is no nerve damage to the spine. If there is, she may not be able to walk. But she was luckier than all the other people on the tram. At least she's alive."

Tears appeared in Salah's eyes. He took a deep breath to hold them back.

"It's all right, Mr. Masri. Would you like a moment before you see her?"

"I'm sorry, Doctor," Salah said. "This was such a shock."

"Yes, I'm sure it was. She is in there," he indicated the room.

—⁂—

Salah swallowed when he saw Noura. She was lying back against the pillows, her eyes closed. She was wearing a white hospital gown. Her arm was in a cast, her forehead and chin were bandaged. There were cuts on her cheeks and dark black shadows under her eyes. *How dare they?* His anger rose. *Erdogan will pay for this.*

Salah went to her side and looked down at her, gently caressing her hand.

She turned her head, opening her eyes with difficulty, and smiled.

"Noura . . ." Salah's voice was gruff with emotion.

Softly, she squeezed his hand. "Not now, Salah."

Without letting go of her hand, Salah pulled a chair forward. "Noura, this was no accident."

"Salah, please."

"They have crossed the line," he said angrily.

"Everything will be fine, Salah. All this will heal."

"I almost lost you, Noura." Tears appeared in Salah's eyes and he bent to kiss her hand.

"It's not that easy to get rid of me," Noura said.

"I will find the men who did this," Salah said, his voice steely.

"Salah, I am really sorry," Noura said, "about what I said before you left."

Salah shook his head and opened his mouth to say something, but Noura silenced him. "No . . . please, let me finish." She took a deep breath. "I am sorry, Salah. I have behaved so badly, so selfishly toward you. And I don't understand why, because you are the man I love. I think it's just that I have been so afraid of losing you."

"I understand, Noura. Please . . . don't think about it. It's all in the past. Just get better. That's all I care about."

"I feel awful, Salah. I never meant to hurt you. It would just be too much to lose you and Khaled within a year."

"I know and I understand."

"Do you really forgive me, my love?"

"Of course! Why would I not?"

Tears appeared in Noura's eyes. "I cannot believe how lucky I am to have a man like you in my life."

"I cannot believe how lucky I am to have a woman like you in love with me." Salah smiled.

"Salah, please make sure that Tante Saydeh and Siran are safe."

Salah nodded.

"Noura . . . ," he began, "as soon as I finish what I have promised Faisal and Lawrence, I am getting out. I swear it to you."

—ᛗ—

Salah spent the rest of May and early June in Cairo looking after Noura as best he could and making arrangements to ensure that his mother, Siran, and Noura were properly looked after, before heading back up to Alexandria, where Nusair was waiting to sail to Beirut.

He tried to convince his mother to move into a house in the British Army compound, but Saydeh refused to move from her home, insisting that the Turks would have to kill her before she left the El-Khalili. So Salah had Magdi organize a round-the-clock close vigil on the house, and Fatmeh moved in temporarily to help Saydeh care for Noura when she came back home from the hospital.

—ᛗ—

Ahmed Jemmal stood in his office, hands clasped behind his back, staring out of the tall French windows at the city that was still at his feet.

"Sir . . ." His secretary coughed discreetly.

"Colonel Erdogan is here."

"Masri has just arrived in Beirut, Pasha."

"What is he up to?" Ahmad Jemmal said, stroking his moustache. "Don't let him out of your sight, Colonel."

Erdogan nodded.

"He is currently with Lawrence and the other two in a café in Hamra."

"Good. Arrest them for spying. Hang Masri and his architect for treason and throw the English in jail. Who do they think they are? Going up against the Ottoman Empire."

Omer Erdogan left the governor's office and hurried back to his own office to get word to his agents, who were sitting inside the café awaiting his orders. Sitting only a couple of tables away, they had overheard Salah and Lawrence discuss the route they were going to take to Damascus.

"All of us, especially you, Masri, will be the perfect distraction," they overheard Lawrence say. "Jemmal won't know where to look."

"We just have to make sure we are not caught," Salah added. "As soon as Charlie and Rabih come back, we'll head north toward Tripoli and cut across the Lebanon Mountains, across the Bekaa Valley and into Damascus."

The two agents smiled at each other.

Suddenly, a group of loud, boisterous young men entered the café, making their way toward the table between Salah and Lawrence and the two Turkish agents. They were noisy and demanding and by the time they'd settled down, Salah and Lawrence had disappeared.

—◦◦◦—

"Do you think they heard?" Salah asked Lawrence as they slipped out the back entrance of the café.

"I hope so. That was the whole point."

—◦◦◦—

"There's a checkpoint ahead," Charles remarked, looking down the long, dusty, mostly desert road that ran along the Mediterranean coastline.

"Why don't all of you go around that hill toward that monastery?" Charles suggested, pointing. "Judging from where they are, the hill's incline will hide you. I'll keep them busy and meet you a few miles up the road where it curves into the bay of Jounieh."

"If something happens, shall we meet back in Gaza?" Salah suggested.

"Very well." Lawrence gave the thumbs-up sign. "Gaza it is."

"I have a better idea," Rabih suggested. "Why don't I go through the checkpoint? I can always say I'm on my way home to see my parents and if they want to check it, it is true. They live outside Tripoli. And you never know, we might have to stop there anyway."

"Good idea," Salah agreed.

"See you on the other side!" Rabih waved.

—◦◦◦—

"Halt!" the soldier held up his hand.

Rabih dismounted his horse and walked toward the soldier. As he got closer, he realized the man was wearing a German Army uniform. Another soldier came out of the checkpoint hut just when Rabih approached. He was Turkish. Rabih could hear two other men talking inside the hut, but from where he stood he couldn't see them or make out whether they were speaking Turkish or German.

"*Identifizierung.*" The German soldier held out his hand. "*Die passe.*"

"*Aa'fwan,*" Rabih said politely, and reached into his pockets to look for his papers.

Rabih stood respectfully as the German soldier unfolded the sheet of paper.

"Moment," the German said, "wait here."

Rabih's heart started to beat faster.

"So . . ." The Turk lit a cigarette.

"Want one?" he offered Rabih.

Rabih shook his head.

"Where you going?" he asked, continuing to pace slowly around Rabih.

"Douma."

"You're still a way off."

"I know."

What is taking so long? Rabih thought. He looked around, wondering where he could go if he had to make a run for it. But there weren't many choices . . . a lonely cluster of trees in the distance, but they could easily put a bullet through him before he got there. His heart continued pounding and he had a strange feeling in the pit of his stomach. He put his hands in the pockets of his tunic, squeezing them together to try and calm his nerves.

"No, no!" the Turk shouted. "Hands where I can see them."

Rabih took them out and was forced to stand with his hands at his side. His mouth went dry. He was trembling. He knew that if he lifted his hands, they would be shaking.

"I'm from Izmir," the Turk said.

Rabih closed his eyes. Ya Allah! he prayed, *please help me.*

"You ever been to Izmir?" the soldier asked.

"Actually, yes, I have."

"And?"

"And what?"

"Did you like it?" the Turk asked him.

"I did."

"What were you doing in Izmir?" He stood in front of Rabih, his hands folded across his chest.

"I . . . uh . . . was there with a friend."

"Huh," the Turk grunted. "You know," he began rubbing his chin, "you look awfully familiar . . . I don't know why."

"Perhaps we saw each other in Izmir?" Rabih muttered, his tongue sticking to the roof of his mouth.

"Yes . . ." The Turk looked at Rabih through narrowed eyes.

The German soldier who had taken his documents came out of the hut.

"Moment, *bitte*." He shook his finger at Rabih.

Both soldiers went to the side of the hut. They were speaking softly, whispering among themselves, and as much as Rabih tried straining his ears, he couldn't figure out what they were saying.

If you're going to make a run for it, now is the time, Rabih thought. He took a couple of steps forward.

"Hey!" The Turk motioned. "No moving allowed."

Rabih stopped dead in his tracks.

"What's taking so long?" he asked.

"Patience . . . all good things come to those who wait," the Turkish soldier replied.

This was not a good sign. He'd been standing at the checkpoint for at least half an hour. Maybe there was something wrong with the document? But what? It was an Egyptian passport. When he arrived in Cairo, he didn't have anything on him, so Salah had arranged for his papers. Even though Egypt was a British protectorate, it was still technically part of the Ottoman Empire and Egyptian professionals and merchants could still travel in Ottoman-controlled territories.

A man emerged from the hut. This one was not a simple soldier like the other fellow. He was dressed in an officer's uniform. As soon as he appeared, the German and Turkish soldiers stubbed out their cigarettes and rushed to stand on either side of Rabih.

Rabih's stomach sank.

"So," the Turkish officer looked at Rabih, "you are Rabih Farhat . . ."

"Yes," Rabih didn't look at him.

"The same Rabih Farhat who started work at the Chemin de Fer Imperiale in Izmir in July 1914?"

Rabih did not immediately answer. He was trying to search his brain for something plausible to say, but he couldn't. There was no way to explain without lying.

"The same Rabih Farhat whose immediate superior was Salah Masri?" the officer continued.

Rabih didn't look at the officer.

"The same Rabih Farhat who worked on the Hejaz Railway with Masri?" the Turkish officer approached Rabih, his hands clasped behind his back, his eyes glinting in anger. He came so close to Rabih that the tips of their noses touched.

"The same Rabih Farhat who betrayed the Sublime Porte by purposely removing bolts and weakening the tracks?" he shouted, his spittle flying onto Rabih's face and wetting his cheeks.

"The same Rabih Farhat who leaked secret information that led to the deaths of hundreds . . . thousands of Ottoman soldiers?

"The same Rabih Farhat who fled like a coward to Cairo?

"Rabih Farhat . . . you are under arrest. You are a disgrace and a traitor to the Ottoman Empire and now it's time to pay for it."

There was nothing Rabih could do. He was completely cornered. He knew he would never make it if he ran. But he also knew he wouldn't make it if he stayed . . . he would only be prolonging the inevitable.

"Take this piece of shit away." The officer spat in Rabih's face. "It's his fault I spent time in that filthy British prison in Cairo . . . now let him rot."

Rabih looked up at him. He was one of the Turks who had followed him into Rania's that first day.

"Yes . . . I am that man," the officer confirmed Rabih's thoughts. "Sergeant Mehmet Celik of the Imperial Ottoman Army."

Rabih stood defeated, his arms hanging limply by his side.

The Turkish soldier took Rabih's left arm and, in the split second the German soldier took to hoist his rifle on his shoulder and take his right arm, Rabih elbowed the Turk in the ribs with all the strength he could muster. The man doubled over and Rabih lifted his knee into the man's chin. The Turk's head went flying backwards and blood spurted from his mouth. Rabih grabbed his rifle and stabbed the German soldier through the heart with the bayonet, killing him immediately. He lunged toward Sergeant Mehmet, who immediately moved aside. The bayonet got him first in the arm and then in his thigh. Rabih twisted it in, ripping his thigh muscle. The Sergeant screamed in pain and fell to the ground, clutching his leg. Blood was spurting everywhere.

Rabih dropped the rifle and turned and ran as fast as he could. He didn't dare look back. *If I can make it to that monastery, I'll be all right. I can claim sanctuary.* Hope rose for a moment, buoying his heart, urging him on. When he was a third of a mile away, a shot rang out in the distance. Suddenly, Rabih felt a shooting pain just below his shoulder. *Don't look*, he told himself. Another shot sounded. This time Rabih felt it below his ribcage. *Dear God!* His pace slowed. He put his hand to his waist and felt something wet. He brought his hand up to his face. It was red. He looked down and saw his tunic soaked with his own blood. He staggered through some long grass and finally collapsed at the base of some trees, his breathing shallow, his heart slowing dramatically. He couldn't feel the tips of his fingers. A cold sweat enveloped him. He tried to focus his eyes but they were dimming. In his mind he saw his parents, his sisters, himself as a young boy running in the orchards around his parents' home in Douma. And finally he saw Rania . . . he saw her smile, twirl around—her silky dresses flowing, the ruffles dancing around her. She held her arms open to him. "Rabih!" he heard her say, smiling invitingly, just before his eyes closed.

—⁂—

Salah paced up and down on the beach, below the spot where they had agreed to wait for Rabih. He pulled out a pack of cigarettes and lit one.

"Salah, we have to keep moving," Charlie said. "We're like sitting ducks here."

"Let's give him another hour," Salah said. "He'll be here. He's never let me down."

"If they have him, they won't be far behind," Charlie said. "We have to go."

"No!" Salah said forcefully. "He's one of my boys. I'm not going to leave him behind."

"Salah, he knows to meet us in Gaza," Lawrence said.

Salah took a long drag of his cigarette.

The sun began to sink. Salah looked out at the sea and the gentle waves playfully lapping the shoreline, leaving a fluffy, creamy foam on the dark brown sand. *Come on, Rabih.*

"There's a car coming, Sir." Charlie was on the top of the small cliff, looking through binoculars. "We really have to go. They'll be on top of us in about fifteen minutes."

"Salah?" Lawrence said.

Wordlessly, Salah mounted his horse and reined it around, spurring it into a gallop toward the thickly forested hills above Jounieh.

As night fell, they rode into a tiny village on the borders of the Bekaa Valley. Salah dismounted in front of a small stone hut with a black roof.

"We can stay here tonight," Salah said, as they tethered their horses to a wooden fence in front of the house.

Salah knocked on the door.

"*Meen?*" a grumpy, gruff voice said from inside.

"*Ana Masri.*"

A small wooden panel in the door slid open and a pair of eyes appeared. They went from frowning to breaking out into a big, beaming smile. The door was flung open and a very tall, large man hugged Salah.

"Brother Salah!"

"Dahmi," Salah said.

"How good it is to see you! What on earth are you doing here?"

"We're on our way to Damascus."

"You're going the wrong way."

"Yes, we know. These are my friends . . . Charles Hackett and Lawrence . . ."

"Yes . . . the one with Faisal. I have heard of you," Dahmi said. "Tell Faisal that the Al-Dahmi tribe will support him. But I will need money and supplies for the men I bring to him."

"Dahmi, we need a circuitous route into Syria. Preferably one that will let us do a little damage to the Ottoman railway lines."

"Yes. I'll take you to Baalbek tomorrow. You can start there."

They set out the next morning and the fifty-mile journey doubled because of the roundabout paths Dahmi took them on. The scenery was spectacular as the plain gave way to the Lebanon Mountains. They walked through mountain passes, crossed streams, galloped across fields, and couldn't help but marvel at the rows of elegant and statuesque cedars that grew on the mountains.

"There's a very big railway bridge just outside Baalbek that could be of interest to you," Dahmi said as they neared the Bekaa Valley.

"The bridge is on the main line of the Turkish railway that runs from Constantinople through Baalbek and Beirut to Aleppo."

—ɯ—

The ancient city of Baalbek in the northern part of the Bekaa Valley stood midway between Beirut and Damascus. Approaching it from the Lebanon Mountains, the town sat east of the Litani River in a plain that gave the land its lush green fertility. On a hill bordering the town was a massive, sprawling ancient Roman temple devoted to Bacchus, Jupiter, and Venus.

Salah and Charles went on a brief reconnaissance mission of the city, making notes on the fortifications and the strength of Ottoman troops in the area before meeting up with Lawrence, who had gone to buy a few things he needed for the explosives.

They left their horses tethered a couple of miles outside of town, and walked through the fields and orchards that surrounded Baalbek until they reached the train tracks.

"There's the bridge." Charles pointed to the large steel and concrete structure about a mile away.

"Package the dynamite in sticks of twenty," Salah said to Lawrence and Charlie, while he busied himself with the cable and fuse.

Working quickly and silently, they carefully placed a package under each end of the bridge and under every bastion, and added a few more packages for an extra special bang. Once done, Lawrence pointed to a small cave at the summit of a nearby hill. The others nodded and Charles led the way while Salah came behind him rolling out the cable.

"Ready?" Lawrence lit a match. All three were lying on their stomachs inside the cave.

The ensuing explosions several minutes later from the first package of dynamite were deafening, blowing the bridge into the sky in a mass of flames and smoke. One after the other, the dynamite packages blasted through, shattering the rails, destroying the infrastructure, and raising dust and stones and pebbles, which showered down on the countryside. The noise ripped downstream, echoing against the mountainside as it made its way downriver.

And then there was silence . . . only a brief dull roar in the distance as the sound traveled.

"Was that the last one?" Charles asked, getting to his knees and dusting the front of his tunic.

"I believe so," Salah said.

"Shall I go and check?" Charles suggested.

"We'll head over and get the horses," Salah said.

"I'll meet you there."

Charles headed down to the bridge. Even though the air was filled with the dust and grime of the explosion, the scenery was still beautiful. High up on the opposite mountain, the cedars had stood witness to the blast. Charles carefully made his way along the burned fuse. He reached the now non-existent bridge, searching around the specific areas where they had placed the bundles of dynamite to make sure there were no unexploded sticks of dynamite that were still smoldering. His keen eyes picked up the shards of the sticks that had exploded. *Good. I think we've accomplished the mission.* He turned and began to walk back. Suddenly, he heard a high-pitched hissing sound. He looked around to see where it was coming from and there, less than a hundred feet away, was a package of dynamite, half hidden in the tall grass. *Oh Lord!* Charles turned and ran. The force of the blast seconds later propelled him into the air, across the field and slammed his body into the earth.

Salah and Lawrence, who were making their way back to the horses, heard the blast. They looked at each other, left the horses where they were, and ran back as fast as they could to the railway bridge. As they came over the hill where they had hidden during the blast, they stopped dead in their tracks. A group of Ottoman soldiers was running toward the explosion. Both men quickly fell to the ground, hiding behind a clump of short bushes that were close enough for them to see and hear.

"Our informant was correct about the explosion," said a man who looked like the officer in charge. "Who did this though?" he said looking around the rubble.

"You!" he shouted to one of the soldiers. "Run back to the barracks and tell Colonel Erdogan about this. He will want to come and see this for himself. "Damn it! I wish we could have caught whoever it was in the act."

"Over here!" a soldier cried out. He dropped to his knees behind a rock and quickly got back up. "Sir! Sergeant! Over here!" He waved to some of the others. "You're going to want to see this!"

The officer and a couple other soldiers came running over. "Good God!" one of them exclaimed. "Is he alive?" another asked. "I don't know." The officer knelt down. "There is a pulse. It's very, very faint. I don't know if he'll make it or not," he pronounced.

"Maybe he's the man who set the charges?" one of the men suggested.

"Get him out of here," the officer ordered. "Take him to the infirmary at the military school. We'll see if he makes it," he said.

"The rest of you . . . fan out and start looking for clues."

Salah looked at Lawrence, gesturing with his hands that they needed to get out of the area immediately.

"Sir!" one of the soldiers shouted. "I found something."

Lawrence froze in his tracks.

"What is this?" the soldier said as he picked up a mangled pistol.

The officer came over and took it from him, twirling it round and around.

"What is it, Sir?"

"Are you blind, soldier?" the officer snapped. "It's a pistol."

"Yes, but I've never seen one like it before."

"No . . . because this weapon is standard British military issue."

The soldier looked scared.

"Damn! Damn! Damn!" the Turkish officer swore. "It's Masri and that Englishman, Lawrence. They're here. This is their doing. Come on! We'd better head back to Baalbek. I have to let Colonel Erdogan know as quickly as possible."

—∿—

When night fell, Salah and Lawrence rode back into Baalbek toward the Turkish military academy, where the officer had ordered Charles to be taken.

"How on earth are we going to get in there?" Lawrence said, as he looked at the tall, wrought iron gates patrolled by Turkish soldiers.

"We're going to have to find disguises."

"As what?"

"Have you ever dressed up as a woman, Lawrence?"

"Is that a joke?"

"No . . . Turkish soldiers never question women. They think it's beneath them to address a woman," Salah said.

"All we have to do is find women's clothes."

"In my case, dear Salah, I think I'll be fine . . . I'm only five and a half feet tall. You, on the other hand . . ."

"Well then you will have to go in on your own. According to what I've been told, the infirmary is on the first floor at the back of the building."

—∿—

Late that evening, Salah, wearing a robe, turban, and scarf covering his face, and Lawrence, dressed as an Arab woman and carrying a pile of clean sheets and towels, walked across the small square in front of the military academy, arriving at the gates. "Are you sure this is going to work?" Lawrence asked.

"Yes."

"Really?"

"Works every time," Salah assured him. "You'll see." He winked.

"My wife is here with laundry for the infirmary," Salah said to the sentry.

"You wait here. She can go in."

Lawrence crept across the main courtyard, walking quickly toward the back of the building and entering through a side door. He walked down a long corridor until he reached the end. The sign on the door said "Infirmary." Softly, he opened the door and peeked in. No one appeared to be on duty.

He went into the main ward. There were a few patients who were asleep, but none of them looked like they had recently been in a bomb blast. Lawrence went from bed to bed, peering at all the men sleeping in white single beds. Charles wasn't there.

As he turned to leave, he saw a nurse rushing in to tend to one of the men, but she was busy and didn't give him a second look as he hurried back to the entrance.

Suddenly, Lawrence had an idea. He doubled backed to the nurse's desk and opened the main drawer. Inside there was a large ledger-style book. He opened it. It was a daily organizer with a list of all the patients and what they needed, what was administered, dosages of medicine given, and all kinds of other details. Turning quickly to the last page, which would reflect what had happened that day, he scanned the entries with his index finger. And there was Charles. He was listed as "unknown." It said that he had severe burns, a broken leg and arm, and some organ damage. But where was he? There was no bed number listed next to his name like there was next to everyone else's.

"*Shoo?*" the nurse said, coming into the reception area. "May I help you?"

"May I help you?" she said again, a bit more forcefully.

Slowly, Lawrence looked up.

"I brought the sheets and towels," he whispered hoarsely.

"At this hour?"

"Yes . . . I forgot to bring them this afternoon."

The nurse looked at him doubtfully.

"But you're not the woman who comes in the afternoon." She came closer to Lawrence.

"No . . . that's my sister," Lawrence said. "Her husband doesn't let her out after dark."

"And yours does?" The nurse's tone of disbelief grew. "You're not my laundry woman," the nurse said. "Who are you?" She tried to grab at the veil around Lawrence's face.

Lawrence turned and ran. "Guard!" the nurse shouted. She went to her desk and quickly wound up the telephone.

When Lawrence reached the gate, he slowed his pace so as not to arouse the attention of the soldiers. He jumped into the sidecar of the motorcycle Salah had running.

"Stop her!"

"Stop who?" the soldier at the gate said, looking around in panic.

"That woman!" the soldier yelled.

"You want me to stop a woman?" the sentry asked.

"She's not a woman, you idiot!" the soldier clapped the young sentry on the back of his head.

Salah revved up the accelerator and they sped off in the dark of night.

A few miles later when they were quite sure they were not being followed, Salah stopped the bike.

"Well, anything?" he asked.

"He was there." Lawrence took off his goggles. "There's a record of a seriously injured man having been brought in this afternoon. But he wasn't there tonight."

Salah lit a cigarette. "They've probably moved him to Damascus. We're going to split up, Lawrence. I'll go look for Charlie. You continue the mission."

CHAPTER SEVENTEEN

While Salah headed to Damascus to find out where the Turks had taken Charlie and what had happened to Rabih, Lawrence headed south to Deraa.

According to Salah, Deraa was a major junction in the Hejaz Railway for both troops and supplies and therefore a major target in the guerilla effort. Lawrence spent two days disguised as a Bedouin, exploring the railway lines on all sides of the junction, and made extensive notes and drawings of the lines north, south, and west and where he was going to put the boxes of dynamite.

He then headed to the market to see Bani, a friend of Salah's, who happened to be the brother of Magdi in Cairo and, like him, also a fruitseller. Bani was to be Lawrence's assistant in the venture.

"Hello, Bani," Lawrence said softly, "I'm Lawrence."

"*Ahlan! Ahlan wa sahlan, habibi!*" Bani jumped up and warmly hugged Lawrence. He held him at arm's length and looked him up and down. "I am so pleased to see you!" he said and hugged him again. "I was wondering when you would appear." He hugged him for a third time. "How are you?" he asked with yet another hug.

"I'm fine, Bani." Lawrence laughed at Bani's effusive welcome, given that they didn't know each other.

"Please, please, come in," Bani said, quickly pulling out a stool for him. "How is my brother, Salah?"

"He is very well, on his way to Damascus."

"Ah! Then he will definitely visit my cousin. Salah loves his wife's cooking!"

Lawrence grinned.

"Now, what can I get you?" Bani rubbed his hands together with glee.

"Well for a start, I need a few boxes of dynamite."

"Oh!" Bani looked perplexed. "How about some coffee to start?"

"That would also be nice," Lawrence replied.

"Right away," Bani said, calling over a young boy and giving him some money to go and get coffee. "And bring some mammoul," he shouted after him.

"How long are you here? We would love to have you for dinner."

"Bani, we really need to get down to business. I need to light up the skies tonight."

"That's too bad. I know all my wives will be most upset. They're all driving me nuts because this war is ruining their social life."

"How many wives do you have now?"

"Just the four . . . you know." Bani shrugged. "It's what's allowed. And I like to stick to the law."

"Now, Bani, here is my list." Lawrence pulled out a piece of paper.

As they were talking, a couple of Turkish soldiers strolled by. They stopped a few feet from the fruit stand. One of them indicated Lawrence with his chin. He turned to his partner and said something. The partner nodded and they began talking among each other, all the while looking over at him.

"I don't think you're going to have time for coffee," Bani said.

"I don't think so either," Lawrence agreed, casually covering his face with the scarf.

"Fruitseller!"

"Yes, Sir!" Bani replied.

"What's fresh today?" The two soldiers casually sauntered over to the fruit stand.

"Everything! Everything!" Bani proudly ran his hand over the display of fresh fruits. "Now over here," he walked over to the far end, trying to distract them. "Look at these beautiful melons. Very ripe, very juicy, just arrived from the Bekaa."

Lawrence sat quietly on his stool. Without making eye contact with them, he could tell the soldiers were looking at him.

"And these grapes?"

The soldiers wouldn't move. One of them took out a piece of paper from his pocket. He looked at it and looked over at Lawrence.

"What about these oranges? From Jaffa?"

"Gentlemen? What can I interest you in?" Bani rushed down to the side of the stall where the soldiers were standing and where Lawrence was sitting.

"Officers?" Bani kept trying to get their attention.

"You! Bedouin!"

Lawrence looked up at them.

"Are you deaf?" one of them said.

"Officers!" Bani came over trying to interrupt. "Figs? Peaches?"

"You're under arrest," the officer said to Lawrence.

"On what grounds?" Bani jumped in.

"He's a deserter from the Turkish Army," one of the soldiers said.

"We've been looking for him," the other said.

"I think you're mistaken," Lawrence said calmly.

"I don't think we are."

"All right, let's go." The soldiers stood on either side of Lawrence.

Lawrence got up. He glanced at Bani, who looked terrified.

"Officers . . . this man is a merchant . . . he's not in the army."

"If you don't shut up, we'll arrest you too!" they threatened.

Bani wrung his hands as he watched them lead Lawrence away. He had to get word to Salah.

"Come here, boy!" he gestured to the little boy who had gone to get them coffee. "Watch my fruit stand and mind you don't give away the fruit for free."

Bani handed him a couple of coins and ran to the post office.

—m—

"Now isn't this a pleasant surprise?" The Turkish officer smiled. "And here I was thinking I was getting a deserter, but who do I get instead? The great T.E. Lawrence, disguised as a Bedouin in enemy territory. My superiors are going to love this. Finally . . . caught red handed."

Lawrence sat in silence.

"You realize you are very lucky, don't you?"

"If they'd known who you really were, my men could have shot you as they would any ordinary spy," the officer continued. "But I'm glad they didn't. Now I can take all the credit for capturing the Englishman who is . . . what do they call you . . . ah yes! The Prince of Mecca."

He guffawed as he paced around a basic wooden table, the only piece of furniture, apart from two wooden chairs, in an otherwise bare room in the Turkish military barracks at the edge of the city.

"Do you have anything to say in your defense?"

Silence.

"Well then consider yourself under arrest in the name of the sultan. As a spy for the allies, your very presence in the Ottoman Empire is punishable immediately and by death. You will be executed at dawn."

Lawrence didn't move a muscle.

"Good. Well, then, I shall see you in the morning at the firing squad, Sir," the Turkish officer said.

"Oh and by the way, we have met before," he added, "which is why I know for sure that it is, indeed, you. It wouldn't do to execute someone we thought was you and then have you pop up somewhere in Syria, blowing up our railway lines, cutting our supplies . . . you know . . . the sort of thing that you're so very good at.

"My name is Omer Erdogan . . . Colonel Omer Erdogan. You arrested me and one of my men last year . . ."

The Old Bazaar in Damascus was teeming with Ottoman and German soldiers. Salah pulled his scarf across his face. He'd stopped off to see Bani's cousin first, where Bani's telegram had been waiting for him. As soon as he'd read it, he headed into the heart of the old city, arriving in time for dinner at the palace of another old university friend, Ali Riza Al Rikabi, who happened to be the current Ottoman military governor of Syria.

"I'd heard you were in the area." Ali Riza hugged Salah warmly. "Except my men can never seem to catch you. Why is that?"

"Because I'm bloody good at what I do."

"Or because I'm bloody good to you," Ali Riza said, cocking one eyebrow.

"I've got a problem, Ali Riza . . . a good friend of mine, an English Special Forces guy, was taken in Baalbek by Erdogan . . . and my old architect, Rabih Farhat . . . he was stopped at a checkpoint north of Beirut," Salah paused, holding Ali Riza's gaze, trying to gauge his reaction. "And . . . Erdogan has Lawrence in Deraa."

A long, heavy pause hung in the air.

Finally, Ali Riza sighed deeply. "All right, Salah. But you only get one chance because we're old friends. Which one will it be?"

—⁓—

Lawrence sat in a corner in a darkened cell listening to the rats scampering around in the straw on the floor. There was one small window with iron bars from which he could see the sky. The silvery beams from the full moon were trying their best to reach in through the bars.

So this is how it ends. I suppose it was inevitable, really. At some point, everyone's luck runs out. Perhaps the only regret is not seeing the campaign through to the end. And all this information I've gathered. What a waste. There's no way to get any of it to Faisal.

He felt unusually calm. Somehow it didn't feel like the end, even though he knew it was. How funny life is, he thought. If someone had told me, when I was younger, that I would die a spy at a firing squad in Deraa, I would have laughed.

"Lawrence?" a voice whispered.

Lawrence's ears perked up.

"Lawrence? Are you in there?"

Someone was at the door. Softly, he padded to the door.

"Who's there?"

"Where are you?" the voice whispered. "Scratch the door you're behind."

Lawrence did as he was told. He put his ear to the door and heard footsteps outside and two people whispering. Suddenly, Lawrence heard keys clinking. He stood back. A key was inserted in the door and turned. The door opened. It was Bani and Salah.

"*Yallah, Yallah!*" Bani said.

Lawrence was shocked.

"I'll explain later," Salah said, reading his mind. "For now, we have to move quickly and silently."

Together they went through a long corridor and stopped at the end, where Bani pulled open a secret trap door. Silently Bani lowered himself, followed by Lawrence and Salah, who shut the door firmly above him. They went through a maze of underground corridors, finally arriving at brick wall that swung open when Bani pushed on a certain brick. It wasn't a large opening and they all had to bend to step out. Lawrence looked around. They were on the stage of the Roman theatre of Deraa.

Salah put his finger to his lips. He hugged Bani warmly and kissed him three times. Bani acknowledged him with a hand to his heart. He turned to Lawrence and hugged him.

Salah took Lawrence by the arm and indicated he follow him. From behind a column, he pulled out a satchel and swung it across his body. They stole across the stage and slipped out of a side entrance, continuing in silence until they reached the desert at the edge of Deraa. There, two camels were patiently waiting for them. Salah paid the man who was waiting with the camels and they set off with only the light of the moon to guide them.

"Are you all right?" Salah asked when they stopped at an oasis in the middle of the night. "That was a close one, Lawrence."

"How did you find me?"

"I called in a favor from an old university friend."

"What about Charlie? Any news? Rabih?"

"I only had one favor, Lawrence."

Lawrence nodded.

"What's next?"

"I've heard from Auda. The tribes are ready," Salah said. "They are waiting for us in Bair."

"Good . . . let's create a little havoc along the way to help him out."

—ᴍ—

Salah and Lawrence spent a little time bombing two miles of track around Minifir. As expected, Ottoman troops quickly swarmed the scene and a repair train was immediately dispatched from Deraa. Salah also placed a mine a little further up the track that wrecked the train that arrived the next day.

The explosion did its job well. Amid the confusion, Salah and Lawrence slipped through the Ottoman net, riding past Amman and continuing southwest, skirting the Dead Sea until they reached Auda's camp.

—ᴍ—

Just before dawn in early July 1917, over five hundred camels stole across the desert toward the Turkish garrison at an outpost on the outskirts of Aqaba. Salah, Auda, and Lawrence rode at the head of the army, which was made up mostly of desert tribesmen whose loyalty had been bought with British gold.

As the sky lightened, the tribesmen positioned themselves in the hills around the Turks. When the sun broke through, Auda gave the signal and they began firing on the Turks. Dust and sand flew, the noise of the gunfire was deafening, and, when the sun rose, the heat was unbearable. Yet, despite the almost constant bullets that were being fired on the Turks, nothing seemed to be happening to the garrison.

Salah ran over to Lawrence, who was reloading his gun behind a rock. "What the hell is going on down there?" he screamed over the noise. "Why haven't we taken the fort?"

"I don't know," Lawrence admitted, sitting back against the rock. "It may be the heat."

"What does that have to do with anything?" Salah turned back and aimed down at the Turks.

"What do we do?"

"I don't know." Lawrence sat up against a rock and pulled his drinking bottle from his holster. "Damn! No water."

"Giving up, Lawrence?" Auda sauntered over.

Lawrence remained silent.

"What kind of man are you?" Auda jibed. "You call yourself my brother? You pretend to be an Arab? One of us?" He gestured around. "You want to be a Bedouin? Then come out of hiding, little white boy . . ."

"Really . . . why don't you take a look around, Auda?" Lawrence said. "Look at your so-called fierce warriors! They shoot a lot, but what are they hitting? Nothing, my friend. Some use they are!"

Auda's eyes narrowed into slits. His nostrils flared and he puffed his chest up. "How dare you?" he growled and stormed toward his men, shouting orders. "Salah come! We will show this white man what we Arabs are made of."

"Auda! Auda!" Lawrence ran after him.

But Auda wouldn't stop.

"Auda!" Lawrence caught up to him. "Look, I'm sorry . . . I didn't mean that."

Auda didn't say a word.

"Auda . . ."

"Get out of my way!" Auda growled.

"Salah . . . ?" Lawrence tried.

"Stay here, Lawrence." Salah mounted his horse.

"But what are you going to do?"

"I'm riding with Auda."

"*Allah-o-Akbar!*" Auda cried and raised his sword.

The entire Howeitat Tribe gathered around Auda. With loud cries of *Allah-o-Akbar*, the hundred-strong group of men galloped down the mountainside screaming, shooting from the saddle, riding straight into the middle of Turkish troops, leaving Lawrence staring after them.

Lawrence crawled forward to the ridge of the crest just in time to see the charge reach the bottom of the hill. The Turks were completely spellbound by the sight of Auda's warriors and appeared not to be able to move. They fired back in the beginning but mostly turned and ran when the Bedouins descended in their midst.

Lawrence watched as Auda and Salah fought fiercely, cutting down the Turks with their swords in one hand, guns in the other. As the fighting intensified, Lawrence lost sight of them in the dust and sand that was kicked up by men and horses. He tried to look for them with his binoculars, but they had disappeared.

Lawrence jumped up. "Come on! *Yallah!*" he cried to the other Arab tribes who were watching, waiting. "Let us help them!"

He quickly mounted his camel and led the rest of the Arabs on camels down into the battle, shooting as he descended the side of the mountain. Suddenly, his camel tripped and fell and Lawrence hurtled to the ground. The fighting was going on all around him. He turned over and covered his head with his arms to protect himself from the hooves of camels and horses as they flew past. He didn't know how long he remained there when suddenly he heard Salah shout.

"Lawrence!"

He looked around and saw Salah running towards him. His face and clothes were black with the filth and dirt of the desert and gunpowder. There was blood on his cloak and a large cut on his cheek and above his eyebrow.

"Salah! Oh thank God you're all right."

"What on earth is wrong with you?" Salah shouted over the din of the battle.

"What do you mean?"

"I saw you coming down the mountain and you shot your own camel in the head."

"I did?"

"Yes."

"Anyhow, what is going on?"

"Auda's taken the fort. The Turks have given up."

Lawrence threw himself into Salah's arms.

—⁓—

That night, after it was all over, they all sat in Auda's tent enjoying a narghile and some tea.

"Auda, I need to go to Cairo," Lawrence said.

Auda fingered his prayer beads silently.

"We have no food," Lawrence started. "We need supplies, we need gold . . ."

"And you think you will get it?"

"I have more chance of getting it if I am in front of them than if I am here and telegraph them."

Auda nodded.

"And I want tell them about Aqaba in person. I don't want to just send a telegram."

"Then go . . . ," Auda said. "I hope you get what you want."

"I hope I get what you need."

The next morning, Lawrence rode into the Sinai Desert, headed for Suez on his way to Cairo, making the hundred-and-fifty-mile trip by camel in just over three days.

Salah went with him.

—m—

Salah was just about to put his key into the door when it was flung open. Tears were rolling down Saydeh's eyes. Immediately, Salah went into his mother's open arms, hugging her.

"It's all right, *imme*. I'm home now."

"Oh my son," Saydeh cried. "My dear, dear son."

"How is Noura?" he asked.

"She is much better . . . recovering well."

"And Siran?"

"Also very well. Growing up. She's a curious little girl. She's already trying to eat on her own!"

"*Imme* . . ."

"Go to Noura. She is waiting for you in my room."

Salah hugged his mother once more and ran in. Noura was sitting on the sofa, embroidering. Fatmeh was sitting next to her holding a pattern open. The two women were smiling.

"Salah!" Fatmeh saw him first and jumped up, running over to hug him. "I am so happy to see you."

Salah hugged her, but his eyes were on Noura.

"I'll be in the kitchen," Fatmeh said and immediately disappeared.

Salah silently walked over to Noura, who had not moved. He sat down next to her and took one of her hands in his and raised it to his lips and kissed it. Still she did not move, concentrating on the other hand in her lap.

"Noura?" Salah said softly. He got up and sat in front of her on the coffee table. He held her chin between his thumb and forefinger and tilted it up toward him. Noura's eyes were shut. She would not look at him.

"Noura, what is the matter?"

Noura's chin began to tremble. Her forehead crinkled and tears began to seep from the corners of her eyes.

Salah went down on his knees in front of her and took her in his arms, holding her close to him, caressing her hair as she clung to him, crying into his shoulder. It was several minutes before she finally quieted down, her sobs turning into hiccups.

Salah cupped her face in his large hands and looked into her eyes.

"I love you, Noura," he said, which brought on a fresh bout of tears.

"What is the matter?" Salah asked again.

Noura looked at him apprehensively, her eyes darting around, evading his. Salah was perplexed. He put his hands on her shoulders, forcing her to look at him.

"Now tell me what is wrong," he said. "Whatever it is, we will deal with it."

"Salah . . . I can't walk."

Salah stared at her. "What do you mean?"

"I can't walk," Noura repeated. "The nerves around the base of my spine were badly damaged."

"Noura . . . !" Salah said. "Why didn't you tell me?"

"How would I tell you? You were in the middle of the desert . . . in the war."

"What do the doctors say?"

"They're not sure what is causing it," Noura said. "They didn't think there was serious damage to my back during the explosion, but now they feel there might have been."

"We will find the best specialists for you. Don't worry."

Salah took her in his arms. "Don't worry," he repeated. "I'm here now."

They sat together locked in each other's embrace for some time,

Noura resting her head on Salah's shoulder. Salah kissed the top of her forehead. She looked up at him and with her fingers, gently caressed his cheek, running them along his jawline and up to his forehead. Slowly, with her thumb, she rubbed his bottom lip. Salah bent his head and put his lips over hers. She placed her hand on his neck and brought him closer as their kiss deepened. Noura arched toward him as his hands slid down to her waist.

"I love you, Noura," Salah murmured against her mouth.

"And I love you, my Salah," she whispered back. "Don't leave me again." Noura pulled back and put her hands on either side of his face.

"I promise. I never will."

Salah looked at her.

"Noura . . . I want us to be married. Immediately. I don't want to wait."

"I can't walk down the aisle."

"I will carry you," Salah replied. "And one day you will walk again. I know it."

Rania was in the kitchen preparing for her usual morning crowd. She was in a good mood, smiling to herself and singing a little tune as she did her chores. She fired up the brick oven with wood and while she waited for it to heat up, she walked around the café inspecting it. It looked good, she thought. Rabih really had done a very nice job. *I'll tell him when he comes back. Now all I need are some new curtains and tablecloths. Perhaps Noura will make me some*, she thought.

She looked at the clock. *I must have woken up early today.* Given that she had a few extra minutes, she decided to have a little breakfast herself. She went back into the kitchen and was pouring herself some coffee when there was a soft knock at the back door.

Through the thin, linen curtains, she recognized Salah.

"Salah!" she said, pleased to see him. "*Sabah al-khair!* What a wonderful surprise! I had no idea you were back. When did you arrive? How are you? I must say you look well!"

She threw herself into his arms and hugged him.

"*Sabah an-nour*, Rania," Salah said a bit gruffly.

Rania noticed the gruffness and wondered what was wrong. Usually Salah was all smiles.

"Well now, sit down and tell me everything," she said. "What can I get you this morning?" Have you eaten already or can I tempt you with some fresh-from-the-oven *manoushe* and olive oil?"

Salah's eyes were serious. It was not like him to turn down food.

"What has happened, brother?" she asked, worried.

"Sit down, Rania," Salah said in a deep voice.

"Why?"

"Rania, sit down," he repeated.

Rania looked perplexed.

Salah sat down in front of her.

She searched his face feverishly. Something was wrong. She could feel it.

Salah closed his eyes and took a deep breath. As he let it out, he reached across the table for her hands and took them in his. He did not look at her. Instead, he cocooned her hands in his in a prayer position.

Rania's heart jumped into her throat. It began beating so hard she could feel it reverberating in the pit of her stomach. "Rabih's dead."

Through her lowered lashes, she saw Salah nod his head.

She swallowed.

She gave Salah's hands a squeeze and gently extricated hers from them. She got up and went to the oven and began to put the small rounds of bread on the oven paddle, readying them for the oven.

"Are you sure you don't want any breakfast, Salah?" she asked in a toneless voice.

"Uh . . . no . . . I'm not hungry, thank you, Rania."

Rania continued to make bread and drank her coffee in one gulp, keeping her back to Salah.

"Thanks for coming by and letting me know."

"Rabih was a very good man," he said.

Rania kept her back toward Salah.

"I'll be going then, Rania."

It was only when she heard Salah close the door that she turned around and opened her eyes. She was haunted by images. Rabih in the kitchen . . . mostly of him in all four corners, standing high upon a ladder, smiling down at her when he would see her come in in the morning. "*Marhaba ya*, Rania," she heard his voice again. She turned around to stop the memories from washing over her and she saw him again, sitting at the kitchen table, tucking into the food she'd served him. "This is delicious," she heard him say. "I love baklava."

Rania ran into the café and slipped behind the bar, crouching down near the coffee machine, her hands over her ears, her eyes squeezed tightly shut as she tried desperately to keep the memories away. "Please, please, help me," she heard him say and when she dared to turn around, a bleeding Rabih, lay slumped over her bar. She stared, watching as his eyes slowly rolled back in his head and his lifeless body sank to the ground.

—∿—

"Noura!" Fatmeh called out, pushing open the door to Saydeh's apartment.

"I'm in the living room!"

"I was looking for Salah," Fatmeh said, coming in. "I was just at the mosque with Imam Ziad and I wanted to talk to Salah."

"He just went out."

"How did he take the news about your . . . ?" she asked.

"He wants to get married! He said he would carry me down the aisle!"

"Oh Noura!" Fatmeh jumped up to hug her. "I am so happy for you."

The two women embraced.

"Fatmeh," Noura started tentatively, pulling away from her. "About Charles . . ."

"You're going to tell me that he isn't coming back, aren't you?" Fatmeh said, nonchalantly.

Noura looked at Fatmeh, speechless.

"I know he's missing," Fatmeh said. "I've known for some time."

"How do you know?"

"He left my name along with his family's with his commanding officer in Cairo to let us know if he went missing or if he was dead."

Noura took Fatmeh's hand in hers.

"I received a telegram saying that he was missing."

"But why didn't you say anything?"

"Because he will come back."

"But, Fatmeh," Noura said, "he could be missing, but he could also be dead."

"No," Fatmeh shook her head. "He's not dead."

"Fatmeh," Noura took her hands in hers. "Salah and Lawrence heard the explosion . . . they took him to a Turkish hospital, but after that they lost him. They don't know where he is."

"Did Salah say Charles was dead?" Fatmeh asked.

"No . . . ," Noura admitted.

"Then he doesn't know if he is dead."

"But the probability is that Charles is dead, Fatmeh . . . ," Noura said, squeezing the younger woman's hand. "You must prepare yourself."

"No!" Fatmeh cried. "Charles is not dead," she said forcefully. "He is alive and he is going to come back. He asked me to wait for him and I promised I would and I will not break my promise."

"Fatmeh . . . please . . . ," Noura tried.

"No, Noura," Fatmeh said gently. "He is alive. I know it. I can feel it. If he were dead, I would know."

Rania was standing behind the bar, wiping glasses, when she heard someone try the door. She looked up at the clock. She wasn't due to open for another half an hour at least. She went to the door and pulled the curtain aside. It was Saydeh and Yvonne. Ya Allah! She really didn't want to talk to anyone this morning, especially since she had a feeling about what they wanted to talk about. Taking a deep breath she reluctantly turned the key.

"Can we come in?" Saydeh asked.

"It's a little early and I'm not quite ready yet."

Yvonne clicked her tongue. "Don't be silly. It's us . . ." She tried to barge in.

Rania stood aside grudgingly, releasing a resigned breath as the women walked in.

"What can I get you?" she busied herself behind the bar.

"Coffee?" Yvonne said.

Rania banged two cups down on saucers and threw two small teaspoons next to them. She pulled out the coffee beans, thumping the container down on the bar, not caring what the two older women thought. *Why the hell are they going through this stupid ritual, pretending as if they're here for coffee?*

She poured the coffee into the cups, spilling it all over the saucers. "*Haraam!*" she shouted.

"Can I help?" Yvonne ventured.

"No!" Rania cried. "I don't need any help. It's just that nothing is ready . . . as I said. You are too early," she added, the frustration evident in her voice.

Her nostrils flaring, her brow furrowed, she pulled out a dishrag and began mopping up the excess that had spilled. She made a little more coffee to fill up the cups and clumsily tried to put them directly under the nozzle from where the coffee was coming out. But, she didn't quite manage and the boiling coffee ran all over her hand.

She cried out as the liquid burned through her skin, tears rushing to her eyes. She dropped the cups and they smashed to the floor, shattering into smithereens. She ran across the shards in her bare feet to get to the kitchen sink to pour cold water on the burned hand. She bent over the sink, standing awkwardly, trying to not let the slivers of porcelain get deeper into her foot. Tears of pain wet her cheeks as she held the red, blistered hand under the water.

"Rania!" Saydeh and Yvonne came running into the kitchen behind her.

"Leave me alone," Rania said, her face hidden behind her hair, which hung down on either side.

"Rania, please, we only want to help . . ."

"Well, I don't want anyone's help!" Rania cried. "I don't need anyone's help."

Saydeh took a step toward her.

"Don't come near me!" Rania growled, still facing the sink. "Get out! Get out! Both of you!"

She whipped around.

"What do you want?" she shouted. "To console me for Rabih's

death? Did you want me to cry on your shoulders and tell you how much I miss him? How much I loved him? Is that what you want? Get out! Get out!" she began to scream. "I don't love him . . . all right . . . do you understand?" Tears started streaming down Rania's face.

Suddenly, she took a hold of a jar of olive oil and threw it against the wall. It smashed, the oil leaving a greasy yellow-green mark on the wall. Rania let out a loud growl and went around the kitchen, throwing everything on the floor, jars, plates, glasses . . . anything she could get her hands on. She pulled down the curtains and ripped the light linen material apart, trampling them underfoot. She grabbed the oven paddle and started to hit the floor. She threw pots and pans against the walls. She overturned the table, kicking everything that was on it, cutting her feet even further on the glass and terracotta shards on the floor.

And when everything in the kitchen was destroyed and overturned and upside down, she looked around and grabbed what she had in the pantry. The flour, the lentils, everything, went flying out of the neatly tied sacks as she stamped and threw them. When there was nothing left, she started beating the walls with her bare fists, drawing blood from some of the sharper edges.

Finally, spent, she collapsed in a heap on the floor, sobbing, her shoulders heaving as she wept. Slowly, Saydeh got up and made her way over to her. She got down on the floor next to Rania and put a gentle hand on her back. When Rania felt her hand, it brought about a fresh bout of sobs.

"Tante Saydeh," she looked up at the older woman. "I . . . I . . ."

"Hush, child." She took her in her arms.

"Tante Saydeh," Rania moaned into her shoulder. I couldn't tell him . . . Tante . . . I didn't tell him . . . and now it's too late. I couldn't tell anyone, not even myself. Oh God! Tante Saydeh . . . I miss him. I miss his gentle presence . . . and he loved me so much . . . and I couldn't love him back."

Saydeh silently held the younger woman in her arms, her own tears pouring down her cheeks.

"He did so much for me . . . he spruced up this dump and I didn't even tell him how much I appreciated it . . . I didn't even tell him how much I loved it . . . how beautiful his work was."

"Shhh, Rania . . . it's all right . . . he knows. Wherever he is, he knows."

"How can he know? He's dead . . . ," she sobbed.

"He knows, Rania. I am sure of it. If it is in your heart, then he knows."

"How could I have been so selfish? My heart is breaking Tante Saydeh . . . oh please, God . . . please let him come back to me." Rania put her face in her hands. "Just for a minute . . . just so I can tell him I love him."

Saydeh motioned to Yvonne to join her. "Hold her," Saydeh said while she reached for her handkerchief.

"Tante Yvonne, I'm so sorry," Rania kept saying as Yvonne rocked her gently.

"Don't apologize to me, child." Yvonne kissed the top of her head.

"Oh God . . . Rabih! I'm sorry . . . ," she cried, her eyes looking to the ceiling. "I'm sorry I pushed you away . . . I was scared. I didn't want to get hurt again . . . and here I am . . . Please. . .please help me . . . ," she begged, her hands clasped up as she stared up at the ceiling.

Yvonne wiped the tears from her eyes and she and Saydeh both put their arms around Rania and held her as hard as they could.

Rania's hand healed, as did all her bruises and scratches, but even the slightest reference to Rabih would bring tears to her eyes. That would take time, Saydeh said, "That heart," Saydeh shook her head, touching her own left breast, "no matter how hard you try. It has a rhythm of its own."

After Rania's meltdown, everyone got together and put her kitchen back together again. Noura made new curtains and tablecloths and napkins for the café and Saydeh presented Rania with a brand new chandelier for the one that got caught in the middle of two flying saucepans and the oven paddle. Yvonne donated a whole set of pots and pans she had received as part of her wedding dowry and never used. And Fatmeh helped Rania with the running of the café in the morning, making the bread and pastries, serving coffee, and cleaning up while juggling her time with Noura.

CHAPTER EIGHTEEN

Back in Europe, US troops arrived in France and Germany began to drop bombs on London. Outside the El-Khalili, the Arab Revolt continued through the rest of 1917 and the best part of 1918. The guerilla campaign that Lawrence continued when Salah stepped down was successful and achieved its primary goal of tying down Ottoman troops and cutting off Medina.

And General Allenby, who replaced General Murray, finally broke through Turkish lines in Palestine, captured Gaza in November 1917, liberated Jerusalem in December, and moved north into the Levant in the spring of 1918.

—∽∾—

"Sir! Governor!" Omer Erdogan ran into Ahmed Jemmal's office in the Grand Serail in Damascus. Seeing the governor seated at his desk, calmly going through some papers, he stopped and saluted him. Omer Erdogan looked filthy. His face was black with gunpowder, which, mixed with the sweat of battle, had created little black rivulets all over his face, seeping down to stain his already dirty shirt collar.

"At ease, Colonel," Ahmed Jemmal ordered, without looking up.

"Governor, we have to leave Damascus . . . please, I must get you out of here."

"Why?'

"The British are at our doorstep, Pasha," Omer Erdogan told him.

"They will not defeat the great Ottoman Empire," Ahmed Jemmal said quietly.

"Ahmed Pasha, please, I need to get you to safety," Omer said again.

"I will not leave."

"Sir, they crossed the Jordan River yesterday and they already have Beirut and Baalbek."

"They have our supply camps in the Beqaa?" Ahmed Jemmal asked.

Omer Erdogan nodded.

"And now they are in Deraa and coming this way."

"Then we will go out and meet them," Ahmed Jemmal said, getting out of his chair.

"Sir, please, it is too dangerous."

"I will not have my troops without a leader," Ahmed Jemmal said. "We will meet them at Tafas."

But despite Ahmed Jemmal's presence, the Ottoman brigades were routed and the governor had to retreat, having lost five thousand Turks over two days. He beat a hasty retreat to Damascus as the Arabs kept on coming.

"Sir." An exhausted and defeated Captain Omer Erdogan stood in front of the governor. "Please, Sir, it's now or never. The Arabs have closed the north and northwest gates of the city. It's all over, Sir."

"It is not over."

"Sir . . . the garrison, the Damascus garrison is retreating through the Barada gorge. From there it is a quick ride up into Turkey. We have to go. Please, come with me, Sir."

"I cannot, Captain," the governor declared. "I cannot leave Syria to the English."

"You will be leaving Syria to the Arabs, Ahmed Pasha," Erdogan said. "They intend for Damascus to be the capital of this new united Arab nation."

"It'll never last, Captain."

Suddenly, explosions sounded in the distance.

"What is that?"

"Those are the English, Sir."

"So close already." Ahmed Jemmal took a deep breath.

"Come, Ahmed Pasha." Omer Erdogan held out his hand. "Let us go back to Turkey, where we belong."

Slowly, Ahmed Jemmal moved. He looked around his office and walked out the door in front of the captain, his head high.

"Quickly!" Captain Erdogan shouted to his men who were waiting outside. "Get the Pasha to safety."

Ahmed Jemmal climbed into a car. "Thank you, Captain." He turned and saluted the young man who was already on his horse.

"Thank you, Sir." Omer Erdogan saluted back.

"Colonel, give the order to destroy our ammunitions," the governor said as he sat down in the car.

"Yes, Sir!" Erdogan turned his horse around and saw a group of British soldiers headed for the governor's palace. They were only a mile away and moving in fast. *I have to stop them, or they'll capture Ahmed Pasha . . .*

Taking a deep breath, he started galloping toward them, his sword raised. He let out a horrible cry as he neared them, spurring his horse, rocking in his saddle as he galloped full speed into the British column.

Captain Omer Erdogan slid off his horse, riddled with bullets and wounded by scores of bayonet points.

Damascus fell to the British on October 1, 1918.

—⁂—

Charles' eyes flew open. He lay there wondering if he'd dreamt the explosion. But no, there was another one. And another one. *What is going on out there?* He got up off the filthy straw he was sleeping on and walked to the stone wall of his cell. He looked up at the tiny, barred window that was on the side of the pitched ceiling. The sky was changing color. It was almost dawn. There was another explosion. He banged on the heavy wooden door. "Guard!" he called out. "What's going on out there?"

There was no response.

"Guard!" he yelled again.

The explosions were much closer now and from the window in the ceiling, he could see smoke. The rats in his cell were scampering around the sides of the walls trying to get out. Suddenly, he heard voices; loud, angry ones that were shouting, but he couldn't tell what they were saying, the words muffled by the thick stone walls.

"No . . . no . . . no . . . !" he heard a man cry out. "Please . . . spare me . . . I have a wife and children!" the man begged, after which Charles heard a bloodcurdling scream. *What is going on?* Charles paced his small cell. He wondered who was out there and whether he should make it known that he was inside.

He heard noises outside his door. "Get them out! Get them all out!" someone yelled. *Oh God!* Charles shivered. This was it. They were killing them all. "Come on! Open all these cells! The orders have come from Damascus. And make sure you get every one of them."

Charles froze in his cell. He was trapped. After a year and a half of enduring a filthy Ottoman prison, he was finally going to die. God knows how they would do it, he wondered as he waited for them to come for him. He heard the cell next to him being opened. "Come on out!" he heard someone say. "Allah!" he heard the prisoner in the cell next to him burst into tears. "*Yallah, Yallah! Khalas!* Get to your feet."

He heard the key turn in the door to his cell. He stood up as straight as he could to face the soldiers. But he was so weak. He hadn't eaten in days, his broken leg had not mended properly, and he limped badly. His shirt was filthy, his trousers were torn and he was barefoot. His hair and beard were long and filled with lice and all kinds of insects. His skin was black with dirt and he was sure he had bacteria in his stomach and who knows what other diseases.

A man dressed as a British soldier appeared at the door. Charles looked at him and was sure his eyes and mind were playing tricks on him.

"You!" the man pointed his bayonet point at him. "What's your name?"

"Charles . . . ," Charles stuttered. "Major Charles Hackett, British Army, Cairo."

The soldier backed out slowly, still aiming his bayonet at Charles. "Sir!" he shouted when he got to the door, looking to his right. "Sir! There's an English soldier here."

Another man came running over. "Thank you, private. Keep moving. Open the next one. Get everyone out of here and into the infirmary."

Charles didn't say a word. He stared at the man who walked in. He was tall with a beard and moustache and a Sikh's turban.

"Who did you say you were?" The officer approached Charles.

"Major Charles Hackett," Charles replied. "Special Forces, British Army."

Suddenly, the man in front of him stood tall and saluted. "Major! Sir!"

"At ease, soldier," Charles said, still confused. "Your name?"

"Captain Sukjit Singh, Sir, third Lahore Division of the Egyptian Cavalry Force."

Charles stared at him, still dazed.

"We've won, Sir," the Sikh told him. "We've defeated the Ottomans. Field Marshal Allenby and the Arabs have entered Damascus."

—⟶⟶⟵—

When Charles woke up again, he was lying in a soft white bed, covered with starched white cotton sheets and a white blanket. He was wearing a white robe and when he looked under the blanket he saw he had no underwear. His beard was gone, as was his hair . . . he was completely bald. He looked down at his arms and they looked clean except for the blotches of red Mercurochrome on his cuts. Charles looked around. There wasn't a single empty bed. He saw men with bandages, casts, legless, armless, eyeless; he saw doctors and nurses running around efficiently, speaking softly to the wounded; he heard a man scream and start to cry.

"What's wrong with him?" he asked his neighbor.

"I think they've just told him he's to lose his leg," the man replied.

"How are you doing?" Charles asked.

"All right, I suppose . . . I've still got all my limbs."

"I'm Charles Hackett." Charles held out his hand.

"Michel Khoury . . . lieutenant."

"Lebanese?" Charles asked.

Michel nodded.

"Where are you based? Beirut?"

"No, Cairo."

"As am I." Charles smiled. "I'm sure we'll see each other then."

"So, Major Hackett, how do you feel?" a doctor with a clipboard interrupted.

"Quite well, thank you."

"You're a tough man, Major," the doctor said, looking at his clip-board. "From what we can tell, they certainly had a good go at you."

Charles smiled ruefully.

"But you seem to be all right," the doctor said. "Unfortunately, you're always going to have a limp because of the way your leg healed. And we'll be giving you some medicines to kill anything you might have caught . . . but you can leave whenever you like."

"Thank you."

"Anything else you need?"

"I'd love a hot shower."

Charles showered, soaping every bit of himself, rubbing his skin with a brush, getting all the dirt out from under his fingernails and other crevices, trying to rid himself of the grime of the last eighteen months. He soaped his head again and again to make sure there was not a single louse left. He stood under the hot shower, letting water run all over him, washing away all those months he had languished in jail, withstanding the horrible torture and the pain, both mental and physical, the Turks had inflicted on him. At one point, he thought he was going to break, but somehow he had pulled through.

He dried himself thoroughly. He was very thin and gaunt and he still felt weak. *Time*, he reminded himself. *Give yourself time.*

He dressed quickly in a fresh army uniform, enjoying the feel of the starched shirt, the jacket and pants that all smelled fresh and clean. He walked out of the bathroom and went to find the reception area to let them know that he was leaving earlier than expected. The nurses argued with him for a bit but soon acceded. He didn't need to be a captive anymore.

"Well I'm off, ladies!" he smiled charmingly at the two nurses at the desk, who both looked up at him and smiled back.

"Goodbye, Major Hackett," one of them said. "We're going to miss you."

"And I will miss you too, Nurse," Charles kissed her hand. The nurse visibly swooned. Charles chuckled and walked through the door after a final wave. Outside, his mouth fell open.

"Hello, Charlie ol' boy!"

Charles walked as quickly as he could and threw himself into Law-rence's open arms.

—⁂—

Charles looked at himself in the small mirror in the little bathroom that was part of his accommodations in the barracks in Cairo. His hair was starting to grow back, but was still very short. He had decided to sport a very trim beard and moustache that was no more than a five o'clock shadow. He examined his face. His forehead was furrowed, the lines around his eyes were deeper, and his usually chiseled jawline was lined. But at least he looked healthier than before. Normal sleep patterns, exercise, and three square meals a day had helped. His leg still hurt a bit, especially during a chilly night, and he had to walk with a cane to walk straight, otherwise, it tended to buckle. But he didn't mind. Lawrence said the cane made him look more regal. And perhaps one day he wouldn't need it anymore. He'd started work with the army physiotherapist and they were hopeful that, with some hard work, he might even be able to run again. He sat down on a chair in his room and put on his socks. He picked up his shoes, inspecting then, making sure they shone before he put them on. Putting on his officer's cap, he gave himself a final look in the mirror, and opened the door. He stopped. He went back to the bathroom and splashed on a little spicy Saint John's Rum cologne. *There,* he said to his reflection in the mirror. *Now you're ready.*

"What do you think?" he asked George, his little monkey who had been left in the care of one of the young assistants in the Arab Bureau.

The monkey stood up and beat his chest, squealing and showing his gums.

"Well thank you, George," Charles said, putting his hand down so the monkey could run up his arm to his shoulder. "I think you look very well too.

"Do you feel like coming to the El-Khalili?" he asked the monkey.

The monkey nodded, squealing and jumped up and down on his shoulder.

"Let's go then . . . perhaps you can wait for me at El Fishawy? Just don't go around stealing food from tables." He shook his finger at the monkey.

With the monkey sitting around his neck, Charles walked down the hall. "You know, it's really good to see you, George . . ."

He went outside to the entrance of the barracks, hoping to get a tram.

"Major!" he heard a voice call out.

Charles turned. It was the lieutenant from the infirmary in Baal-bek. "Khoury! What are you doing here?"

"I'm back on duty, Sir."

"Excellent to see you up and about."

"Who's the little creature?"

"My pet monkey, George," Charles introduced them.

Michel laughed.

"Where are you going, Major? Can I give you a lift?" He pointed to a motorbike and sidecar parked at the curb."

"I'm going to the Al-Hussein mosque."

"So am I . . . what a coincidence. Come on! I'll take you," Michel offered.

"That would be very kind, thank you."

"Not at all."

"Why are you going to the mosque?" Charles asked, getting into the sidecar.

"Actually I'm going to the El-Khalili."

"Really?"

"Yes, my father has a few shops in the souk, and I'm going to see a couple of friends who are also back from Palestine. Their father has a fruit stand, and unfortunately, one of their brothers was killed a few months ago," Michel added. "So I'm going to pay my condolences."

"Don't tell me . . . was his name Hisham?"

"Yes!" Michel replied. "Why? Did you know him?"

"Yes . . . he was with me when it happened," Charles said. "A freak sandstorm. He was very young, no more than eighteen."

Michel nodded. "So you know his father, Magdi?"

"I do . . . I had an assignment in the souk some time back, so I got to know it quite well."

"It is a confusing place."

Charles agreed. "Where is your father's shop?" he asked.

"He's got several," Michel said, "but the main one is an antique chandelier shop on Zuqaq al-Hamra . . . next to a café that was run by one of my father's best friends, but he passed away and I think he left the café to his nephew and his wife."

"So you know Rania's Café?" Charles laughed.

"Not very well, but I've passed by very often . . . she's quite a beauty, Rania."

"She is," Charles agreed.

"But . . . ," Michel sighed, "all the beautiful ones are always married."

They stopped at a crossroad and waited for the traffic policeman to give them the go- ahead.

"I believe Rania is a widow." Charles turned to Michel and cocked an eyebrow meaningfully.

—⁓—

Charles' heart started beating stronger as soon as he saw the Midan Al-Hussein.

This is where he'd been waiting for her. He remembered how she had run across the square, her hair flying around her, her face flushed and her eyes sparkling with excitement.

"Thanks, Lieutenant."

"Anytime, Major." Michel Khoury saluted.

"I'll see you around the barracks."

"Or perhaps right here in the El-Khalili." Michel smiled.

"Yes, indeed!"

"*Ma'asalame.*" Michel waved casually. "*Allah ma'ak.*"

After the motorbike drove away, Charles stood for a moment and took a deep breath, looking around. There were times when he'd thought he would never see it again. He never quite knew where he'd gotten the resolve to stay alive, especially the nights when they had thrown him brutally back into his cell after beating and torturing him for information about the movements of the Arab Army and Lawrence. Was it the memory of her face? He wondered now as he walked toward the entrance to the souk. Did she still look like that? Or was it simply a picture he had kept in his mind and the reality would no longer match. Suddenly, he stopped. Had she even waited for him? What if she'd gone back to her husband? No, he said to himself. She'd given him her word. She wouldn't have gone back on it. Charles took a step and stopped again. But on the other hand, he really couldn't blame her if she'd changed her mind. After all, they didn't know each other at all well. They'd really only spent that one evening together. Filled with uncertainty, Charles made his way across the square. He saw a man pushing a wheelchair with a woman in it out onto the square and another woman walking next to him.

The woman took over the wheelchair and carried on toward the souk, leaving the man behind. There was something familiar about him, but Charles couldn't see that far. His eyesight wasn't what it used to be. Suddenly, the man saw him, stopped dead in his tracks, and stared at him, but the sun was in Charles' eyes and he put his hand up to shield them. Slowly the man started walking toward him. And then suddenly he came into focus. Charles stopped and smiled, his eyes moist when he saw a slightly bigger Salah come running over, his tunic clinging to his stomach, his waistcoat flapping in the wind.

Salah was openly crying when he reached him, throwing his arms around him.

"I thought I'd lost you too, Charlie." He choked up, hugging his friend as hard as he could.

"Well," Salah sniffed, wiping his eyes with his handkerchief, suddenly embarrassed about his emotional outburst in the middle of the Midan Al-Hussein, "shall we go have a coffee or something stronger? I know Rania has some whiskey behind the bar."

"How is she, Salah . . . Fatmeh?" Charles asked.

"You will see for yourself soon enough." Salah smiled. "Come!" he said in his big booming voice.

"So how the hell are you?" Charles slapped him on the back.

"Me? Oh well I'm very well! Noura has agreed to marry me."

"Really? Why?"

"Very funny! But I must say you look very well . . . ," Salah said as they walked away. "No hair though."

"Yes, well, it'll grow back."

"You'll come to the wedding, of course . . ."

"When is it?"

"Sometime soon . . . honestly I can't remember the date." Salah laughed. "My mother and Noura . . . I'm leaving myself in their hands."

"I would, old friend . . ."

And the two men walked along the old, narrow cobblestone lanes and alleys, enjoying each other's company, talking as though no time had gone by and nothing had happened.

—⁓—

"So how do you feel being a divorced woman?" Noura asked Fatmeh as they sat together in the salon.

"I feel so much lighter."

"I can imagine," Noura said. "Now, after we finish our tea, do you want to help me continue with the uniforms or shall we start my wedding dress?" Noura's eyes shone mischievously.

"Oh let's start the dress!" Fatmeh agreed with equal enthusiasm. "I'm so excited for you, Noura." Fatmeh spontaneously hugged her. "And I'm so happy for you. You couldn't have found a better man than Salah."

"I know." Noura nodded. "I am very lucky. And what is important is that Siran will not grow up fatherless."

"But . . . in addition to having a father for Siran," Fatmeh started tentatively, "you are . . . in love with him? Aren't you?"

Noura looked up at her. "Completely and with all my heart."

—⁓—

"Noura!" they heard Salah's voice call out from downstairs.

Noura and Fatmeh looked at each other and grinned at the coincidence.

"Yes!" Noura shouted back. "We really need those new telephones in this house so we're not yelling from floor to floor." She turned to Fatmeh.

"Noura, is Fatmeh with you?" Salah boomed.

"Yes!"

"I'm coming upstairs to get you."

"What's all this about?"

Fatmeh shrugged.

"Noura, I have to show you something outside," Salah said when he came upstairs and swooped her up in his arms.

"What?" Noura looked at him, puzzled. "What about Fatmeh?"

"Oh!" Salah said quickly. "She can wait for us . . . !"

"Noura, I'll go and continue the ironing," Fatmeh said as Salah took Noura away.

"No! No!" Salah said, a hand firmly on Fatmeh's arm. "Just wait right there, Fatmeh! Don't move! We'll be right back. Really. Please! Just wait!"

Shaking her head, wondering what was going on, Fatmeh went back into the salon. She walked to the window and looked outside. Salah and Noura were just below the window. Salah was saying something and Noura's hand flew over her mouth. Fatmeh tried to strain her ears to hear what they were saying but there was too much street noise.

Suddenly, she heard a noise behind her. She froze. Chills ran down her spine. A figure appeared in her line of vision. She didn't dare turn. She quickly closed her eyes to stop the tears that had formed, and put her arms around herself protectively.

Slowly she turned and opened her eyes. The minute she saw his shiny, polished shoes, the tears started to fall. She looked up at him, her chin trembling, unable to speak.

Charles also had tears in his eyes.

And then suddenly she was in his arms, crying into his neck. "Charlie . . . ," she sobbed. "I knew you weren't dead. I just knew you were alive . . ."

Charles couldn't speak. Finally, he lifted his head to look at her, caressing her face, pushing her hair back. He smiled. She was just as beautiful, if not more so. He ran his thumb over her lips and she kissed it. He held her chin between his thumb and forefinger and searched her face. She placed her hands around the back of his head and brought it forward. She closed her eyes as he bent his lips to place them over hers, gently, growing in passion until she opened her mouth and their tongues met, feeling, exploring, and probing, hesitantly at first and with more confidence as their kiss deepened.

Charles pulled back and looked at her. Fatmeh opened her eyes, her lips still parted. He still held her face cupped in his hands.

"It is only the image of you that kept me alive, Fatmeh," he said simply. "It was the thought of you waiting for me that kept me going."

Fresh tears appeared in Fatmeh's eyes.

"You are the most beautiful woman in the world to me," he told her. "I don't think I can let you go."

"You don't have to," she said.

"But what about your husband?"

"It's over," Fatmeh smiled. "The imam divorced us . . . today, as it turns out."

"Then," he said as he very slowly went down on one knee, "will you have a wounded soldier as your new husband?"

Fatmeh sank to the floor on her knees and put her arms around him. *This is what love feels like,* she told herself. This is what she had only dreamed of up until now. What she felt right now in this moment . . . the warmth in her heart . . . was the feeling she wanted to capture and keep with her forever. And she knew she would always have it, as long as Charles was by her side.

—⁓—

As promised, Musa Nusair married Salah and Noura, although not on the *Tree of Life.* The wedding ceremony was held in February of 1919 in the Jardin des Plantes in Zemalek, where Salah had first kissed Noura and told her he loved her. The only people there were the immediate family and friends . . . Saydeh, Yvonne, Takla, Charles, and Lawrence. Fatmeh and Rania had stayed behind at the café to organize the reception.

Noura wore a dress she'd made of white netting lined with satin silk that shimmered when she moved. It was a simple, v-neck empire-silhouette design with short puffed sleeves. The fitted bodice ended just below the bust, making her look longer and taller. The gathered skirt was long and loose and flowed around her.

And just as he had promised, Salah carried her down the aisle.

Afterwards, everyone went back to the Khan el-Khalili. Rania's Café was packed.

The café erupted with loud ululations and cheers as people clapped and shouted their congratulations when Salah brought Noura in, placed her gently at the long farmhouse table, and sat down next to her.

Noura glowed on Salah's arm, shielding herself from the showers of rose petals and grains of rice that came down over their heads.

The party was in full swing when Fatmeh noticed a new face.

"Who is that?" she nudged Rania.

"Who?" Rania looked around, her dark hair swinging around her.

"Over there." Fatmeh tried to discreetly indicate with a tilt of her head.

Rania looked over and across the room, her eyes met the smiling eyes of Lieutenant Michel Khoury. He inclined his head, acknowledging her. Embarrassed, she smiled tightly and looked back at Fatmeh.

"So? Who is he? And why is he looking at like you like that?"

"Like what?" Rania blushed.

"Like . . . you know!" Fatmeh winked. "He clearly thinks you're beautiful."

"*Ya, Fatmeh! Bas!*" Rania scoffed. But secretly she smiled to herself. She looked up again, searching for him over the heads of the crowd that had gathered around the bride and groom. She saw him sitting with Charles and Lawrence. He was talking to them and suddenly they all laughed and he turned and caught her looking at him. Rania blushed and quickly tried to pretend to be serving drinks. But whenever she could, she stole a glance at him.

Fatmeh noticed but didn't say anything. *So much has happened at this café*, she thought. *So many stories have begun and ended here. It feels like* One Thousand and One Nights.

"What are you smiling about?" Charles asked, coming up behind her.

"Well, I just think that everything is going to work out."

"Really," he turned her around to face him.

"Yes," she said confidently. "I do."

—⁂—

At the old farmhouse table, Salah took a hold of Noura's hand. She looked up at him, her eyes shining.

"Noura, I will never let anyone destroy this," he said, gesturing to the two of them. "It hurt me immeasurably to destroy the railway that I had built, but us . . . if anything or anyone threatens us, they will have to kill me first."

Saydeh came over and put a huge wedding cake in the middle of the table and began lighting the candles.

"Salah," Noura whispered into his ear. "I want to stand and cut the cake with you."

"I'll hold you up."

"No."

"All right, you two," Musa Nusair said before Salah had time to react. "Time to cut the cake."

Noura put her right hand on Salah's shoulder. A hush fell over the crowd and all eyes focused on her. Noura put her left hand on the table and slowly lifted herself up. The crowd murmured their surprise. Once she was standing, she took her left hand and placed it over her right on Salah's shoulder.

The crowd began to clap and cheer. Salah had tears in his eyes. Gently, he took Noura's hand in his and stood, cautiously. She stumbled, but he was right there and quickly put his arm around her waist to balance her. He looked into her eyes. She, too, had tears in her eyes. Noura reached for the knife and Salah put his hand over hers.

Carefully, they cut the cake. The crowd cheered again.

Salah turned Noura toward him.

"A kiss! A kiss!" the crowd demanded.

"I am the happiest man in the world, Noura," Salah whispered to her.

"Please don't let me go, Salah."

"I never will." Salah slowly and gently kissed her.

Cheers went up as everyone congratulated the happy couple again. Salah sat down with Noura at his side. He saw Michel making his way over to Rania. He saw Lawrence and Musa Nusair laughing. And he saw Saydeh, Yvonne, and Takla moving through the crowd, making sure everyone was eating and drinking to their heart's content. And here he was, still alive and holding the woman he loved in his arms.

EPILOGUE

The Sinai and Palestine Campaign of the Middle Eastern theater of war came to an end when Damascus fell to the British and Arab troops on October 1, 1918. Faisal ibn Hussein and the Arab troops rode victorious into the city and the Arab flag flew proudly over the governor's mansion.

The British and their allies had won. The Ottoman Empire had been defeated. The Arabs would now have their independence. Or at least, that is what they expected. After all, it was what the British had promised them in return for their revolt against the Turks.

But it didn't quite work out that way.

On October 3, Faisal was told by Edmund Allenby that things had changed . . . that Syria was to be under French protection, guidance, and financial backing and that a French liaison officer would assist him every step of the way. The Arab naturally objected. Allenby was forced to pull rank, saying that he was commander in chief and Faisal would have to accept the situation, at least temporarily, until matters were settled at the peace conference in Paris.

Lawrence, horrified, returned to England the following day to begin lobbying the British government to honor its original promise to the Arabs. He even went so far as to gain an audience with King George V, in front of whom he caused a scandal, refusing the medals the king wanted to award him because he was so outraged over Britain's betrayal of the Arab cause.

At the peace conference in Paris that began in January 1919, the most important and pressing piece of business on the table was how to punish Germany. It was really only after the Treaty of Versailles was signed in June 1919 that the Allied Powers turned their attention to the Ottoman Empire and the Arab demands.

Lawrence convinced Faisal to come first to Britain, where he managed to drum up a modicum of support before going to Paris. He prepared a speech for Faisal, presenting the Arab point of view to the delegates and diplomats, which Faisal delivered in Arabic. Lawrence then delivered the speech in English and French. Lawrence hoped fervently that perhaps the Americans would understand and back the Arabs, especially since the American President, Woodrow Wilson, was an advocate of self-determination, urging that all nationalities within the former Ottoman Empire be assured "an absolutely unmolested opportunity of autonomous development."

But the Europeans had other ideas. Britain and France were adamant about maintaining their colonial empires and expanding them, especially with the discovery of large quantities of oil in the Arabian desert.

The British and French also wanted to loosen Islam's hold on the region by promoting a secular government. But, as the historian David Fromkin wrote, "these foreign powers trying to impose their own order would not be welcomed in places whose inhabitants for more than a thousand years have avowed faith in a holy law that governs all life, including government and politics."

To further complicate matters, in addition to the Sykes-Picot agreement with France in 1916 (according to which Britain would get Mesopotamia and Palestine, France would get Syria and Lebanon, and the Arabs absolutely nothing), the British also announced its support for a "national home for the Jewish people in Palestine" in 1917 in a letter known as the Balfour Declaration, written by the British foreign secretary, Arthur Balfour, to Baron Rothschild, a leader of the Jewish community in Britain.

So in the end, despite Lawrence's efforts, the Arab point of view was completely ignored and the British and French promises made by Henry McMahon to Sharif Hussein of Mecca in 1915 disappeared like footprints in the desert sand.

By the time the Treaty of Sevres, the peace treaty between the Allies and the Ottoman Empire, was signed in August 1920, a year and a half after the peace conference began, the Sykes-Picot agreement came into effect. Britain and France received "mandates" from the newly formed League of Nations to oversee much of the former Ottoman Empire, where they created several new states and installed figurehead rulers.

Even at the time, the Americans believed that the lines being drawn in the sand by the British and French, lines that did not take into account race, religion, and tribal loyalties, were creating "a breeding place for future war."

The British mandate for Palestine included present-day Israel, Jordan, and the West Bank and Gaza Strip. In 1921, on the land east of the Jordan River, Britain carved out Transjordan and placed Faisal's brother Abdullah on the throne.

West of the Jordan River, the issue of a Jewish homeland played out over the next two decades. Most Arab leaders opposed the creation of a new Jewish state in Palestine, where the population was largely Arab.

In 1920, Syria became a protectorate of France, claiming a special responsibility for safeguarding Christian enclaves in the Ottoman Empire. France carved out Syria's coastal region into the separate state of Lebanon, whose legitimacy the Syrians still don't recognize.

In 1919, there was no Iraq. To create the new nation in ancient Mesopotamia, Britain cobbled together the Ottoman provinces of Baghdad, mostly Sunni; Basra, mostly Shiite; and Mosul, mostly Kurdish.

—◊◊—

Egypt probably fared best. It remained a British protectorate, achieving full independence in 1922, but British troops remained in the country until 1956.

—◊◊—

Today, three generations after the end of World War I, the American president's aide was right in his dire prediction for the Middle East. The question is, will the conflicts there ever cease?

ACKNOWLEDGMENTS

My sincere gratitude to Duncan Macaulay for being by my side when I wrote this book; to Gay Walley, my friend and editor, for her inexhaustible patience; to Blanca Rosa Roca for her eternal confidence.

ABOUT THE AUTHOR

Maha Akhtar is a journalist, author, and speechwriter. A contributor to *Departures* magazine, she also writes about wine for several influential restaurateurs in New York City. A graduate of Bryn Mawr College, Akhtar started her career in the music business as assistant manager for the Cure. Six years later, she moved into public relations for Zagat Survey before entering CBS News, where she worked closely with Dan Rather on the *CBS Evening News*. Akhtar is the author of two memoirs and two novels previously published in Spanish. She lives in New York City.

BARCELONA BOOKS

Barcelona eBooks is a spin-off of Roca Editorial, a prominent publishing house in Barcelona. The digital books company was founded by Blanca Rosa Roca, Barcelona eBooks CEO, and Michael Seay Gordon, vice president. Roca Editorial and Barcelona eBooks encourage a cultural exchange and make it possible to seek out the world's best books for publication in both the Spanish and English languages. In Spain, Roca Editorial already publishes E. L. Doctorow, Nicholas Sparks, Christopher Paolini, Michael Connelly, Noah Gordon, Robert Crais, Edward Rutherfurd, Don Winslow, and John Verdon.

FIND OUT MORE AT

WWW.BARCELONAEBOOKS.COM

Barcelona eBooks is one of a select group of publishing partners of Open Road Integrated Media, Inc.

Open Road Integrated Media is a digital publisher and multimedia content company. Open Road creates connections between authors and their audiences by marketing its ebooks through a new proprietary online platform, which uses premium video content and social media.

Videos, Archival Documents, and New Releases

Sign up for the Open Road Media newsletter and get news delivered straight to your inbox.

Sign up now at
www.openroadmedia.com/newsletters

CPSIA information can be obtained at www.ICGtesting.com
Printed in the USA
BVOW05s1028090915

416364BV00001B/1/P